WHY WE CAME TO THE CITY

ALSO BY THE AUTHOR

The Unchangeable Spots of Leopards

WHY WE CAME TO THE CITY

Kristopher Jansma

VIKING

VIKING
An imprint of Penguin Random House LLC
375 Hudson Street
New York, New York 10014
penguin.com

LIBRARY OF CONGRESS CATALOGING-IN-PUBLICATION DATA
Names: Jansma, Kristopher, author.
Title: Why we came to the city / Kristopher Jansma.
Description: New York : Viking, [2016]
Identifiers: LCCN 2015044555 (print) | LCCN 2015047243 (ebook) | ISBN 978-0-525-42660-8 (hardback) | ISBN 978-0-698-15213-7 | ISBN 978-0-698-15213-7 (ebook)
Subjects: | BISAC: FICTION / Literary. | FICTION / Coming of Age. | FICTION / Urban Life.
Classification: LCC PS3610.A5873 W48 2016 (print) | LCC PS3610.A5873 (ebook) | DDC 813/.6—dc23
LC record available at http://lccn.loc.gov/2015044555

Printed in the United States of America
10 9 8 7 6 5 4 3 2 1

For Leah

CONTENTS

I

II

I

We do have Prayers, you know, Prayers for forgiveness,
daughters of mighty Zeus . . . and they limp and halt,
they're all wrinkled, drawn, they squint to the side,
can't look you in the eyes, and always bent on duty,
trudging after Ruin, maddening, blinding Ruin.
But Ruin is strong and swift—
She outstrips them all by far, stealing a march,
leaping over the whole wide earth to bring mankind to grief.
And the Prayers trail after, trying to heal the wounds.

—Homer, *The Iliad* (trans. Robert Fagles)

What can go wrong will go wrong.

—Murphy's First Law

WHY WE CAME TO THE CITY

We came to the city because we wished to live haphazardly, to reach for only the least realistic of our desires, and to see if we could not learn what our failures had to teach, and not, when we came to live, discover that we had never died. We wanted to dig deep and suck out all the marrow of life, to be overworked and reduced to our last wit. And if our bosses proved mean, why then we'd evoke their whole and genuine meanness afterward over vodka cranberries and small batch bourbons. And if our drinking companions proved to be sublime, then we would stagger home at dawn over the Old City cobblestones, into hot showers and clean shirts, and press onward until dusk fell again. For the rest of the world, it seemed to us, had somewhat hastily concluded that it was the chief end of man to thank God it was Friday and pray that Netflix would never forsake them.

Still we lived frantically, like hummingbirds; though our HR departments told us that our commitments were valuable and our feedback was appreciated, our raises would be held back another year. Like gnats we pestered Management—who didn't know how to use the Internet, whose only use for us was to set up Facebook accounts so they could spy on their children, or to sync their iPhones to their Outlooks, or to explain what tweets were and, more importantly, *why*—which even we didn't know. *Retire!*, we wanted to shout. *Get out of the way with your big thumbs and your senior moments and your nostalgia for 1976!* We hated them; we wanted them to love us. We wanted to be them; we wanted to never, ever become them.

Complexity, complexity, complexity! We said let our affairs be endless and convoluted; let our bank accounts be overdrawn and our benefits be reduced. Take our Social Security contributions and let it go bankrupt. We'd been bankrupt since we'd left home; we'd secure our own society. Retirement was an afterlife we didn't believe in and that we expected yesterday. Instead of three meals a day, we'd drink coffee for breakfast and scavenge from empty conference rooms for lunch. We had plans for dinner. We'd go out and buy gummy pad thai and throat-scorching chicken vindaloo and bento boxes in chintzy, dark restaurants that were always about to go out of business. Those who were a little flush would cover those who were a little short, and we would promise them coffees in repayment. We still owed someone for a movie ticket last summer; they hadn't forgotten. Complexity, complexity.

In holiday seasons we gave each other spider plants in badly découpaged pots and scarves we'd just learned how to knit and cuff links purchased with employee discounts. We followed the instructions on food and wine Web sites, but our soufflés sank and our baked bries burned and our basil ice creams froze solid. We called our mothers to get recipes for our old favorites, but they never came out the same. We missed our families; we were sad to be rid of them.

Why shouldn't we live with such hurry and waste of life? We were determined to be starved before we were hungry. We were determined to decrypt our neighbors' Wi-Fi passwords and to never turn on the air-conditioning. We vowed to fall in love: headboard-clutching, desperate-texting, hearts-in-esophagi love. On the subways and at the park and on our fire escapes and in the break rooms, we turned pages, resolved to get to the ends of whatever we were reading. A couple of minutes were the day's most valuable commodity. If only we could make more time, more money, more patience; have better sex, better coffee, boots that didn't leak, umbrellas that didn't involute at the slightest gust of wind. We were determined to make stupid bets. We were determined to be promoted or else to set the building on fire on our way out. We were determined to be out of our minds.

We couldn't stop following the news. Every ten seconds we refreshed our browsers and gawked at the headlines. Dully, we read blogs of friends of friends of friends who had started an organic farm out on the Wachito River. They were out there pickling and canning and brewing things in the goodness of nature. And soon we'd worry it was time for *us* to leave the city and go. Go! To Uruguay or Morocco or Connecticut? To the Plains or the Mountains or the Bay? But we'd bide our time, and after some months or years, our farmer friends would give up the farm and begin studying for the LSATs. We felt lousy about this, and wonderful.

We missed getting mail. We wondered why we even kept those tiny keys on our crowded rings. Sometimes we would send ourselves things from the office. Sometimes we would handwrite long letters to old loved ones and not send them. We never knew their new address. We never knew anyone's address, just their cross streets and what their doors looked like. Which button to buzz, and if the buzzers even worked. How many flights to climb, and which way to turn off the stairs. Sometimes we missed those who hadn't come to the city with us—or those who had gone to other, different cities. Sometimes we journeyed to see them, and sometimes they ventured to see us. Those were the best of times, for we were all at home and not at once. Those were the worst of times, for we inevitably longed to all move here or there, yet no one ever came—somehow everyone only left. Soon we were practically all alone.

Soon we began to hate the forever cramping of our lives. Sleeping on top of strangers and sipping coffee with people we knew we *knew* but couldn't remember where from. Living out of boxes we had no space to unpack. Soon we named the pigeons roosting in our windowsills; we worried they looked mangier than the week before. We heard bellowing in the apartments below us and bedsprings creaking in the ones above. Everywhere we saw people with dogs and wondered how they managed it. Did they work from home? Did they not work? Had they gone to the right schools? Did they have connections? We had no connections. Our parents were our guarantors in name only; they called us from their jobs in distant, colorless, suburban office parks and told us we could come home anytime, and this terrified us always.

But then came those nights, creeping up on us while we worked busily in dark offices, like submariners lost at sea, sailing through the dark stratosphere in our cement towers. We'd call each other to report: a good thing happened, a compliment had been paid, a favor had been appreciated, an inch of ground had been gained. We wouldn't trade those nights for anything or anywhere. Those nights, we remembered why we came to the city. Because if we were really living, then we wanted to hear the cracking in our throats and feel the trembling in our extremities. And if our apartments were coffins and our desks headstones and our dreams infections—if we were all slowly dying—then at least we were going about that great and terrible business together.

LIVING VICARIOUSLY

Irene Richmond ran down the narrow foyer, helping guests get out of their coats, which were dusted with flakes of snow that had been coming down heavily all day and still drifted lightly onto the hotel balcony. Coats that cost more than she earned in a month and that were works of art themselves. Hoods lined with fox fur imported from Finland. A quilted sateen coat filled with goose down and patterned in the latest Japanese style of concentric circles. A long vest made of rabbit. Mongolian lamb's wool. Irene got a thrill from just holding them, but it was always short-lived. By the time the guests had finished warning her not to crease the collars or wrinkle the hems, there was someone else making an even more fashionable entrance.

During rare pauses, she checked her phone for messages from George and Sara. Nothing. And nothing from Jacob either. Twisting in front of the hallway mirror, she reseated the bobby pins that kept her blond hair up off her shoulders. She liked the way her neck looked in the golden light by the door. An elegant extension of her one bared shoulder. She hoped it wasn't too much. Abeba had said only to look nice, but Irene had sensed an implication that she not look nicer than the guests. Juliette then added that it was important to look hip, which Irene took to mean young, vital, and strange. Therefore: cerulean leggings, crochet sweater dress, peacock feather necklace, and a braided skinny-belt. Irene hoped these projected the artistic, professional image specified. Every job had its uniform.

She checked her eye shadow, which made her irises look a shade darker, almost black instead of blue. She rubbed at a spot beneath her left eye that had been there for a month now but had only recently begun to feel sore. *Buzz* went the door, and she was off to collect a giraffe-print bolero from the next artist or heiress to stagger in on midnight-black stilettos.

The K Gallery's annual holiday party at the Waldorf Astoria was always an impressive affair. All year Irene and her friends looked forward to this night, the second Friday in December. Not that they didn't go out other nights, not that living in the city wasn't sometimes glamorous, but never anything compared to this. There were seventy-eight people on the exclusive guest list, and renowned chef Marc Herradura was catering. Honest-to-God movie stars attended. Last year they'd seen that guy from *The Office*, and the year before that, Cyndi Lauper! This was that other New York: always around them but never visible. For this one night it belonged to them too.

Even with the first big storm of winter going on outside and flights canceled at JFK and LaGuardia (only Newark soldiered on), they had nearly full attendance. All day the gallery's owners, Juliette and Abeba, had been commanding Irene from one end of Manhattan to the other. They'd thrust her into snow-capped cars in Chelsea with a wrought-iron baboon skeleton (a steal at just $300,000) whose shrieking head had extended dangerously out the window into traffic. Wearing a pair of Abeba's oversize duck boots, Irene had sloshed across the posh lobby of the Lexington Avenue hotel, aching under the weight of a moldy yam encased in bile-green polypropylene (starting at just half a million).

Five years ago, when she'd first begun working at the gallery, Irene had gotten a thrill simply from being *near* such valuable art, but by this point she was considering telling the driver to take her and the oversize photograph of Trisha Birch's genitals (one million flat) to the George Washington Bridge so she could hurl it out into the Hudson. Or maybe she would just keep going. On and on, out of the city. With the money this one photo was worth, Irene could paint all day and all night for another twenty years. Or start her own gallery. Or institute a progressive artists' colony where young dreamers could take up their own work. She could help them avoid the eighteen-hour days, the perpetual temper tantrums, the name-dropping, the ego trips, the talentless and tormented. Except that, of course, outside New York City, the Trisha Birch photographs were more likely to get her arrested for indecency than for theft. *Maybe in L.A.*, she thought. *Maybe in London. Maybe on Mars, or Neptune.*

Juliette and Abeba were not terrible bosses, but they had all the fussiness of artists without the brilliance. They had an eye for slick marketing and could start a trend like nobody's business. But the higher the K Gallery climbed in the Chelsea scene, the more Juliette and Abeba drank sickening amounts of Campari and spoke of selling everything and setting sail for the Marquesas like Gauguin. Rule one of living in the city, Irene had learned—as soon as you got there, you had to begin threatening to leave. She was theoretically putting money aside for a trip to France from which she privately imagined she'd never return, though it seemed like the same $350 or so kept entering and exiting her savings account; meanwhile the trip got more expensive and the exchange rate got worse and the gallery took up more time.

Still, it was, as they said, a living, and far from a bad one. Even when she'd had to examine Teacup Yorkie feces to see which should be threaded alongside diamonds on a necklace for the Bryant Park show. Even cataloging seventeen years of Percy Bryson's toenail clippings. But she had legit benefits and enough money to pay for a cramped studio apartment on East Fourth Street, where she could paint at night without disturbing a roommate. Plus she wasn't starving. If not trips to France, her paychecks covered a vintage dress or two and movie tickets and bar tabs and green tea smoothies.

Buzz! At last it was them: George Murphy and Sara Sherman.

George wore a wide smile and a black pinstripe suit. Was it new?

It was. Sara had gotten it for him last week at the Macy's pre-Christmas sale, to wear to his postdoc interviews. Irene kissed his cheek and inspected his penny-coppery hair; it needed cutting. Irene could never resist the urge to ruffle his head lightly, for luck.

"We made it!" George announced. His cornflower-blue eyes met the room over Irene's shoulder and then fixed on her. When he spoke to her, or to anyone, they never drifted an inch. His three favorite words were, "Did you know—" and after saying them, he had a way of lowering his voice as he told you something terrific about some distant galaxy he was researching out at the North Shore Observatory, as if Andromeda B were a restaurant you might want to check out sometime. He seemed to want nothing more than for others to find him handy to have around. Swiftly, he could explain to you: the mechanics of an elevator, the science behind a hailstorm, or the electric spark between your fingers and the fringe of your dress. A good Catholic boy from Columbus, someone had raised him right; George Murphy was attentive in a city of the attention-deficient, and for this he was always looked after.

"No one's ever on time to this thing," Irene said. "Here, give me your coat."

But George was already hanging it up by himself.

Sara slid in for a kiss from Irene. "Some big accident on the LIE," she explained. Irene told her she looked stunning, and Sara said she must be mental; she'd come straight from the gym and was sure that she must *reek*, but of course she did not. Her long purple dress was discreetly sequined. Raven-haired and slender-jawed, Sara forever made Irene itch to break out her charcoals and sketch dark, elegant lines. No matter that she was technically not of the artsy crowd at this party—inside an hour, half the people there would believe Sara was the one throwing it. She'd glide from one conversation to the next, sometimes drawing one or two along with her until no one was a stranger to her, or to anyone, anymore. "Did you know" were also Sara's three favorite words, followed not by a fact but by a person. She always knew someone you knew: a girl in your prom limo, your YMCA summer camp counselor, the barista at the coffee shop you frequent, a man you met at that bar in Chiang Mai, the boy whose hand you held on a third-grade field trip to the Museum of Natural History. Some people never forgot a face; Sara never forgot a connection.

George played with his skinny knit tie in the hall mirror. "*Six-car* pileup. I've done this commute every day for five years, and I've never seen a crash that bad."

Irene watched as the mirror's golden, thorny frame transformed George into a portrait: *Man in Crooked Necktie*. She wished she could tear the Claude Lozarette off the farther wall, melt the pigments off the canvas, and use them to paint George right there on the mirror's surface—why not?—but the moment passed. The knot was fixed; he'd stepped away.

"Sorry. I had to change in a Starbucks bathroom that smelled like dead aardvarks and—"

Sara interrupted. "Oh, speaking of—this is for you." She dug an oil-stained brown bag from her bottomless purse.

Irene peeled back the paper to reveal a single, smushed vanilla cupcake. Little rainbow sprinkles formed a lopsided swirl, winking up like stars.

"They made us *buy* something. Can you believe it?"

In fact, Irene could *not* believe it. First, Sara was a rotten liar, and second, everyone knew Starbucks was one place you could use the bathroom without paying for something; it might as well be rule two of city living.

George winked at Irene as she helped slip off Sara's coat. "Someone was afraid you didn't eat today," he murmured.

Sara pretended to object, but Irene kissed her cheek again. "Well, did you?" Sara inquired, and before an answer was given, she reached up to poke the faint spot beneath Irene's eye.

Irene snapped her head to one side. "I had some grapes."

She already regretted telling Sara about last week's CT scan, which meant she'd just keep worrying and eventually she'd ask about yesterday's follow-up appointment.

"Jacob here yet?" George asked, absently trying to take Sara's coat so he could hang it.

Irene yanked it back. "Not yet. But he's always late."

"But *we're* late."

"He's always later."

Then, as Irene moved to close the door, she saw someone approaching—a young Korean man who was shyly inspecting the wall. It took two seconds to see that he didn't belong there. Distantly, she remembered him from somewhere. He wore a sharp, gray Armani suit and held, in one hand, a bottle of Bollinger Blanc. *Who brings champagne to a catered party?* Irene wondered as she tried to remember which gallery he worked for. She wasn't entirely surprised to see Sara give the boy a bear hug.

"William *Cho*? What are you doing here? Irene, did you know William? He was in Art History II with McClellan. You sat in on that one."

Irene didn't hesitate to grip his wet, gloved hand in welcome. He was very thin, with cheekbones that she was sure she'd have remembered if he'd had them back in college. *People don't just go around getting cheekbones*, she told herself. Or coal-black eyes like that either. She liked the girlish line of his upper lip; he bit it nervously whenever he looked at her. Normally she wasn't very interested in shyness, but something about him was making her blush.

Sara turned. "George, you remember William."

They shook hands politely. "Sure! William Cho, right? We met at that newspaper party with Lisa Schmidt. Sara took over as features editor after Lisa went to Madagascar with that guy with the Rhodes . . . honey, what was his name?"

Sara knew it (Henry Fordham, Jr.), and also that the girl's name had been Lisa *Schlick,* but from the look on William's face, Irene guessed he didn't know either of them.

"Hang on!" George said, "Before we get caught up, let me grab us all something from the bar."

It was understood that Irene had to wait until the guests had finished arriving, but Sara said anything involving St. Germain would be terrific. It was only then that William thrust forward the bottle of champagne that he'd been cradling like a football.

George seized it with grateful hands. *"Damn.* This is nice stuff, William."

"I stole it," William abruptly announced.

"Like, you boosted it?" George asked. "Don't tell me you *boosted* this."

Sara laughed. "Boosted? What are you, a thirties gangster?"

George winked at her while William clarified. "Yeah. I mean—no. I didn't rob a liquor store or anything. But it's been under the coatrack in my boss's office since last Christmas."

Turning the bottle over, George peeled a shiny gift tag off the bottom. " 'To Lenny. From the Berg-Geldorf Family!' Well thank you, Berg-Geldorfs! I'll see if the guy can put this on ice."

He clapped William on the back. Then, while Irene and Sara turned their attention to William, he slipped into the main room with every appearance of happiness.

Truth be told, however, George was feeling unusually nervous. His mind was elsewhere. Ordinarily the gallery Christmas party was his best excuse all year to get all dressed up and feel metropolitan, but this time he was in no mood. He looked around, smiling at everyone and no one in particular, as a sensation crept up his spine that somehow they could tell that he was from the Midwest, that these artists could see the sleepy cornfields in his complexion. Not like he'd grown up on a *farm*. Fairfield Beach was ten miles from Columbus. His parents had belonged to the yacht club. But tonight he wasn't feeling very yachty. He was counting on a few drinks to settle his nerves. The accident had been over on the eastbound side, but everyone on *his* side had been rubbernecking like their lives depended on it. Like they'd never seen a crash before. *Oooo look at the flashing lights! How exciting!*

He looked up to realize that the bartender was eyeing him. "Do you have a bucket of ice we could chill this in?"

The graying-haired man frowned. "This isn't a nightclub. I don't do bottle service."

Poor guy looked exhausted. George smiled and took a twenty out of his wallet—the only thing in there—and slipped it into the tip jar. This both worked and didn't. The bartender took the bottle and plunked it into an empty punch bowl that he angrily began to shovel ice into, resentful at the implication that he could be bought, even if he could be.

George fidgeted with the button on his new jacket. Open, the fabric whooshed backward like a cape when he walked too quickly. Closed, it made him look uptight, almost as bad as that William guy. George couldn't remember having seen him in college, not once. He was quiet, polite, and finely dressed, which meant that Jacob was going to hate him. Just knowing how much Jacob would hate him was making George sweat. Where was Jacob anyway? How was he always, always later than the rest of them? How did he know? Why wouldn't he just *show up*, so he could be mean to William and the girls could get upset and George could swoop in to set things right and they could all go home?

When the bartender had finished sourly shoveling the ice, George ordered something off the ornately printed menu called a Death in the Desert. It tasted sickeningly of licorice. He thought about asking for something else—open bar and all—but didn't want to show weakness. He gulped the drink down and pretended to be deep in appreciation of a nearby painting of a man eating his own bowels. If there was one real artist there, it was Irene. Over the years he'd seen the most outrageous, beautiful things come off her fingertips. She had a sort of effortless, infinite control over the thickness of a line, or the shade of oils, and the proportion of lightness to shadow. Walking through the city's museums, George was often sure that he'd just seen one of her paintings out of the corner of his eye.

"*Wan'nother?*" the bartender grumbled.

"Death in the Desert," George said. "That's a pretty hard-boiled name."

"Iss'a poem. All the drinks got names of poems." He tapped the company logo on the napkins: *Dead Poets Society Functions.*

"Cute," George said. "So no living poets? Couldn't get a Billy Collins in a tall glass?"

"The Wasteland is pretty good," the bartender offered. "Got tea-infused bourbon in it."

George was soon handed a cloudy gray drink that tasted like neither tea nor bourbon. In fact it tasted like nothing at all, which was fine by him, so long as it made the party a little blurrier. Then he got Sara a Faerie Queen, involving St. Germain and blueberries, and resumed scanning the room. Finally he put his finger on it. Last year more people had been dressed up. A *lot* more. In fact he couldn't see *anyone* else wearing a suit, except for William. Had suits suddenly gone out of style? There were an awful lot of piratical mustaches going on around him. Two—no, three different guys with muttonchops. What was the point of looking different in exactly the same way as everybody else? No wonder all their dumb art was so dumb—edgy but harmless. Pairs of safety scissors in gilded frames.

He turned, and his eyes locked with Sara's. She was chatting with William over by the doors to the balcony. She gave George just the quickest, tiniest smile, and it shattered him like a pane of glass. Could even one of these people paint *that*? The feeling you get when you're having a crappy night and the woman you're about to propose to smiles your way. With his right hand, George reached across his chest and patted his left jacket pocket. There was the impression of a small jewelry box, containing a diamond ring that had belonged to his father's mother's mother. He would give it to Sara tonight.

"Everyone says Gaussman's going to be the next Rosenquist" came Irene's soft, sweet voice behind him. She was speaking to a very tall woman and gesturing toward a longish painting of various bright-colored Web site logos. George liked it—at least it was colorful.

"I *loathe* Rosenquist," the very tall woman said.

Irene made a face behind the woman's back as she said, "Obviously. But that's why—"

Just then they both heard familiar belly laughter. It was Jacob, at last, speaking to an elderly woman in a fox stole. "Did you skin that yourself? The workmanship's incredible."

"George!" Irene sang lightly as she passed him. "That's the curator of the Morrison!"

He didn't know what that was, but it didn't matter. He was the designated extinguisher of Jacob's fires. Still holding Sara's drink in one hand, George pushed across the room.

As he arrived on the scene, Jacob was inspecting the woman's fur: "You can hardly see where the hounds got him."

"Where've you been, Jake?" George asked, looking apologetically at the elderly curator, who took her chance to break for the next room.

After taking a sniff of Sara's drink, Jacob helped himself to a gulp. "Ah, Georgie Porgie pudding and pie. Long day up at the asylum." Jake clucked his tongue. "Had to wrestle a kid to the ground who thought he was a goddamn ninja."

Jacob Blaumann worked as an orderly at Anchorage House, a private rehabilitation institute up in Westchester. He kept a short, dark scholarly beard, which if he ever shaved would grow back during a commercial break. Of course Jacob didn't watch television, or own one, and the real reason for the beard, George knew, was that a boy Jacob madly desired in their sophomore year had offhandedly commented that it made him look "less pudgy." Likewise, Jacob had worn the same brown tweed jacket every day since he'd found it at Goodwill and Irene had said it made his shoulders look broad. These things went right to his head, it was true, but so what? It was his confidence, more than anything, that George had seen work its magic on all manner of men in bars, train stations, Whole Foods freezer aisles, and library carrels.

Once Jacob had written poetry, but now he was just a poet. He specialized in a certain type of epic that was a tough sell in an age of text messages. "At least my poems don't fit on a square of toilet paper," he was fond of saying. Now he tended a herd of mental patients who, upon occasion, needed to be held down and syringed and straitjacketed. A job he'd found on craigslist, believe it or not, which put his size and his psych minor to unexpected use.

"George," he began, slinging an arm around his old friend, "I'd like to go to a fox hunt sometime. What do you say?"

"Oh, at least once before I die." George sighed wistfully.

"Let's set one up right along Madison Avenue. Get some hound dogs. Floppy ears. Keen sense of smell. You and I follow on horseback, naturally. One of us plays a bugle."

"You *know* I used to bugle with the Columbus Philharmonic."

Jacob lifted a cupped hand to his lips. "TOOO DOOO! TOOO DOOO!"

Most of the people in the room were looking at them now. George ceaselessly enjoyed his former roommate's irreverence, since he couldn't often bring himself to be rude. With Jacob it was just the opposite: if he ever had impulses toward politeness (and Sara firmly believed he didn't), they were soon drowned out by whatever he was shouting. George liked to think they complemented each other in this way, each living through the other when it suited.

"Bunch of rubberneckers!" Jacob scoffed, no quieter.

George grinned. "Speaking of, I got stuck behind this six-car pileup today on the—"

"Hang on. Where's the bar in this joint?"

"Over there. You'll like it. All the drinks are named after poems."

Jacob glowed like a thousand-watt bulb. "Who couldn't love this town?"

Irene shot them an unappreciative look from across the room and then rubbed nonchalantly at her left eye with the back of her right hand as she schmoozed another donor. Feeling George staring at her, she stuck her tongue out at him and made bug eyes at the green-plastic-encased yam that perched at his end of the bar.

George rubbed his stomach and pretended to be hungry. She gestured silently at the moldy yam, and he scratched at his chin as if considering it. He pantomimed taking out a checkbook and writing many, many zeroes.

"Shut the fuck up!" Jacob bellowed. "They have a drink called The Wasteland! Though it *ought* to be two words: Waste, space, Land. That's the actual title. Nobody gets that right. Even if it is highly overrated," he went on, "it can't touch 'The Bridge.' Hart Crane? Now there's a poem you guys ought to make into a drink. With hints of the East River—"

He'd have gone on, but he got distracted. "Hey, why's that Korean kid look so familiar?"

George ordered two more Wastelands, plus five flutes of William's champagne. Now everyone was there. Now things could really get started.

William Cho never ceased to be amazed. Here he was in the penthouse of one of the most luxurious hotels in Manhattan, in the midst of a great spiral of artists and patrons. Strange accents buzzed past his ears. A Persian woman passed by with owl feathers braided into her hair. There was snow blowing around out on the balcony, and beyond it more snow was falling a hundred stories to the streets. A Somali man by the window gestured wildly, his platinum watchband glinting in a spotlight. Diamonds ringed the neck of a white girl on the bathroom line, who couldn't be older than twenty. She and a Brazilian boy of about the same age studied a twisting glass sculpture that reminded William of a tidal wave, frozen solid. And here he was among them, feeling strangely rich by association, not least because he was standing there talking—being talked *to*, really—by Sara Sherman, of all people.

William didn't kid himself that Sara actually remembered him. Back in Ithaca, these four had traveled nearly everywhere as a pack. While every other college clique experienced seismic shifts and occasional mergers, they had never grown apart. "The Murphys," people had called them. William had especially adored Irene, the doe-eyed beauty who'd been habitually late for Art History II. The persistent rumor on campus was that she wasn't actually a student but a townie who had nevertheless been elected Treasurer of the Ballroom Dance Society and had several pieces put up in the Digital Media gallery—all without paying a cent of tuition. William didn't have a hard time imagining why doors opened for her. She'd used the library, attended lectures, and spent nights in the dorms, forever popping up where least expected, haunting the school, simply *belonging*. William had never spoken to her or her friends once in four years.

Now they were all at the same party. It wasn't, of course, a coincidence.

William had been living in Murray Hill and working at Joyce, Bennett, and Salzmann, a boutique downtown investment firm with its fair share of wealthy partners and wealthier clients. He'd been there for three uncomfortable years. Even before Lehman Brothers and Merrill Lynch had sent everyone into a panic, William had been worried about getting laid off. Just like college, the real world was all a game of who you knew. When the bosses began sending pink slips to the print server, they'd start with the people they didn't care for—or even remember. William knew he had no presence. Not at JB&S. Not anywhere. He always skipped the big holiday party, the weekend retreat at Bennett's house in East Hampton, and even the celebratory lap around the island on Salzmann's yacht after the Fontainebleau merger had come through, thanks largely to William's own analyses. He had spent those evenings like all the others: at home in his apartment watching old movies. Which is what he'd have been doing the night of the party, if he hadn't seen Irene two weeks earlier at the gallery.

Mr. Joyce had sent William downtown to pick up a monstrous mural of deboned chickens that his wife had commissioned from an artist named Xeer Sool who was, apparently, very hot just then. And there she'd been! Irene Richmond! In greasy overalls, beautiful as ever, trying to help an angry Austrian sculptor bolt ceiling fan blades together at precise thirty-nine-degree angles. She didn't look up, but William knew she'd never have recognized him if she had. He had been wallpaper at school. If they made beige wallpaper you couldn't even tell wasn't paint. It didn't matter. He could not get her out of his head. He had actually had dreams about her—always in black and white, as if she were in one of his movies.

Then the following week he'd seen the invitation for the K Gallery Christmas party arrive with Mr. Joyce's mail. He knew Mrs. Joyce would be in Vail with her husband anyway and wouldn't be able to go. So, just like the champagne bottle, he'd stolen it. The Dow was in free fall. They were probably going to fire him anyway. Still, it had been a week of hemming and hawing before he'd decided to go as an envoy of Mrs. Joyce's—merely hoping to catch sight of Irene again. He'd never for a moment imagined he'd speak to her, let alone that she'd be twenty feet away, smiling at him.

For her part, Irene was mainly happy that Sara had someone nice to talk to, since she still had to schmooze for work and George and Jacob could never be pried apart. She knew odds were good that Sara would try to adopt William. Sara was forever picking up strays—after all, she'd once been one of them. Irene did notice that

William kept looking over at her. Looking at her and then looking quickly away, that is, as if she were the sun and he might damage his retinas if he stared too long. She waited until he stared again and raised her champagne flute in one hand.

William looked away so fast, he thought he'd pulled a ligament. Or whatever you had in your neck. What would she think of him, leering like that? Oh. Except that now she was mouthing "thank you." What on earth for? Oh. For the champagne. All right then.

Sara was explaining that George had become an astronomer as he'd always planned. Well, a researcher. Well, a research *assistant*. But at a quite respected observatory and certainly on his way to gaining faculty status when his research was completed. She was beckoning to George and Jacob so wildly that they finally had to come over. "Jacob was in classics too. You must have been in some of the same classes!" Sara insisted, "That department was the size of a postage stamp. There were only four professors—Douglas, Jones, Khan, and oh! the alcoholic one. Wilfrey!"

"Why do you have the 2003 classics faculty memorized?" Jacob asked.

Sara tapped her right temple. "Like a steel trap."

Jacob looked at William. "Well, mine's a hunk of Swiss cheese. I swear I just can't remember you. Nothing personal."

Sara knew he was lying. Jacob *did* remember him, and it damn well *was* personal that he was pretending otherwise. Why would he do such a thing? Jacob could be a jerk when he wanted to be, and he nearly always wanted to be. Over the years she'd tried to introduce several new friends to the group, but they never lasted.

This time would be different though. William was blushing every time he caught sight of Irene. They were perfect for each other. At least a lot more perfect than the awful people that Irene had crashed in and out of bed with lately. Sara mentally reviewed the full 2008 batting order: Connie the bitter divorcée; Sasha the former figure skater with the "mild" coke habit; "Cowboy" Lenny who had turned out to be "Cult Member" Lenny; and Anne, a Lower East Side chef with a mean streak longer than the wait at her restaurant. But now there was something softening in Irene's stance when she turned toward William.

"I wish I'd stuck with classics," William confessed. "I ended up at Yale for my MBA."

"You make it sound like you tripped and fell into it," Jacob said.

Sara flicked his ear. "Ignore Jacob. He hates anyone who went to Yale."

"Why? Did he go to—Sorry, did you go to Harvard?"

"No," Sara said wryly, "Yale rejected him, and his ego never recovered. You'd think Harold Bloom personally came over and strangled his puppy."

Jacob was pointedly ignoring the both of them now. He and George were whispering to themselves about something or other, though not as quietly as they thought they were. William stood alone, pretending to look out the window at the falling snow, trying not to appear to be eavesdropping on the boys' conversation—even though they were standing right next to him and not even bothering to be quiet now that Sara had walked away.

"*Here*," Jacob was saying, "in front of everybody? You're the living worst."

"It's our anniversary," George explained, so cheerily it seemed forced.

"It is beyond lame of you to keep celebrating all these anniversaries. Eight years since you first made out! Eight months since you took your first trip together! Five years and six months since you first bumped uglies! Are you both in middle school? It's revolting."

"Can you be quiet?"

Jacob shrugged. "We may never know."

"She'd want me to do it here," George tried again, "with our closest friends."

Jacob snorted. "What'll you do if she says no?"

"She's not going to say no."

"I forgot you can predict the future. You should look at my stock portfolio sometime."

"You don't have a stock portfolio. You barely have a couch."

"I've still got half my bar mitzvah money in Nintendo stocks, and don't insult the blue foldout! We bought that couch together, remember? And I've bumped more uglies on it than—"

William decided it probably wasn't a good time to offer to take a look at Jacob's portfolio, or to tell him that his own picks were still doing better than expected, despite the Dow being down about five thousand points since October. Actually he hoped to talk to Jacob about poetry—William had done his thesis on *The Iliad*—but the guy showed zero interest, and so William decided it was probably just as well that he take off. He moved away toward a waiter with a tray of duck meatballs smothered in bulgogi sauce. After he grabbed one and ate it, he realized the leftover toothpick was the perfect excuse to wander toward the kitchen, where Irene and Sara were whispering about something else. They didn't notice him as he dumped the toothpick and began looking for a napkin to wipe his hands.

"So what did she say at the follow-up?" Sara was asking.

"I don't know! She checked it out." Irene refilled her champagne flute from the bottle William had brought, which she'd reappropriated from the bartender and was hiding behind an Estelle Danziger gigantic toy nutcracker with immodest genitalia.

Sara held her flute out for a refill. "I hope she did more than take pictures this time."

"They—I don't know—I think she stuck a needle in there."

"Well, did she or didn't she?"

"She scraped it or something. I didn't look."

"Sweetie, you are hopeless."

Irene looked crushed and laid her head on Sara's shoulder. Sara told her that it was all going to be fine.

William wished he had any idea what they were talking about, but before he could hear more, he noticed Jacob blazing a path across the party toward the girls, with George a step behind. William pretended to be only just coming upon them all again.

Jacob was in mid-rant. "I'm opposed to the whole institution! I'm pissed as hell they want to legalize it for us. Not having to get married was the only advantage we used to have over you people. That and our get-out-of-the-army-free cards . . . I swear, next they're going to figure out how to get me pregnant."

Sara shot George a quizzical look, and George shrugged.

William figured this was as good a time as any for him to make his exit, so he tapped Sara on her shoulder and, faking a yawn, said, "I should get going." He reached in his pocket to grab a business card, but before he could get there, he found his hand intercepted by something else—by another hand, divinely smooth and soft.

"Don't be ridiculous!" said Irene. "You've barely said a word to me yet."

William felt his whole body choke up. "Hello," he managed to say.

"Hey, Sara, could I see you on the balco—" George interrupted.

But Sara was busy. "Jacob, did you know William did his thesis on *The Iliad*?"

William nodded. "I worked with Professor Douglas. On the paradox of fatality and divinity . . . I mean, the idea that to some extent the mighty Olympian gods were restricted by the Three Fates, that they were some kind of independent panel—"

"Sure, sure," Jacob interrupted. "So what translation do you like?"

"Lattimore."

Jacob coughed. "Lattimore? Come *on!* Fagles or Lombardo, even, did it *way* better. Christ, I can't believe they let you into Yale with *Lattimore*."

Irene spoke mischievously, "Hey, don't knock my man Lattimore. Besides, *I* heard Fagles and Lambada were total quacks."

"Hopped up on bennies, translating into the dead of night. A trail of broken hearts behind them."

"Oh, you be quiet," Jacob poked her in the side.

"Hey," Irene pouted, "we've been here how long? How about a hello?"

Jacob bowed toward her. "My liege."

William felt his face turn red. He'd never known people who ricocheted so swiftly between obnoxiousness and affection. He supposed they had had a lot of practice over the years.

He tried to return to familiar ground. "Well, Fagles makes it sound very *nice*, but—"

"Nice? Nice? This is Homer we're talking about, not a Hallmark card! *Nice?* My God!"

As Jacob began a familiar tirade about society's overuse of certain adjectives and their eventually being rendered meaningless, George excused himself to the bathroom. Nobody noticed him slip away. There was a bit of a wait, so he polished off another tasteless Wasteland while he stood in line. The drinks were blotting out the surrounding party but also having the unfortunate effect of amplifying his nervous thoughts. He thought splashing a little cold water on his face might do the trick. At last he got inside, where there was relative peace, and took three long deep breaths.

The bathroom was all white marble and great Greek arches. It was the only room in the suite that hadn't been redecorated with contemporary art, and as he washed his hands and splashed cold water on his face, he appreciated the refreshing, comfortable hotel art—the white cliffs overlooking a Minos seaside, a round bronze platter covered in faux verdigris, the cherubic statuary above the bath.

Alone at last, he let his expression fall and stared into his own eyes in the mirror. His hair was everywhere, and his suit jacket was too tight in the shoulders somehow. He wasn't used to feeling nervous and self-conscious. He'd been perfectly fine until that stupid accident—but he didn't want to think about that, tonight of all nights. Delicately, he took the engagement ring out of his pocket and placed it on the countertop in the light. He'd never understood before. *Why diamonds?* he'd always asked. *Seems kind of arbitrary.* But now that he was looking at the ring and trying to imagine putting it on Sara's finger, anything less seemed unworthy, impermanent. What he'd said to Jacob was the truth. He couldn't imagine any scenario in which Sara would say no. It had been such a foregone conclusion for so long that he was now worried only about doing justice to their decade together.

He nudged the ring with his fingertip. Would it fit? He'd measured her finger with a little piece of string one night while she'd been sleeping. But what if he'd done it wrong? The ring seemed too narrow. He nudged it again. The drain in the neighboring sink was wide open, and a deep chill ran up and down his spine. He hadn't realized. *Don't knock it into the sink. Don't bump it. Pick it up carefully . . .* Jesus! He lowered his fingers like an arcade crane, from directly above. Even being careful, it slipped just a little. He thought his head would explode. His head or his heart. But he had it, and he was lifting it, and he would not drop it.

Still, some perverse imp inside his head was making him imagine it: his sweaty fingertips would loosen; he would try to grip it more firmly, but it would slip even more. Then he would hear it—the dread *clink* of the band against porcelain. He would look down into the basin just in time to see it *clink* again. He would reach in to snatch it, but he would only knock it closer. It would bounce around his groping hand like a glittering mosquito and then be *gone*. Gone. Down the drain. Lost forever.

He clenched the ring tightly in his fist, feeling the diamond pricking his palm. He thought about praying for some kind of reassurance, but someone was jiggling the knob. God, he couldn't wait until it was over, and he could wake up tomorrow feeling good again. Gently he put the ring back in the box and the box back in his pocket. He felt as if he might vomit, but then the doorknob was going again. There were people waiting.

The party simmered a little longer but never quite boiled. Four or five people made an attempt at dancing ironically to the Czech folk music being played off somebody's iPod, and then there was a lot of laughing, and there was no more dancing after that. Someone almost knocked into the Chevrolet bumper, and someone else passed out in the attached bedroom, and someone was saying the caterers were nearly out of food, and someone else was saying the bartenders would only be on until two and why not grab a cab down to this new club on Allen Street, and then the suite was half empty.

Irene barely noticed. People seemed far more willing to put their own coats on, now that they'd had a few drinks, and Abeba walked out with an arm around a buyer for the Goldman Sachs building. A minute later Juliette shoved an envelope into Irene's hands and ran after her. Neither of them came back. Then, more or less without warning, it was all over. Irene got a text message from Abeba that said, *Going tpo Jersey thxz v much for all hlp.* Irene gave the caterers their checks and tips from Juliette's envelope, and the bartenders kindly left behind a few half-empty bottles, and then there was no one left but them.

This had never happened before, in the years they'd been coming to the party, and they were as thrilled as young children allowed to stay up long after the adults had gone to bed.

"I'm going to defile some of this so-called art," Jacob roared.

"You can't defile it," Sara shouted. "It's already disgusting."

"I shall hump the moldy yam!" Jacob announced. But its green plastic case proved impenetrable, so he settled for miming fellatio on the wrought-iron baboon.

"What kind of art do you make?" William asked Irene nervously.

Irene, through her laughter, managed to say, "Nothing like this."

"To the balcony!" Jacob cried, grabbing a fresh bottle of champagne in one fist and shoving the door open with the other. Freezing air rushed in, and flakes of snow danced around their heads before being obliterated by the room temperature.

"The hotel wants us to stay off there!" Irene shouted.

"Then they should have locked it!"

"You realize it's snowing. Like, a lot," George said, even as he followed Jacob out. The dark tops of the neighboring skyscrapers waved like great trees in the wind, and it took him a moment to realize it was he who was leaning, not them.

William took his jacket off and offered it to Irene as they stepped outside. She took it gratefully and held his arm to keep from toppling over on her heels.

"A gentleman!" Sara cried, sticking her tongue out at George. He had gotten his jacket halfway off before remembering what was in the pocket. Then he got stuck getting it back on.

"I'm a mess!" he laughed.

"Uh-oh." Sara was always a bit delighted when he'd had too much to drink, as if he were a child who had eaten too much cotton candy at the county fair.

"There. Is. A. Hot. Tub." Jacob said, staring over onto the far corner of the balcony, like he'd just spotted the shroud of Turin. "There is a hot. Tub."

"It'll be freezing!" Sara shouted.

Jacob skidded and slid as he raced over to the enormous plastic tub, which was covered by a thick pad. He pressed his hands against the covering, and his eyes rolled back into his head.

"It's warm!" he cried. "It's warm!"

"Not like anyone packed a swimsuit!" George shouted.

"As if you all haven't seen me naked a dozen times before," Jacob shouted as he tore off his sweater and began in on his buttons.

"*William* hasn't! Jacob Blaumann, you put your clothes back on this instant!" Irene cried.

But it was too late—George was already helping him push the cover off. The two of them were no better than fraternity pledges when things like this came up.

Irene was worried that Juliette and Abeba might decide to return after all, or that some guest might come back looking for a forgotten purse or phone—but she was so tired of worrying. Worrying about her job and her doctor's appointment. She began to undo the tie on her dress. The cold air felt wonderful against her sore muscles, and her feet ached to be free from her shoes.

"Irene!" Sara was screeching.

"Come on, Mom," Irene said, handing William his coat back again.

"William! Sorry about this—we're not usually quite this *reck*less."

His face was red hot despite the subzero air. "I think I'll go."

"Seeya!" Jacob shouted, as everyone caught a glimpse of his ass lowering into the water.

"William, don't!" Sara screeched. "I'll be *so* embarrassed if you leave."

Would she really? If they met twenty years from now, would she remember? *That time in the hot tub at the Waldorf when we all got drunk and you left?* William bet that she would, and that he would, and he was so tired of remembering all the times he had left before things became insensible. Plus, Irene had gotten her dress off at last. He wanted to look but didn't dare. Instead he looked up at the red blinking lights on top of the building. Years ago his father had told him they were there to keep planes from hitting them.

Half dressed, George rushed back inside to stow the jacket safely on the couch.

"Now *this* is living," he heard Jacob shouting.

"Get bathrobes!" Sara yelled. "Or towels or something."

George dug two terrycloth robes out of a closet and grabbed a pair of towels from the bathroom. When he came back out onto the balcony, he found that his three friends—and William—had all gotten into the bubbling tub. The girls' underwear had gone see-through, but they kept their shoulders level with the water. William kept his eyes fixed on the stratosphere.

"Come on in, you big baby! We're not going to look," Jacob bellowed.

George undid his shirt while the girls hooted and hollered, and by the time his pants were off, Jacob was doing old-timey stripper music. "Da da da DA . . . Da da da DA . . ."

"No small bills!" George joked. "Fives and tens only, or I'm going right back inside." He thumbed the elastic of his Superman-blue boxer briefs, just enough to make Sara and Irene shriek, and then he climbed into the hot tub and dunked his head under at the sound of the popping champagne cork.

After coming back up and taking a long sip from the bottle, George turned to William. "After tonight we're either going to be best friends or you'll never talk to us again."

"My night with The Murphys," William joked.

"Oh my god! Do you remember? People used to call us that!" Sara cried.

Eventually George began to talk to him about people they'd known in common at school and then people who'd been at Yale. It was like they'd always been friends.

Yale. Despite appearances, Jacob was, slowly, beginning to stew. He expected that William imagined they did this sort of thing every weekend, but this was actually a first for the four of them. And he'd expected to feel triumphant—this, after all, was *exactly* the type of thing he was always trying to get them all to do. He was their ever-present diversion. Player of panpipes; God of wine; their much-needed anarchic spirit. He was the one who, back in the early years, had always insisted they should do shrooms and consummate the obvious tensions between them in some sort of orgy. They'd laughed, but he'd been perfectly serious. He'd wanted George, and George had wanted Irene, and Irene had been in love with Sara and George too, probably, so why not? Everybody had been in love with everybody—except him.

And now that they were there, sitting in a hot tub on the top floor of one of Manhattan's most exclusive hotels, he was steadily feeling less and less like a child left home alone without the grown-ups around and more like they *were* the grown-ups. All that glorious sexual tension had petered out. They sat there as platonically as brothers and sisters sharing a bathtub.

And now George was going to propose? Of course Jacob had known this would happen eventually. It had been coming for years now—the end of all this. No more drinking champagne in hot tubs at three in the morning or joking about fox hunts. The end of the years that they'd spent discovering this city like strangers in a strange land. Now they were just here. Now half of them would be married—hopelessly monogamous. Why would anyone do such a thing? Now they'd be just another lame, sexless couple and he'd be left with Irene.

George was trying to make the story of his commute sound exciting, again, and Irene was telling William and the others about her day—about the car rides with the art. And William was saying how much he really liked some of it—how he'd taken an elective at Yale called "Art After Warhol."

Jacob found himself laughing uncontrollably. "Art?" he was saying, shouting, spitting. "This crap isn't art. This is what happens when people who *hate* art try to make art."

Irene was nodding.

William felt emboldened. "But what does *art* even mean today in an age of commercialization—when the drinks we're having all night are named after poems and poets, just to make a buck?"

Jacob snorted. "*The Waste Land* is the fucking *Waste Land* no matter who misnames a drink after it. Fuck it. Two words or one, you can't cheapen it after the fact."

"Hear, hear!" cried Sara.

William rose. "Well, that moldy yam in a box makes you ask yourself, what is art really? Ultimately it's a question that we can never really answer."

"Sure we can. I'll answer it right now," Jacob said.

"But—" Irene began.

"No! No *buts*!" he was crying, and to illustrate his point, he lifted his great white rear out of the water. "It's always but, but, but, but, but."

There were shrieks and groans as Jacob reseized the watery floor.

"Real art obliterates artifice. *The Night Watchmen* doesn't jump out at you and say 'Hey! I'm just a bunch of paint!' No. It makes you forget that it ever had to be created in the first place. It makes you tremble before it. If anyone's trembling in front of a yam-in-a-box, it's because they're laughing. Or puking."

Nobody was arguing with Jacob at this point, but he was all revved up and couldn't stop.

"Art makes you feel things nobody ever taught you to feel before, because you're feeling what some stranger felt when he, or you'd better bet *she*, made it. It's living vicariously. It makes you love from inside someone else's heart and hate with the acid in someone else's guts. It's the only thing on this planet that can make us leave the pathetic smallness of our insignificant speckness and not just connect but *become* someone else. It's got to be metamorphic, or it's just fucking television."

Then Jacob stood, triumphant, and exposed himself to everyone. The snow swirled around his head as he brought his hand to his lips and cried, "TOOO DOOO! TOOO DOOO!" He saluted George, marched out of the tub, went inside, and passed out facedown on the couch.

"William," Irene said, "come help me get a towel over him so he doesn't die of pneumonia or something."

William looked away until Irene was in her robe, then climbed out to join her. They went inside together, and it was the last that George or Sara saw of either of them until morning.

Alone together at last, George moved around to Sara's side of the hot tub and put his arms around her. She laid her head against his firm shoulder, and they sat that way, in silence. The sky above was pink-gray and starless, as it always was in the city. They gazed across Lexington at the office windows. Far below were taxi horns and car alarms and the rumble of the M102, going south from Harlem to the East Village. These were the noises of their great, unsleeping city. The familiar creaks and groans of their home.

George hoped he looked calm, even though he was cursing himself for not bringing the ring back outside. He didn't know where he would have hidden it, exactly, but this seemed like the moment he'd been waiting for. But how to get back inside and come out again? Could he say he had to go to the bathroom? That'd kill the mood.

He was overcome with a feeling of rightness, as if for once his outside matched his in—and yet he was stuck. To get up would be to ruin it. And as they sat there, the silence lengthened, and he began to worry it had gotten too long, and so he tried to think of something to say—but the only thing he could think of was the accident he'd seen on the way back from Long Island. He didn't want to think about it, but there it was. A perverse pricking began on his lips. He had to say *something,* and the only thing he wanted to say would, again, most assuredly ruin everything.

"I saw a dead body today." God, the relief to say it out loud.

Sara gasped and squirmed around to look him in the eye. "At work?"

George shook his head. "No. On the LIE. That accident I told you about. A guy died."

He had nearly missed it. He'd been sitting in traffic, thinking about Sara and what he would say to her that night at the party. He'd been watching the snow start to fall and checking the ring in his pocket every few minutes. Then at long last, he'd come to the head of the bottleneck. Having been sitting in the car that whole time absolutely fuming about rubberneckers, he was eager to speed angrily ahead. He wasn't going to look. He wanted to prove that he was above such petty gawking.

But then he had. At first all he had seen was a green Isuzu with a great big hole in the windshield. He had been taken in by the size of the hole, and then he'd noticed that there was no one in the car. *Of course*, he'd thought, *they've gotten him out by now. He's back by the ambulance getting insurance forms filled out*. But then George thought—what if? What if he had sailed through the glass—headfirst—the initial impact almost certainly knocking him out, if not killing him instantly? What if he had gone straight through the glass and been launched into the air (George could see it happening in slow motion, as in a terrible soap opera), and then had landed on the pavement and crumpled—

And then George had seen it. The body. Not his imagination's pale little TV version but real, there, on the pavement. Right where the horrid calculator in his brain intuited it should be, given the weight of a grown man versus the resistance of a windshield versus the momentum of sixty-five miles per hour rapidly become zero, launching him into flight while gravity, that sick constant, pulled him to the pavement. Right there. The man was there and not there at all.

Thank God the man's face had been turned away; the body was hunched over, head bent to the pavement as if he were merely praying.

All this had happened in just three or four seconds. Soon the honking of the other impatient drivers brought George back to reality, and he'd sped off. But in that brief instant, he'd felt that man's impact with the glass as if it had been his own. He'd felt his own knees hitting the pavement—his own face coming down, hard.

He had been trying to shake that feeling the whole night, and only now that he'd mentioned it to Sara was the feeling easing. He stroked her neck gently with the side of his hand. It was a moment before he realized that she was looking down. Long, dark tendrils of hair fell around her face.

George could see that she was crying. "What's the matter?"

"Nothing."

"Is it about the accident?"

Sara shook her head.

He began to panic. "Did Jacob say something to you?"

She sobbed. "Irene went back to the doctor."

George shushed her gently. "It's going to be nothing. She's young. She's practically a vegan. She's basically Wonder Woman. Don't worry."

But Sara *would* worry; George knew that. In fact he loved it when she worried about things, because it made him confident for the both of them. That was the best part of love, he thought. Better than sex or not waking up alone or cooking without having to halve all the ingredients. Sara made him braver, and George made her calmer. Vicarious. That was what love could do. This was the reason he wished he'd thought of, before.

A few light nudges with his nose made Sara turn up and close her eyes to kiss him. The snow was really picking up now. Sleepily, they watched the flakes dancing down across the street into the rising steam above St. Bartholomew's and all across Midtown. Down it came, over the Village and the Bronx, blowing across both dark rivers and along the whole of Long Island. Piling high on the steel guardrails and concrete medians, and the roads that ran through the city and out in all directions.

George knew the time had come. Ring or no ring, this was his moment, and it would never be quite like this again. He loved this woman, and he knew he would never stop loving her—first, better, always, most. He could see Sara's heart pounding. Somehow she always knew what he was about to say.

FIVE IN A MILLION

1

On Tuesday, George Murphy arrived at the office to discover that his star was on the verge of collapse. Perhaps in some metaphorical way, but also actually—237 Lyrae V, a prestellar core in the Ring Nebula that George had been studying for the past four years was experiencing a highly unexpected gravitational collapse. This, at least, according to the note he'd found on his desk that morning from Allen Ling, his cubicle mate at the astrophysics department of Brookhaven University. He had scrawled *"She's gonna blow!"* at the top of a spreadsheet whose rows and columns—much to George's annoyance—did appear to delineate the variations in temperature and density that might characterize the beginning of a collapse.

Not looking up, George said, "You are a delight to work with."

Allen, who was on the phone with someone at the European Space Agency, paused from speaking rapid-fire Spanish just long enough to flip George the bird and spin toward his computer, where he was seriously bungling a game of Snood.

George felt it all slipping fast away. All throughout his two-hour commute on the icy LIE, he'd been thinking of exactly how to tell his coworkers that he had finally proposed to Sara. Fatherly Dr. Cokonis had certainly been asking long enough when he would finally "make an honest woman out of her" or, as Allen preferred, "put some bling on that shit." But now this would be the main business of the day—hell, if not the month. George's doctoral and now postdoctoral research centered on what were called prestellar cores, essentially huge clusters of cosmic gases that sometimes collapsed into young protostars. Allen had been predicting this fate for 237 Lyrae V all year, despite George's lovingly constructed models that suggested the contrary.

Privately, George imagined himself as a sort of astronomical Darwin, creating algorithms that could hypothetically be used to better predict the stellar landscape millennia from now. The earliest results had led him to identify dozens of cores that were on the verge of becoming stars—but discouragingly, none of them yet had. His formulas had also revealed several highly stable cores, like 237 Lyrae V, in the Ring Nebula, which were statistically unlikely to ever reach T Tauri status, with orbiting planetary bodies and asteroid belts and all the rest. It was these predictions on which his entire project was based, but if Allen was right, it was all about to be disproven on a grand scale.

It took George a half hour to confirm Allen's data, and another hour to rerun the numbers through a series of algorithms on the computer, which spat out even more numbers, which then had to be rechecked. None of them looked hopeful. George simply willed it not to be true, and after another hour he could think of nothing to do but call Sara. As he dialed, he anticipated the relief he'd feel in complaining about this devastating development—but as her phone rang, he hesitated. He didn't particularly relish the idea of Allen overhearing such a breakdown, and he didn't see how he could ruin Sara's day with worrying. She'd been so excited to tell everyone at the *Journal* about the proposal—

"Hey, you!" her voice came on the line.

"Hey, yourself," George said, more smoothly and cheerily than he felt by a mile.

In the background he could hear the busy hum of Bistro 19, one of their group's go-to spots. Sara was cutting out of work early to have lunch with Irene to keep her mind off the fact that the doctor might call with the biopsy results. According to Irene, they had said they'd know something "later next week," which made George think there'd be no word until Thursday or Friday, or else they'd have said *We'll call first thing.* But he knew it was important to Sara, even if not to Irene, to be the sort of friend who insisted on having lunch with you when the doctor was probably not going to call.

George cleared his throat. "So, some stuff came up over the weekend. I'll have to stay late tonight to get it straightened out."

He could hear her disappointment as she said, "But Irene got us all tickets to see *The Death of Eurydice* tonight."

"Oh, right. Well, the thing is that one of the most important prestellar cores in my research is undergoing some pretty surprising shifts."

"Sweetie, your star will still be shifting tomorrow. It's not like you can stop it."

George wanted to argue, but at the same time he realized that she was right—if the prestellar core really *was* collapsing, that really meant it had already collapsed, more than two thousand years ago, because all the information they were collecting right now had actually been traveling at light speed across space for two millennia, and so whatever was happening was all over and done already, one way or the other . . . but that didn't change the fact that his research, here and now, might all be a complete and total waste of time. Four years of his life shot—a blink in the existence of 237 Lyrae V, but a long time to him, especially at the start of his career—

Sara broke in on his long silence. "Fine, I'll see if William can take your ticket then."

"Don't be mad."

"I'm not mad."

"Good. And see if you can find out what happened with him and Irene on Friday."

"I *can't* ask him that." A pause and then, "Though I might ask *her* if she ever shows up."

"There you go. You're a reporter. Do some digging!"

"I'm an *editor.* I edit *other* people's reporting. If you can call it that."

"Just a joke," he said. There was a long sigh. "Everyone's really excited about our big news," George lied, his voice low so Allen wouldn't hear.

Then a happy noise. "Here too! I'm already making up a guest list. You should get the home addresses of anyone you want to invite from the department."

"Let's invite everyone but Allen," George said, louder now, earning another middle finger from his office mate.

"Good luck with your star. There's an after-party thing. Meet us there, okay?"

He released a long sigh. "Just text me the address?"

"It's in Greenpoint."

Long sigh, *redux.*

"Love you."

"Love you too."

He got off the phone. He didn't know what to do next. He closed his eyes. How could this be happening? He had to remind himself that Allen wasn't capable of collapsing a giant molecular cloud of gas, a hundred times larger than their solar system. But that didn't stop him from resenting his colleague, who had been ascending with Machiavellian precision through the department by subtly undermining the research of others.

George had fallen in love, thirteen years ago, with the dream of all the infinite things in the universe still to be discovered, of theories to be pieced together and daring connections made. The Allens of the world, however, seemed to outnumber him at every turn . . . researchers who didn't look out into the universe, pondering, but instead busied themselves attending conferences and reading abstracts, looking for flawed research to tease apart or supposed discoveries to disprove. George knew, in theory, that the world—the universe—needed these doubting Allens to check the ideas of the dreamers, but he wished they didn't enjoy it quite so much.

George called Jacob, whom he could usually count on for sympathy in these matters, but his friend didn't answer. If he was up at the asylum, he couldn't usually pick up.

"Kaaaaaaa"—George heard Allen shouting behind him—"BLOOEY!"

"Are you in the third grade?" George asked without turning around.

"I wish. Okay. So I just got off with the guys in Madrid. They're getting us some time on the Messier Telescope tonight to get the last of the data."

"Us? Don't you have the Phoenix-13 all afternoon?"

"That weakass telescope can't get us the readings we need. Come on."

"Again, who is this *us*?"

Allen shouted, "You and me, G-man! I'm telling you—this is exciting shit!"

"This is a catastrophe, Allen." George pointed to the shelf full of black three-ring binders, identical except for the steady fading plastic, moving leftward, as they went back in time toward his first research years. "Four years in those. Two thirty-seven Lyrae V was supposed to be *stable*."

"That's what makes it so interesting, G-man. She ought to be one of the most stable cores in the Ring Nebula, right? I mean, from what you've found so far, it should take a goddamn supernova to collapse two thirty-seven. Only there's not one. So we've got to ask ourselves, in the words of our great scientific forebears—what the fuck?"

"Allen—"

"I'm saying, George. It's not too late to get on board with this paper I'm writing."

"*You're* writing?"

"Okay, okay—we're writing. We're going to watch the collapse in real time, G-man. That's rare as shit. We're talking 'target of opportunity.' We're talking you and me are going to get time on the motherfucking *Hubble*," Allen said, standing quickly. "Look, I've got a lunch with Cokonis. I'm going to catch him up on all this. Think it over. If this is what I think it is, you don't have a lot of time to start writing grants." He was practically skipping as he left the cubicle.

"Oh, and by the way, I'm getting married . . ." George said to the empty air. There was a long quiet, and then steadily he heard the clack of keyboards and the squeak of chairs from the other cubicles all up and down the hallway. The click of phones being put back into their cradles, the hum of fluorescent lights, the scuffing of rubber soles on carpeting.

Allen was right. George knew it. He had been massively wrong about everything leading up to it, but aside from that fact, 237 Lyrae V's collapse could actually be huge for them. Shouldn't he want that?

George rolled his chair over to Allen's computer, where he'd left the interface open for the Phoenix-13 telescope. Pausing the data stream Allen was downloading, George's fingers typed in the set of complex coordinates without conscious thought: Right ascension of $18^h\ 53^m\ 35.079^s$. Declination of $+33°\ 01'\ 45.03$. There was a long pause as the telescope, twenty-five hundred miles away in Arizona, adjusted its mechanized gaze to a completely different part of the universe. The sheer scale of these little keystrokes still floored George some days and still briefly distracted him from the heinous particulars of his job—that morning consisting of ten e-mails in two hours from Cokonis about getting the next round of grants written up, about publishing his next paper, about presenting at a conference in Wichita.

The images began to come up on the screen. The Ring Nebula, aka Messier 57, aka NGC 6720. A planetary nebula in the constellation Lyra, a great reddish ring of fire surrounding an iris of blue-green like ocean water. On the sad little computer monitor, George couldn't see much detail, but he knew it glowed like an ember on the big infrareds . . . and that it was, in its way, an ember, left over when a star exhausted its supply of hydrogen and the outer layers pushed outward and it became a red giant. He zoomed the telescope to its maximum point and found his little core inside the nebula. Just a hundred thousand years old. Practically an infant in cosmic terms, emitting no light, only heat and gas, but he knew it was there.

He'd first seen the Ring Nebula in AP Physics C. Mr. Pix had put it up on a color transparency, explaining, "Every once in a while, a dusty red giant star can become a nebulae, like M fifty-seven, here, which contains an unknown number of nebulosities, and in this way, one dying star becomes a kind of breeding ground for new ones."

George had been stunned. Until then they'd been so fixated on heat death and entropy and black holes that he'd never stopped to think about the fact that the universe was constantly generating new stars. Against all the data it now seemed as if 237 would become one of them. But, as Sara had reminded him, its fate was sealed. Whatever was happening had happened already. The weak light he could see had left the star two millennia ago. It had all been over and done with back in the days of Babylon and Plato, when the first astronomers had turned their lenses toward the black sea above them and ventured to look more closely at those white shining spirits. His little dot was just one in 400 billion, but George didn't care. It was his, and he whispered to it, there in his cubicle, "Don't you die on me."

2

How exactly like George, Sara thought, to ask someone to marry him at three in the morning, when she couldn't call everyone she knew. She considered this while waiting for Irene to arrive for lunch—already twenty-five minutes late. Maybe there had been news, and Irene had decided to bail. She was a disappearance artist, Irene was. Days or weeks could go by without contact, either because she was working on a new piece or because of something personal. She could be maddeningly private. Evading the circling of an impatient waiter, Sara pretended to be on her phone while she replayed the weekend's events in her mind.

For the first two minutes after George had asked, she'd said almost nothing but "Oh my God" until George reminded her she technically hadn't said yes yet, and so then she said yes for the two minutes that followed. But after those four minutes were over, she had wanted nothing more than to burst into the bedroom Irene and William had vanished into, except maybe to call her parents in Gloucester, except maybe to call her sister in Vancouver, except maybe to call Sue, her best friend from third grade, and then there were her grandparents in Sacramento and Austin . . . but it was still after midnight there and everywhere else.

"Let's call your cousin Peg in London!" Sara had shouted, leaping from the hot tub and hardly pausing to wrap herself in a towel before rushing to find a phone.

"It's only eight there," George had said.

"Call her, call her, calllllllll her!" Sara had screeched happily. While George hunted down his phone, she continued to make erratic squeaking noises.

"I don't have her new number," George concluded after investigating his contacts list.

Sara grabbed the phone and began flipping through, looking for people to call. "Do you ever clean this thing out? You still have your RA's number from freshman year." Then she clapped. "Jacob! Let's tell Jacob!"

She was inside the hotel again before George could catch up to her. There they found Jacob wearing nothing but couch cushions.

"Wake him up!" Sara insisted. "He's your friend."

"You've known him practically as long as I have!"

"But you knew him first," she insisted. "So technically he's your friend."

George thought about this. "Does that mean I get to tell Irene too?"

"Don't be ridiculous. She's a girl. It's completely different."

"Completely different according to who?"

"Polite society," she insisted. "And it's 'according to *whom*.' "

George looked dubiously downward at their naked, snoring friend and begrudgingly poked him in the shoulder. Sara had to hand it to him—Jacob seemed neither polite nor social as he made a half-snarl and shifted, exposing one gigantic pale buttock. She sighed and gave Jacob a hearty slap on the back of the head. When this succeeded in opening just one of the boy's bleary eyes, she looked at him squarely and said, "George has something to tell you."

The bloodshot pupil had swiveled in its socket toward George, who stammered at it, "We're . . . um. We're engaged!"

There'd been a short silence, and then, in a growl from deep beneath a throw pillow, Jacob had said, "Engaged in what exactly?"

"To be married, you ass!" Sara shouted happily, bouncing on the couch beside him.

Jacob snorted, closed his eye, and said, "Does this mean Sara'll finally stop being a puritan priss and move into your place?"

"Obviously," George said, just as Sara said, "*George's* place?"

They paused, each sure the other was joking.

"Who's moving in with who?" George had asked.

"With *whom*," Jacob and Sara both corrected him at once.

That matter had still not been settled. And Jacob hadn't been the last to ask. Her parents had asked almost immediately, as had his. It was ridiculous that George imagined she could move into *his* place. It was hardly big enough for even one person to move around in. Granted it was on Riverside, in a beautiful prewar building, a stone's throw from the park and close to Zabar's. And of course it was insanely cheap, which was why George had remained in this prison cell, with its single sad window that wasn't wide enough for an air conditioner. And people never believed her when she said this, but his shower was inside his kitchen! The toilet, then, was in another room the size of a coat closet, with no sink. But the worst thing by far was that his bed folded up into the wall. Yes. George Murphy, her soon-to-be husband, slept on a Murphy bed.

Sara's apartment, all the way across the island on York Avenue, was vastly superior. The railroad style wasn't all that convenient for living with Karen, a former coworker whose boyfriend, Troy, now spent every night and most of every weekend there. But it would be perfect for her and George, if Karen could be convinced it was high time she moved out to Westchester, where she and Troy both worked now anyway.

The waiter was circling Sara like a shark now, trying to get her to give up the table. He was new and didn't know that she was there practically all the time. He kept asking if perhaps she'd like to wait at the bar until her friend arrived. Sara pretended to take important calls from the office when he approached, her thoughts flitting to *The Death of Eurydice*. Some artsy friends of Irene's were in it and had given them all tickets. But now Irene was saying she was too busy, and George couldn't make it, and Jacob flat-out said he could make it if he'd wanted to but didn't want to. Rude. Well, William had already written back to say he'd be delighted to come, and Sara could hardly wait to see him. She hoped he might inject a bit of civility into the group.

Sara came out of her reverie to find the waiter hovering again.

She coughed and ordered another coffee, though she was jittery enough from the first two cups. It was strange being there alone. Since they'd come to the city, this had been where they'd all gathered by default for brunches, lunch breaks, and late-night bull sessions. They'd last been there a week ago, though actually—no, they hadn't all been there. Jacob hadn't been able to make it. And it had been trouble, as it always was, when one of them was missing. Whenever all of them were anywhere together—picnics down at the Battery, visits to see a new exhibit of Edwardian Court costumes at the Met, an investigatory meal at a new restaurant—no one said a cross word. If anyone did (most often Jacob), it was seen as genuinely good-natured . . . However, whenever someone was missing, that person almost instantly became the subject of speculation, criticism, and suspicion. It was as if the person's absence left a hole in their mutual fabric, and the others couldn't help but pull at the fraying threads around the hole, as if to say *Something ought to be here. How has this happened?*

Just last week they'd been right here in Bistro 19, without Jacob, because he was out on a date with a new boy. *Isn't he still secretly dating his boss?* Irene wanted to know, even though his arrangement with the boss had been open from the get-go and they all knew it. Then George had started calling the new boy "Siddhartha," because Jacob had mentioned that he lived this, like, monastic lifestyle, though not for religious reasons but just because he was sort of OCD about clutter and—here was the worst part—were they ready? They'd met at a coffee shop when Jacob had seen him finish reading a copy of *Angela's Ashes*, get up, wipe down his table, clear his cup, and then *throw the book in the trash can.*

Irene couldn't believe it. What George wanted to know was, had Jacob seen the Siddhartha guy's place yet, and was it, like, completely spotless? Sara hadn't been able to help herself from asking if Siddhartha had seen *Jacob's* place yet, and Irene and George had almost lost it. None of them, not once in six years, had seen Jacob's apartment.

It was somewhere way up in East Harlem, and as far as they could tell, he never stayed there. Either he slept with a current or past boyfriend, or he stayed up in Stamford with his boss and took the train in as if nothing were at all strange. But it was strange. For one thing, he wouldn't tell any of them where the apartment actually was. Sara thought it was because he'd bitten off more than he could chew in terms of the neighborhood, all blustery and believing that he could fit right in, only to find, as she'd explicitly told him a hundred times, that he didn't feel safe, but of course he couldn't admit that, and kept renewing the lease just to make the point.

She checked her phone again. Still no message from Irene. She texted Jacob to see if he'd heard from her. She texted Irene a question mark. She texted George a smiley face and admitted to herself, then and there, that of course she'd move in with him in a heartbeat—even into that tiny closet-toilet apartment. She'd live with him in a refrigerator box, in a nursery rhyme shoe, a teepee, an igloo, or a fortress made of couch cushions. Let the doubters doubt. Let the future be unsure. In a city of eight million, they'd always be two, together, and that was the beginning and the end of it. Then, just as she was about to get up and head back to the office, Irene rushed into the restaurant, her hands up high in breathless apology.

3

Jacob lay in bed with a poem wadded up inside his mouth. A dry, papery obstruction. The toxic stinging of ink along the ridge of his tongue. He reached in with two fingers and tried to pull it out, even as his throat, in some sort of horrible reverse gag reflex, tried to contract and swallow the poem whole. Just as his fingers hooked onto one pulpy piece of it, he felt his esophagus swell and take the whole thing in like Jonah's whale. He pulled, gagging, on the edge of the paper, but it ripped, leaving just a scrap pressed between his fingers. His nightmare ended with a gasping breath, the poem ingested again—*again! every fucking night!*—and his bleary eyes staring down at the ripped fragment of paper he'd torn free. On it was the first line, in handwriting so messy he couldn't read it.

And then he'd woken up, and that too, had vanished.

It took him a moment to be sure he wasn't really choking. He could still *feel* the lump in his throat. As he got his breath back, he tried to think of where he was. *Pete's apartment*, he thought, when he saw Pete snoozing on the right edge of the mattress. *He worked from home on Tuesdays and Fridays. Which means that I am in Morningside Heights. Again.*

Moving softly so as not to wake the slumbering Pete, Jacob found his pants on the floor, next to the copy of *Breakfast at Tiffany's* that Pete was *still* finishing. What was it, like a hundred pages? He squeezed himself out of bed and slipped into the bathroom with the blue jeans, button-down Oxford, and brown tweed sports jacket he had worn the night before. He looked out the window at the white light of early afternoon. He remembered he had a night shift up at Anchorage House.

He closed his eyes and tried to see the words from his dream. It was *there* somewhere; he could hear its footsteps just around the corners of his head. Impulsively, he grabbed his cell phone and texted Dr. Boujedra. *Oliver—Under the weather. Won't make it up tonight.* It was a message he sent at least once a week. One of the perks of his relationship with his boss was that he could usually get away with playing hooky when inspiration seemed about to strike—or even on days when he just couldn't handle spending eight hours in the presence of hallucinating, drug-withdrawn, suicidal teenagers.

Back in Pete's bedroom, Jacob picked up the Capote. It was the only book in the apartment—practically the only thing in the apartment. Pete owned one pot, one frying pan, one plate and one cup and one fork, a tacky lamp made out of conch shells, the mattress he slept on, one set of sheets—sky blue, with white puffy clouds—a yellow towel, and a cardboard box that contained his three outfits. One dressy, one for loafing around, and one to wear while washing the other two. He had a refrigerator and a stove, only because they'd come with the place, and both were always empty. His apartment was really quite large for a Manhattan studio, and Pete made good money working at Eco-Finance Apps or iPod Banking or something like that. He didn't belong to any cult or ascetic belief system that Jacob could discern.

You're such a weirdo, thought Jacob as he kissed sleeping Pete's cheek goodbye. Then he slipped out through the blank white door, which locked behind him with a click.

Jacob hurried down chilly Broadway and bustled up the icy iron ziggurat of the 125th Street station, just as the downtown number 1 train groaned onto the aboveground platform. He hardly had time to admire the view as he blew aboard just before the doors cinched shut. Morningside Heights yawned before him, and he tried to feel the immensity of the entire island, of the steel tonnage beneath his feet. He willed the whole labyrinthine mess of it to vibrate up his calves and forearms.

He had the first line—*he had it*—of an epic poem. Or at least it was nibbling on the little gleaming hook that dangled from his spinal cord. He reeled all the way in and recast, way out into the deep white city: the literal soul of a thousand poets who'd come before him; the fishing grounds of two thousand others who'd gotten up earlier, read longer, worked harder, breathed deeper. Still, couldn't he just snare a little Langston? Snag some Allen or Frank? He barely dared dream of angling for Walt or for Hart—those two slippery silver sturgeons, each eighteen feet long and weighing, together, a metric ton. Guarding their salty eggs, that humble caviar. Walt, the monstrous Methuselah, with his prehistoric whiskers in the murky bottom. And Hart, the lithe Leviathan, his steel-cabled fins propelling him through the upper currents. Jacob blinked twice as the ground outside the windows rose upward on each side, and in an instant he was underground.

Though the 1 train was quiet in an early-afternoon sort of way, Jacob transferred to the express 2 train at 96th Street, hoping to move even more swiftly south to Fourteenth Street and the coffee shop that he required to sit in and write this poem. It was the only place he could breathe easily enough to tease it out. The challenge, as always, was to hold this impish idea in his threadbare net until he could get there.

Jacob's mind traveled back to a high school biology class where, eighty pounds lighter and half as hairy, he had seen an article in a *National Geographic* magazine showing an African tribesman extracting a deadly parasitic worm from one of his legs. He grinned with blindingly clean teeth at the camera, as he displayed his affected leg. The onyx flesh was powdered with whitish dust, except for a circle about the size of a quarter that he'd been keeping clean. From a tiny, oozing wound emerged the freeloading worm, thick as a spaghetti strand and, according to the caption, more than *four feet long*, curled inside the man just beneath the flesh. The only way to extract it was to coax its little exposed wormy tail around a piece of twig. Then at a rate of one quarter-turn per day, the worm could be slowly spooled out of the wound. Any faster than this, and the alarmed worm would break its captured tail off, and the whole thing had to be started over. Between turnings, the twig and its wormy passenger had to be taped down onto the man's leg so that he could continue to run and hunt and live.

Disgusted, fourteen-year-old Jacob had been unable to rid his mind of the image and, worse, of the idea. Ten years later he found himself haunted by it nearly every day. For this was what writing poetry had become: a delicate extraction, done in quarter-turns, where the slightest jostling meant starting all over.

It hadn't always been that way, Jacob thought, as he slipped out of the 2 train. He hurried now, as he traversed the long white corridor between the 1-2-3 and the Brooklyn-bound L. In high school he'd written like blinking. On the backs of napkins. In textbook margins. On the edges of his desks. On the dividers in the bathroom stalls. On the chalkboards of empty classrooms. He wrote so easily that he hardly minded giving his little quatrains and sonnets away. He imagined them being found someday by younger versions of himself, who would then be inspired to continue the tradition of guerrilla poetry at Moses Maimonides Elementary School.

In college, he wrote only after four a.m., an hour he'd known intimately. He had to wait until everyone he knew fell asleep—when all excitement was over. With his friends falling down into couches and onto curbs and against the springs of others' beds, Jacob would scramble up the nearest sturdy tree. It didn't matter how drunk or how high he'd managed to get. He liked the feel of bark against his palms, the brush of branches on his stubbled cheeks. He liked to imagine that it was his way of tapping into his most primal self—a Paleo-Jacob who still hunted with spears and made fires with flint. But the truer reason was that he'd discovered that the fear of falling was just enough to keep him from going to sleep. More than once his friends had woken up to find him snoring in the embrace of an old oak tree's roots on the North Quad, having barely made it down before losing consciousness but with a completed poem safe there in the tweed pocket.

In this city without climbable trees, he'd taken to early rising and writing on boyfriends' fire escapes. And it was this way, just on the other side of four a.m., that he'd penned his great epic, *In the Eye of the Shitstorm*, and that, really, had been the beginning of all the trouble.

Looking back on it all now, Jacob could hardly believe he'd even attempted it. One thousand, nine hundred and thirty-two lines (in honor of the year that All Real Literature had died inside of Hart Crane, when he'd jumped into the Gulf of Mexico) and told in thirty-three sections (one for each year that Walt Whitman had worked on *Leaves of Grass*). *God,* Jacob thought, *what a pretentious little ass you were.* It didn't matter; he missed the confidence that had permitted it. Missed the fury that had blinded him to all paying of bills, all feeding of self, all sleeping at night until it was finished. It had taken him two weeks, and he'd begun to believe he'd never really recovered.

The poem had come after the suicide of his uncle Miles, a man from St. Louis who at forty-five had been able to fix anything motorized or mechanical. He had taken Jacob fishing for the first time when he was a boy out on the Missouri River. He had also been the first gay man Jacob had known. Miles had been thought to be just a happy bachelor by the rest of the Blaumann family. Only Jacob, at eight, had known the truth, after seeing his uncle embracing the shadow of another man behind a boathouse. It was their secret and Jacob had kept it, even after Miles swallowed a pharmaceutical cornucopia in the back of a Dodge Dart parked near the river.

His poem, *In the Eye of the Shitstorm*, was about his other great childhood idol, the only other superhero he'd ever believed in: Michael Jordan, hanging himself from the backboard of a basketball net in a Brooklyn schoolyard. The poem dipped in and out of the troubled life of the iconic athlete, circling the legend but never landing. The main character, in fact, wasn't the great Number Twenty-three at all. Jacob's "stroke of genius" (according to his editors at the Roebling Press) was beginning the poem just *after* the paparazzi and police had cleared the court of the body.

They have, in their thoughtless hurry, left behind the enormous pile of, well, *shit* that Number Twenty-three left beneath the basket when he'd strung himself up. A nameless janitor is brought in on a Sunday morning to remove the excrement. Most of the thirty-three epic sections, and the 1,932 lines, detailed the life of this nobody, as he makes various attempts to clean the famous man's fecal matter from the tarmac. He eventually settles on using his hose to steadily wash it all toward a drain on the edge of the court, where the crap begins to spiral in great Coriolis circles, forming a veritable hurricane of shit, the central image of the poem.

The Mariani Prize committee had particularly loved the "deft handling of pop-cultural allusions" (fearing litigation, Jacob had referred to Jordan throughout only as "Number Twenty-three") and his "unblinking insight into modern racial discourse" (Jacob had never quite figured out what that meant). Among the other accolades they'd heaped upon the poem were that it was "unabashedly obscene" and that he was "a man's poet like none since Bukowski"—misguided sentiments that made Jacob retch. Four years later these praises were braided together into the strands of a noose that he'd cinched around his own neck.

Reading *Shitstorm* sickened him now. He'd been angry as hell those two weeks when it had poured out of him. At the time he thought it honest, full of pure rage. A mirror held up to the sickness of the world. But as time had passed, he had come to realize that under all the sly references and ballsy profanity, his poem had only one monotonous undertone—the same shrill buzzing that had been in his head that whole week, in the wake of his uncle Miles. Beneath all the rest was only one sound. It went *fuck you and fuck you and fuck you and fuck you and fuck you and fuck you.* And that was all.

Jacob tried to shake all this from his head as people poured onto the train at Union Square. The car was crowded, and the swell of Brooklyn-bound bodies began to prick at something inside him. He felt hot and sick and shaky. He felt the worm begin to break, but with his eyes squeezed tight, he thought he might make it. He was so close. Just two quick stops, and he'd be free. He would coax it all out at last.

"Ladies and gentlemen," came a quaking voice behind him.

Not now, Jacob begged, keeping his eyes shut tight. But he could smell unwashed skin. He could feel hot breath passing his ear.

"Ladies and gentlemen, I'm sorry to bother you," the voice continued. "I need some money so that I can get something to eat. I'm really sorry to bother you, but I'm very hungry."

It wasn't the usual affectless mumbling that Jacob and most city residents had adjusted their internal dials to ignore. It wasn't the drone he'd heard a million times before, on sidewalks and street corners and in subway cars just like this. This man sounded really awful. This man sounded dead already.

"Ladies and gentlemen, I need your help. I don't know what I'm going to do. I swear to God, I'm really scared, everybody. I really don't know what I'm going to do."

Somehow Jacob felt the ugly twinge in the man's tone. It wasn't "I don't know what I'm going to do to survive" but "I don't know what I'm going to do next." It wasn't desperation to live; it was a fear of knowing the only options he had left. These weren't the pleadings of a man just trying to make it to tomorrow. They were the quaking last words of a man headed for the nearest bridge unless he got a dollar. But Jacob's wallet was empty. He didn't even have a quarter. He'd spent his last ten on a bottle of cheap wine, which he and Pete had barely touched, and which Pete had emptied down the drain last night before sending the bottle shuddering down the trash chute. Jacob winced. If all he'd had were a hundred-dollar bill, he'd have given it to the man just to make him be quiet.

"Please," the man begged, "I swear to God I don't know what I'm going to do."

The doors opened at Third Avenue and Jacob moved toward the platform—it wasn't his stop, but he didn't care. He'd walk across the state to get away. As he got out onto the platform, he heard the doors closing behind him, and momentarily seized by some perverse imp, he turned to get a look at the man. His dark skin was powdered with some strange white grime. Jacob looked into his eyes. The worm snapped. The train pulled away from the station and left Jacob there. The lump in his throat had sunk deep down into his guts now, and he was sure it was never coming out.

4

The call had come just after lunch, thank God, as Irene knew there'd have been no keeping Sara from joining her for the appointment if she'd known about it. The gallery was closed for two weeks heading into the holidays, and so Irene had been wandering around the Village, getting lost in the nexus of Bleecker and Christopher Streets and Sixth and Seventh Avenues, ostensibly doing some holiday shopping. She'd already found nice leather boots for Sara, though Irene wasn't going to tell her they had been purchased at the Pleasure Chest. At her favorite vintage store, Mel's Secondhand Shop, she found, for George, a thermos with Einstein's face on it that said REALITY IS MERELY AN ILLUSION, so that his coffee would stay warm on his way out to the observatory. She thought about William when she saw a scarf like the one Bob Dylan wore on the cover of *Blonde on Blonde* that she could see him in, that is, if she ever actually did see him again.

Sara had gone on and on about William at lunch, and about fate and how seeing him again after so long meant that it was. Fate. Irene said she preferred to make her own fate, but secretly she was glad that, in this case, the forces of fate, via Sara, would certainly throw her back into his path again soon. So she got the scarf and had them wrap it. Heart beating heavier then, she went to the back where they had a lot of old books and found an illustrated book of Italian fairy tales for Jacob. They'd first met in an Italian class that she'd been sitting in on and that he'd failed spectacularly.

It was just after this, having wandered into a pet shop down the street, that the woman called from Dr. Atoosa Zarrani's office at Mount Sinai Hospital to say that the results were in and the doctor could see her that afternoon to go over them.

"Unless you're busy? Are you at the zoo? In this cold?"

"Oh no," Irene had answered. "I'm in a pet shop. I was thinking about buying a bird."

The woman had laughed. "Birds can be a lot of work. I have two sulfur-crested cockatoos at home."

"Is that a good kind?"

"I wouldn't recommend them to a beginner."

"It's just that I have this beautiful bird cage," Irene confessed. "It was there when I moved into my apartment. I guess the last tenant left it behind. Anyway I just keep my jewelry and things in it, but sometimes I think to myself—I don't know, maybe I'd like having a pet."

"Well," the woman had said, "you think about it. And if you need some time, I'm sure we can find you an appointment tomorrow."

Irene had taken this as a good sign. Surely if there was something wrong, the woman would have orders to get her there pronto. Plus, the woman wouldn't be telling her to buy a bird if she thought she was dying. That'd be irresponsible. So nothing to worry about.

And that was how Irene came to find herself, a few hours later, sitting in a little room at Mount Sinai Hospital with bare walls and a table bolted to the floor. Her shopping bags were at her feet, and she tried to keep the one with the purple silhouette of a dominatrix with a cracking whip facing the wall. To kill time, she flipped through the book of Italian fairy tales and thought happily about what type of bird she might get, until she looked up to see a tall Persian woman in a lab coat coming into the room.

"Richmond? Irene?"

They shook hands, and the doctor sat down and began leafing through the report she was carrying. Irene recognized the jagged, illegible signature of Dr. Von Hatter at Park Avenue Pathology, where she'd gone for the biopsy. Irene noticed the clear, commanding letters beneath it: DR. ATOOSA ZARRANI. *Not. Messing. Around.*

"You came by yourself?" the doctor said, looking around as if someone were hiding.

Irene looked around too, as if she couldn't remember, then shrugged. Why didn't the doctor just get on with it? She felt sick. That couldn't be a good sign.

"Usually people bring a friend, or a family member."

Irene nodded as if taking this under advisement for next time. She searched the doctor's large dark eyes for some clue as to what she knew that Irene did not.

Dr. Zarrani smiled and then laughed a little to herself. "This morning a woman brought her doorman—a little Hungarian gentleman with red epaulets and a hat."

Irene smiled, feeling almost at ease, just as Dr. Zarrani cleared her throat and said, "Ms. Richmond, you have cancer."

Irene looked down quietly. She reached across herself and adjusted the sleeve of her shirt. Her first complete thought was that she shouldn't get a bird after all.

Eventually she said, "Well, shit."

Dr. Zarrani continued in a calm and even tone. "The biopsy revealed that the lump under your eye is a malignant osteosarcoma, which is the most common form of primary bone cancer. Tumors in the arm are most likely, but they can also present in the legs and skull. We'll have to do a more thorough scan to be sure that this is the only tumor, but it's small, and we're optimistic that this hasn't metastasized yet. Of course we'll need to do more testing to be sure. Very likely a CT and a bone scan, probably an MRI of your head and neck."

Irene felt dizzy. "Where did it come from?" she asked. Then she rolled her eyes and said, "Wow, sorry. That's a pretty stupid question, right?"

Dr. Zarrani shook her head, a little dark hair falling in front of her eyes before she quickly brushed it back. "Not at all. Some cancers do have known causes, although you're correct that we don't know for sure what causes this type. There have been a lot of studies. We don't know if it has a genetic component. Environmental causes are possible. We've looked at fluoridation in the water, dietary factors, dyes, preservatives, too much red meat, exposure to radiation, pesticides, BPA in plastics, artificial sweeteners, certain types of viruses, high tension wires, using cell phones . . ."

"And nothing?"

"Nothing conclusive."

Irene looked away at the blank wall. She wanted to just climb into it and disappear.

"The long-term survival rate for osteosarcoma is fairly high. Sixty-eight percent."

"Sixty-eight percent doesn't *sound* fairly high."

"Sixty-eight percent isn't bad. And you're lucky in a sense. Because you're so young."

Irene took a deep breath and shifted her gaze to the floor now. It, too, offered nothing. "See, now to me that seems distinctly *un*lucky."

Dr. Zarrani smiled a little. "Sixty-eight percent is taken across the board, over all cases. Including very young children whose immune systems aren't anywhere near strong enough to handle the treatment. Osteosarcoma affects children quite often, actually. Again, we don't know why. And then there are the elderly, who generally don't have the strength to pull through either. What I'm saying is, because you're young and otherwise healthy, if we take this thing head on and act quickly, your chances are going to be very good."

A weight that Irene hadn't quite noticed suddenly seemed to lift from her shoulders, even as the knotting in her stomach got worse. She leaned forward as if she were at a board meeting—arms bent at the elbows, fingers pressed together.

"So what do we do?"

"A team of specialists will review your case."

"Oh, but I like *you*," Irene said, smiling crookedly. Was she really flirting with this woman who was telling her that she was maybe dying? Used to being confused, Irene was completely bewildered now.

Dr. Zarrani seemed about to say something but stopped herself before it came out. "I'll be head of your team, but you'll need a plastic surgeon, a chemotherapist, a radiologist—"

"Radiation?" Irene said, touching her eye.

"It helps to kill the tumor. Though this is delicate because radiation will likely permanently affect your vision in the eye, because the tumor is so close."

Irene stared blankly down at the table, bracing herself for tears that were not coming. "No. That's not going to work," she said. "I'm a painter. Well, more sculpture lately. Doesn't matter. Thing is, I'm really going to need both my eyes."

"I see," Dr. Zarrani said softly. "Well, as I said, we'll have a specialist take a look."

"That's nonnegotiable," Irene said, even as she intuited from Dr. Zarrani's gaze that this wasn't a negotiation. "Oh fuck," she sighed finally, easing back and looking up at the blank ceiling. After a moment she peeked back again. "What are the odds?"

"Well, as I said earlier, around sixty-eight percent generally—"

"No, I'm sorry," Irene said, shaking her head. "I mean what the odds are that I'd . . . I mean, why me? Is this, like, super rare? How many people get this?"

Dr. Zarrani nodded. "Extremely rare particularly for someone your age. As I've said, it's most often seen in very young patients or the elderly. It—well, it isn't the sort of thing you see often in healthy twentysomethings."

Irene laughed. "So I'm just lucky then?"

"You could look at it that way."

"I really couldn't," Irene said. "I guess my mother always said I was one in a million."

Dr. Zarrani smiled. "Osteosarcoma affects about five people in a million, across the whole population."

"You know that off the top of your head?"

"I'm very good at what I do. Which is why I'm confident that we can get through this together."

Irene nodded, scanning the bare walls again. "You know, you should really put some art on the walls in here. Everywhere else in this hospital there are, like, banal *Water Lilies* prints and that sort of thing. You know? Stuff that can kind of fade into the background. But then if you really *need* some art to look at—like if you've just been told you have a thirty-two percent chance of dying—then there'd at least be a Monet print to distract you."

"Perhaps you could paint—or sculpt—us something," Dr. Zarrani said.

Irene smiled. "If you can cure me without ruining my eyes, I'll paint this whole hospital."

Dr. Zarrani stuck her hand out, over the open file, across the table, and Irene shook it.

"We'll begin in a week. It may take a few hours. And do bring someone with you next time," Dr. Zarrani suggested.

Irene shook her head. "I'm not close with my family," she explained. "Actually, I left home when I was sixteen, and I haven't spoken to them since. But don't worry. I can handle this on my own."

Dr. Zarrani shook her head slowly, and Irene couldn't escape her sharp disapproval.

"I'm sorry, Ms. Richmond, but I've seen Navy SEALs who couldn't handle this on their own. You're going to have to have some help. You'll need people to get you to treatments and take you back again. You're going to feel sick all the time. Someone's got to make you eat because you won't want to. You're going to need prescriptions filled and insurance claims filed and dressings changed. You see those Lifetime movies with cute little children and pretty ladies who are always stoic and brave and solemn. They might throw up once or twice, some hair falls out, they get a little thinner . . . but that's nothing. That's just for starters. Listen to me when I say this. You are about to go to war with your own body. That's the best way to describe it."

Irene felt every fiber of herself, sick and well, tight with fear.

What the hell did she know about going to war? Metaphorically or otherwise.

She nodded and the doctor seemed satisfied. "If you don't have friends you can trust with something like this, we can arrange—"

Irene stopped her quickly. "No, it's not that. It's—you know, my friends are great—"

Surely Sara would let them take out both her own eyes to save one of hers. Jacob and George would carry her to and from chemo appointments on their backs if she asked.

Dr. Zarrani seemed to know already. "Ms. Richmond, you can't save them from this, I'm sorry."

And that was when Irene, finally, began to cry.

Embarrassed, she looked down into her lap, the book of fairy tales still open to the page she'd been on when the doctor had entered. There was a beautiful silvery illustration of an enormous cloud over a still gray sea. It caught her so suddenly that for a second she forgot where she was and what she now knew. In the fairy tale, the North Wind was speaking to a Shining Fish who had no courage.

"La speranza è l'ultima a morire," the North Wind said. Unlike Jacob she hadn't failed the class. In fact she'd been one of the best students in the room, according to their teacher, Mrs. Marzocco, even though she'd gotten no credit for it or for any class.

The wind was telling the fish that hope is the last thing to die.

5

William, for the second time in four days, found himself at a party where he knew practically no one. First a suite at the Waldorf, now a basement apartment in Greenpoint that was jammed with actors. The ceiling was two inches above his head, and several others had to stoop. After the show, before William quite realized what was happening, Sara had whisked him onto the 7 train and then onto the G. William never felt comfortable being back in the boroughs. He'd grown up out here, after all, in Flushing. This felt like returning to dry land after months at sea. The buildings were too short; the streets too quiet. Driveways and fences! They'd followed the chummy cast members past Polish restaurants and a pencil factory and an odd, freestanding water tower like the sort you'd see in Kansas somewhere by the highway—to a little basement apartment with a hobbit-size door. One by one the actors had piled in and now were sitting around on the bare floor in a circle, drinking warm white wine from plastic cups and leaving periodically to smoke skunky weed in the back alley.

"I've recently begun listening to my whole hip-hop collection again," one of them said to William. "Grandmaster Flash is a *whole* different experience on vinyl."

The stranger wore a corduroy jacket and was drinking beer out of a brandy snifter, which William suspected he'd brought from home. Everyone else had plastic Solo cups and not, like, the nice ones. He reeked of pot and he kept smacking his lips together as if his beer were sawdust.

"I'm sorry," William replied politely, "I don't think we've met."

The boy's red eyes widened. "I thought you were someone else." Then he backed away in a hurry and moved off across the room, before William could say that, once upon a time, he'd had a Run-DMC record himself.

George and the surly Jacob weren't talking to anyone else either, but at least they had each other. They sat by the host's bookshelves looking utterly exhausted and talking as if they'd been parted for weeks by dreadful battles. They exchanged stories of office politics, writer's block, graduate research, and homeless panhandlers, all while wincing at the warm PBR cans in their hands. Every few minutes one of them would pull a hardcover down, remove the dust jacket and swap it with another from elsewhere on the shelf. Neither offered an explanation. William kept trying to excuse himself, but they were too engrossed in their talk of poems and planets to even look at him. He could have left, and they'd never have noticed, but he was still holding out that Irene would show up.

They had slept together three nights ago, after the last party with Sara and her friends. It was unusual for William. Not just to sleep with someone he'd met hours earlier, but to sleep with someone like Irene. He'd known while it was still happening that he'd never get over it. And things had gone well—at least he'd felt so at the time. But then in the morning he got the impression that perhaps it—no, that *he* had been a mistake. Not an error or a lapse so much, because neither of them had been very drunk. There had been no impairment. But a mistake and the sex had been merely a miscommunication, like a game of telephone played badly.

The next morning the excitement had been all about Sara's engagement, and Irene had left after breakfast without even a kiss or a phone number. Now William guessed he was somehow supposed to act as if nothing had happened. As if he didn't remember every microsecond of the evening, as if he hadn't been replaying it on the 35mm film reels of his mind ever since. It felt a little shameful, really, as he'd watched it that afternoon right through a meeting with the partners and during a Sunday phone call with the London office, and on the walk home as he passed thousands of people on the sidewalks. But they couldn't see it, he reminded himself—even if it were projected as high as the Empire State Building and as wide as the Battery. It was all in his head, and in the head of one other, who remained a ghost.

All weekend he'd been miserable and afraid to return Sara's calls.

He drank deeply from his cup of warm wine and wished the red plastic container would, instead, swallow him up. He looked around the party and wondered if anyone would even notice if he spontaneously disappeared. It was a bit like watching the play. He was still there, in their audience, almost as if, hours ago, the curtain had gone down, the bows had been taken, the cheers had risen, and everyone in the orchestra and all the people in the mezzanine had gone home . . . but for the actors, the whole thing just went on and on.

"How was the show then?" George was asking. It took William a moment to realize that he was speaking to him.

"It was fine," William lied, thinking that it would be rude to say otherwise in such a small room, filled with the very people who'd produced the play. They'd clearly worked hard and created something from nothing—wasn't that praiseworthy?

Both George and Jacob stared at him, clearly expecting some elaboration. But William simply couldn't think of a positive thing to say. He swayed a bit and tried looking at the ceiling where a bare bulb in a fixture dangled with great intent. But when he looked back, the boys were still waiting for him to speak. And William, exasperated at the party, at the days of waiting for Irene to call, at the bad wine—finally snapped.

"It was really, really awful. Really. God. Awful," he confessed in a whisper. George and Jacob looked both delighted and not surprised. As William described the awfulness in detail, he tried to keep his voice down, but he soon realized it was utterly unnecessary—the actors were all so loud that they wouldn't have heard him with a bullhorn in hand.

"All the dialogue was in rhyming couplets. Not sure *why*. Or why there was line dancing. And the guy who played Hades shouted all his lines. And, well, Eurydice couldn't sing, so I have no idea why they put her in the lead role . . ."

George and Jacob each looked over at the girl in question, the frightfully thin hostess of the party, with breasts so enormous that her every movement seemed a complex balancing act.

Jacob commented wryly, "I can't imagine."

"You could count her ribs through a parka." George concurred.

William went on to describe the highlight of the play: the moment when the actor playing Orpheus had slipped and crashed into Cerberus, whose three papier-mâché heads had gone flying into the wings.

George began telling them all about his star, collapsing two thousand light-years away, but then got distracted by the skinny actress as she rotated a tray of Bagel Bites in her tiny toaster oven. George left to go see if they were almost ready and then Jacob began telling *him*—William!—about the homeless man he'd seen on the subway that day and about how he felt silly now for getting so worked up about it. William was vaguely aware of a buzzing sound on the chair beside him. He looked down and saw Irene's smiling face on the cell phone that lay there.

"Oh, get that?" Jacob said quickly. "That's George's. Irene probably got lost coming out of the subway again."

William lifted the phone, almost not wanting to answer it because if he did, her smiling face would vanish from the display. And he'd have to think of something to say to this girl, who'd slept beneath him last week and awakened a total stranger.

He hit the green button to answer the call. "Yes? George Murphy's phone. This is William Cho."

There was a silence on the other end. Then, static. Then, "William?"

"Irene? Can you hear me?"

More static. Then a strange sound he couldn't identify. "William?" she said again. William thought Jacob must be right. She sounded lost—scared.

"Hello? Irene?" he said, louder. The actors were all so *loud*. And the hot-water pipes were clanking above them—how could the skinny girl ever manage to sleep?

Jacob pointed to the street. "You'll never get reception in the alley. Head out front."

William hurried to the little hobbit door and ducked out onto the quiet sidewalk.

" . . . William? . . . Are . . . there?"

William raced out, past the trash cans, lined up for the morning, and the tightly bundled stacks of newspapers that were ready for recycling. He eased between the cars, parked neatly in their rows. He was desperate to hear Irene. He fought the urge to tell her *insane* things: that he had been missing her all weekend; that he hadn't washed his shirt from that night because it still smelled like her. He wanted to tell her that he was sure he loved her, even though he'd only known her for eight hours, during five of which he'd been asleep.

He ran out into the dark street without even looking—if a truck had been going by, he wouldn't have noticed until ten seconds after it had hit him.

Finally he could hear her clearly. Finally he could make out the strange noises on the other end. Full-on, reckless sobbing, more painful than any in the songs in the musical.

"Irene, where are you? What's wrong?" He ran down the street to the corner, so he could figure out exactly where in the enormous city he was. He wished it all away. He wished every borough, block, and street away.

"William, I—William, I'm at a coffee shop across from Mount Sinai."

William kept running. He looked around, as if maybe the hospital were nearby. And then he remembered he was in Brooklyn and it was on the East Side of Manhattan.

"Are you okay? Were you in an accident? Hold on, I'll find a cab—"

The crying stopped, and he heard her clear her throat.

"William, I've got cancer. I've got . . . osteosus . . . I forget the name of it already. Bone cancer. This lump under my eye. Only five people in a million have it."

He knew he ought to turn around—go back to the party and tell her friends. That was what she wanted probably. After all, they'd known her for years. He hardly knew her at all.

"You're going to be fine!" he yelled into the phone. Not even his phone. He knew he should go back to the party and tell George. But he was still racing down the street. As long as he could hear Irene there on the other end, he knew she'd be all right. He ran past the water tower, past the pencil factory, past the Polish restaurants. He ran all the way to the water's edge to a dark wooden pier. Black as the Styx, the East River rushed by.

"Don't tell anyone," she said.

He realized she was still sobbing into the phone.

"I don't know why I even called. Don't say anything to Sara or George or Jacob or anyone, all right?"

"I won't, I won't," he was saying. "Shush." He didn't make a *shhhhhh* sound, just said, "Shush."

It took him a second to realize that she'd begun laughing, softly.

"What's so funny?" he wheezed.

"Nothing," she said. "It doesn't matter."

He didn't understand. He tried to catch his breath, but each inhalation was like battery acid, each exhalation like cumulus clouds leaving his lips.

"Where are you?" Irene asked, her voice a bit steadier.

He gazed across at the dark skyline. Hundreds of thousands of feet of glass and steel rose up into the blackness like a great Necropolis, and she was in there, somewhere.

"William? You know, this is stupid. I'm just going to go home."

"No, I can't really hear you," he said, turning from the river to run back toward the party. "Hold on."

Irene's breath was in his ear again. He looked back over his shoulder at the water and the majestic city beyond it. Holding the phone tight to his ear, he ran three and a half more blocks before he realized that the signal had dropped.

FISH EYES AND NO EARS

At first, having cancer seemed to be largely a matter of paperwork. Irene tried to remain composed as the grandmotherly clerks at Mount Sinai looked crossly at her forms, their expressions never failing to falter as they handed her fresh ones. Irene wondered if they were having an interdepartmental Ugly Christmas Sweater contest or if the drop-stitched Rudolphs, Frostys, and Kringles had perhaps been knitted by their cats. She reminded herself to not get snippy. These people were trying to help her.

With some pharmaceutical-sponsored clipboard on her lap, Irene attempted to hold her head high without getting it in the tinsel of the plastic fir trees, or knocking the light-up snowmen from the wire branches. Christmas was consuming Mount Sinai Hospital with virulent glee. Everywhere Irene looked, she could see prickly wreaths, looping garlands, and glitzy ornaments. Stockings were hung with care in every single elevator. Toy trains looped through banks of fake snow. Handsomely wrapped gifts with oversize bows were stacked neatly in hallway corners, although these were just for show. Irene had kicked one accidentally, and the hollow tower had toppled. The décor had seemed laughable at first, and then depressing, but now, after spending an entire morning filling out forms, she was coming around to it. Who was she to judge what it took to bring a little cheer to those stuck at the hospital over the holidays? After all, she was about to number among them.

Eventually Irene was shuffled onto the sixth floor: Head and

Neck Cancers. Though it seemed apropos, considering the location of her tumor, she found the little sign above the waiting area annoyingly absurd. *I've got head cancer,* she thought to herself. *Cancer of the head. Just all this up here is no good at all. I'll get myself right on the head transplant list. Pop on the head of a nice quiet schoolteacher from Ann Arbor and be done with it.*

Grace, Irene had always believed, was a double-edged blade to be kept laced at her hip at all times. To appear unperturbed by all that was perturbing you eased both your own mind and the minds of those around you. So she wished to appear the cool lieutenant, marshaling the harried hospital staff as they hammered keyboard keys and strategized the times and locations for her first two chemotherapy appointments. This worked, until she caught a glimpse of her reflection in the glasses of one of the old ladies behind the counter and was thrown by how stretched and blurry she appeared: precisely the way she felt.

The woman's great gray head swayed from side to side and her tongue clucked behind fuchsia-painted lips.

"Oh dear," they all seemed fond of saying, as they reached for their telephones, "let me just call someone and see about this."

The problem was the question marks. Irene was full of them. Allergic reactions to medications: *?* Name of previous primary care physician: *?* List previous hospital visits, in order, and by purpose: 1. *Tonsils removed, 1992 or 1991?* 2. *Fell down and hit head on a brass Dalmatian statue. I was 5 or 6? No concussion.* 3. *Horrible stomachaches, turned out to be lactose intolerance, which went away suddenly. Not sure when.* Immunizations and vaccinations: *Probably all the standard ones for kids? Nothing after 1998.* Father's medical history: *Male-pattern baldness, rosacea, near-sighted, ???* Mother's medical history: *???*

"I have primary bone cancer." She tried to get used to the way these words felt on her tongue, and she'd point to the small lump below her left eye socket. "I have a malignant osteosarcoma." It wasn't at all noticeable until you noticed it.

The day passed in excruciating baby steps. By the time darkness fell, Irene had visited practically every floor in the hospital, never once escaping the sight of glittering snowflakes.

Finally cleared to begin her first two-day chemo dose the following morning, Irene walked across the dark street and broke down crying in the back corner of a MetroStop Bakery over a bowl of scalded corn chowder. None of the servers seemed to find this odd. She looked down at the mascara smudges she'd left on the edge of the paper tablecloth. She'd expected to get a bit farther than *this*. She hadn't even seen a single needle, scalpel, or IV! To quiver in the face of medieval instruments seemed reasonable; to be undone by grainy Xeroxes did not. At eight a.m., she was to report to the twelfth floor for chemotherapy, which would take a few hours to be infused through a vein in her arm.

Irene waited for the mascara stains to dry a little. Then she carefully tore a perimeter of paper around them and slipped the scrap into her purse, not yet sure how or if she'd use it in some new piece she'd been constructing late at night in her apartment.

While her fingers were in her purse, they pulled out her phone, even as she forbade them to do it. *Everyone's gone for the holidays,* she reminded them. Still, they thumbed through her contacts. Sara was at George's parents' place in Ohio for Christmas. Jacob was in Tampa, or as he called it, "the land of decrepitude," with his mother and father for the final few days of Hanukah. She hadn't wanted to ruin anyone's holidays, so she hadn't told any of them about her diagnosis yet.

The only person who knew was William Cho. Irene studied his picture. Her phone had downloaded it on its own, from where she didn't know. Dressed in a black suit and black tie, William looked somewhat startled against a blue Sears background. She wished she knew how to change it; this puzzled man was nothing like the delicate and curious boy she'd spent the night with a few days ago. The more she looked at this un-William, the more she wanted to see the real one again. She had bought him that Dylan scarf, but it was still back in her apartment. They hadn't spoken since the last time she'd sat in this same café right after the diagnosis.

He would probably still be in the city; his parents lived in Queens. She tapped the star key every so often to keep the screen from going dark and taking him away.

867 Video was dead, and from the owner's stares, William got the distinct impression that he was the sole reason the store hadn't closed up yet. Perhaps William was keeping it open in a larger sense as well, for the trend among his coworkers was to have DVDs—no, Blu-rays now—conveniently delivered to their doors, or better yet, streamed to their TVs. "How do you have time to go to a store?" they asked him at work, when they saw his rentals sitting on his desk waiting to be brought back. "Didn't they all close?"

But William had nothing *but* time to go to the store, even so close to Christmas. Especially now, as his office was closed. He loved stores because he never knew what he wanted. He had to touch everything until his fingers selected the right one, generally without his permission. He was doing just this when his phone rang.

The owner, Arturo, whose left eye was lifeless and listing, called out to William as he set down the copy of Alfred Hitchcock's *Suspicion* so he could answer the call.

"Forty-nine cents I got that for! Not a scratch on the disc! Stupid teenagers that ran the Blockbuster on Seventy-eighth Street didn't even know who Cary Grant was. I told them, 'This is an American god, you cretins! This man could act circles around your Bin Diesel, your Channing Tater, your Catrina Gomez!' "

Expecting a call from his mother, William answered the phone without glancing at the screen.

"Annyeonghaseyo, eomeoni."

"William? Is that you?"

At the sound of Irene's voice, he gripped the rack of classics unsteadily.

"William," she continued cheerfully. "Sorry to bother you. I'm sure you must be busy right now, but I was hoping I could ask you a favor."

"No," he said quickly. "I mean, no, it isn't any bother. How are you feeling?"

"I'm feeling fine. No change. But it's my building. Practically in the middle of the night, the super came around just now to tell us we have to ev*ac*uate because of some kind of infestation. Pill flies or sharp beetles or something like that. Thank god it's not bedbugs, but anyways, I just ran out—stupid me—without packing a thing, and I'm terrified to go back. Everyone's out of town, and I need a place to sleep if it's not too much to ask. Just on the couch or somewhere, I'm not picky. I don't want you to think I have the wrong idea—"

Wrong idea? William wanted to ask. Which idea was wrong, exactly? The idea of them sleeping together again? Or the equally ineradicable idea that they were nothing more than two more people who ought never to have slept together in the first place? He kept his mouth shut, which was about all he trusted himself to do.

"I know that things have been—well, I don't know *what* they've been. Sorry for babbling on like this. I know it's—shit."

"No," William blurted. He instantly wished he'd just let her keep going; he wanted nothing more than her babbling on and on. But now she'd fallen silent and clearly expected him to say something. Panicked, he stared down at Cary Grant on the *Suspicion* DVD cover. *Each time they kissed,* the tagline read, *there was the thrill of love . . . The threat of murder!* Cary Grant's lowered eyebrows bespoke a smoothness that William wished he possessed.

"Good," he said, trying to sound Grant-like, "I'll let the doorman know you're coming."

"William, you're the best," she sighed.

"Don't mention it," he said, lifting the DVD.

Irene sighed happily and ended the call.

William texted his address to her phone and then rushed over to Arturo with the DVD in hand, hoping that if he hurried, he might be able to study a scene or two before Irene buzzed up.

"One of Hitchcock's best," Arturo said, looking adoringly down at Joan Fontaine in her low-cut red dress. "Except for the ending, which RKO made him change—"

But William could hardly hear him. He paid and left the store, thinking at first he'd buy some of the Bollinger Blanc she'd liked last time—or get a bouquet of roses that he could throw into a vase, only he didn't think he owned a vase—and moreover, this wasn't what Cary Grant would do, he was fairly certain. Cary Grant would never be so presumptuous. She said she didn't want him to think she had the wrong idea. Whatever else, that probably meant he ought to play it cool. Cool like Cary Grant.

William left the video store feeling stone-jawed. This lasted two thirds of his way home, when he slipped on a patch of ice and slid into the branches of one of those Christmas trees out for sale on the sidewalk.

Irene went over immediately. She'd thought about going back to her place for his scarf, but she didn't want to waste time and risk him losing interest. William greeted her at the door and said he had just been watching an old movie and asked how she was feeling. But she cut him off—she didn't want to talk about that. She instead gushed that she *loved* old movies and that she would have to insist they watch the rest together. She hated to interrupt when he was being so generous. But after an hour passed, sitting there on the couch watching Grant and Fontaine flirting, Irene found it difficult to focus.

William's apartment distressed her. More and more, Irene felt as if she were watching the movie from the set of another movie. Not only was his place achingly coordinated in maroons and teals and mahogany leather, but it was filled with showroom-style homey touches. On one wall above a sideboard hung a gigantic bronze architect's compass, surrounded by framed black-and-white photos: a medieval cathedral apse, a Roman atrium, the gable of a seaside cottage. She was positive these were not vacation photos but the kind of black-and-white "art" pictures that you could get twelve for ten at IKEA. She was grateful that he didn't have a single Christmas decoration up, but she'd have preferred an evergreen to the inexplicable basket of neatly arranged branches that sat in the corner. It was like something you saw in a magazine, not anything that a real person owned. Steadily, she became convinced that she was sitting in the completely fabricated living room of a completely fabricated person.

Irene excused herself to use the restroom, and William paused the movie. On the way down the hall she looked for evidence of a personality, photographs of friends or kitschy mementos, but she found nothing. William's family was Korean, yet she couldn't spot a single piece of art with any Asian influence whatsoever. She knew that he had studied classics in college, but the only Greek object she saw was a small urn, filled not with significant ashes but with potpourri that didn't smell of anything anymore. What sort of self-respecting bachelor owned potpourri? In the bathroom Irene found a mirror whose frame was strategically flaked of its paint, and a little soap dispenser adorned with tiny, irregular mosaic tiles, as if some artisan a millennium ago had carefully glued them onto a Crate & Barrel sanitizer pump. On the way back to the couch, she checked his bookshelf to be sure the spines had been cracked. She was relieved to find that, at least, William wasn't the full Gatsby.

It didn't help that he himself was speaking like a movie character. "Could I pour you another glass of wine?" he asked when she got back. Once he did, he looked up as if he'd just surprised himself with the thought and said, "Pass me the clicker, if it's not too much trouble. The sound is a little *dim*, wouldn't you say?"

"You smell like pinesap," Irene said as she passed him the clicker.

"Ah, yes. I had a run-in with a tree salesman out on the street. Nice fellow, though he shouted a bit when I ran off."

"Are you being British?" she asked.

That seemed to catch him somewhat, and his cheeks reddened in the way that she remembered. "Not intentionally, no. I suppose I should take that as a compliment."

"Should you?" Irene asked under a sigh.

William didn't hear, now the volume was up.

When the movie was over, Irene was tired but too uncomfortable to sleep. She didn't want to stay in the false-living room. Nor did she want to go to bed with this false-William.

"I think maybe I should go," she said finally.

William looked sad. "Oh! Well. All right then. Wait here. I'll call for a car."

"The city's full of cabs, William," she said. "Cabs and sidewalks and trains. Christ, what I wouldn't give to be on a *train* right now."

"Sorry if you didn't like the film," he said stiffly.

"The *film* was fine," she said.

"You're upset." He frowned without quite pouting.

"No, not at all," Irene said, getting up to leave. She didn't know just what sort of coaxing it was going to take to get him to relax, but she was pretty sure she had 68 percent less time for it now than she'd had a few weeks ago. It had been a ridiculous idea to come in the first place.

"Where are you going?" he asked, as she was putting her boots back on.

"Look, William—"

"No, I mean, I get that you're leaving. It's just, you said you couldn't stay at your apartment tonight, and I know Sara said everyone was going out of town. I was worried that—well, do you have anywhere else to go?"

Irene tossed her coat over her shoulders angrily. "You don't need to look after me, all right? I have *lots* of places to go."

This always happened. Guys—especially nice ones like William—were always trying to persuade her she needed to be taken care of. It was only the losers and fuck-ups who left her to take care of herself. She tried to remind herself that William didn't know her whole history. All the worse places she'd slept than a bug-bombed apartment, which hers wasn't even, though again he didn't know that.

Her left arm kept getting jammed in the sleeve. She couldn't bend her elbow after all the blood they'd taken that afternoon, which only made her more upset.

"I've got friends all over! I'm serious. I could walk over to Penn Station right now, get on any train at all, and I'd be *fine*."

William was standing there, nodding, rocking a little on his heels. Irene had her coat on and was at the door. Was he really just going to stare at the floor and not say anything?

"Well," Irene said finally, "what?"

He looked up at her. "Well, what what?"

"What are you *doing*?" she specified.

He stopped rocking. "Sorry. Just thinking. Sorry."

"What about?"

"The film. Movie. The ending," he sighed. "Originally Hitchcock wanted Fontaine to write a letter to her mother saying she knows Grant's a killer but she loves him so much that she'll die for him. Then she drinks the poison, and it *would* have ended with Grant mailing the letter. But the studio felt that it should end with a killer being brought to justice—so they forced Hitchcock to change it so Grant attempts suicide."

Irene couldn't believe he was still talking about the film—movie. Whatever. "That's completely absurd," she said.

"Right. I agree. Someone that confident and controlled would never consider suicide—"

"No, *that's* not absurd," Irene interrupted. "He's an arrogant prick. And killing yourself like that would be the ultimate act of arrogance."

This brought out the red in William's cheeks again.

"What I meant is it's absurd to think he could really kill *her*." The flush spread; Irene stepped closer to him and the couch. "In that first scene, right after I came in, where they're walking outside together and it's all very romantic and then he calls her Monkeyface, and she gets angry? No self-respecting murderer would call a woman Monkeyface like that. Hitchcock must have known that."

Suddenly Mount Sinai felt miles and miles away.

Irene looked into his dark eyes and said, "So I think you should hurry up and give me a nickname like that right away, so I'll be sure you're not a murderer."

William laughed. "I can't! You're, well, um—too beautiful to make fun of."

She stepped back a little. She hated that word. *Beautiful*. It meant nothing; it was too unreliable. What if they took out her eye? If her hair fell out in chunks? If her facial muscles lost their grip? Would he still say she was beautiful?

But William kept going. "I guess, if you pressed me, I'd say your face is a little . . ."

"What?" Irene urged. "Come on, I can take it."

"Well, it's your ears, actually. They're really tiny. It's almost like they're trying to climb back into your head."

"They are not!" she shouted, jumping up to find a mirror.

"They are too. You've basically got no ears."

"No ears?" she shrieked at her reflection in a black-framed mirror without any discernable character, but it wasn't her ears she stared at. It was him, behind her, smiling shyly. She turned and he grabbed her, and they collapsed together against the couch.

"Don't worry," he said, pushing her hair back as if to study her more closely. "It's really very becoming, No Ears."

"You take it back!" she shrieked.

Gently he brushed her hair back and kissed one of her allegedly nonexistent ears.

"There they are!" he exclaimed.

"There *you* are," she said. At last.

Irene slept heavily on top of William, right there on the mahogany leather couch, and he didn't dare budge for fear of waking her. She'd told him all about her day at the hospital and the first treatment, which would begin in just a few hours. Just before she'd nodded off, he'd made the mistake of asking why she didn't have any family to visit for the holidays, or to take her to the hospital, for that matter. *I left home when I was sixteen,* she'd explained. *I won't get into all the reasons I had to go. I just never belonged there. People get born into the wrong families sometimes. Just like souls wind up in the wrong bodies occasionally. I have a very old soul. I think my soul belongs in the body of someone who's already a hundred and ninety-five.*

William couldn't quite tell if she was kidding, but in the shadows, he could imagine her on top of him, all wrinkled and bird-boned, with hair as gray as moonlight.

Not like you, she'd continued. *Your soul's very young. It's a boy's soul. Now don't be angry—see, that's just what I mean—there's no reason to be angry. Your body's plenty manly. But inside you're boyish. The way you took my clothes off, for one example. Kind of awestruck. Slow. It's what I like most about you. Your soul is so boyish actually that it is almost girlish.*

He hadn't reacted especially well to this comment, and he regretted it now, as he lay there, replaying it all, and watching her dreaming.

So? she'd replied, *I like a girlish soul. And a girlish body too, if we're going to be honest. In fact, you should feel special because I haven't slept with many boys. Far more girls than boys.*

William hadn't covered his surprise at this well either, and he was so flustered that he didn't shift his lap away from Irene in time to cover his inevitable reaction to the idea of Irene with another woman.

You see? she had teased. *Boyish.*

Later, he asked again about her real family, and why she'd left them, but she was either pretending to be falling asleep or really nodding off.

I left them because they weren't my family, she mumbled. *I thought Alis-ahh was my family, but she said I was always leaving her.* These were the last words to fall from her mouth before she slept.

William wasn't sure he'd heard her right. What sort of a name was "Alis-ahh"? Had she said *Alissa* or *Alicia*? Had he misheard?

So he sat, awake and unwilling to move, until the sun rose up over Queens.

Irene woke up at seven, vaguely aware she had only an hour to get to the hospital to begin her first day of treatment. She'd had one of the strangest dreams of her life—Dr. Zarrani had said it wasn't uncommon for cancer patients to get them. Dreams like full-on acid trips. Surreal visions that didn't always end right away when she woke up. The doctor had called them "healing dreams" but hadn't explained what exactly was healing about them. Irene barely had time to think about it, however. She was hectically running around the apartment. When William asked why, she told him she had to get ready for her first infusion.

"Just wear what you had on yesterday," he said.

"That's—don't be ridiculous." She thought about taking back what she'd said about him being girlish, but she thought that might please him too much, and besides, when she opened up his wardrobe (made of real wood that was faux-weathered), she discovered that his closet was filled with clothes that she could easily wear. A pair of jeans that must not have fit William since college were a bit torn in the knees but looked quite good on her with the cuffs rolled and a yellow necktie as a belt. She spotted a pink dress shirt and rolled the sleeves around her elbows, cinched it in the back with a rubber band, and tucked that into the waistline of the jeans.

"If I didn't know any better, I'd think you had a girl living here with you," she said, detaching a silvery pull cord from his window shade and retying it as a necklace.

"We're going to a hospital, No Ears. What does it matter what you look like?" William groaned. She saw his eyes were sunken and bleary.

"It's my first day, I have to make a good impression! Do you have any makeup?"

"Why would I? Let's go! You look beautiful!"

"What did I say about that word?" she chided. "Come on, you don't have anything? Who doesn't have some concealer lying around for bad skin days? Or some lipstick a girlfriend left somewhere?" She eyed him curiously as she lifted a white panama hat down from his hat rack. "I know you've had girlfriends. Don't tell me you bought this for yourself."

William placed it on her head. "It was a gift from my mother."

Irene took the hat off and studied it. "It's excellent. I'd like to meet this woman."

"If you will hurry up and get to your appointment, you can meet her tonight."

Her eyes widened. She hadn't expected him to take her up on it, but suddenly she wanted to meet Mrs. Cho very badly—if anyone could help uncover the real William beneath all this showroom furniture, it would be her.

He went on. "We're having a big family dinner for Christmas Eve. You'll love it. It's like my own personal circle of hell."

Irene clapped eagerly.

William began to say firmly, "If you keep delaying and we miss your appointment, then we'll never get there in time . . ." but Irene was already halfway out the door.

They made it into the hospital just in time, and Irene enjoyed the holiday decorations much more now that William was there to look aghast alongside her. After filling out some more paperwork, they met with Dr. Zarrani, who guided them around the chemotherapy suite as if it were an apartment they might be interested in buying.

"No elves or reindeer in here!" Irene said.

"The design was done around the concept of a Japanese Zen garden," she said. "You come in over here past the waterfall sculpture to check in each morning."

All the light came from great brass lanterns, and to one side of the waiting area was an actual sandbox filled with rocks and little rakes, which two children were busy attempting to demolish. The tables, covered in magazines and catalogs, were all made of polished stone, and trimmed bonsai trees divided the waiting area to make it more peaceful.

Dr. Zarrani stood stiffly. "I know it seems silly, but studies have shown an improvement in patient recoveries."

William balked. "What, like through some ancient Shinto magic or something?"

The doctor led them back into the infusion area. "It has to do with the patient being more relaxed and inspired to face the hard work ahead."

"Aesthetics are important, William," Irene snapped. "Hence, why I wanted to look nice."

"You look *very* nice," Dr. Zarrani said to her as William raised his hands in apology. "Now take a seat here by this blue . . . pagoda thing. The nurses will be out soon to begin you on doxorubicin and cisplatin. It takes a few hours, so I hope you brought a good book."

Irene eyed the nearby *Vogues* and *Cosmopolitans* suspiciously. She'd read the same ones yesterday in the waiting room.

"I can run out to a bookstore and find you something," William offered.

"Well . . . ," Irene said, looking mischievous as she pulled a heavy volume out of her purse. "I took this off your shelf this morning. I hope that's all right."

He did look a bit startled at the sight of his copy of the *Iliad*, the Jacob-disapproved-of Lattimore translation, surely filled with old college notes and underlinings, but he shrugged, not knowing, Irene was sure, that the notes and underlinings were precisely why she wanted to read it.

"Can I wait here with her?" William asked the doctor.

"For eight hours? Don't be absurd. Go buy your mother something for Christmas. And get some sleep. I know you were wide awake all night."

William wanted to stay until they started, but Irene wouldn't hear of it.

"You go or I go," she said. So William went.

Dr. Zarrani came in to start the drip. "The doxorubicin distorts the shape of the helix, which prevents it from replicating, and then the cisplatin binds the DNA to itself, which triggers a kind of self-destruct order inside your cells."

Irene felt her nervousness quieting in the comforting hands of the doctor, as she scrubbed the crook of Irene's elbow with a cotton ball soaked in yellow antiseptic. Irene had thought that they'd inject something into her face, not her arm.

"How do the drugs know to go from there all the way up to my eye?"

"Unfortunately, they don't," Dr. Zarrani explained. "Normally we'd do surgery first, but in the interest of not damaging your eye, we'll start with this and hope it shrinks the tumor a little. The chemo drugs go into your bloodstream and go everywhere. They'll get the tumor but also everything else."

Irene sat up straighter in her chair. Not a surgical strike then, she thought, just a full-on scorched-earth policy. And then she remembered her dream from the night before. She'd been crawling, for what seemed like hours and hours, through a barren desert. Finally she'd come across a great black leaf, and she'd hidden in its shade. But once there, safe, something very strange happened. She'd begun to spit, uncontrollably. Great threads of saliva flowed uncontrollably from her mouth, and she'd felt drier than ever as she'd writhed about, trying to stop. Only when she'd thought she'd desiccate completely like a mummy in a tomb did she realize the great threads she'd released weren't saliva but silk. And while she'd been writhing, she'd inadvertently, or perhaps instinctually, woven this silk into a great shimmering womb, its walls glistening with cool dew. She'd been just about to climb inside and sleep for a thousand years, when she'd woken up on top of William.

"Now this will sting a little bit," the doctor said.

There was a terrific pinch, and then Irene could feel something alien inside her arm. It would be there for hours, and she would keep on feeling it there, long after.

William had already found gifts for everyone in his family except his mother. So he stopped at a Salvation Army a few blocks from the hospital, where he spotted an enormous and truly heinous pink vase covered in golden chrysanthemum blossoms, on sale for five dollars. The gift itself wasn't as important as how little he'd paid for it. Any present that came from a retail store she'd return later and then complain about how much money he'd spent. Always she had seen the *exact same item* for a tenth of the price at some church sale just a few weeks earlier.

As a boy, he had once spotted a beautiful silk kimono on sale at the gift shop of the Guggenheim, where he was taken on a class trip to see an exhibit on Eastern Art. He'd sold his collection of Aqualad comic books to Mi-cha Yu so he could buy it. But then Christmas morning arrived and his mother opened the gift. "What is this?" she'd asked, so he'd told her, "A kimono" and she'd given him a withering look. "Kimonos are Japanese. We are *Korean.*" She'd dragged him all the way back to the Upper East Side to return it, but since the Eastern Art had gone out and the Monets had come in, they no longer stocked the kimonos. Furious, his mother had flung it deep into a guest-room closet, where it hung still.

William walked down Third Avenue with the vase under one arm for blocks and blocks, trudging over the snow that was still unshoveled in many places. As cold as he was, William kept on walking without fully thinking about just where he was heading, though his feet seemed to have some idea. The storefronts were quiet; the roads were empty. It wasn't often, he thought, that you got to have the city to yourself.

By the time he realized where his feet were taking him, he was far closer to Fourth Street than to the hospital, where he knew he ought to turn around and go. Something about the way that she had taken his *Iliad* off the shelf had struck him, as if it actually belonged to her. Without thinking, he had found himself lifting the keys from her purse while the doctor had been explaining the chemotherapy to her. He'd thought he could surprise her—run inside, despite the bug-bombing, and bravely grab a bag of clothes to wear to dinner that evening. She couldn't show up wearing William's old blue jeans and a necklace made from a curtain chain. As he came down Avenue A toward her block, he told himself that she'd be delighted.

But by the time he got to her building, he knew he was kidding himself. Irene would surely *not* appreciate what he was about to do, but his mind was unquiet with questions. Where was she from, and why had she run away? The thought that maybe she had been abused, or worse, was difficult to push aside—even though she'd assured him it hadn't been that. Who was "Alis-ahh"? Had he even heard her properly? Was she one of these girls that she claimed to have slept with?

Irene's building was a crumbling brownstone with trash cans around the entrance that were chained up and overflowing. The ground floor windows were covered with boards, and the boards were covered in long-faded concert posters. He opened the door and walked up three flights of crooked stairs; the railing became more bent the higher he climbed. Hadn't she said her whole building was being fumigated? There was no sign on the front door, and he could hear people in the other apartments. He climbed all the way to the fifth floor and came to her door, expecting to find a department of health sticker, or caution tape on the knob, but there was nothing out of the ordinary. The cheap vase still tucked under his left arm, he slowly unlocked the door and stepped into Irene's apartment.

Looking around, William could see haphazardly discarded blankets and workout clothes heaped on the floors and over the top of the bathroom door. The apartment was filthy, from the overfilled sink to the paint-peeled ceiling. He stepped over the remains of a Sunday *Observer* and several brown boxes filled with flea market objects: glittering marbles, rusty doorknobs, a tangle of wiring, old movable type letters, several novelty wristwatches, bookends shaped like cartoon faces, dozens of Barbie dolls still in their individual packages, empty mirror frames, children's soccer trophies, and a plethora of silk flowers. He was just about to ask himself what on earth it was all for when he saw the far end of the room.

The end nearest the window was relatively cleared of junk. It seemed to be a working area. Sketch pads lay open on a low coffee table, with pages covered by rough lines of blue ink. Against the paint-flecked walls of the apartment were perhaps a dozen paintings of different cities and landscapes, neatly stacked from smallest to largest. Badlands and prairie grass. Arching, shadowy bridges and marshes at twilight. An Albuquerque desert and an icy Alaskan plateau. Against the opposite wall were several half-finished collages and combines, made from odds and ends. Marbles, painted like eyeballs, were pressed into putty, numbers and bits of maps were connected by hairy bits of yarn, above a backdrop of still, mounted butterflies and gigantic death's-head moths. It was all assembled on a heavy plywood base. William thought it looked like a corkboard belonging to an elegant serial killer.

William looked through a few of the dresses on the floor but couldn't tell which, if any, were clean. He noted her size on one of the labels, thinking that if he just bought her a new one, he wouldn't have to admit he'd broken in. Didn't you have to put things away if someone was spraying for bugs? Wouldn't it smell weird, only half a day later? The more he thought about it, the surer he was there had never been a pill fly infestation. But why had she lied to him? If she had just wanted to come over, she hardly had to make up a reason. She must have known that.

Just then he saw a box wrapped in white ribbon, with a card on top that said "For William." He picked it up and gently shook it, but there was no rattling inside. What could it be? Should he have bought something for her? He wanted to open the box, but then she'd surely know he'd broken into her apartment, so he set it back down where he'd found it.

His eyes fell on a brass birdcage by the window that was filled with jewelry boxes. He stepped lightly over to the cage and carefully searched for any kind of door. Puzzled, he reached through the bars, but they were barely spaced enough for a single finger to go in and fish out an earring or a necklace.

"How the hell did you get the boxes inside?" he asked the empty room.

Then, just as he was about to back up again, he noticed a small book covered with soft black leather, wedged between two of the jewelry boxes. He tried to snag the book, but no matter how he tipped or turned it, it wouldn't pass between the cage's bars. Sweating despite the pervasive chill in the apartment, he stood on his tiptoes to try to make out what was inside. If he squinted, he could just see what appeared to be—yes, names and addresses! An address book! Perhaps, somewhere inside there was an entry for an *Alissa* or an *Alicia* or an *Alis-ahh*.

Where on Earth are you from? he asked as he tried to flip the pages through the bars. *Who* are *you?* Then the book slipped a bit from his hand, and a half-dozen black-and-white photographs slipped out and fluttered to the bottom of the cage. There were some old train ticket stubs in there too. William felt around to gather them. Baby photos? Old school photos? A bucktoothed, no-eared middle-schooler, not yet run away from home? William had to crane his neck awkwardly in order to see clearly, but by bracing his foot against the windowsill, he was able to inch upward a little further and get a good look at—Irene's naked body.

William dropped the photos in his surprise, and they fell again, some now outside the birdcage, getting utterly and hopelessly out of order. Extracting his hand from the cage door, he bent over to scoop up the risqué photographs. Irene's body was ethereal and light against dark sheets. The poses were seminatural and rather unpornographic. In one, her breasts were exposed but blurry, the focus on her lips and the tip of her nose, her eyes crossed daringly as she studied the ash trembling at a cigarette's end. In another, she twisted sideways in a black river of sheets as if it were carrying her off. In a third, Irene lay with her back to the camera, eyes fixed out of a window, as if she were planning an escape. William could see the photographer's apparently female hand reaching out at the bottom of the frame, as if trying to coax her back. He flipped the photograph over and saw handwriting—not Irene's:

Tu es toujours sur le point de me quitter. —Alisanne

Alisanne! That was the thing, the name she'd been saying as

she fell asleep. He fumbled with his phone a minute, typing the inscription into Google. It struggled a little until he found a second bar of signal closer to the window, at which point it spat out the result.

"You are always about to leave me," he said aloud to no one.

William had had enough. He stacked the photographs together again as neatly as he could, slipped them into the back pages of the address book, and wedged the whole thing between the jewelry boxes again. *It's too much,* he told himself, as he stepped out of the apartment. "It's too much," he said to himself. *It's too much.* Shutting it all behind him, he trudged back down the half-collapsed staircase and pushed out onto the snowy sidewalks of East Fourth Street.

He made it all the way to Fifty-third Street before he changed his mind again. By Seventy-eighth, he saw a high-necked red dress in a shop window. He bought it and had it gift-wrapped.

Irene thought she'd never been happier than she was walking down the streets of suburban Flushing with William's arm on her recently bandaged one, heading toward the home of Mr. and Mrs. Cho. William was flustered, she imagined because they were late. Still, she didn't even mind that he'd asked her "How do you feel?" five times and "Are you feeling all right?" six times since she'd checked out of the hospital. For she was telling him the truth: she felt *spectacular.* In the eight hours she'd been stuck in the chemotherapy chair, she'd done five preliminary sketches for new sculptures, read six chapters of the *Iliad* (and William's touching accompanying thoughts), and—the pièce de résistance!—had found a certain page twelve of the fall 2007 Pottery Barn catalog.

"J'accuse!" she'd cried, when he'd come to collect her at the end of the day. She'd flung the open catalog into his worried-looking face.

"How do you feel?" he'd asked, batting it away.

"I feel," she said with a deep breath, "*incredible.*"

William looked confused and studied the catalog a moment. "I don't understand."

"This is *your* apartment, William! What—did you just pick up the phone and call the eight hundred number and say, 'Give me a page twelve, please'?"

He blushed again. "Not exactly, I—"

"William!" she cried, pulling at her hair with both hands. The other patients in the room were staring at them, delighted for a bit of real drama after several dull hours of talk shows. "William, you are a *person*! You possess, within you, a person*ality*. A personality that can—no, which *must*—be expressed in the things that surround you!"

She lifted up his copy of the *Iliad* like a battle-ax.

"Listen to this, Mr. Cho! 'If the gods actually know our fates and still try to meddle and wage their wars in us, then there must be some purpose in our *choosing* one of the many paths to that end. Man must have free will, or else why would the gods themselves bother?' "

"So?" he'd said. "Just some notes. They don't mean anything."

"They mean," Irene shouted happily, "that you aren't a page twelve, William Cho!"

This victorious cry still rang in her ears as she rushed arm in arm with William over the icy pavement, wearing the new red dress that he had bought for her as a Christmas gift. Somehow he had managed not only to select something she might have bought herself but also to get the proper size. She wondered if he had slyly checked the label on her clothes the night before as he'd undressed her, already planning this gracious surprise. And as he fumbled with the stack of gifts beneath his arm and hurriedly tried to warn her about his parents, she felt that he was her very own dark horse—that she would bring him out of himself and into the world, just as she had been herself, once.

"My father is quiet. Silent, generally, so don't be offended if he doesn't say anything. And my mother is—strange. She works in the community here as a sort of a healer, I guess. Not like a doctor. It's a family thing—back in Korea her mother was a *mudang* . . . like a shaman-kind-of-medicine-woman-kind-of-thing. So she's bonkers, basically. I don't know. She thinks she talks to spirits and gods, and people pay her to, like, channel—"

"William. Everyone's got a crazy family. Take a breath."

"Well, not all of them speak to the dead, that's all I'm saying. Actually there's one other thing," he whispered as he stood awkwardly a few inches from her. "My parents won't like it if they think we're dating. Because you aren't Korean. Not that we are dating. But we should make sure they don't think we are."

Irene knew she ought to be upset at this but simply couldn't feel it. She looked at him mischievously. "You know I'm just using you for your body."

Again William turned six shades of red. She dragged him up the steps of his own house and rang his doorbell. In moments they were greeted by a tall woman who studied them from behind the screen door.

"Come in, hurry!" she said. "You'll get caught in the storm!"

"It's beautiful out!" William said as she took the presents from him and bustled them both inside. Irene looked up at the sky, which was soft and pink from the cast-off light of their city. There wasn't a dark cloud anywhere in sight.

Inside, they took off their coats and laid them on top of an old washer and dryer, atop a heap of others. Irene shook Mrs. Cho's hand, which was covered in large rings. As the woman turned to address her son in stern Korean, Irene was delighted to see that the woman's hair was dotted with more of these tiny rings, glinting like silver salmon backs leaping upstream.

"Mom, this is Irene." William said.

Mrs. Cho looked up at her. "We are so glad you could come. It's always good when William has a friend."

He blushed.

"I love your hair," Irene said to Mrs. Cho.

She blushed, a slighter shade than her son, and gripped Irene's hands between her own pair, giving them a shake. She seemed about to say something when she pulled away, her eyes filling with curiosity and worry. "Not feeling well?" she asked.

Irene tried to smile. "I've never felt better, Mrs. Cho. Honestly."

But Mrs. Cho stood there, lips pursed, inspecting Irene as if she were a thin crack in a wall that might get larger. William hissed something at her in Korean, which she ignored, and then he hissed again, and she sharply spoke back to him without taking her eyes off Irene. Something about it made Irene feel as if she were back at the hospital, being scanned in the echo chamber of the MRI machine. She felt a quick dizziness, as if the tiles beneath their feet had lurched an inch upward, and then it was gone.

Mrs. Cho reached up with one ringed hand and seemed about to clap Irene on the shoulder, when her thumb flicked higher, passing directly below her left eye. Irene's hand jumped up nervously and brushed Mrs. Cho's hand away. Awkwardly, Irene pretended to be picking at an errant eyelash, as William barked at his mother, and she finally stepped back.

"I hope we haven't missed dinner. It smells incredible."

Something about the look in Mrs. Cho's spectacled eyes continued to make Irene uncomfortable as she said, "We are just sitting down!" and graciously led them into the next room.

Irene tried to settle herself, cooing over a hung portrait in the family room of young William and his brother, dressed in some sort of ceremonial garb, but the deeper into the home that she got, the harder she felt it was to draw in a proper breath. Following the glinting rings in Mrs. Cho's hair, Irene had the oddest sensation of descent, as if the room were on a slight slope, and they were all leaning a bit against it in order to stay upright.

They paused at an open double door, through which Irene saw a great library filled with books, and a Christmas tree in the far corner surrounded by presents. Mrs. Cho stepped inside to leave the presents that William had brought, while they both spoke more amiably, in their private singsong language. Irene closed her eyes a moment and tried to pierce through the spicy, strange scents that were coming from the dining room and breathe in the evergreen. But all she could make out was dry sawdust.

In the dining room they found the rest of the Cho family, and Irene was quickly introduced to Mr. Cho (who gave a warm grunt but spoke not at all) and William's older brother, Charles, who sat with his wife, Kyung-Soon, and their daughters, Charlotte and Emily. The girls chirped to each other as Irene was seated beside them. Emily seemed not quite able to look at her without immediately looking back down at her coloring book, whereas Charlotte couldn't seem to look at anything else. Irene shook everyone's hands, and there was jubilation as William and his brother began to catch up on something or other.

Spread out on the table was a colorful and strange feast. Irene had ordered Korean takeout food before—kimchi and bibimbap and rice cakes—but she had never seen any of these dishes. Crispy brown pieces of grilled pork, cucumbers stuffed with something crimson, and a plate of spongy-looking squid caked in sesame seeds. In the center of the table was an enormous snapper, its red scales seared brown from careful grilling, but its head still on and staring slack-jawed at Irene as she tried to get comfortable.

Ordinarily, Irene loved trying new foods, and everything smelled mysteriously delicious, but the uneasiness grew inside her gut as she sat there at the table. Before she could quite get talking to anyone, Mr. Cho looked backward and began addressing a painting of Christ on the cross that hung on the wall above his chair. Irene wasn't quite sure what was happening until she saw everyone lowering their heads, and the shy hand of little Emily gripping the edge of hers. Mr. Cho began to pray in a croaky tongue. Irene closed her eyes and tried to feel grateful—for the food, for the company, for the dress even, but somehow these thoughts were hard in coming. She never felt comfortable praying. She always felt like a liar, afterward.

Once Mr. Cho was finished, they all continued to chatter in Korean. Irene could barely detect the tone, let alone the meaning. It made her a little dizzy at first—and then a lot. Just minutes ago she'd never been happier; she tried to trace her steps back to it, but the way was lost. The crook of her elbow stung where the IV tube had been. There were still little black smudges outlining the places where the tape had held it down. She picked at the sticky edges. The lump beneath her eye was sore, and it made her wonder if the cisplatin and the doxorubicin were already binding with the tiniest and most intimate fibers of her being. It was *surely* in there and in everywhere, from the roots of her hair to the soles of her feet. The nurses had warned her of dizziness, irritability, and nausea. She tried to look delighted as she was at last introduced to Charles and Kyung-Soon.

"Charles is my older brother, and of course, he's a doctor, so my parents like him best," William explained.

"It's true," Mrs. Cho shrugged mischievously

Charles tried to wave this away. "William's the one who got into Yale."

"You went to medical school!" Kyung-Soon squeaked, as she passed Irene a bowl of a magenta soup filled with clams, shrimp, and tofu delicately carved in the shape of small fish.

"In Rochester," Charles teased. "Irene, if you ever want to see a fish out of water, find a Korean in Rochester."

She politely stirred her soup, watching the fish swirl around in their lava sea. "I spent a little time near Rochester, actually. On this farm just outside New Hope?"

"New Hope! Christ, what were you doing out there?"

There was a quick volley of Korean as, Irene gathered, Mrs. Cho reprimanded her oldest son for taking her Lord's name in vain. Mr.

Cho said nothing but gestured emphatically to the painting of Jesus. Charles raised his hands again in defense against the barrage of strange words, fired at him like pleasant bullets.

"My stars," Charles corrected himself in a genteel falsetto, "whatever were you doing on a farm outside of New Hope?"

"Farming?" Irene grinned, despite the faint but blinding halo that was forming around the chandelier above the table.

"William said you were an artist of some sort?" Kyung-Soon piped sharply.

William explained, "Irene's a bit of a Jack-of-all-trades."

"A Jane-of-all-trades," she offered, and was met with a rapid-fire exchange in Korean.

Irene couldn't tell what they were saying, but brotherly teasing was the same in any language. Mrs. Cho's mouth opened, and she began to smack her fork in the direction of her two sons, trying to get them to behave.

"What's going on?" Irene whispered to Emily, who was scribbling with crayons.

Charlotte whispered, "Daddy says you are Uncle William's girlfriend."

Irene raised her hand to her mouth playfully. "Uh-oh!"

Emily began to giggle but still wouldn't look at Irene directly. In her coloring book was a blue Santa with a golden hat. The rest of the family was still arguing, and Irene was trying to remain composed as best she could. Outside, the wind was picking up, and the girls watched eagerly as fresh snow began to fall. A few flakes at first, and then great curtains of white.

"Have you been good? Have you asked Santa Claus for anything?"

Charlotte immediately began to tick off a grand list of the things she'd requested of Harabeoji Santa in exchange for her sterling behavior: several dolls of very specific brand and style, nail polish like her mother's, a big-girl bicycle, skis, an elephant (of what size, she didn't explain), and a dress like Jill in her homeroom had. The list went on and on, and Irene pretended to be very interested as she ate her soup and watched Emily shading delicately in her coloring book. She sang softly to the crayons as she plucked them from the flimsy box and inserted lilac trees and ghosts into a sleepy, snowy town of Bethlehem.

"Could I?" Irene said slowly, taking a red crayon out of the box. Emily studied her with eyes like her grandmother's, penetrating and large. Then she allowed Irene to shade in a small barn on the edge of town. It was only when she looked up and noticed William staring at her that Irene began to feel dizzy again.

"Are you okay?" he mouthed, not subtly.

She waved, even as she felt the room lurch a few degrees clockwise and back again.

"I call a cheek!" Charles shouted eagerly.

Irene looked over in time to see that Mr. Cho was carving up the gigantic snapper and passing portions out to his sons.

William protested. "The cheek's the best part! Irene should get one—she's a guest!"

"She's *your* girlfriend. Give her yours."

They began to bicker again in Korean, and Irene graciously accepted the delicate cheek meat that Mr. Cho placed on her plate.

It was only then that Irene noticed Mrs. Cho was leaning over the carved fish, rolling her ringed fingers lightly over the bony carcass, and *singing* something. "What is she doing?" she asked Emily breathlessly.

"She's a witch," Emily whispered, the first words she'd spoken aloud all night.

Irene was about to say that it wasn't nice to say such things about one's grandmother, when Mrs. Cho ran the tip of her knife along the scaled, pink face of the fish and, with a gasping sound, plunged her fingertip into the small gap behind its eyeball and popped it out.

Irene lost her balance, just for an instant, but that was all it took. She felt her whole stomach heave inside her, a ship tossed in a tempest of bile. The pink, glassy fish eye rolled an inch or two like a wobbling marble, leaving a translucent trail behind it. Irene tried to clamp her mouth shut. She felt something rising inside her, boiling against gravity, up her esophagus. She grabbed her napkin and held it to her lips, her throat flexing and seizing.

Charlotte shrieked, "Grooooooossssssss!"

Irene was able to keep herself from vomiting all over the table, catching a little with the napkin and choking the rest hotly back. William was shouting at his mother, who was still singing and going for the other eye now. Charles and Kyung-Soon were shouting at Charlotte. Even Mr. Cho was barking something, apparently back at the sympathetic Christ above his head. Irene felt Emily's small hand squeezing on her wrist, not in panic but in comfort. She had a look, as if Irene were her doll and Emily meant to drag her to the other room to safety. But Irene couldn't keep her eyes off the fish, from Mrs. Cho's knife as it fumbled at the edge of the other pink eye. The tip of the knife again slipped into the space between ball and fish skull, and with a squishy *pop*, the second eye was loose and everyone was silent.

Calmly, Mrs. Cho plucked the two eyeballs off the tablecloth and placed them onto a small white side plate. She looked up at Irene and politely offered her the plate. Irene took a deep breath, feeling a bit steadier as she stared down at the plate's two gelatinous passengers.

"Eat these," she urged kindly. Then, as if confused that Irene didn't understand, Mrs. Cho added, "They'll make your eye better."

Irene covered the spot under her eye and looked over at William with no small amount of horror.

William, speechless, just waved his hand at his mother to put the plate down.

"Ew. *Total VOM*!" Charlotte snapped. "That's like the grossest thing ever."

"They're considered a delicacy," Charles said, trying to lighten the moment.

Irene knew she was a guest in the home of another, but surely this was something beyond grace. And why exactly was she wasting so much time and energy trying to be gracious anyway? She was exhausted. She could feel wet splotches on her red dress, where drips of vomit had gotten past the napkin. Now she would have to spend the whole ride home marked with stains. What had she done to deserve this? This, which was the cure? What had she done, even, to deserve the disease? So why was *she* sorry? She should be alone in her apartment with no tree and no fireplace and no presents and no family. She was full of poison. She wanted to be quarantined, sent to Siberia, put out on an ice floe. She'd stayed too long in the city. She'd forgotten to keep running, and now Death had caught up to her. Now He stared at her, from the surface of a porcelain plate, through these two roseate eyes.

Irene reached out and plucked the fish eyes off the plate. She held them in the open palm of her hand like a pair of dice. Then she popped them both into her mouth and bit down against their jellied circumference. A bursting of fishy goop clung to the back of her tongue. Charlotte screeched again, and William stared in horror. For a moment, Irene thought she might throw up again, but something about Mrs. Cho's gaze kept her stomach still. Just then she felt a small hand, Emily's, patting the belly of Irene's dress. *There, there,* she seemed to be saying. *Isn't that better?*

The storm outside was far too heavy for anyone to leave that night, so William set Irene up on the pullout couch in the study. They waited until the girls had placed a bowl of black bean noodles on the edge of the fireplace for Harabeoji Santa, and then when they were safely asleep, Charles helped William build a fire in the fireplace. William apologized for the five hundredth time since dinner. Irene was back to acting normally, back to pretending that everything was "Fine! Absolutely fine!" but William knew better. He could see the panic behind her eyes, even after his mother brought down some old clothes for her to change into.

"I wish you could sleep down here with me tonight," Irene said, pouting. But William could feel it—she was lying. There was this imposter look about her; it was hard for him to put his finger on. It was the way she'd sounded when she'd first called. Like Joan Fontaine in the movie.

"We'll have to leave tomorrow for the hospital before the girls are even up to open presents. But I have something for you," William said, taking a rectangular pile of silk out from the pile of extra clothes that his mother had given him for Irene. "Merry Christmas."

"Oh, William," she moaned, touching it. She unfolded the parcel, and it became a beautiful silk kimono, covered in butterflies and weeping trees and winding rivers. "It's—"

"It's a little old," he apologized. "But I promise it's never been worn."

Irene began to cry a little, and William couldn't think why. He moved in to comfort her, but she pulled away, as if she were contagious and might infect him.

"I feel awful," she said. "I bought you something but I left it at my apartment."

Irene slipped the loose kimono on over the billowing pajamas that Mrs. Cho had given her. William was stunned at how beautiful she looked in its folds. There were tears in her eyes.

"I'm sorry," she said, kissing him on the forehead tentatively, as if she weren't sure it wouldn't leave a mark.

"What for?" William asked. And though she had lied to him over and over, and though she had refused, again and again, to tell him the truths he wanted her to tell, he said, "You've done absolutely nothing wrong."

"Give me time," she said lightly, as if it could be a joke.

He left her there and went up to his old bedroom to sleep. In the morning, she was gone. The only sign of her was a little water on the floor by the front door where the snow had blown in on her way out and then melted.

William took the subway back down to her apartment, but the main entrance was locked and no one answered. He followed someone through the front door, went upstairs, and pressed his ear up against her door. It was ice cold, and there wasn't a single sound inside. He called the hospital, hoping, but the nurses there said she hadn't shown up yet for her appointment. Dr. Zarrani called back, worried, and told William that if Irene didn't come in for the second half of her dose, they'd have to start all over again. She asked him if he might know where she would go. Was there anyone else she might be staying with? William said he didn't know, that he didn't really know that much about her. He didn't know where she was from. Would she go to Sara's, up north? Then he thought about the photograph and its inscription. He hopped in a cab and asked the driver to take him to Penn Station.

The train station was empty on Christmas morning. Silence hung in the open terminal like a kind of fog. Most of the shops and restaurants were closed, their grates rolled down and locked tight, garlands hanging heavy above the archways, as if they knew that by the next morning they would be taken down and thrown away. William found Irene sitting on a bench, still wearing the stained red dress. She sat by the big clapboard train schedule, reading William's copy of the *Iliad*.

She looked up at him when she saw him coming. "Can't you leave me alone?"

"Dr. Zarrani said you have to come in before noon today or they'll need to start over."

Irene shook her head and clapped the heavy book shut. "I'll call her."

"To tell her what exactly?"

"That I'm going away for at least a month, maybe more. I'm sorry, William, we both know it wasn't going to work out with us. I can't explain. I'm just like this. I'm—"

William looked down at his phone and read off the words he'd translated the day before.

"Tu es toujours sur le point de me quitter."

Irene frowned as William sat down on the bench next to her. He knew he had badly mispronounced the line. "I went by your apartment to get you a dress the other day. There weren't any bugs. And I saw the gift you got me . . ."

"It's a scarf," she said softly.

"And I saw the dirty pictures in your birdcage. I saw what that girl wrote to you."

Irene didn't seem upset or violated. She just looked tired. "See? It's not just you, William."

"I actually wouldn't have thought that it was."

She looked up at him. "Oh, no?"

"No," William said, and then kissed her forehead once before patting the book as if to say goodbye to it. "I didn't think I mattered that much to you, No Ears."

He hadn't really meant it to be cruel, only true. There was nothing about her that belonged to him. Everything he knew about her, he'd stolen.

Irene watched William walk away, and then for several more minutes she watched train after train departing. There was one heading for San Francisco, but she didn't want to go there, not really. She didn't want to go to Boston, St. Louis, Raleigh, or Chicago either. She'd been to all those places before, and there were other Williams in each of them. Irene kept reading about Ajax and Hector and Priam. Warriors lacing their armor on for battle in one refrain, only to lie slain and forgotten in the sands of the next. All for some "beautiful" woman whom none of them really cared about at all. Irene flipped backward and forward. The men all died and died again. Trains arrived; trains departed.

Irene flipped to the page where William had written his note. Was there some God or gods who knew her fate? She stared up at the wide empty space above the clapboard. Bakersfield. Albuquerque. Pittsburgh. Burlington. Two dozen tracks to the end. Twenty-four places to die. *Man must have free will,* William had written, *or else why would the gods themselves bother?*

She sat up straight and closed the book. She rested her hand on her hip. There was still a faint fishy taste on the back of her tongue. She stood up and walked past the tracks to the tunnel for the subway. She rode to the hospital. She apologized to Dr. Zarrani and said there had been an accident on the 5 train and she'd been stuck, underground, for an hour. The doctor said she'd make some adjustments, but they hadn't lost too much time. Before the nurses hooked her up to the IV, Irene changed into the kimono. Its loose arms fell gently over the elbow where the tube went in, and she felt a great freedom as she drew and drew, nothing but fish eyes. Cold, with dead black pupils staring out at her.

When the dose was over, Irene took the subway home, and was so flushed she had to pull her coat open with only the kimono underneath. People stared, but she didn't care. It was New York, and there were stranger people than her in every neighboring car. The thought comforted her.

She had already arrived in the place she belonged. Once she was safely inside her apartment, she turned on the heater. There was a loose thread at the sleeve of the kimono that had been tickling her all day long. She tugged, and more silk came away in her hand without breaking. She pulled and pulled at the thread for minutes, until there was no cuff, and then only half a sleeve, and then no sleeve at all. She let the thread fall around her feet.

William called. She didn't answer. Sara called. She didn't answer.

In a week Sara would be back in the city and she would have to tell her everything, but not yet. She kept pulling until the collar and the bodice and the hem and the other sleeve were all entirely unraveled. Soon the silk thread was piling up to her naked waist. She unraveled the rivers and trees and the carp that swam in circles. At last she unraveled the final stitch. She felt safe and warm as she burrowed into the nest of silk. She had eaten almost nothing since the fish eyes, but she wasn't hungry. She closed her eyes as she pulled the silk in around her. She wanted nothing more than to rest there in that enormous cocoon, for days and weeks, and then emerge—free of poisons and tumors and heartsickness. *With wings*, she thought to herself, as sleep finally came.

A SUBJUNCTIVE MARCH

Sara could no longer tell one day from the last or the next. Irene had told her about the biopsy results right after she and George had returned from New Year's, and now it was March. What had happened to the intervening weeks was a mystery worthy of study by George's counterparts at the theoretical physics laboratory. Sara suspected that something had happened to the very fabric of time itself. It was always March. Sara didn't even need to see the gray dawn outside the one tiny window in George's apartment to know it was out there, dismal and petulant.

She woke up each morning to the sound of her husband-to-be trying to extract himself from the Murphy bed without waking her. She dreamed of it closing up like a Venus flytrap with her inside. With her eyes nine-tenths shut, she breathed heavily so George would believe she was still dozing as he moved around the tiny apartment, from the toilet-in-the-closet to the shower-in-the-kitchen. Coffee dripped behind the spray of the shower. She peeked when George emerged, sopping wet, and proceeded to barrel about the apartment in his towel, trying to simultaneously pour the coffee, check the weather on his phone, and (on alternate days) water the plant. There was a hard deadline, always, of seven o'clock, because that was when George's car was due for ticketing, and his panic grew and grew as the minute hand worked its way around. Already there were four parking tickets that George was fighting, plus a speeding ticket he'd gotten on the LIE, another from Riverside Drive, and a third he hadn't yet told her about but that she'd seen hiding under a notebook and seemed to involve driving the wrong way down a one-way block in Tribeca.

Lying in bed, she imagined how much more smoothly things would go if people just listened to her. If her roommate, Karen, saw reason and moved out of their bigger apartment, regardless of whose name was technically on the lease. If Irene would not always wait until the last possible minute to text to say if she needed someone to take her to the hospital or pick her up. If Jacob would read the book she'd bought him for Hanukah. If Irene would hurry up and tell Jacob about the whole cancer thing, instead of always waiting for the "right time," which was clearly never. If she and George would find the perfect glamorous yet intimate place to hold their wedding so she could finally mail the save-the-date cards she'd already bought and addressed. If William would sign on to Facebook again because even though she was mad at him for leaving Irene at the train station, she was also sure that they would make a great couple once she was all better.

Sara snapped to as George, showered and dressed at last, kissed her cheek to say goodbye. "Hey. When will I see you?" he whispered in her ear.

She opened her eyes. It was nearly seven. How had that happened?

"Irene's meeting me to see an apartment in Morningside Heights during my lunch break, and then I'm going to try and get down to Battery Park tonight to see a place for the wedding. But I still have the 'Hip Spring Break Destinations' column to edit. Sheldon quit last week, so it got reassigned."

"You're already doing the six articles that Meegan left behind when *she* quit."

Sara was too tired to get into that. "So I might just do that at the coffee shop until they close."

George nodded, "Allen got us time on the Gerber satellite tonight, and he wants to go over the materials for the conference next month. And somewhere in there I have to find ten minutes to talk to that guy at Cornell. Someone's on leave and might not come back. They don't know when they'll know."

"You want to move back to Ithaca?"

"I don't want to move anywhere. I just want a job."

"Okay. We'll just live in this closet forever then."

"I like this closet. As closets go, this is a good one."

Sara arched an eyebrow. "Oh yeah? Why's that?"

"Well, I've been checking, but so far, this is the only closet in the city that has you in it."

She couldn't help laughing at the thought of George bursting into an apartment, opening the closet doors, and doing an apologetic about-face.

"Run away with me," Sara said suddenly.

George laughed. "You want to elope?"

"I want to go to France."

"Oh, is that all?"

"Come on. I'm serious. We've been talking about this forever! You, me, Irene, Jacob. Freshman year we found those berets at the Salvation Army, and we *promised* we would go someday. Remember? We watched all those Godard movies."

George groaned, still pained by the memory.

"We've put this off for a third of our lives already. And I'm saying we should really think about going while we still have the—while we all still can."

George checked his watch nervously. "Well, okay, but only if you have a few thousand dollars lying around I don't know about."

The thing was, she did. And while she loved that George always forgot, he *did* know she did. Before her grandfather, C. F. Sherman, had completely lost his marbles, his accountants had set up various accounts for her and her sisters. Trust funds, essentially, though she never called them that because it gave people the wrong idea:

snobby and spoiled were immediate conclusions. In college, even though she'd worked part time every single semester and interned in the summers and paid for all her own books and meals, the fact that she didn't *have* to, technically, had still occasionally caused friction when Jacob panicked about his loans and Irene had needed to sometimes sleep on their couches or raid their pantries when her latest fling had kicked her out.

Sara found it much easier to simply pretend the money wasn't real and to live paycheck to paycheck like everyone else. Her mother kept telling her to just get a broker, hire a wedding planner, get a cleaning service, go to the tailor. But Sara refused to pay others to do what she could manage to do herself. If everyone else could do it, then she could too. Twice as much of it, even. And meanwhile she always looked forward to the days ahead of them, when everyone's hard work would pay off, and George would have tenure somewhere, and Jacob would get a Fulbright, and Irene would sell her art for thousands, and they could all finally travel together, with all their future children tagging along behind them.

Sara stroked George's cheek. "Hurry up. You're going to get a ticket."

He groaned. "See you at the end of time, then."

"See you at the end of time," she replied, with another quick kiss before he dashed out the door. When the door finally closed behind him, Sara cautiously untangled herself from the sheets, closed the bed, fixed her hair, brushed her teeth, and pulled on the clothes she had laid out carefully the night before.

Sara had learned of Irene's cancer in the back of a taxi, sandwiched between the door and a human-sized cocoon made of iridescent silk. She had come down to Fourth Street to help extract Irene's latest artistic creation from the living room and transport it to the K Gallery, where Irene intended to hide it in the back of the storeroom until she figured out just what the hell to *do* with it. They had been heading up Sixth Avenue when Sara observed that it was an unusually large piece for Irene.

She had sighed. "I know. Any bigger, and it'd be installation art."

Sara had complimented the cocoon, which really was quite stunning and had an almost wet texture somehow, from the way the silk shone in the murky January daylight.

"So what happened?" Sara had asked.

"What do you mean?" Irene had replied.

"I mean what came over you? Why'd you make it?"

Sara realized now (knowing what she knew by March) that Irene must have been about to tell her the story of Mrs. Cho's kimono, but couldn't do so without explaining how she'd spent Christmas Eve at the Cho household, and that she couldn't explain that without first explaining how she'd broken down and called William from the MetroStop Bakery by the hospital, and that she couldn't explain that without first explaining why she'd been in the hospital. Irene had traced this long invisible thread of events back and had landed where she needed to begin, which was to say, "Well, the biopsy results came back positive."

Sara ignored the apparent non sequitur and hugged Irene firmly. She had been ready for this since before the holiday party.

"Everything's going to be okay. We're going to beat this thing, no problem." She pulled her phone from her purse to start hunting for the relevant numbers. "Luther said he knows someone at Sloan Kettering and someone else at Montefiore. We should make appointments right away for a second opinion, and then our health columnist, Dr. Sammy, he said he'd talk to us about treatment options anytime."

But Irene had actually seemed annoyed by this. "Actually," she said, "I started chemo a few weeks ago. At Mount Sinai."

"A few *weeks* ago?"

"It only took a few hours for three days. Now I've got a little time off before the next round. It wasn't so bad. I feel pretty good, and they're very optimistic. I just didn't want to ruin everyone's holiday. It's silly."

"*Silly*? Irene, this is serious."

"Don't you think I know that?"

"Who else knows? Does Jacob know?"

"No," Irene sighed. "William's the only one who knows."

"But you barely know him!"

"He was here, and I got scared, I guess," Irene had said matter-of-factly. "It doesn't matter. He sort of left me at Penn Station. He's probably waiting for me to call him, but—"

"You told him you had cancer and he—what?"

It had then taken a good twenty minutes to back up and get the whole story before the cab driver deposited them, and Sara helped Irene navigate the cocoon into the storeroom. And though it had all seemed fine at the end of the day, Sara continued dwelling on it. They had always told each other everything. So why hadn't Irene told her right away? It killed her that when it was all said and done and Irene had been cured, this would still be there between them.

All Sara wanted was to take care of Irene: shuttle her to and from her doctor's appointments, make her chicken soup from scratch, sit with her on the couch watching *¡Vámonos, Muchachos!*, and wait until Irene fell asleep to pick her hair off the pillows. But Irene refused to allow any of this. She insisted on acting as if nothing were any different than before, like the rest of the world.

For instance, it was insane that Sara still had to wake up and get to the *New York Journal* on time and spend the bulk of her day in a gray cubicle, covered in orderly columns of Post-it Notes and tacked-up newspaper clippings. While her friend *had cancer.* She just *had* it. "I mean, hello?" she felt like saying to her dry-erase calendar. "Are you serious with this shit?" It was still totally full of precise, centimeter-tall lettering and meticulous color coding: red appointments, green deadlines, blue editorial board meetings, purple social engagements, yellow holidays, and intern schedules in brown.

Even though Irene had been adamant about sticking with Dr. Zarrani at Mount Sinai, Sara still went in to discuss the situation with her boss, Luther Halles, the editorial director. He gave her a few numbers—well, actually he told her to look the numbers up in his Contacts list—and said she could use his name, of course, for anything anytime.

"You could do a piece on this," he said, rolling his Mont Blanc pen between his fingers. She did a quick mental check of whether she needed to order him more ink. "Even a multipart thing, you know? Young, invulnerable people with cancer. It's compelling stuff."

Sara hummed. "I'm not sure my friend would go for that."

Luther got up and began pacing. The way he walked, he sort of led with his head, which whipped this way and that, tugging through his neck as if pulling the rest of his low, reluctant frame behind him. "Tell her this is important. Others can learn from her."

She wasn't sure that was on Irene's list of current priorities.

"Hey. Does she have health insurance?"

Sara nodded. Juliette and Abeba were keeping Irene on the payroll.

"She works at this gallery in Chelsea."

Luther made a face; it would be a better story if she didn't have insurance, Sara supposed, with all the headlines about the legions of young people who were coming off their parents' plans into part-time work and their parents' basements. There was no room now for them here, with her whole graduating class on idle, waiting for this financial crisis thing to end. Now the people above them couldn't retire and wouldn't be promoted and so she and everyone else were stuck in assistant purgatory. Still it was better than being back home.

"The other thing is that I might need to take three weeks off," Sara said as seriously as she could. She knew he knew she had the days saved up and he'd been dreading she'd try and use them. "Once she's finally feeling better, I'm taking her to France."

Luther didn't reply, and didn't really need to, as his eyes alone suggested that this wasn't happening. She knew she'd be better off asking him to rename the paper *The Daily Sara* than asking for multiple weeks off. She was the paper's unofficial closer. Whenever someone quit or was fired (which happened every other week), their abandoned projects were usually given to her to finish. Meanwhile she represented the paper in the Classroom Journalism Initiative and served on a steering committee for the new Web interface. When Luther traveled, Sara was the one trusted to book his hotels, dinners, cars, and flights and to find people to take his unused Knicks tickets if there was going to be a game. She spoke to Mrs. Sigrid Halles (a former Miss Norway runner-up) at least three times a day and kept track of the major life events of their children Laetitia and Laurence.

He seemed aware that this was a lot of work for one person, or at least he had given her a 5 percent raise last summer when she'd complained about it and given her a new title as head of the mentorship program, which meant she had use of the two interns. But using them was far more work than doing it herself, for both were clueless. They were only six years younger, but they were hopeless. God knew what they would do to the place if she were gone for three weeks.

Luther sat back down and pushed a stack of files toward her, which he'd finally signed after a week's delay. "Why don't you all go use my beach house? Shelter Island is great this time of year. It's absolutely beautiful."

"In March?"

"Oh, totally. I wouldn't go swimming, but there are some excellent vineyards, and you'll have the town to yourselves. It's primal,

I'm telling you. It's so relaxing. I go out there some weekends just to think. Be in nature. Commune with the pounding surf and the wide-open sky. Check with Sigrid about it. We're lending it to her nephews until early April, but you can have it for a couple days after that. It'll be perfect. A long weekend on Long Island! On me."

Sara thanked him with enough false gratitude that he'd be satisfied and promised she'd think about it, even though the idea of staying in her boss's house—even his vacation house—made her feel awkward.

On her lunch break Sara went up to check out the Morningside Heights apartment. Since they'd arrived six years ago, the rents had climbed far faster than their pitiful raises. She found herself feeling grateful the housing market had just spectacularly collapsed (though she knew this was awful) because the rents weren't increasing for the first time in six years. But they weren't going *down* either. Occasionally she and George did find places that seemed within reach, but the listing would disappear before they finished their application. No matter, they had always already begun to get cold feet.

Because George couldn't realistically come in from the observatory on his lunch break, Irene joined Sara to see apartments sometimes during the week. Most of the time she was either just coming from or going to an appointment at Mount Sinai, but she never said more than "It was fine" or "They don't know if it's working yet," when Sara asked how it was going. Nothing would be determined until April, when this latest round of chemotherapy would be finished and new scans would be taken. That day they met by the steps of St. John the Divine and hugged, and Sara thought she noticed Irene wince a little from her light touch through her red pea coat. She looked pale, for sure, but then so did everyone; the sun hadn't been out in weeks.

"Have you spoken to Jacob yet?" Sara asked, as they walked past the sculpture garden and down to the corner of 110th and Amsterdam.

"I saw him yesterday. He yakked my ears off about his stupid boss for an hour. They have this rule, apparently, where they don't talk at work, except Jacob has to always wave hello to Oliver when he walks by his office, because everyone else does and so it might look suspicious if Jacob didn't. But Jacob says that he'd rather just never say hello to anybody ever, *including* Oliver—"

This wasn't what Sara had meant, but then a tour bus roared by, its double-decker top filled with elderly Europeans wearing complementary ponchos just in case the solid gray sheet of a sky made up its mind to rain. The tourists snapped photos of the cathedral as the bus idled at a red light, and then the light went green and they roared along toward Columbia University and the Apollo Theater beyond.

"Here's the building!" Irene shouted. A hand-drawn sign taped to the door announced the open house, and the door itself was propped open with some wadded-up coupon circulars. Sara wrinkled her nose—the front hall was badly lit, the mailboxes were covered in permanent graffiti scrawl, and there was a distinct M. C. Escher lilting to the stairs as they walked in. At the first floor they knocked on the appropriate door and waited. A moment passed, and then the door swung open to reveal an elderly man wearing mascara, rouge, and a blond beehive wig. He wore a cerulean silk Ralph Lauren bathrobe that was tied just loosely enough to make his biological sex undebatable.

"Oh!" Sara almost knocked Irene backward down the rickety staircase.

"Yes?" he asked, as if nothing were odd at all, looking them up and down eagerly.

"We're here to see the apartment?" Sara managed, eyes flitting from the wig to the open bottom of the robe, to the side of the doorframe.

"Come on in," he said. "You know it's only a one-bedroom, don't you?"

Sara had to purse her lips to stop giggling as Irene slipped an arm around her waist.

"Oh, we'll only need the one bed."

The man laughed, and the gruffness gave away his masculinity even more than the powdered-over Adam's apple.

"Let's come back another time," Sara said, trying to wriggle gently away from Irene.

"Come on," Irene said, reaching up to brush some of Sara's raven hair from her forehead. "I'm sure Ms. . . ."

"Daphne."

"I'm sure Ms. Daphne doesn't have all day to show us around."

But Irene took her sweet time poking around the closets and the kitchen, seeming to relish the way Sara kept close at all times. "Oh, your mother would *hate* this wallpaper. It's so perfect!" Irene said as she ran a hand over the velvety-floral patterns in the living room.

"It's all original," Ms. Daphne explained. "At least since the sixties."

"You've lived here that long?" Sara asked.

"Oh, honey," he exclaimed. "You're making me feel old now."

Irene dragged Sara through the door into the bedroom, where an old armoire hung open, revealing an assortment of beautiful gowns. Sara's eyes wandered instead toward the mirrored vanity, which was overflowing with heavy-duty makeup. Ms. Daphne blew into the room after them and then eased himself onto the low-slung bed, which rippled unnaturally as he stretched out on it.

Irene hooted. "There's a water bed! Sara, come try this out."

Sara stifled a laugh as Irene bounded toward a spot on the bed, then felt a pang. How could Irene have cancer and be goofing around like this? There she was, making herself comfortable on the water bed and wiggling her eyebrows suggestively at Sara.

Ms. Daphne clapped his hands together. "For another three hundred I'll leave the bed. Don't worry, it's very sturdy!" This offer seemed to, finally, break Irene. She began giggling uncontrollably, which made Sara start to giggle as they excused themselves and rushed out, nearly tripping down the stairs. The girls didn't stop running until they were back in the park, winded. For just a moment it felt like nothing had changed at all.

"I could kill you!" Sara shouted, as Irene leaned against a low rock wall for support. "He . . . was this close to getting us in the bed!"

Irene was practically crying, she was laughing so hard. Then she leaned over the wall and threw up what looked and smelled like a grapefruit that she'd had for breakfast. Sara rushed off to a nearby kebab truck for napkins. When she got back, Irene was cleaning herself with a fistful of snow she'd scraped off the wall. They each caught their breath.

Finally, Irene stood and threw one arm around Sara. "Totally worth it," she declared.

Sometimes Sara called George without even realizing, on afternoons like that one when she was wandering through Times Square on her way back to the office after a late lunch. She just found her phone against her ear, ringing. Then when George picked up, she didn't know what to say.

"What's up, buttercup?" he asked brightly from the other end of the phone. In the background she could hear Allen playing a loud video game, blowing up aliens with rocket launchers. "Could you turn that down?" she heard George say.

"We're taking Irene to France. I've decided."

George laughed. "Did you also decide to rob a bank, because—"

"No," Sara said. "I'm going to pay for it. I'll call my mother after work and tell her I'm taking it out of my grandfather's money."

This was what she called it to George, and even to herself, though it wasn't really her grandfather's anymore and hadn't been since she was fifteen and his great decline had begun. Slowly he had lost the ability to form cogent sentences, to walk, to lift a spoon to his mouth. Sara's mother had set up the pool house for him and his nurse, and at night she'd sometimes heard him howling out there. Her parents and sisters never talked about it, then or now. Then one day Sara had come home from school to find a note on the refrigerator saying that they'd all be going to his funeral on Saturday. She had tried to tell George all of this, but he didn't really understand. How could he? And so now it was just she who knew firsthand what happened when the human body began to come apart at the seams. Who knew there wasn't time to waste. That illness cared nothing about money or fairness or the things you planned to do later.

George hummed over the phone. "You think Irene's going to be comfortable with that?"

"People have done worse things to other people than buy them trips to France."

He laughed and didn't take it further. "Hey, did we ever think about the New York Public Library for the wedding?"

"They're booked solid." Sara was hovering under the low blue marquee for the Letterman show, a block from her office.

"For when?"

"Forever."

"How about Disney World?" George offered.

"Don't say that unless you're serious."

"I'm *not* serious."

"Because you can't joke with a girl about getting married in Cinderella's castle, mister."

"I'm not serious! I'm not serious!" George shouted.

"You can get the character of your choice to officiate."

George thought a second. "I want Quasimodo then."

"You would."

"Hey, next to Quasimodo I'm going to look *good*."

"You always look good," Sara said, leaning into the receiver as if she could kiss him through the mouthpiece. The smell of the pizza at Angelo's filled her nostrils as a street sweeper swarmed by, picking up the torn ticket stubs and the spilled salads of the afternoon's tourists; the shows would be opening in only a few hours, but the sidewalks were already teeming with high school classes and church groups and seniors who'd been bused in from New Jersey. They were all clinging tightly to one another, looking overwhelmed, scared to walk too far in any direction. Everyone kept checking phones and wristwatches. *How much time before dinner? Let's not be late. How long will* that *line take? How many blocks is it? Let's just stay here and stare at the American Eagle billboard. I heart New York.*

"Gotta run," George said. "Cokonis is calling on the other line."

"See you at the end of time," she said.

Back in the office she killed an hour Googling "osteosarcoma causes." She always came up with nothing, even after going up to the thirty-eighth page of hits. She was amazed how many different ways there seemed to be to say it: *unknown*. Does not have a concrete cause. Little is known about the etiology. The causes are not known. Scientists have not found the exact causes. The cause is not yet established. There are no known or apparent causes. One time she found, "While the causes are still unclear, doctors believe that his type of cancer starts with a DNA error in the body's cells." She'd thought she was on to something until she looked up "DNA error" and was met again with *unknown*. The causes are not known. Etc., etc.

She got up to make a cup of coffee in the pod machine in the kitchen. As it gurgled and spat, she lifted a sunflower-yellow packet of zero-calorie sugar and snapped it back and forth with her finger to compact the crystals inside. She imagined, in thirty years, opening a newspaper and seeing the headline: CANCER CAUSE CONCLUSIVELY DETERMINED. And everyone would go, "Damn, it was *riboflavin* the whole time! How did we miss *that*?" She ripped open the pack of sugar substitute, emptied it into the coffee, and threw away the paper. Then she returned to her desk to find one of the interns waiting to confess that she'd broken the copier by forgetting to remove a staple from a three-page memo. These were the winners who'd gotten this chance while others their age sat at home. These were the people whose parents were too important for them to be fired. Dealing with the copier would take up what remained of the hour, just as the afternoon before had been lost to the other intern forgetting P came before Q and an hour's filing needing to be redone.

What was another hour? What was another afternoon? Sara wanted to waste as many as it took to get through this awful month.

At seven o'clock Sara changed into a strapless sea foam dress that she'd had tailored from a bridesmaid's dress used during the previous summer and headed downtown to meet Jacob. They were scheduled to check out a high-end seafood restaurant in Battery Park as a potential wedding venue. The planners hadn't been able to get her in on a weekend day but had gotten the members of the Marcuso-Gerber Wedding to permit them to come see the space in action that night. Ordinarily Sara would have warned Jacob that they were only slipping in and out without bothering anyone, but given the oppressive weight of this March on her shoulders, she rather hoped he would get her out on the dance floor, or maybe start several fights with Marcuso cousins, or at least swipe her a slice of wedding cake that she could sink her troubles into.

Walking down Broadway, past the line outside Letterman and past the smells of Angelo's once again, Sara dug her phone out of her purse and called her mother, only to discover that she had already missed a call from "Home." No matter how many times she tried to impress upon her parents and her sisters that, between the hours of eight and six, she "worked," that is, "had a job," and therefore couldn't take personal phone calls, they always, always called then and seemed annoyed and surprised that she was ignoring them. Such was the tone exactly of the voicemail then from Sara's mother.

"Sara sweetheart, we *really* need to know the date for the wedding. We're supposed to go to Ireland for three weeks in June next year and we have to book the flights now, but we can't until we know if we should be in New York. You can still do it in Boston, by the way. Are you going to get a block of rooms? Hotels in New York are so expensive, we really want to reserve those right away, especially if you're thinking about September, because that's move-in for colleges and . . ."

Sara jammed on the delete button so hard that she thought she felt the glass crack on her phone screen, though George kept telling her this wasn't possible. How exactly was she supposed to worry about wedding planning? She didn't care at all. All she needed was enough space to successfully fit two hundred friends and family members, a five-piece band, a Unitarian minister, four steaming tables, and a three-tiered cake covered in vanilla buttercream—and yet nothing felt right.

She and George went to place after place. The rooftop of the NoHo Hotel and then an old ironworks called The Smithy, which had been converted into a medieval-looking space. The elegant Russian Dance Hall, the slick and seedy Club 99, and the Bronx Botanical Gardens. George had vetoed Guillermo's on the Water in Hoboken ("I'm *not* getting married in New Jersey") and a huge ballroom inside one of the former World's Fair buildings in Flushing. ("Really? Your mother is going to let you get married in Queens?") There was brief talk of being married in the Lower East Side Tenement Museum and doing a kind of Dickensian thing. There was a short investigation into what it would take to join the Rosicrucian Order, because Sara liked the Grand Lodge but it was only available for qualifying Masons. In one weekend alone, they had toured the Central Park Boathouse, a church converted into an artist's collective, the Morgan Library, and NYU's South Asian Institute. As with the apartment search, she was overwhelmed by a plurality of possible futures, each of which seemed as impossible to reach as April.

While she waited for Jacob to come down on the bus, Sara milled around the far-downtown neighborhood. Even under a heavy coat, she was freezing in her dress. She paced up and down Bowling Green and up past the mouth of the Battery Tunnel. Her face felt heavy with makeup, her hair tight in its twist. She willed herself to stop craning her neck every ten seconds looking for Jacob, and to stop checking her text messages and to just take that particular moment in. To hold on to the lingering crust smell of French bread still emanating from the closed Au Bon Pain up the block and to keep the resilient greenness of the grass in front of her. Keep the prickly chicken-skin bumps on her arms and the way they felt under her palms as she rubbed to stay warm. Keep the angle of the shadow that belonged to the elevated walkway, which was closed and dark, and the stairwell leading up to it was chained off. Keep the chains clanking in the cold gusts of a passing black town car. *It's too quiet down here,* Sara thought. She could feel the particular wet chill of the Hudson from a block away, but she couldn't see it. The buildings were too new even though this was the oldest part of the city.

Finally she saw Jacob coming from up the block wearing a black top hat and tails, which he'd rented from God knew where. He had on the patent leather shoes and a little cane thing with white tips. He looked like a pudgy Fred Astaire.

"Oh my god, you look amazing!" she yelled.

"I know!" he said. "I mean, so do you!"

He hugged her and felt her shivering. "Why didn't you meet me inside somewhere?"

She lifted up her arms as if to say that she had no idea, but Jacob thought she was pointing across the street, toward the high fences that marked off the construction site there, and the hundred-story cranes that stood sentinel overhead.

"Oh, I know. Can you believe it? Eight years later and still just a fucking hole in the ground?"

Sara didn't know what he meant, until she realized that she'd been standing there—trying to live in the moment and to be observant and aware—for twenty minutes directly across the street from Ground Zero without having even the slightest idea that this was where she was standing. The shame of this made her slump into Jacob's shoulder. She'd never really known the city before the towers had fallen—just one class trip in high school to the Natural History Museum and a family excursion to see *Cats*. It had happened the third week of Junior year, two years of eager progress suddenly derailed into twenty-four-hour coverage of gray ash and bafflement. Her parents calling to report that so-and-so's father was all right and that so-and-so's father was missing, and weepy firefighters, and angry men in suits on CNN, and then shock, and then awe, and then tough and solemn boys in desert camouflage on FOX. And for years after it had felt like progress could be measured only in how much closer they were to rebuilding that wide and brilliant world and then gradually accepting that it would never be rebuilt—that it, too, remained a hole in the landscape.

They walked a little farther and came up to the railing and looked out over the Hudson. A thin crescent of silver moon hung above Jersey City, and Sara tried to squint enough to see the time on the Colgate clock, glowing like an ember at the foot of the huge skyscraper there.

"What's up with you lately?" he asked. "Every time I see you or Irene it's like you're trading off periods or something. At least let George and I have a turn."

Sara paused, ready to tell Jacob everything and deal with Irene later. "I'm stuck in a subjunctive mood," she said finally.

"A what?"

"Come on. You're a poet. The subjunctive. Indicating that everything is possible and contingent. Hypothetical. I'm just having a subjunctive month."

"A subjunctive March," Jacob agreed.

Sara looked down. There beneath her three-inch heels was the cold white concrete of Manhattan. An inch beyond them, on the other side of the railing, was the cold, dark roiling river. Here was city, and there was not. Ever shifting though it might be, there was an edge to the city in every given moment. Its beginning and its end. It was a finite thing, after all. And inside the city was *one* apartment for her and George. And *one* place where they would exchange their vows and cut a cake and dance to a cover of Bon Jovi. And Irene would tell Jacob at *one* moment, just as there had been indeed *one* moment when Irene's DNA had erred, and just as this very moment now the chemotherapy was either repairing this error or the cancer was growing. Time would tell, as sure as it would also pass. It could not be March forever.

"Come on," Jacob said, "let's go crash this wedding. It'll give me a chance to explain why you don't really want to get married."

Sara giggled, though she knew he wasn't entirely kidding.

"First . . . you really just can't tie down a guy like George. He's got insatiable appetites. He's got the soul of a rock-and-roll legend inside that nerdy shell. He's like . . . you know who he's like? He's like Meat Loaf in there. That's right, there's a four-hundred-pound, sweaty animal locked up in there who would do *any*thing for love."

Sara was laughing so hard, she could hardly breathe. "Thank you," she said, giving Jacob a kiss on the cheek.

"Let's make out," Jacob said. "I'm in love with you. Don't marry that other guy."

"Sorry. You missed your chance," Sara sighed.

"Can I at least sleep in your attic once you get all lame and have a billion kids? Maybe make a little den, up above the garage."

"Nope," Sara said. "I won't have you coming and going at all hours of the night, bringing your conquests to breakfast. What would my billion children think?"

They went on like that for hours. And they did go to the wedding, and they did drink themselves sick on champagne cocktails until they were escorted out by the bride's brother, a greaser named Mikey who tried to get Sara's number even as Jacob was attempting to kick him in the shins. And Jacob promised, he *promised*, he'd come to Long Island for a long weekend at Luther's beach house in April. Just the idea filled Sara with happiness all the way home, where she burrowed into the Murphy bed beside George, already sound asleep.

SHELTER ISLAND

George liked solving problems. Finding the square root of *x* using the Babylonian method. Unjamming the printer in the department office. Determining the number of Sun-like stars in a Brightest Cluster Galaxy based on the ratio of their luminosities. Tracing the most efficient possible route between his parking spot on Riverside between Seventy-second and Seventy-third, and the Borders outside Grand Central from which Jacob had consented to being (in his words) "kidnapped," and down to East Fourth Street for Irene. Then back up through the Queens Midtown Tunnel and the Long Island Expressway, in early Saturday morning traffic, with a quick detour around an accident near Hauppage, and then onward until exit 70 brought them to the Sunrise Highway. Then Route 51 and the North Fork, where they'd take the ferry over to Shelter Island where Sara's boss Luther took his family in the summertime, but which for this one weekend belonged to them, for nothing.

It was important to appreciate nice things when you could. Fine wines, good friends, free beach homes. It would be just like old times, back in the dorms. They'd be up all night talking, playing charades and gin rummy, counting stars from the rooftop.

George had a slight headache, the likely result of the whiskey he'd had at one that morning to celebrate the e-mail he'd gotten from an AAS committee member in Belgium inviting him and Allen to speak at the June conference in Pasadena about their mounting discoveries in the Ring Nebula. People were talking about it. Physicists anyway. Terabytes of new data every day that he and Allen were gathering on 237 Lyrae V's collapse.

He took a long sip from his Einstein thermos, its contents still warm after almost two hours. It was a relief to be leaving the city at last. Get the past few months behind them. Sara had been up half the night, packing and repacking, and now she was asleep in the passenger seat. In the rearview mirror he could see that Irene was texting on her phone and Jacob was dozing. George was glad that they could finally start focusing on what lay ahead. Jacob had booked tastings at some vineyards Oliver had recommended, and Sara had researched the best local seafood spots. Best of all, Irene had been steadily improving since her fourth chemo treatment at the end of March. Dr. Zarrani had seemed to feel things were going well when George had picked her up from the last infusion.

"You may see the lump under her eye getting smaller, although don't overinterpret this," Dr. Zarrani had urged. "Sometimes there is some shrinkage due to liquid loss, but that isn't necessarily indicative of cancerous cell death. Call me immediately if she feels swelling beneath her arms or an ache in her jaw, as this could indicate spreading to the lymphatic systems."

How on earth could Irene's jaw possibly be connected to her armpits? George wished he'd paid better attention in AP Bio.

"Obviously changes of any kind could be relevant," Dr. Zarrani stressed to Irene. "Call the office anytime, and we'll see you next week for fresh scans. Then we'll know where we are."

He and Irene had celebrated with a pint of Cherry Garcia on the sidewalk, followed by two pints of Guinness and a round of Big Buck Hunter at McIntosh's Bar on the corner. Back at home that night, George had done something he hadn't done since college. He'd waited until Sara was asleep and then got up to pray. That Irene would soon be herself again, and that by extension Sara would be herself again and that he could be himself again. It had been a long time since he'd prayed, and it didn't feel right, but maybe his words were getting through, because here they were, all together as planned, in a car headed to the end of Long Island, to meet the ocean at the horizon.

Luther's house wouldn't be available for another hour, because a cleaning service was coming to get things ready for them after Sigrid's nephews' departure for Norway that morning. So George decided their first stop should be at The Blue Anchor, where they kicked things off with raw oysters and Bloody Marys made of freshly juiced heirloom tomatoes from the hothouse garden out back. They sidled up along a long bar facing the bay and the still-rising sun. There was hardly anyone else there.

"Isn't this fun?" George said, raising his oyster shell up until everyone did the same. "Cheers!"

Sara forced a smile as she slurped the slimy, briny creature from its shell. Something was clearly still bothering her. Jacob belched as he set his own shell down and said, "Delicious. Now, would anyone mind telling me what we're doing out here? In April?"

Sara half-choked. "Sorry. Horseradish." She was trying very hard not to look at Irene, who had *promised* that at some point that weekend she'd finally tell Jacob what had been going on. George wasn't holding his breath.

"Do we always need to have a reason?" Irene asked.

"Think of it like spring break," George chimed in.

"Sure," Jacob said. "All those times we went on spring break. Remember Cancún? When I did that body shot off of Mark McGrath? No? *Me neither.*"

George knew Jacob would just keep pushing until something snapped. The only hope was diverting him.

"Don't look but I think the oyster shucker is staring at you."

They all turned cautiously—except for Jacob, who half stood and craned his neck just to get a look. There indeed the burly, bearded man was looking back at them, not that there were many others to look at. Giant tattooed tentacles wound around his muscled arms, curling out from the white straps of his apron and disappearing down into his gauzy white gloves, which never stopped moving, automatically maneuvering a knife blade between the closed shells.

Jacob grunted dismissively. "You'd think by now you'd know my type."

"He's breathing," George pointed out helpfully.

"He's *adorable,*" Irene corrected. "And he's staring right at you."

She swiveled on her stool, and the morning light glanced off her cheekbones such that George could just make out the reddish lump under her eye. Was he just imagining it, or was Jacob looking at it too? Sara definitely was.

"I'll go talk to him," George offered. He'd had plenty of practice being Jacob's wingman when Jacob didn't want him to be.

Over Irene's cheers and Jacob's protesting, George slid back from his seat and marched confidently across the room. He had successfully solved the problem of the foul mood; now he hoped to begin phase two, beginning a memorable story that they could tell each other over and over again that weekend and always. They had just begun their second round of Bloody Marys, and he was feeling very good after the long drive. A second drink always suffused his worries in the pleasant buzz of uvula and the sting of nostrils. Painted a little haze on everything. Amplified the timbre of Irene's delight as George smiled at the oyster shucker as they began to chat.

"Sorry, but where are these oysters from? They're excellent."

"We farm them just out there by the Shelter Island ferry. Can't get 'em fresher."

He held one up to show George. It was about the size of his open palm, dark and stony and still alive when the man slipped his knife into the thin slit and gave it a firm twist, cracking the shells apart before cleaning grit off the meat and placing it still in the pearly shell on a silver platter covered in crushed ice.

George pointed back at Jacob. "My friend was just wondering . . . we passed all these vineyards on the way over. But we don't want to just drink the tourist stuff, you know? What do *you* drink around here?"

He watched as he momentarily looked up at Jacob, his knife slipping for the first time, just catching the glove. A small red splotch appeared on the glove, amid the dried, darker blotches of past slip-ups. He dipped the blade down again into the shell and in one swift motion flipped it straight up into the air. Like lightning, his other hand came around and caught the oyster in an empty glass. He repeated this trick and then poured a shot of vodka over each. Then he scooped a little cocktail sauce onto each and squeezed a lemon over them.

"For me?" George asked.

"You asked what I drink around here. Plus your friend looks like the jealous type."

George winked and tapped the side of his glass against the shucker's. He wasn't wrong: no sooner had they each swallowed their oyster shots than George heard Jacob calling from the other side of the room, "When you and your new best friend are done over there, could you get us another round?"

The man looked over at Jacob as he began to crack open a fresh oyster. "Tell your friend to open his mouth."

"*That* is never a problem," George replied, and called over. "Hey, Jacob, open wide!"

Jacob turned on the stool and opened his mouth.

Without breaking eye contact, the man loosened the gray bivalve and positioned his knife underneath. Then in a fluid motion he flipped the oyster again, this time in a long arc, fifteen feet across the floor of the restaurant. Jacob had to lean back just slightly, enough to make Irene shriek in fear he'd fall, before, in one spectacular moment, he caught the projectile in his mouth and swallowed it whole. The girls cheered as Jacob stood up and walked over, grinning.

"You've got my attention," he said.

Jacob took his sweet time getting the phone number of the oyster shucker, and Irene took a detour down to the docks, claiming she needed to collect some loose shells and gull feathers that he imagined might find their way into a painting sometime in the near future. George soon saw her walking around with phone out, frowning and trying to catch a signal. But he didn't care, so long as everyone was happy.

Sara pulled him aside as they approached the car. "Did you see Irene take her Neulasta this morning?"

George hadn't, but he said, "I'm sure she did. She's fine."

"I should have reminded her before we left."

"I'm sure she remembered."

"I just have a bad feeling. We don't even know where the nearest hospital is."

"Nothing is going to happen. Dr. Zarrani even said a trip would be good for her."

"She also said Irene should have had the tumor removed."

"No, she said she thought it would be *better* to be thorough, but it probably wasn't necessary, and considering that it would possibly permanently ruin her vision in that eye, it'd be better not to do anything until we know if the chemo is working."

"I know. I'm just worried."

"It's going to be fine. The scans are going to come back clean."

"Don't *say* that!"

"What? You think I'm going to jinx it? That bump under her eye is basically *gone*."

"But you told me she said that doesn't mean anything! I wish you'd take this seriously."

George sighed. "I am."

He tried to put his hand on her shoulder to pull her close, but she remained firmly planted just a bit too far away from him, her eyes narrowed.

"How much did you have to drink in there?"

"I thought we were supposed to be celebrating, for God's sake."

She crossed her arms—a bad sign. "All you've had to eat today are oysters, and you had the two Bloody Marys plus a shot at the bar. Maybe you want to let someone else drive?"

"I'm fine," he said, trying to sound nonchalant. "Don't worry so much, okay?"

"I'm just saying Jacob's a lot heavier than you are. It doesn't affect him as quickly."

"He has the tolerance of a nun. He hardly ever drinks unless we're all out together."

He realized too late that he wasn't helping his case exactly by reminding Sara that, in contrast, he had at least two drinks every night, whether they were out together or home alone. He was about to take it back, to try and explain what he'd meant, when he heard Jacob and Irene coming back over the gravel.

"Who does she keep texting?" George asked. "We're all here."

"Don't ask," Sara said.

"What's the problem?" Jacob called out.

"No problem," George said loudly, unlocking the car. "Let's go."

They only had to go around the corner to find the ferry that went to Shelter Island. George drove the car up onto the prow of a beautiful, barnacled service boat that went back and forth across the gray water all day long, buoying Benzes and Lexuses to the otherwise unreachable shore. As they moved out across the water, George stared at the spot their oysters had come from and wished that they weren't now churning around quite so unpleasantly in his stomach. Fortunately the ride was soon over, and they only had to go a half mile up the hill to reach Luther's beach house at last.

From the end of the driveway, they could only see how enormous it was. Three stories, shingled in impressive gray wood, with white trim. It had two garages and a kidney-shaped pool on one side. It was only when they got closer that they realized the pool was covered in thick green algae. The yard was scorched dead in patches and overgrown in others, littered from one end to the other with crumpled silver and blue Michelob Ultra cans and the jagged remains of two twenty-four packs of Dos Equis bottles. The cardboard boxes these had come in, presumably, were also in the yard, as were about a hundred red Solo cups, some used BIC razors, half-empty Herbal Essences shampoo and conditioner bottles, several cans of spilled paint thinner, and a wheelbarrow filled with what appeared to be the past century's collection of withered *Redbook* magazines. A grimy hammock hung limply from a bolt in a leafless tree; the pole that had once supported its other end was, for some reason, sunning up on the garage roof.

"Was there a hurricane or something we didn't hear about?" Irene asked.

Jacob whistled. "What, was Abu Ghraib all booked?"

Sara had both hands on her cheeks, jaw open. "The nephews," was all she could say. "The nephews. The nephews."

George trudged carefully up the walk, leading the way through the shattered glass and scattered cigarette butts to the door, which was slightly open. It was too much to hope that the inside would be unmolested, as it turned out. Everywhere he looked were more empties, more dead houseplants whose pots had been repurposed as ashtrays, more greasy pizza boxes, more melted plastic forks and spoons. Every single inch of the kitchen counter was taken up by liquor bottles. Fat ones, tall ones, green ones, brown ones. Handles of vodka with plastic screw tops. Liters of soda bottles used for mixers. Buckets of dirty water, perhaps once ice. A folding card table lay in three pieces on the floor, streaked with crusted white powder. Chairs were overturned, lightbulbs were broken in their sockets, molding Chinese food containers stood open. Either the cleaning people had never come, or they had arrived and done an abrupt about-face.

"It's like Hunter S. Thompson, the Marquis de Sade, and Amy Winehouse hung out in here for a month!" Jacob seemed to be nearly in awe.

Irene reached down into a pile of sheets and pulled out a silver-sequined bra, each cup of which she could have sat inside of.

"Oh. My," she said. "Looks like the nephews made some friends in town."

Jacob trudged over to look at it more closely, crunching down on the brim of a straw hat as he did. "Hope there's not a thong in there too."

Sara was supremely annoyed. "Luther's going to think *we* did this! What the hell? We're going to have to clean all this shit up."

Jacob kicked an open can of Spaghetti O's across the room. "How about we just set the place on fire and tell him it got hit by lightning?"

Sara looked around again. "Why does *every*thing always have to be a disaster?"

A disaster. Jacob was soon telling them how this word came from the old Greek: *dis*, meaning "bad," and *aster*, meaning "star." Bad star. From back in the good old days when such misfortune could be attributed to the continual and predictable realignments of the cosmos. It was soon agreed that they'd go wine tasting first and deal with the mess when they got back. Swiftly they were back on the ferry. Sara was trying not to seem furious behind a pair of round retro sunglasses. Jacob hung out the window like a loyal hound dog, his ears all but flopping around. Irene kicked at the back of his seat as she sifted through the bag of shells she'd gathered. George hunted for a radio station everyone liked, which was impossible because Jacob hated everything, so finally they settled on a country station that nobody liked, just to punish him.

The outing at least got off to a decent start. At Raphael Vineyards they did the tasting and then split a bottle of First Label Merlot on the back porch, while Jacob talked to the server about skydiving and ended up with another phone number. After that it was Bedell Cellars, where Sara thought to mention that she and George were looking for a wedding venue, which got them a twenty-dollar discount on a bottle of blanc de blancs. They soldiered on to Shinn Estates, then made one last stab at a nice time at Paumanok, but by then it was midafternoon and they were all exhausted, having forgotten everything they'd tasted except that there had been an awful lot of it. George had felt himself slipping deeper into a fuzzy warmth with each visit, a sense of all being right with the world, with the exception of Jacob, who kept reeling him back into dissatisfaction. At some point they all agreed that lunch was in order, and so they got some cheese and bread and cured meats and set out to have a picnic in the green expanse overlooking the vineyard.

Sara had picked out the cheeses for each of them from a glass-enclosed aging cabinet. As she handed them to George, she explained her thinking. "You get a triple crème brie. For me, an Alpine . . . nutty, but firm." For Jacob she went with the cheese with the most pretentious description: a Romano the color of earwax and with a "dry, granite texture" with a "saltiness hiding its butterscotch undertones." Finally, for Irene, an Auvergne Blue—punchy and velvety, streaked with dazzlingly beautiful molds.

George almost regretted that in a few minutes they would all be devoured, except that nothing was making Sara happier than seeing her companions lying on her mother's enormous old Scotch-patterned picnic blanket—he knew she'd packed it with just this tableau in mind. She took out a camera and began taking pictures of first the cheeses, and then of all of them on the blanket, and then the fields of grapevines beyond. It was perfect.

Except Jacob, naturally, was on about something. "Look at all this old machinery and shit they have on display out here. Like they need to make this place seem more *real*? Like . . . oh, well *now* we use giant machines to plow our fields and squeeze our grapes, and our bottles are made for ten cents apiece in a factory in Mexico, and our corks are made of plastic . . . but we're in touch with our heritage, gosh durn it!"

George looked over at Sara. She looked annoyed again. He felt a heat rising up all around his temples, the warm suffusion of his wine-buzz beginning to feel like real drunkenness, and he shot Jacob a cease-and-desist look. George reached for Sara, wanting suddenly to kiss her deeply and blot out their friend's forever blathering, but she eased him off before he could do more than peck her quickly on the lips.

"Here it is! Shellacked, of course, to preserve that rusty veneer forever and ever! In a hundred years I wonder what people will stand around staring at, thinking it's so quaint and authentic? Oh, look at that cute little cellular phone! Look at that funny hybrid car! Just imagine how hardworking and pure-hearted people must have been back then!"

"Christ. Do you have to be such a snob?" George shouted. This came out a bit meaner than George had intended.

Jacob returned the sentiment. "Do you have to be such a wet blanket?"

George was about to reply when Sara tried to grab his hand. "Come take a walk."

"He thinks because he got one poetry prize, he knows better than other people."

"I *do* know better than other people," Jacob snapped. "Most people can't do math in their heads, much less write a poem."

Ordinarily George would have backed down. He knew there was no getting Jacob to apologize. It was just his nature. But George's head hurt and he knew there was nothing left between him and the inevitable evening spent cleaning someone else's house.

"You know you don't get a medal on your deathbed for having been right most often. You just lie there alone because everyone you ever loved hates your superior guts."

His friend held up his hands to call for peace. George couldn't remember a time Jacob had ever backed down before. Irene stood up and pulled her phone back out of her pocket again, walking around with it stretched out toward some phantom signal. George was finally about to ask Irene who she was texting when Sara, finished with her cheese, took George's keys from his jacket and walked over to the driver's side door without a word. She leaned twice, sharply, on the horn to announce that they were moving on.

The final stop was Lenz Winery, and it seemed pleasant enough from the front—wide swaths of brown vines being forced to grow straight up, and a building with huge oak doors that hung invitingly open. Inside were a half dozen other visitors, milling about the long bar in the back and wandering off occasionally to sample chutneys, mustards, and vinegars that were displayed along the walls. George bought five tastings for the group, and soon a white-bearded man was easing a bottle over each and pouring out a perfect mouthful of something the color of sunlight. He and Irene both took sips and swished them around in their mouths.

"We're supposed to taste ginger and apricots," Sara read.

"That's ridiculous," Jacob said, downing his tasting in one gulp.

"It says it right here," Irene said, pointing to the card in Sara's hand.

"They just make that stuff up to make it sound fancier," Jacob snorted. "Wine is wine."

"Well, it doesn't taste like any Chardonnay I've ever had before,"

Sara said, leaning over the counter to catch the man's attention. "I want to ask him how they do that."

"Oh, like he's going to tell you the truth," Jacob scoffed, before wandering off to admire some salami hanging in a nearby display.

"This one's wonderful," Irene said, reading the card, " 'Tastes like bluegrass with notes of honeysuckle and hominy'? Well. I don't know about that, but I like it."

George took a sip and was inclined to agree. He was about to suggest they buy a bottle of it when he noticed Sara nudging the silver spittoon toward him.

"This is so good!" Irene sighed.

"Let's get a bottle of it," George said, taking another sip and pointedly swallowing.

"It's only the second thing we've tried here!" Sara replied. "Let's have the others and then see which we like the most."

"But Irene likes this one," George said.

"Yeah, I like this one," Irene agreed.

"But you might like the next one even more."

Just then Sara finally got the attention of the man behind the counter. "Why does this taste so different? I usually don't like Chardonnay."

"Well, you're used to California Chardonnay," the man behind the counter answered with a smirk. "It's much cooler over here, so I can harvest the fruit over the period of a couple of weeks. There's time for different flavors to develop, and we can mix them together to create a much more complex wine. California is much hotter, so they don't have time to let the fruit mature in stages. It's all simpler, more one-note over there, whereas here the wine's got real complexity and sophistication."

"Like a true New Yorker!" George quipped as Jacob wandered back over.

The man behind the counter stooped below a low crossbeam as he fetched up a bottle for George. "You're joking, I get it, but there's truth to it. The people are part of the wine. The wine is part of the people."

"It's the circle of life . . ." Jacob began to sing, before Irene stepped on his toe.

The man continued. "We call it the *terroir*."

"That sounds fancy," Sara said.

"It's how we speak about the soil it's grown in. The weather. Out here we're surrounded on three sides by water, so that affects the vines. We get less sunshine than California, but we also get a greater variety of climates throughout the year. And we're part of the terroir too, if you get my drift. Let's say one year I'm standing there in the dirt in New Zealand, and the mud that's still on my shoes from the Rhineland the year before becomes part of the next year's harvest. We had this big brass band out here last summer during one of the weddings, and, well, those vibrations carried through the air and got into the soil and the vines. That music is in the grapes now. Everything is connected, and everything has a lasting impact, no matter how briefly it's here."

George felt Sara's hand gripping his tightly as the man finished his speech. Even Jacob was silent as they toasted again. He stayed silent right up until the end, when he approached the man and asked for four bottles of the Chardonnay made from "bluegrass, hogwash, and fairy wings."

The sun was heading down, and there was no more avoiding it. For the third time that day, they boarded the Shelter Island ferry and crossed the water. Nobody spoke as they got out of the car and faced the mess, which seemed even more humongous in the waning light.

Sara found some buckets and brooms in a hall closet and sent George and Jacob down to the basement to see if they could locate some trash bags. They climbed down the old stairs together, saying nothing, moving through the dark with George's cell phone screen up as they hunted along the cinderblock walls for a light switch.

"There's a pull-chain thingy here I think," Jacob said from somewhere behind him.

George moved closer with the white rectangle of light in his hand. "Sorry," he said, "about before. I guess I had a little more than I realized."

Jacob grunted in what George guessed was an acknowledgment, if not an acceptance, of his apology. George could admit he had crossed the line, but there was no reason anyone had to be worried about him. He always suspected it was because none of the others had ever seen a real drunk before. George had known plenty. Bad alcoholics, back home in Ohio, at the bar his grandfather had owned and where he'd spent a few hours every day after school. Those shapeless men. Hard, but helpless, leaning low down on their stools. Nothing like him.

"It's no big deal," he said. "It's not like I have to be drunk all the time. It just makes me happier when I'm already happy, you know?"

This statement hung there in the dark basement for a moment. With a defiant click, the chain in Jacob's hand snapped down and the basement lights came on. They found themselves standing in front of a network of shelves, where the tiny colored noses of bottle after bottle peeked out from the shadows of perfectly fitted boxes. There had to be hundreds. It was hard to see how far back it went. A fur of dust lay over everything. Jacob's cries of glee bounced off the high, curving stone ceiling as he pulled bottles out two at a time.

"1991 Cabernet Franc. 1961 Grand Cru. 1984 Bordeaux . . . 1944 Cuvée . . . Holy shit, this bottle's older than my father."

George breathed in deeply as he ran a gentle hand over the smooth curve of the glass. He imagined all that had gone into the air and the soil and the vines. 1944. In the middle of a world war, some farmer had harvested his grapes and split his oak trees and dried and charred the wood and forced the slats together with bands of metal. Outside there had been horror and fear, but in this bottle he'd hidden something made from holy sweat. Someone had corked it and set the bottle down with a prayer, knowing he'd never drink it. It was for sons and grandsons. It was waiting for some future, for someone. George wished that it had been waiting for him. Reluctantly he slid the bottle back into its place.

When he looked back again, Jacob was bearing down on him. "All right. Enough. Are you going to tell me what the hell is wrong with Irene or not?"

George froze. "What do you mean?"

"She's been texting that psycho ex of hers, Alisanne. I looked at her phone."

"She is?"

"Yeah, all this shit about how they need to talk and there isn't time to waste."

"Damn it," George cursed.

"She's not writing back, thank God, but clearly something's going on. The last couple of months you three have all been on another planet. So what is it? Did William do something to her?"

"No, no," George said. "I can't—I'm not supposed to say anything."

"Enough drama—. This is too much. Even for her. It's not like she's *dying*."

George felt as if his heart had stopped, and he must have looked like it had. Jacob glared at him for another minute, then suddenly his face went slack. Without another word he turned and marched up the stairs.

George followed after him and came up just as Jacob reached the top of the stairs and pointed at the girls, who were scraping dried eggs off the stovetop.

"—the fuck didn't you tell me?" Jacob shouted.

For a moment everything was frozen. Then Irene threw her sponge down and walked out through the sliding-glass door that led onto the porch and began running at top speed into the spiky, sandy-colored grass that stretched between them and the foggy bay.

Jacob went after Irene—stubby legs tripping and stumbling with every step over the uneven terrain.

George was about to follow when Sara grabbed his wrist. "Let's give them a minute."

"I swear I didn't say anything," George said lamely.

"It doesn't matter." Sara looked relieved, and suddenly George realized that he had—*eureka!*—solved the problem. The truth was finally out, and Irene could blame it on him. But it would be forgiven, as it always was.

They cleaned in silence for a few more minutes. Then they walked along the path where they found Jacob embracing Irene in a low trench of dune grass that stretched long and empty in either direction. The surf pounded against ancient black rocks and loosed a white spray that danced in the air for just a moment before falling into the sea again.

"It's just not fair," he heard Jacob saying as they got closer.

"There's no such thing as fair," Irene said softly.

"Why didn't you tell me?" he asked.

"I didn't want you getting all moody about it."

"I don't get *moody.*"

George watched the waves pounding the shore, each surge of salty water carving another molecule off the stones. In a hundred years the shoreline would be ever so slightly nearer. A hundred years ago, it had been ever so slightly farther out. A hundred years before that, it had been farther still. Hundreds of years from now it would carve in so far that it collapsed the house. Two hundred and fifty million years before, the continents had been fused. Maybe in another two hundred and fifty million years they'd all smash back together again.

George and Sara sat down next to their friends. Irene smiled at him and he took a deep breath. Sometimes it paid to take the blame. Now there would be peace at last, and they could get on with their fun weekend. They'd clean for a few hours until the house looked better than new. He'd make jokes about hazmat suits, and they'd find more plus-size underwear, and Irene would begin sifting through the junk looking for sculpture pieces that complemented her seashells, and Jacob would call up Billy Budd from the oyster place and they'd talk, long into the night, just like they used to.

"If I don't make it—" Irene said slowly.

Sara immediately cut her off. "Don't say that."

"Seriously, Irene. You seem *much* better—" George began, but stopped as she shook her head.

His stomach turned to lead as Irene slowly lifted the left sleeve of her shirt to reveal another lump. It was the size of a golf ball.

He didn't know what to say, but Sara seemed to have it covered. "Has that been there since before we left? Irene, I swear to *fucking Christ—*"

George knew Sara was right. Irene had known it. Probably she'd even known it that day in Dr. Zarrani's office. She'd hidden it so she wouldn't spoil the trip. He wanted to run into the ocean and pound back at the waves until they were still. He looked into the wide gray sky. For what reason—what reason could possibly exist for this? What plan could it be part of? And if there *was* Something out there that had known about this, well then fuck Him and fuck His plan and fuck whatever it had all been written on.

"I'm just saying. If I don't make it," Irene repeated, "heaven had better look like this. It's absolutely mythic."

George wished he could believe in it, but just then he couldn't. Sara looked ashen.

"I wouldn't like it by myself. Just me here all alone," Irene went on. "But I guess you and George would be along soon enough."

She put her arm around Sara, and Sara fell into her, leaning on Irene's shoulder—on the good side. Irene kissed Sara's forehead and reached her hand out for George. "Jacob, I don't know. I guess we'd visit."

He laughed. "Jews don't believe in hell. Though we're not too sold on heaven either."

"Good thing you're a terrible Jew then." Irene smiled. They sat there for a while, quiet in each other's company.

George ran his fingers through the dune grass. Then, all at once, another solution came to him. "Fuck it," he said suddenly, "I'll be right back."

He turned and stumbled back through the sand toward the house. Inside he went through the messy kitchen, past a table filled with sticky, half-empty liquor bottles, to the basement door. Taking the rickety steps three at a time, he came to the bottom and soon located the dusty green bottle that Jacob had picked up earlier. He ran his fingertips over the year. 1944. The glass was cold against his palm as he went back upstairs and returned to his friends on the beach.

"What's that?" Sara asked immediately. "Is that Luther's?"

"Yes," George said. "Or Luther's father's. Or his father's father."

"So we're just stealing it?" Irene asked.

"No," George grinned. "The Norwegian nephews did."

Jacob laughed, deep and proud, and then took out a pocketknife and started prying the cork loose. It came out in several pieces. Sara didn't object as Jacob took a long drag from the bottle and sighed. "Now *that* is a terroir."

George raised the bottle to his wetted lips and tipped back. God. It was the most incredible thing he had ever tasted. The taste grew in his mouth, pulling on an alternation of taste buds. It made no sense, but he thought he could *hear* its taste. It tasted like a requiem he'd heard as a boy in the Basilica of the Sacred Heart. A priest his father had known at Notre Dame had died, and they'd driven five hours to South Bend for the service. God, it was still going. A few notes at first, gradually swelling in sequence to an offertory, and then Communion—every flavor at once, until it was almost too much. The retreat then was welcome, sweet. And then, just at the very end something new—an aftertaste bound to linger deep in his memory. Like sitting in the basilica, the sound of the requiem in his ears, and the sure feeling that his father's friend had been a good man, and was in a better place now. Up on the ceiling there were angels with outstretched wings, perfect golden circles haloing their heads. Some floating on clouds against the light, and others hovering, weightless, against the dark of night. It was the same dark of the sea beyond them, the same as the clouds that passed above.

They passed the bottle around until it was drained. After a long time they all walked back to the car again. Irene agreed to call Dr. Zarrani's emergency line on the way back. They'd set up an appointment to have the new tumor looked at as soon as possible. As for the house, they would leave it as it stood, minus one very expensive, very empty bottle of wine, which was now nestled under Jacob's armpit as he climbed into his seat.

Sara looked back one more time before they left. "We were never here," she announced.

George drove slowly up the darkening highway, back to the city. The girls whispered for a while, and Jacob stared out the window. Before long everyone else fell asleep and seemed so peaceful. George drove on. It occurred to him that everything he was experiencing now, they were missing. Sadness waited for them, just past the edge of their dreams. It would be patient for hours yet to come, just as his own sadness seemed to hover just beyond the magnificent afterglow of the wine. Great patterns of light streamed across the window like red and white comets. He was unworried, and he didn't know why. It was just so much easier for him to believe, when he felt this way, that there *was* some reason, and that there was another reason just alongside it why he didn't need to know what it was.

JACOB IN THE WASTE LAND

They returned to the city, and in three days Shelter Island seemed as distant to Jacob as Tierra del Fuego. He closed his eyes on the train up to Anchorage House in the morning and tried to summon a vision of that sandy shore reaching out toward the ocean, but all he could see was the alien lettering in the tunnels south of the Wakefield stop. He tried to remember the dark smell of the sea, but its scent had already been overwritten in his memory by the puke he'd had to wipe off the face of a nineteen-year-old psychotic named Thomas who believed himself to be a submarine. "HMS *Sybil*, lowering periscope!" the kid had shrieked. "Dive! Dive!" before losing his lunch all over the television set in the common room. "You forgot to shut your hatch," Jacob had reminded him, as they passed arm in arm down the hall to the nurse's station. He tried to recall the feel of sand beneath his feet and the taste of oysters. "It's dark down here," Thomas had whispered, until finally the HMS *Sybil* had gone quiet.

A dry heat welcomed them back. By the first week of May, it was approaching eighty-five degrees in late afternoon. Still, Jacob persisted in wearing his tweed jacket up to Anchorage House each day and back to Irene's at night. "It's very breathable," he told her when he arrived at her door, drenched in sweat. He passed several evenings helping her shuttle some of her older paintings into storage at the gallery and trying to clear space in the living room by sorting through the piles of odd crap that she'd amassed. "Keep that Baggie of tulip bulbs, but get rid of that Oktoberfest hat—no, keep the feather, actually. Do you think you could pry just the runners off that toy sled for me? I know there's a screwdriver here somewhere."

Jacob didn't mind. He wanted to help, and he was no good talking to doctors. He kept sending Irene into hysterics at inappropriate moments. Once an MRI had to be redone because he was making her giggle so much. Irene sweet-talked the technician into printing the blurred scan anyway, and she'd given it to Jacob as a thank-you.

His other main contribution was trying to get George to unclench, but whenever Jacob called him out for moping around, mute and worried, George acted utterly surprised that anyone would be worried about *him*. He stared at the *New Yorker* articles that Jacob thrust at him in the waiting room and then minutes later looked up in complete confusion. "Was this—what? I'm sorry, which article? Just a second, I have to go to the bathroom." Jacob had never seen anything like it—the man had to pee practically every half hour. He wanted the doctors to check George out for Nervous Dachshund Syndrome. (That was the one that got to Irene so badly that the MRI had to be done over.) George claimed all the fluorescent lighting was giving him headaches, but Jacob didn't buy it. The last two visits Sara had wound up asking him to simply take George to a bar somewhere so he'd stop agitating everyone.

The date for Irene's surgery arrived as abruptly as a summer thunderstorm. Sara had been through three hundred hoops to make sure they had permission to wait in the recovery room, when regulations permitted only family. Jacob appreciated the effort but politely declined. The thought of sitting around in a sterile room for ten hours on a Saturday, watching *¡Vámonos, Muchachos!* reruns on her laptop and waiting for an update was just about the worst thing he could imagine. Irene said she understood, and instead he took the day before off and stocked her apartment with half a Rite-Aid's worth of gauze, Chicken & Stars soup, Assure milkshakes, instant mashed potatoes, and a case of bottled ginger soda in case of nausea.

That night after dinner, Irene snuggled into his arm while Jacob read her his favorite poems with his Patrick Stewart impression, which always made her laugh. He watched as her eyelashes brushed the bump below. In a few hours the lump would be sitting in a stainless steel tray, and below Irene's eye would be a raw abscess. He read much of the night and took the train up to work in the morning, while Irene headed to the hospital to meet Sara, George, and the scalpel.

After a long shift, Jacob tried to take his mind off the situation by going out with Oliver for dinner at Szechuan Garden in Stamford. Oliver wouldn't pry into what was going on with Irene. He had that singular gift among therapists of getting patients chatting about the weather or the rising price of stamps. Then suddenly they would crack open like walnuts, exposing their deepest secrets. Jacob suspected this was why Oliver liked him, because while Jacob never kept his thoughts to himself, he persistently refused to be cracked.

Oliver was telling a story about growing up in East India. "When I was a boy, my father and I used to go on these long walks through the banyan forests, and we'd play games to see who could correctly identify the greatest number of trees."

Even though Oliver got away with telling most people he was in his early forties, he'd really be turning fifty in a year. He didn't look it, which was all Jacob cared about. A high forehead that was still topped with bristly black hair and eyebrows to match. Talking about his father always resulted in a goofy grin that made him look adorably younger still. His father, a native Algerian, had brought their family to Kolkata when Oliver was still young, to join the staff at a major hospital there. He had lived there for only a few years before being sent off to boarding school in England, but he spoke, often, about those golden days with unflagging sentimentality, which annoyed Jacob almost enough to discount all the grinning that came along with it.

He waited for a pause and then said, "*My* father used to pay me a dollar a day to massage his feet after work. He had terrible arches and was too stubborn to get the right sort of shoes. He'd get these hard corns the size of quarters. I don't know how he got them sitting at a desk selling supplemental life insurance all day. He'd make me scrub them off with a pumice stone."

He loved to watch the quick rise of Oliver's right eyebrow when he received surprising information like this. It was as if the information were being weighed on an old mechanical scale. "You must have been very close then, at that age," Oliver said.

"About as close as a king and his court jester. An inch from applause or beheading, any given day."

Oliver stroked his chin, "And why didn't the queen do the massaging?"

A bit too quickly, Jacob said, "The queen did *more* than enough."

"Had you always wanted to be a poet?" Oliver asked, changing tacks quickly and startling Jacob with his aim. This was how it worked—score a point and then veer away.

"Nope," he said.

Oliver now had only two options, the first being to press him "Well, what then?" but he'd go with the second, a long, tense silence. A *Stille Nacht* in the trench warfare of their conversation. Jacob would be damned if he'd cave, like a patient on his couch, and answer the question. Jacob had never told *anyone* what he'd wanted to be as a child. Oliver's intuition had led him to the right spot.

It wasn't a typical embarrassing juvenile wish, like wanting to be a fireman or a professional wrestler or a helicopter pilot. No, it was far weirder than that. Long ago he had sworn he wouldn't tell, and he never had. Not to his mother and not, in all his nights of drunkenness, to Sara or Irene. Not even George knew this particular secret, and he knew Jacob's ATM pin (3825, spelling FUCK on the keypad), the music video he'd first gotten off to (Aerosmith's "Love in an Elevator" on MTV late one night at his grandparents' place in Daytona Beach), and the name of every boy Jacob had ever slept with—or at least the ones whose names he'd known. Never being hung up about anything was a source of pride for Jacob, but this secret he'd sworn he'd never tell. He'd sworn it to God. And even though he didn't believe in God anymore, thinking about saying it still made him sweat.

Jacob switched from the tea to a *large* glass of red wine and though he was still picking at his own food, reached over to grab the menu wedged between the soy sauce bottles and began counting up the available items. Fifteen appetizers. Nineteen special items. Eight vegetable dishes, including "dynasty shyimp," which he didn't think was a vegetable, typo or no. Four chow meins, nine diet items, and twelve dim sum options. Five kinds of egg foo yong and six fried rices. Four lo meins, five mei funs, and four side order options. Seven items marked "our most popolur enteree," distinct on the menu from the "top ten best sellers !!" Twelve kinds of soup, and twenty-three special combination platters.

"There are one hundred and thirty-four different things you could eat here," Jacob announced to Oliver, who was finishing his beef and scallops combo, the number-two special.

"That seems like quite a lot," Oliver replied, as he dabbed brown sauce from his lips.

"It *is* a lot," Jacob said. "But it is still a *finite* number of things. And yet you eat here *every* night. And I'm not being hyperbolic. I mean, I'm not exaggerating—"

"Yes, Jacob. I went to Oxford, and I know what *hyperbolic* means. And I know—"

Jacob knew he knew. They'd had countless meals together at Szechuan Garden and had this same argument practically as many times.

"You eat here *every* night. You don't eat at any of the hundreds of other restaurants in Stamford. Nor do you ever go to eat in Manhattan, which is just a train ride away—"

"If you'd ever let me come over to your apartment . . ."

"—where there are literally thousands of restaurants. And Brooklyn and Queens, which are, as we speak, in the midst of a dawn-of-the-century culinary renaissance where Michelin-starred chefs are grilling foie gras in aluminum-sided diner cars! No. You choose to eat every meal in this one place."

"You're really very fixated sometimes," Oliver said in his best therapist's tone, pressing the tips of his fingers together in the same way as always, so that his hands became a little cage over his heart. "Consistency can be as much a virtue as variety. Besides, I like it here. These people feel like family. And the restaurant is only four doors down from my flat. But since you know that already, I have to conclude that this isn't what's really bothering you. Is it?"

"What do you think it's about then?" Jacob fired back. He was simply dying for Oliver to bring up Irene. To say something idiotic like "you know she'll be fine" or "she's lucky she's so young" or "I'm sure your companionship means so much to her."

But instead Oliver said, "I think maybe you're feeling some guilt about the lopsided shape the commitment in our relationship has taken."

What a passive-fucking-aggressive way of saying that, Jacob thought. Feeling competitive, he skipped the *passive* in his own response.

"You mean how you sit around in your flat listening to Beethoven and watching *Animal Planet* while I fuck other people?"

The words drew just a drop of psychic blood before Oliver regained his maddening calm.

"I'm a monogamous person," Oliver said calmly. "You know this about me."

It was true. Throughout his boarding school years, Oliver had pined away for the same allegedly straight classmate, except for Saturday mornings, when he'd come over to Oliver's to fool around.

Adopting this same confusion, Oliver had actually married a woman at age twenty, whom he hadn't cheated on once in the three years before they'd separated.

"Moreover I know that you are not, and you also know that this is perfectly fine with me. You're young—"

"I'm not *saying* that right now. Aren't you listening to me? That's not my point!"

"Then what *is* your point?"

Jacob thought he might rip his hair out by the roots. "My point is that you are a *mental health professional*!" he shouted, so loudly that it jolted a nearby couple from their cell phone screens. He imagined the fish in the tank rushing behind their fake, red rocks—

Oliver didn't raise his voice even a decibel. "And?"

"The owner here bought you a tie clip on your birthday this year!"

"It's your own choice to order the Dragon & Phoenix every single time."

"Actually I get the '*Dargon* & Phoenix' every time, thank you very much."

Oliver rubbed his eyebrows. "My point is that I never order the same thing twice."

"But you *do*! There are three hundred sixty-five days in a year and one hundred forty-six menu items, which means that you *must* eat the same thing at least two and a half times every year."

"And you never eat the same thing two and half times in a year? You've probably had 'Dargon & Phoenix' at least twenty or thirty times with me here by now."

"Yes, but I have also eaten a Guaco-Taco from San Lupe and spanakopita from the Olympic Flame Diner and chicken à la king from Bistro 19! This week alone I've had *three* kinds of frozen yogurt!"

Oliver grinned the way he always did when he was sure he was about to win. "But that's what you *always* get at those places."

"Meaning?" But Jacob could already feel the point sliding away from him.

"Meaning why is it wrong that I order different things from the same restaurant every night, and *right* that you order the same things from different ones?"

Jacob opened his mouth, but no fire came forth. Why *should* it be wrong? Wasn't it more wrong that they had such a glut of dining options that they could eat somewhere different every night of the year, without repeating? That morning on the train Jacob had read an article in the *New Yorker* about a mountainous area of China roughly the size of France; its slopes were dust, and its citizens were malnourished if they weren't starving. What sort of God created all men equal but then said *fuck it* when it came to the corners of the earth? What did the old lady mopping the floor in the back think about him leaving a third of his "Dargon & Phoenix" on his plate?

The look she was giving him was the same sort that the crones in the cafeteria of Moses Maimonides Elementary had once cast his way when he'd eaten only the Hydrox and ignored the rest of his lunch. And how had the rabbis explained it? *Because we are the chosen ones, beloved of God*, had been the line until about third grade, at which point they began to add *Because we were slaves for centuries, and then we wandered in the desert for forty years, and then we lived in unfriendly lands for more centuries. Always strangers, always scapegoats. Killed in Crusades and Holocausts that everyone else has forgotten.* For their ancestors being forever fucked over, then, the logic seemed to go, it was okay for the Blaumann family to be better off now. There was often the suggestion that probably it would be only a short while before someone figured out how to take it all away again.

This interpretation had reigned until he'd been bar mitzvahed and begun taking practical accounting and economics, at which point the reasoning became nonsecular: *Because you are a participant in a prosperous free economy, in which the work your parents do is valued at a certain amount by the invisible hand of the market, and soon you will take your place in this grand system yourself, and through savings, investments, and avoiding the temptations of credit, you too will deserve privileges and comforts that others do not.*

"*Hazan et hakol*," Jacob muttered.

"A rabbi?" Oliver asked. "Is that what you wanted to be when you were a child?"

Jacob shook his head. He half wanted to tell him—it was just nonsense and stupid superstition. So he'd sworn. So what? Was he going to be struck down there in Szechuan Garden? He opened his mouth to just *say it* after all this time, but the instant he did, he felt the phone in his pocket buzzing. He took it out and saw Irene's picture on the screen.

"Hello?" he said, almost before he'd actually answered it.

"It's Sara" came the voice on the other end, the sound of an ambulance backing up somewhere in the distance. "Irene's fine. I took her phone because I get no reception in here."

"Did she go under all right?" Jacob asked softly.

"We should know something in a couple of hours," Sara said, and Jacob could tell she was at the end of her rope. "But George is losing it over here. He needs to go for a walk, and I have to finish these articles by Friday."

"You want me to take him to the park or something? Let him play in the dog run?"

Jacob smiled, just long enough that Oliver smiled.

Sara, however, sighed short and sharp. "I don't care *what* you do with him, but if he stays here another minute, I'm asking the nurses to sedate him."

"Tell him to meet me at the Bistro in an hour," Jacob said, as Oliver called for the check.

They walked back to the flat. Kissed and made up. Oliver insisted he take an umbrella and called him a cab down to the train station.

From the Hell Gate Bridge, Jacob saw his city, lit up and unreal, as ever. The tip of the Empire State Building was the electric blue of a urinal cake. It was half obscured by the fat clouds above, smoke thick, soot black, but reflecting everything beneath it. Broadway's streetlights, the Times Square spotlights, the postgraduate apartment $4.99 IKEA track lights, the cigarette embers leaning out the windows of the Frederick Douglass Houses. A trail of white headlights flowing over the Triborough Bridge into town, and the ghostly trail of red brakelights limping back out through the jam.

At Grand Central, Jacob clutched Oliver's umbrella in front of him like a shield, pushing past the crowds on the stairs and in the station and then on the sidewalks, under a white wash of streetlights, past the pale hordes in Bryant Park and Rockefeller Center. He tried to visualize what must be happening to Irene. He held it in his head like a poem, words and images and process. Awesome, in the old-fashioned sense of the word: inspiring of awe, to the point of humbling. The things they knew now, the things they could do.

Less than fifty blocks away, in a sterile room, Irene was dressed in a loose white gown, laid out like a drowsy queen, the doctors circling around her like humble servants. According to what Sara had relayed to him from Dr. Zarrani, a tube would deliver pure oxygen through a mask, attached by an elastic strap. Clips would be attached to her fingertips and beige cups suctioned to her breastbone to measure the rate of her heart beating, the pressure of her blood. Lower down, a squid of electrode wires would creep across her thorax and out to her wrists, taking pulses back to the electrocardiogram—the EKG—while a pulse oximeter and a capnograph measured the oxygen and carbon dioxide in her blood. The first tumor would be removed via a periorbital excision, during which an invasion of her eyeball itself could—ideally—be ruled out. If not, they'd have to remove the eye itself, but the doctors had said there was essentially zero chance of this happening. Then, while a plastic surgeon began an ophthalmic reconstruction, the surgeons would move to the left arm, where the second tumor could be removed—along with a significant portion of the ulna to ensure that the cancer was fully contained. The extracted bone would be replaced by a graft from the iliac crest, this being the superior border of the "wing of ilium" (Jacob liked the delicate, angelic sound of that) along the superolateral margin of the pelvis.

The truly good news here, according to Sara—who had taken on the role of interpreter between Irene's doctors and the rest of them—was that the preliminary lymph node biopsy had come back clean, and the doctors believed there was a far superior chance that the postsurgical radiation and the second round of chemotherapy would have a lasting effect on the cancer, now that they were in the—again, less-than-ideal—situation of metastasis. Irene had progressed from stage one to stage two, which meant that the initial lump had sent off phalanxes in search of new territories. It had come down the mountainsides and into the valley of her elbow. But it hadn't yet gotten to the ports. The lymph nodes, which traversed her whole body, were still unconquered. If only he could write it, somehow. If only they were words on paper, not facts in Irene's body.

At Bistro 19, Jacob found George right where he expected, on the burnished brass stool at the far right, leaning heavily against the gray marble bar top. His top two buttons were undone, and his powder-blue sleeves rolled to the elbows. His dusty brown hair showed traces of fingered agitation, though now his hands were clasped as if in prayer around his whiskey glass. Jacob thought he looked like an off-duty priest having a word with his heavenly employer. Or he was only staring up at the grape-stained light coming through the old Tiffany chandelier, which hung elegantly above the bar with its leaded-glass vines and little winged cupids.

George loved the ugly thing. To him, they conjured up the old New York—European money, Cole Porter, high style. "I'm gonna have one of these in my study someday," he'd say in awe, when the third or fourth whiskey had hit him. In the back of his mind, Jacob planned to buy George a lamp like it someday, whenever their ships came in.

Jacob decided to keep his jacket on but stowed the oversize umbrella in the stand near the door. George hadn't even noticed him entering, he was so absorbed by the lamp. "Bless me, Father Murphy," Jacob sighed as he flung his weight onto the stool, "for I have sinned."

George looked down at his watch. "All right, but let's save some time, and you just tell me the ones you *haven't* committed."

"I'm fine on graven images," Jacob said after a second's thought. "Never killed anybody. And I suppose I don't exactly covet my neighbor's *wife*."

George clicked his tongue. "Nuh uh-uh! 'Nor his manservant, nor his maidservant, nor his ox, nor his ass . . .' "

"Oh well, if you want to get into the fine print."

"I just know how you can be around oxen, that's all."

George downed his whiskey and motioned for another from Flo, the no-nonsense French grandmother who worked behind the bar, whose hair had been dyed to a fire it had never known in youth. She topped off George's glass with J&B and then began making Jacob his usual—a gin martini with two onions.

"I can sing all the books of the Old Testament to the tune of 'Ten Little Indians.' "

"Please don't," Jacob said, as George began to lift an imaginary microphone to his mouth. "I've had enough flashbacks to Hebrew school for one night already, thanks."

"Awww. Did Dr. Oliver try to get you on the couch again?" George joked. "Metaphorically, I mean. Not literally. I mean, literally's fine too, but—oh! Hey, guess who's here? Look over in the corner there."

Jacob turned casually in his chair and looked into the dark, rear corner of the restaurant, where he recognized the narrow profile of William Cho. He was wearing a well-tailored gray suit with a dark wool tie. He had clearly just had his hair cut, perhaps at the request of the girl seated across from him, sharing his order of the mahi-mahi. She was maybe a few years younger, also Korean, with liquid black hair that spilled over her bare shoulders. Her great dark eyes were fixed lovingly on William. His were looking back.

"It's William, right?" George was saying.

Jacob saw William swivel slightly in his chair, noticing them at the bar and stiffening, twisting around to keep his back to them and his face toward his date.

George looked annoyed. "It's pretty ballsy of him to bring a date here. He knows this is one of Irene's—I mean, he knows this is our place."

Jacob hummed in agreement. It *was* ballsy of William. Uncharacteristically ballsy. He watched William, who was clearly pretending to listen attentively to his date while not so slyly looking at the two of them in the reflection of the mirror on the far wall.

George did a few quick twists on his stool and nearly slid off. "So. You were saying. About Oliver? He's been picking your brain again, has he?"

"What did you want to be when you were a child?" Jacob sighed, but George thought he was asking, not answering.

"The winner of the Nathan's hot-dog-eating competition. What did you want to be?"

"A carpenter," Jacob lied.

"What, like you wanted to build houses?"

"No," Jacob said, "I mean I wanted to be Karen Carpenter."

George made an inaudible crack about bell-bottoms.

Jacob shook his head. "I really need to break this thing off with Oliver."

"Never a good idea to date the guy who signs your paychecks, I've always said."

"You're marrying a woman who shares your bank account," Jacob reminded him, as Flo finally came back and pushed his martini toward him. He pulled the tiny cocktail sword from the onions and let them settle into the conical bottom of the glass.

"A man's got to have his secrets," Jacob continued. "How are you going to pay off all your mistresses if you don't have any money of your own?"

George hummed for a moment, as if considering the possibility. "I can't think of anything more terrifying than having a mistress," he said finally. "I can barely keep track of Sara. You ever watch that show about that Mormon guy with all the wives? He's got three wives, and he spends the whole time trying to keep them from killing each other. No thanks."

"You don't *marry* all of them! That's the whole—have I taught you nothing?"

"You taught me how to make chili once."

Jacob sipped at his drink as he launched into a long tirade about the antiquated concept of marriage, how it had originated as a way of transferring property, a means of arranging for the exchange of goats and camels. How in the twenty-first century women especially ought to be fighting this old-fashioned way of thinking, this imperialism of the heart and the sex organs.

He was hardly feeling drunk at all yet. He wished he hadn't had coffee on the train. But how else was a man supposed to stay awake long enough to get properly obliterated?

Then George went on about Sara, and the wedding planning, and God knew what else, Jacob stared down into his martini glass. The two little onions stared back up at him. He was exhausted, and his stomach was a great un-Pacific ocean of alcohol and caffeine. His bones ached in a way that he could feel them, independent of his flesh, and it made him feel like a skeleton in a Jacob suit. God. He didn't want to be pain-in-the-ass Jacob. Not tonight. He wanted to be fun-and-funny Jacob. Court-jester Jacob! Did other people get as tired of being themselves as he did? How could they manage it, when most of them seemed so goddamn dull?

What were William and his date talking about? *What did anyone actually talk about?* The dry weather? His boring job? Her ambitions to someday work in fashion?

George leaned back a bit too far on his stool and nearly fell. "Be right back. Going to hit the loo. Keep an eye on our friend over there. I want to be able to give Irene a full report on Mr. Cho's hot date when she gets up."

Jacob sighed and took advantage of George's absence to check his phone for messages from Sara. But there was nothing. He saw that William and his date were pretending to squabble over who paid the check. *Oh my goodness, who will win?* Jacob wondered, rolling his eyes as she acquiesced and permitted him to pay. *And what did you want to be when you were a child, William?* A spineless, self-important, soulless jerk? A hypocrite who studied literature before going into finance? Someone who beds the finest woman in all of Manhattan and then ditches her the second she needs help? Jacob had half a mind to stalk over there and lay him out, right onto the plate full of obsessively picked-over fish bones. But he remained seated, tracing something out on the surface of the marble bar, writing the ancient characters in the sweat from his drink: מיוחד לא אני. Once Jacob had been forced to write it five hundred times in a notebook.

What did you want to be when you were a child?

It was the day he knew he could never become this thing.

The two ladies began to count out their bills and fish through their change purses for the *exact* right amounts. Jacob's father had done the same after every meal, as if a penny wasted here or there might be the difference between starvation and survival. Never tipping—not even when they'd gone to the Gramercy Tavern and Jacob had dipped his jacket sleeve in mustard, and the waiter had scrubbed it out with club soda for them—even then his father had left the exact bill, down to the rotten penny, and left without a word. Sometimes Jacob's mother would still pretend to forget an umbrella or pen, then rush back to find it and slip a few dollars onto the table—a few dollars of the pitiful allowance that Jacob's father gave her each week to cover the costs of groceries and housekeeping . . . not because he couldn't afford more—a lot more—but because he didn't trust her with it.

"Get you anything else?" Flo was asking.

"Just the check," Jacob said. He didn't feel drunk at all, but it seemed like George had had enough. He looked over and saw that William and his date had left. The bill came, and he almost sent it back. How could there be only three drinks on it? From George's slump and dreamy eyes, Jacob would have sworn that he'd tossed back three on his own before he'd even arrived. When everything was settled, Jacob got up off the stool and went back to the men's room to see what had become of his fine feathered friend. The little door marked *Hommes* was locked, however, from the inside.

"You fall in?" Jacob called.

"No, no," George called back. "Sorry. Just a minute. Texting Sara something."

Jacob thought he sounded drunker than when he'd left.

"That's disgusting, George. That's how people get parasites."

He could hear George shuffling around clumsily. Jacob sighed. "We're all settled up. I'm going outside for some air."

Jacob stepped out onto the sidewalk. It was a few moments before he realized that he had left Oliver's umbrella inside, and so against all his principles, he texted George to please grab it out of the bin before he came out. Great winds rushed down the valley between the dark buildings. It was surprisingly quiet, there on the cross street. In fact, Jacob couldn't see another person all the way down the block in either direction. How often did that happen in Manhattan, he wondered, even at this hour?

Both lanes of Fiftieth Street were being ripped up, so traffic was being diverted around the block. No construction crews were working so late, but the lanes were still closed off by fat barrels, striped in orange and reflective white. Somewhere several young women were screeching about something or another, but only an echo reached Jacob's ears. The wind blew westerly, carrying empty soda bottles and discarded Subway sandwich wrappers. A chewed-up looking scarf. A mashed-down cardboard box. Swarms of cigarette butts. He watched them scatter over the broken blacktop, heading out toward the avenue. Far off, by the old Lehman Brothers building, he watched two tall men in dark coats with briefcases exit a gleaming white revolving door. Glass, of course. They were all glass these days, the doors, the buildings too. Transparent but tinted. Delicate but impenetrable. Lessons learned, after 1929, were limited to making sure the windows no longer opened. No one liked to see their stockbroker sailing down past their thirtieth-story window. Jacob remembered the time Irene had taught him to press his hand against the building glass. It vibrated, alive. They built them to be slightly flexible, she'd explained, so they could lean this way and that, in high winds.

Then, at his back, Jacob felt a rush of cool air. He turned, expecting to see George at last, but instead it was William Cho.

"Were you still in there?" Jacob asked.

William nodded cautiously. "Yeah. I bumped into George in the bathroom. Or I mean, he bumped into me. Then he locked himself in a stall."

"He's pissed," Jacob said coolly. "You broke up with our friend when she was sick."

He expected William to make some excuse, but the boy made no motion to deny anything.

"So she finally told you she's sick?"

Jacob's face twisted. He hated that he'd been the last to know, but especially that William had been the first.

"And I guess you hate me too now?" William asked.

Jacob coughed. "Well, that's not really fair. I hated you before."

William nervously kicked at the wall. "How is she doing?"

Jacob didn't feel like telling him anything. "What happened to your date?"

"I put her in a cab," he said, extending his thumb over toward the avenue.

"Seemed like she'd have been happy to go home with you."

"She's the daughter of a woman my mother knows through her church," William explained. "I tell her I'm not interested, but they don't care. 'But Sung-Lee went to Harvard to study art history! And now she works for an important pharmaceutical company,' and I say, 'Good for her.' She says, 'But Sung-Lee's father owns four spa complexes in Passaic County.' Eventually it's easier to go on the date than to explain to my mother that I'm in love with a white girl with no family who's dying of cancer and won't return my calls."

Jacob didn't want to laugh but couldn't help himself. Then the door to Bistro 19 squeaked open again, and out spilled a very drunk George, his arms wrapped tightly around a dozen umbrellas. He looked up in surprise at William, then at Jacob, then back down at the umbrellas in his own arms. There were floral patterned ones and small beige ones and green ones, and there in the middle of them all was Oliver's black one, from Harrods.

George didn't quite seem to know how he'd come by them all. "Which was yours?" he asked.

Jacob broke down and laughed until he thought he'd cry. William, not sure what else to do, laughed too, and George laughed so hard, he dropped the umbrellas onto the sidewalk. The two boys hurried to help him pick them up, and then it seemed like they ought to book it before anyone realized what George had done.

Suddenly the night seemed young, and before any of them quite knew it, they were in a cab, umbrellas stuffed in every pocket, the sounds of horns and motors bringing them down and east.

The driver let them out below Union Square, which was mobbed with the usual late-night crowds of skateboarders and spectators. Little brunette girls in wool caps emerged from Whole Foods, burdened down with reusable bags. Yuppie couples headed out of Craftbar and into karaoke bars. Kids trying to look dangerous while sipping Jamba Juice outside the Best Buy. An old man lingered by the windows of an antique emporium, looking at an $8,000 Louis XV armchair—if he was worth a million bucks or homeless, Jacob couldn't tell.

"Here's what I propose," William said. "We're going to get royally smashed. And I'm going to tell my bosses that you're looking for legal advice about your investments. And they'll pay for it. Tell me something, George. Are you looking for new ways to invest your money?"

"Am I ever!" he cheered. "You know, I've got this bottle-cap collection back home in Ohio, but I really hate having all my assets tied up in beverage futures."

William grinned. "What if I told you I could turn those bottle caps into a triple-tax-free retirement account? Let's discuss it further over drinks."

"Let's!" George shouted, as if Willy Wonka had just invited him into the chocolate factory.

Jacob raised his hands to the full moon. "You know, with this sort of responsible behavior, it's hard to fathom how you all managed to destroy the American economy."

"Rats to the economy," William said. "I hope we all end up on breadlines." George was already half inside the bodega. He emerged in a moment with three cans of Red Bull, which tasted to Jacob like an emulsion of toothpaste and motor oil but provided a jolt sufficient to make them feel like college freshmen once again. *This shit's going to give us all cancer,* he nearly said, but realized it wouldn't have been funny even under other circumstances.

They began at a quiet Greek place called Smyrna, more or less because it was the nearest visible restaurant with a bar in front. William's AmEx had soon procured them a round of cocktails involving metaxa and brandy, plus an order of braised baby octopuses to share. Jacob grew listless as William and George actually *did* become deeply engaged in a conversation about the capital gains tax, SEP accounts, and something to do with paying for Sara's contact lenses with pretax dollars. Boring. Jacob gulped at the brandy concoction but only felt further lost inside the brown fog of his own head. Oliver, Irene, Rabbi Kantrowitz, the scent of his father's corn-riddled feet—everything he had intended to obliterate came crowding in.

The bartender, a hipster kid in a peasant vest whose mustache and goatee were devilishly curly, brought them all a round of complimentary ouzo shots. They downed them all in one, with a cry of *Opa!* at the bartender's gleeful count. Jacob felt the kid's eyes lingering on him afterward, and so when he excused himself to the closet-size restroom a minute or two later, he wasn't entirely surprised when the kid followed him in.

"Won't your friends miss you?" he asked mischievously. The single hanging light in the bathroom was dim against the deep, violet wallpaper but cast handsome shadows over his face.

"Those two?" Jacob said. "They're not my friends. The Asian guy's actually a Shaolin monk. Don't let the suit fool you."

"And the other one?" the bartender giggled, as he closed his eyes and eased close enough to graze his mustache against the bridge of Jacob's nose.

"He's my priest," Jacob said, breathing in deeply, letting the smell of his cologne fill his nostrils . . . something vaguely like currant jam that lifted away the smells of the restroom, and the memory of worse smells: of his father's feet, of Thomas's puke.

"I was guessing you were Jewish," he said, opening one eye as if to check.

"I'm a rabbi, actually," Jacob said. "We walk into bars looking for a punchline."

He pressed his lips to Jacob's. The brown fog began to clear as Jacob turned his eyes up to the ceiling and arched his back. Something started up in his guts like a four-stroke engine, throbbing, waiting.

"My name's Jeff," the bartender murmured.

"Nice to meet you, Jeff."

"This is where you tell me your name," he breathed.

"I—I—" Jacob tried. He tried to say his name, or maybe he did; he was past knowing or caring. With eyes clamped shut, he felt the quickening of his heart and let its echo mix with his own breathing to fill his ears. He felt Jeff's hands move down over his chest and then lower. As the sensations rose up his spine, he tried to intercept them at the base of his skull, to convince himself that they weren't being induced by the hands and lips of a total stranger but by someone else.

What came instead was the long-lost memory of a boy named Isaac. Jacob's first kiss, during swim class at school. Jacob was uncomfortable enough at this but then, unwilled, the image changed in his mind to that of George, and feeling loathsome enough already, he finally settled on the one person he knew he could keep in mind: Oliver. *How awful,* he thought, *to cheat on your boyfriend and then imagine you're with him.* He shuddered, half at Jeff's touch and half at his own mental use of the word *boyfriend.* And it wasn't cheating, was it, when just a few hours ago they'd been discussing the openness of their arrangement?

Jacob began to imagine what might be happening if Sara hadn't called. If George could have held his shit together a little better. He wouldn't be there, in the violet restroom of a Greek restaurant with hipster-bartender Jeff, but home. Well, Oliver's home . . . which by now felt more like home to Jacob than his own. They'd be in the cradling softness of the cracked leather divan, smelling the faint perfume of the laundry Oliver had carefully laid out on all the windowsills to dry throughout the day. Oliver didn't trust dryers and preferred to do the washing by hand, as he'd done at school. Up on the wall, the blowup of an old French magazine cover of a gentleman in a silk top hat, rakishly low on his head. Jacob tried to hear the music in Oliver's study. He'd have on something familiar. The Eighth Symphony . . . just loud enough to mask the sound of an Animal Channel special on the elm bark beetle, which had introduced Dutch elm disease to North America. Not the beetle's fault really, but a fungus it carried. Jacob had liked the name of the fungus—*Ophiostoma ulmi. Ophiostoma ulmi. Ophiostoma*—

It all came swiftly to an end. Jacob swayed, low, and felt everything ebbing away. Jeff moved his head away to one side, and Jacob felt cold. *La petite mort*, Jacob remembered every time. *The little death*. What better way to describe it?

When he got back to the table, George and William had moved on from IRAs to the topic of Irene, barely noticing his absence. Jacob quickly got their bill from the other bartender—Jeff was no longer anywhere to be seen—and slid it to William, who signed it and pocketed the receipt wordlessly, while George detailed the trip to Shelter Island and the discovery of Irene's second tumor. He paused just long enough to bequeath a tall beige umbrella to a shaggy-haired gentleman next to him, and by the time they'd gotten back out onto Twelfth Street, the current surgeries had been outlined, and William was looking green-gilled. They ambled along the sidewalk, past the Strand and down Fourth Avenue, looking for a bar called Queen Elizabeth's that William had heard about.

Not finding it, they ended up in a Brazilian restaurant, mostly because George had to pee again, and in the meantime Jacob and William had two caipirinhas apiece and made pleasant small talk.

Then, in exchange for a scarlet umbrella, their server told them where to find Queen Elizabeth's, through an unmarked door in the back of an Indian restaurant named Shantih. They had a few drinks there, which all seemed to involve egg-white foam, and after that Jacob couldn't remember much. A sports bar. Some New Zealanders. George handing out umbrellas like party favors. They had called Sara at some point, to check in. No news. Was George okay? she asked. Depended on what she meant by okay. Don't be cute. Can't help it. So she'd be sleeping in a hospital chair all night while they gallivanted around the city? He'd offered to send George back there, and she'd hung up.

Jacob remembered mostly feeling as if his feet were stuck with tar to the sidewalk, although at other times as if he were drifting like a loose barge through Greenwich Village. And he remembered thinking he'd never been happier in his life. He'd long forgotten whatever beef he'd had with William, and whatever worries he'd felt for George. He'd obliterated the name Oliver from his mind and thought he had no father on this earth. Who Irene was or where, or what might be being pumped into her or carved out of her—all were questions he'd forgotten how to pose. That which was Jacob was coming apart.

His last, hazy memory was of standing out on the sidewalk, staring in confusion at the flooded street. He remembered George asking, "Hey, when did they put a river through here?" as Jacob had felt a sopping wetness in his socks. Passing cars were throwing up black waves in confusion.

"A water main burst on Sullivan!" someone—he thought it was William—was saying. George had opened up the last of his umbrellas—a huge yellow one—and was attempting to climb into it so as to sail home again. Jacob pitched backward and all he could see were the tops of buildings and a starless sky. The last thing he remembered feeling that night was William's surprisingly strong arm around his shoulder. Jacob was already half dreaming that

George was now rowing them downstream in the yellow umbrella. The things he thought and saw were connecting nothing with nothing, and everywhere there was the roar and flash of fire trucks.

The boy lived in a "not very Jewy" part of Westchester. At least that's what his mother said when his father wasn't around, which, thank God, was fairly often. Things had a way of working out like this for the boy. His father sold supplemental life insurance and was generally best avoided. His mother did everything for him, and as far as the boy could tell, his father never did anything for her. She had even become Jewish for him, something she brought up a lot, which was why the boy was Jewish, but his father acted as if this were no skin off her back at all. The boy did as many nice things for her as he could think of, to try to make up for it all. His mother told him how special he was at least once a day and sometimes more often.

Every morning his mother drove him thirty-five minutes up 684 to go to Moses Maimonides, the school his father had picked out for him to attend. He was in the third grade. He asked if he could attend the school right down at the end of their street, and his mother said no; it was just for Catholics. He didn't know what that was, so she explained that a Catholic is a kind of Christian, which is someone who believes in Jesus, who lived a long time ago and who Christians thought was the Messiah. That last part was in the Torah, which he had at school, about a man who would come to bring all the sinners on earth up to heaven. Anyway, they thought it was Jesus, who'd be back later, but other people, like them, disagreed and thought whoever it was hadn't come around yet. The boy asked why it mattered if he'd come and gone or not come yet, and his mother said that this was a good question.

When he asked his teacher, though, he got sent to Rabbi Kantrowitz's office. But Rabbi Kantrowitz agreed it was a very good question, and then took out a big, dusty book called the Talmud and showed the boy where another rabbi from a long time ago named Maimonides, whose name was now on the side of the boy's school, had written about what the world would be like when the Messiah finally showed up.

" 'And in that time there will be no hunger or war, no jealousy or rivalry. For the good will be plentiful, and all delicacies available as dust. The occupation of the entire world will be only to know G-d . . . the people Israel will be of great wisdom; they will perceive the esoteric truths and comprehend their Creator's wisdom as is the capacity of man. As it is written, *For the earth shall be filled with the knowledge of God, as the waters cover the sea.*' "

This sounded pretty good to the boy. He asked if Rabbi Kantrowitz was the Messiah, and the rabbi said no, the Messiah would be a very, very special person. The boy was about to ask, *Could I be the Messiah?* when he was shooed off to class.

The more he thought it, the more he was sure it could be him. He was the best in the whole grade at math, reading, *and* history. He knew every possible statistic about the Chicago Bulls by heart. He had won a prize for the best essay about what the world of 2010 would be like (undersea villages, connected with tunnels). He was patient with all the other boys, despite them being stupid when it came to subtracting large numbers, and sticking their fingers up their nostrils, and forgetting how to spell *pepper* or what the capital of France was. There were other things too. The boy had once, when no one else was around, levitated a spoon with his mind. He couldn't do it again later, when his mother was there, although she said she'd definitely seen it vibrating. The boy could sometimes make his favorite songs come on the radio just by thinking about them. Every day the evidence grew more impressive. He began looking forward to the day when he'd fix all of mankind's problems.

But it was hard to know that he was the Messiah and not be able to tell anyone else. The only boy he thought he might be able to trust with his secret identity was Isaac Schechter, who sat up front in all the classes and nearly always got the answers right, except when it came to long division. The boy had wanted to be friends with Isaac for a while, but his father wouldn't allow the boy to invite Isaac over after school because he said Isaac was a "sissy." At school, Isaac had speech therapy during normal lunch hour, so the boy couldn't sit with him, and he already had Zeke as a lab partner. Finally, during swimming at gym class, his prayers were answered (of course), and the boy and Isaac were paired up. God had made it happen.

For three wonderful weeks, during swim class, he and Isaac covered the same position in water polo games. They changed in the same corner of the locker room. They always compared how pruny their fingers would get in the water. When Isaac got cold, his lips turned a little blue. Isaac didn't mind sharing his towel if the boys got splashed near the pool. Secretly, the boy splashed his towel on purpose, just so they could share. He didn't really know why. He just knew that he liked knowing the towel had been on Isaac's skin just before it was on his.

The final day of swimming came, and the boy gave Isaac a special signal they'd devised, which meant to dive when the teacher wasn't looking. Underwater, sound traveled better than in the air, and more important, all the people up on the surface couldn't hear you.

"I HAVE TO TELL YOU A SECRET!" the boy shouted.

Isaac pointed to the top. Both boys went up to the surface and took really deep breaths. Then the boy put his hands onto Isaac's shoulders, and Isaac put his hands on the boy's, and they pushed back down under the water. All around them it was blue and still. This was what it would be like in heaven, the boy thought. When God covered the whole world with the sea. Warm water covered him like a blanket. His hair lifted lightly from his scalp. Far away, the other boy's legs were kicking and swirling up white tornadoes of bubbles. Isaac's hair was floating like a halo around his head.

They were gripping each other's arms to stop from rising up. Isaac's dark eyes were searching, and then the boy saw his blue lips open to release a big brilliant bubble. And then they were kissing.

The boy wasn't sure if he'd started it or if Isaac had, but he never wanted to stop. He felt dizzy, and the water around him began to burn with an intense white light, and he thought he could hear the voice of God from all around him, calling his name—

Then in an instant it was all over. Mrs. Cogen, the gym teacher, had pulled them both to the surface. She was very angry. She marched him straight to Rabbi Kantrowitz's office before he'd even dried off or changed his clothes. There he sat, damp and shivering, in an old cantor's robe, until she finished telling the rabbi what had happened.

When Rabbi Kantrowitz took the boy into his office, he asked why the hell he had tried to drown poor Isaac. The boy didn't realize, and wouldn't realize until he was older, that neither the rabbi nor Mrs. Cogen knew that they had kissed. The boy explained that he had only been trying to tell Isaac something important. A secret. And the rabbi had demanded to know what it was, so the boy tried to tell him that he wasn't like the other boys. That he was special. He wanted to cry out, *I'm the Messiah! I was sent to unite the tribes of Israel! I am the one who wrestles with the angels. I am the one who will prevail with God.* But these things all seemed silly the moment he considered them out loud.

The rabbi took the boy to an empty classroom and handed him an empty pad of paper. Carefully, he wrote something in Hebrew at the very top of the first page.

מיוחד לא אני

The rabbi said that it meant "I am not special" and that the boy would write it on every line on every page until it was full.

This took the rest of the afternoon, long past the time when the other boys were sent home. His hands ached and ached. He thought maybe his mother would rescue him from this punishment, but she didn't come. When he finally finished, his father came to take him home. He didn't say a single word to the boy. When the boy looked up at his father, he saw that he looked a lot like him—a little large, the same bristly hair, the same big hands.

He thought about Isaac's blue lips. His hands still throbbed, but it was his heart that ached worse than anything else. *I am not special,* it beat. *I am not special. I am not special.*

The words were stuck in his mouth like a piece of paper, all wadded up. They were like the first line in a long, long poem that might take a lifetime to finish writing.

Jacob woke up to George's snoring. Very slowly he came to the conclusion that he and George were lying side by side on the blue pullout couch they'd bought at the Toronto IKEA during their junior year of college, when they'd lived in a row house off campus.

However, as Jacob slowly recalled, he and George were no longer in college, and they no longer lived on East Street in Ithaca. The blue pullout resided now in *his* apartment, which meant that he was *also* in his apartment, which meant that *George* was in his apartment as well. This would have been bad enough, but then, very slowly, Jacob gathered from the sound of dishes being washed that someone else was there too. A third person. William Cho.

Jacob's first instinct was to rise, thunderous from the bed, kicking and swearing until William was halfway back to Queens. But his body was in no condition for thundering. His throat was Death Valley dry, and even trying to form swear words was taxing his bruised brain.

He remembered that William had still been there at the end of the night, his face sweaty in the flashing red lights of the fire trucks. William had been supporting him and carrying George on his other arm. Jacob could still hear the echo in his ears: water, roaring behind the buildings.

"Coffee," Jacob rasped, his vocal cords raw. He tried again, raising his voice above the rushing of the sink. "COFFEE!"

"Shush," William said.

Jacob found it superbly irritating that he actually *said* the word instead of making a shushing noise, but then he figured there wasn't much he wouldn't find superbly irritating in his current condition.

William came over with a glass of water.

"This isn't coffee," Jacob croaked.

"Coffee's just going to dehydrate you more," William said. "You should have had water last night when I was trying to make you."

Slowly Jacob remembered being in the back of the cab, trying to cool his sweaty cheek against the cold passenger-side window. "Were you in the cab last night?" he finally asked, slowly rising to his feet. Carefully, he crossed the treacherously piled floor to get to William by the sink.

"You and me and George. Who you're going to wake up, by the way, if you keep shouting like that. This place has a hell of an echo . . . I've never seen ceilings this high. You've got more fly space than floor space in here. What is this, like ten by twelve by thirty?"

"Twenty-eight and a half," Jacob corrected, and though he knew full well it was a bad idea, he still craned his neck back to look up at the thick oak beams in the ceiling. The act made him so dizzy, he had to sit down on the floor and lean his head against the fridge. The plastic door was wonderfully cold and smooth. He closed his eyes and thought he might just go back to sleep, but then a baby outside began wailing, so close that he could also hear its mother, crying back at the child to "please, *for the love of God, stop crying!*"

"Lot of people out there," William observed, pointing up to the barred windows, which were halfway up the high walls—too far up to see out of, but they could see the people's shadows drifting like ghosts through the apartment. They could hear little bits and pieces of their voices—muffled and sounding like a confusion of other languages. Their shadows crawled upside down the walls, and somewhere above them, Jacob and William heard the insistent pealing of bells. It was Sunday.

"You live in the basement of a church," William stated.

"Thank you, Captain Obvious," Jacob replied, eyes slitted.

"When we came in last night, I thought we had to be in the wrong spot. But then your key fit the side door. I couldn't believe it. Is this even legal?"

Jacob groaned and moved his mouth fruitlessly. Far too much effort to explain that he was sort of unofficially subletting it from the priest, the brother of a Greek Orthodox guy he'd slept with (off and on) in college who'd hooked him up with the keys when Jacob had announced that after graduation he'd be moving to the big city. What had seemed at first like Divine Providence (avoiding the months of craigslist ads and fleabag brokers that George and Sara and Irene had dealt with that first summer) had quickly become a sort of hell. The place came to feel like the kind of dungeon people got thrown into during the Spanish Inquisition. Jacob felt at times like a boy who'd fallen into a well and decided he might as well decorate.

Though *decorate* was a term best used loosely if at all. Jacob chewed his lip and looked around at the disheveled heaps that were his worldly possessions. The blue pullout couch, a flimsy bookshelf, and a desk made of milk cartons and an old door he'd found in the alley. These were the only pieces of furniture he possessed. The walls were bare except for a few rough starts of poems that he'd stapled, in haste and at odd angles, onto the flat surfaces around the desk. On the bookshelf was one framed photograph, of himself in a tuxedo posing alongside George, Sara, and Irene at the prize ceremony for *In the Eye of the Shitstorm.* The jittery MRI printout that Irene had given him was held to the fridge with a magnet from Szechuan Garden.

The apartment was boiling in the summer and freezing in the winter. His every noise echoed, making him supremely self-conscious of every movement. He had recurring dreams of being trapped at the bottom of an enormous empty swimming pool, only to wake up and find that in a sense, he was. And yet it was so cheap and peculiar that he couldn't justify leaving. He'd settled instead on two rules: he'd spend as many nights as possible in other people's beds, and he'd never allow George or the others to see the place—knowing full well that they'd force him to admit he'd made a terrible mistake.

Jacob felt an odd pinching in his stomach, distinct from the unease of its still containing half a liquor cabinet's worth of booze.

"We've got to get George out of here."

"Why not let him sleep it off?"

"George hasn't ever been here. *No one's* ever been here." He tried to rush back over to the couch and promptly hip-checked the bookshelf, which teetered unsettlingly.

William shut the water off and shook his hands to dry them off. "You pulled your pants off in front of me the night we met, but no one's allowed in your apartment?"

As anxious as Jacob was, he couldn't deny this. "How'd you even know where I lived?"

"It's on your old Blockbuster card. Though I notice you don't seem to have a television."

"It had an abrupt meeting with a thrown remote control during the 2004 Oscars."

"Not a fan of *The Return of the King*?"

"I was pulling for *Seabiscuit*. Look, why the hell didn't you just take us to *your* place?"

William's face reddened a little, and he squinted at the adjacent wall, which was badly cracked through the plaster. "You'd just have made fun of it," he said at last.

Jacob snickered happily. "Your page twelve?"

William almost dropped the cup he'd been washing. "She *told* you?"

"No, she told Sara. Who told George, who told me."

A flash, like lightning, flickered over William's face, and Jacob was for the first time frightened of what was about to come forth. But before William could erupt, the entire room was filled with a thundering noise from outside—the sound of a garbage truck hitting the curb, then the lighter sound of the men opening the bins' heavy iron lids, designed to keep the rats out. Jacob had been so grateful when they'd finally been installed, two years ago, and he'd no longer had to scramble past vermin to get to the door. But as with everything, there were trade-offs. Now the lids clanged loud enough to wake the dead or, failing that, an extremely hung-over astronomer.

George jolted up, looking around for the noise. "Where—?"

Jacob watched as his oldest friend made the same mistake of staring up too quickly. He could actually *see* the blood rushing from his head. George rolled over and planted his face into the soft dark safety of the couch cushions.

"—the hell are we?" George managed, his eyes darting above the cushions accusingly.

Jacob sighed and faced the humiliating prospect of surrender. *I am not special*, he thought. He just liked that they had always thought he was. Even if he'd known, years earlier than the rest of them, that it wasn't true.

"My brother's apartment," William said quickly. "A friend of our father's runs this church, and he rents Charles the room under the table."

While George took another try at inspecting the ceilings, William wandered casually to the bookshelf and set the photograph of them all at the awards ceremony facedown so it was out of sight.

Jacob stood still, not really sure what to say.

"I thought your brother was a doctor," George said to William. "With kids and stuff."

"Let me guess," William said. "Irene told Sara, who told you, who told Jacob? Yeah, well, he works over at Columbia Presbyterian, so he crashes here between shifts."

Jacob was a bit stunned—George seemed to be buying it.

"Hey! Jacob and I bought this same couch, back in the day." Smiling like a fool, George eased himself from the bed, stretched like a sandy-furred cat, and released a long sigh. "I am going to go throw up," he announced as he padded off to the bathroom in his dress socks, undershirt, and a pair of blue boxer shorts with sandwiches on them.

From the bathroom they could hear the seat of the toilet as George knocked it back against the basin, followed by the sound of him emptying his stomach. "You didn't have to do that," Jacob said to William, who returned to washing the last of Jacob's dishes. "Really. You didn't have to do any of this. You could have left us down there in the Village."

"I suppose," William agreed, cheerful now for some reason. "But then you wouldn't owe me one, and I couldn't make you take me to see Irene."

William passed him a sudsy beer stein.

Jacob dried it off. "And here I thought you were just doing all this out of the goodness of your heart."

"Hell, Jacob. It's not like I'm the Messiah or anything."

Jacob froze, nearly dropping the stein on the counter. "How'd you—did I, um—did I say something last night?"

William smiled cryptically. "You were pretty drunk. I doubt it'll hold up in court."

Jacob felt a fury rising, but when he opened his mouth to release it, what came out was a sigh of relief. Hearing it out loud wasn't as terrible as he'd thought. And who'd believe that he'd confided in William, of all people, if he ever were to repeat it?

"Well," Jacob said, "you're the one who went to Yale."

A gruff vibration came from a pile of clothes near the couch. Jacob fished around in George's discarded pants and thought, for a second, he had found a phone in the back pocket. Only the object he extracted wasn't a phone at all but a slim silver flask with an engraving on the side: *Coriolanus Crew 1967 League Champions.* Jacob vaguely recalled being with George when he'd picked it up at the Salvation Army their freshman year. The flask was not quite empty.

Jacob unscrewed the cap and caught the scent of J&B—George's favorite. With a sinking in his heart, he at last understood why George had kept rushing off to the bathroom in the hospital and at Bistro 19. He couldn't decide if he wanted to smack him or crush him in his bare arms.

Whatever ambitions Jacob had held as a boy—to hear the voice of God, to wrestle with angels, to unite everything—he knew now that he'd become too selfish, too discontent, too upset. Maybe that had always been true, but especially after Isaac, he'd known for sure that Jacob Blaumann was no Messiah. He'd never been as good as the boy he thought he'd been. Nobody he knew was that good. Nobody could possibly be.

Then on his first day of freshman year he'd walked into a small room with bunked beds and shaken hands with George Murphy, who in ten years had proved to be the kindest and most generous person Jacob had ever known. And for all his griping, he'd needed George to be the good things that he'd long ago given up believing in. Only now his savior had been holing up in men's rooms, sipping scotch, trying to numb the world's unfairness.

"I think it's your dad calling?" William said, lifting up Jacob's phone.

Jacob almost laughed—why would his father be calling? He stared down at Oliver's picture on the phone, feeling the buzz in his hand until the screen grew dark. "I'll call him back later," Jacob lied.

William seemed about to say something, when they heard the buzzing again now, not from Jacob's phone but from inside George's shoe, down near William's foot. On the screen was Irene's lovely face, framed in black. Jacob motioned for William to answer it.

William pressed the big green button on the screen and held it to his ear. "Sara? It's William Cho. George is just in the bathroom—what's the matter? Did something happen?"

Jacob felt the rush of a hundred voices all at once, his blood vessels and neurons and toenails and eyelashes all screaming in every language at once. He heard the sound of the toilet flushing in the bathroom as William tried to calm Sara down on the other end of the line.

"Shushhhhh," he said, "Shushhhhh. Shushhhh."

THE DISAPPOINTMENTS

JULY

William counted his disappointments on both hands. There was, one, the ninety-eight-degree heat burning through the window of the bus, as it, two, crawled through Staten Island traffic. Three. He was there, on a weekday afternoon, because, four, he had finally been laid off at Joyce, Bennett, and Salzmann. At first he'd been almost glad to have it over with, but then, five, none of the other firms had been hiring. Six, his severance and savings were being so rapidly consumed by his rent that it seemed like only a matter of time before he would be forced to move back home again. He was vexed by a peculiar curdled milk smell, seven, emanating from the woman in the row ahead. Also, the periodic vibration of his phone alarm in his right pants pocket, which he couldn't reach to disable, eight, reminded him that he and Irene were now a half hour late, nine, for their appointment with a guy named Skeevo, ten, whom she had been buying pot from lately (it helped with the nausea, as well as her overall mood), but who today had called about something else that he wanted her to see, all the way in Staten Island, down near the Fresh Kills Solid Waste Transfer Station.

And yet, despite two hands' worth of disappointments, William caught a reflection of himself grinning like an idiot, all the fingers in his reflection's left hand holding all the fingers in the reflection of

Irene's hand, and all the fingers in his reflection's right hand playing gently with the reflection of her hair.

William was aware, at least as long as Irene was around. Aware of the faint burned smell that always got jumbled up in her hair, postradiation. He'd gotten used to it after a month. How many more weeks of treatments did she have left? One? Two? Time was rushing laughably by. Not like the past several months, when he'd buried himself in work (for all the good it had done him) and rerouted his heart on dates with the Society of Korean Daughters of His Mother's Friends. But now William was sitting beside Irene, aware of the vibrations of her throat against his shoulder as she awwed at a little baby in the next row, happily gumming the leg of a Barbie, naked except for one black glove.

His phone buzzed again; it was wedged directly against Irene's outer thigh. She looked away from the baby, craned her head up at him, and whispered, "Is that your mother calling again, or are you just happy to see me?"

She looked so damned ridiculous trying to give him sexy eyes while the left one was covered with a black felt eye patch. She'd bedazzled it with rhinestones in the shape of a skull, claiming it was an ironic statement about Damien Hirst. William said it made her look *more* like a pirate than the eye patch alone. Irene said that was the irony. William didn't understand, or care.

He didn't care about a lot of things far more important than that. He didn't care that he was unemployed. He didn't care that he'd forgotten to make his June credit card payment and would now be charged a one-hundred-dollar fee, the first time this had happened in his life. He was actually a little excited. Ordinarily, he would have carried the guilt of that hundred dollars around in his gut like a bullet for the rest of the year. He'd have cared that the socks he put on that morning were not only two different shades of blue but of different thicknesses, such that his right foot ached and sweated while the left was fine. He'd have been distraught that Irene was still sick—worse, maybe, even than before. He *did* care, of course. It was just that these cares, like all the others, were wiped from his mind now that she was holding his hand.

In moments when he was alone, the circuits in his brain containing these ordinary cares and fears overwhelmed all others, and he couldn't even sleep. But when Irene was around, even the disappointment he felt about her big surgery not going smoothly seemed to clear.

The morning after their epic night of barhopping, Jacob, true to his word, had brought William back to the hospital. While Sara had been dealing with the still jelly-legged George, William had slipped around the cheap curtain that hung around Irene's recovery bed. He had been worrying about what to say: that he was sorry for leaving her in the train station; that he had woken up every day since then thinking of her before even remembering what planet he was on; that he had tried to call her dozens of times; that he had compulsively been donating to the American Cancer Society online at work; that he had run in a 5k to raise money but it turned out that he was a lot more out of shape than he expected and had limped the last 3k on a strained ankle. But the second he'd seen her lying there, these worries began to evaporate from the inside of his head.

She'd looked nearly concave, with thick bandages wrapped over the area surrounding her left eye, and her right eye fixed on the TV high up in the corner. But that right eye had swiveled to him. The lid around it had snapped up like a cheap blind. She'd seized his hand, pulled him to her, and locked her lips onto his. An alarm went off; she'd pulled off her pulse monitor clip and yanked her IV stand half over. A squat Dominican nurse had rushed in and threatened to put Irene into restraints. William had had to walk two laps around the ER. When they released Irene, the two of them had gone directly back to his apartment—actually no, they'd made one stop, back to her place to pick up some clothes and the scarf she'd bought for him at Christmas, which had remained wrapped and on the counter. *Then* back to his place, where she'd stayed every night since.

In a week she'd sold her bed on craigslist and rid herself of every other unneeded belonging, so she could maximize the work space in her East Fourth Street apartment. Every day she worked there but refused to show William, or anyone, what she was making. She never even spoke about it—but she always arrived at William's itchy to return, talking only vaguely about working on something larger, something that she and Skeevo seemed to be into together.

Even now, Irene seemed quietly elsewhere as she and William followed the other passengers off the first bus and toward the next, an S62.

She looked down and said, "You don't need to hold my hand."

But she didn't pull away.

"But I like holding your hand. 'I wanna hold your ha-a-a-and . . .'" William tried to sing.

She screeched and tried to cover his mouth with her other hand, but he persisted.

"'Oh, please . . . say to me-e-e-e-e. You'll let me be your man . . .'"

He finally had to stop when, on the held-note, Irene got most of her fingers into his mouth, and he could no longer form words.

"OKKK FWINE YLOOOU WIHHN."

Irene let him go and shot him another look that was difficult for William to decode without being able to see her eyebrows. The second bus smelled refreshingly of burned Dunkin' Donuts coffee.

Once seated, Irene turned to William to explain. "I can still see out of the other eye. I'm not going to wander into traffic."

"I didn't think you were."

The eye was fine. They had gotten the tumor out from beneath it without any damage to the nerves. It was still swollen, though, and with the thick black stitches there, it freaked people out. Hence the eyepatch, which still freaked them out but in a kinder way.

After the first tumor had been removed, the doctors had planned to head in for the one on her elbow, when one of them had noticed some swelling under her armpit. Thinking it might be a reaction to the anesthesia, they'd run a fresh scan, only to find suspicious shading on one of her lymph nodes. Just days earlier they'd done a complete battery of PET scans and found everything clean, but now there was definitely something. They stopped before beginning the surgery on her arm.

Now she had a "compromised lymph node." This was, as Dr. Zarrani put it, "a big disappointment." The cancer had gone off the skeletal rails and passed into her glands, from whence it could travel, fluid borne, to distant organs. It meant that the first rounds of chemotherapy had done very little, possibly nothing, and that they'd have to "really crank it up a notch now." It meant adding ifosfamide and etoposide to the poisons they were secreting into her veins each day in the chemo lounge. But William wasn't thinking about that now, only about the coconut smell of her hand lotion and of Irene's relief when she learned she wouldn't to have keep her arm in a cast all summer—and so would still be able to work on her sculptures.

The S62 bus squealed to a halt just to one side of the Staten Island Mall. William followed Irene off the bus into the mall parking lot. Steadily, the rest of the people headed toward the forty-foot-high signs for JC Penney's and Loews Cinemas. Irene pulled William in the opposite direction, crossing one vast parking lot after another—each a little less crowded than the last—until they seemed to be a half mile from the actual mall. Irene danced over the cracks in the pavement, as if to not break the back of some mother somewhere. That was another mystery that William had a hard time thinking about. Where was her family in all of this? He became preoccupied by the light glinting on her legs as she leaped.

Far off in the distance, William spotted a red pickup truck parked by a chain-link fence. Hitched up behind it was a little two-wheeled U-Haul trailer with its orange rolltop up. A man who William presumed to be Skeevo was rifling through the odd items inside.

He was tall and wore a grease-stained flannel shirt buttoned to the top and to the wrists. His pants were ripped, revealing kneecaps the same mocha-tan color as his neck and hands. Despite the July heat, he was wearing a half-disintegrated hand-knit winter cap.

Irene let go of William's hand. Disappointment settled in as she moved farther away, and it grew measurably along a neat curve in his mind, like a once-meager debt accruing interest. He walked faster, trying to reduce the distance between them. With each stride he felt the load leveling off. By the time he got to her side again he was out of breath, but happy again. He shook Skeevo's hand as if they, too, went way back. William didn't even mind that his grip felt like a car door closing on his hand.

"What'd you bring me?" Irene asked, moving around to the back of the U-Haul and beginning to sort through the scrap. Things clanged and scraped.

Keeping his eyes on her, William shook Skeevo's hand and introduced himself. "You work over at the dump?" he asked.

"Kind of," Skeevo replied. "It's not really a dump anymore."

"The Staten Island dump isn't a dump?"

Skeevo cast his eyes out past the fence, across the busy highway, toward several enormous green hills. "The Fresh Kills Landfill's been closed for, like, ten years. It was supposed be temporary—you believe that? Back in 1947 . . . then you know, one thing leads to another, and soon enough it's the biggest landfill in the world."

Irene had fully disappeared inside the U-Haul, and William was feeling at an utter loss. Then she emerged with a single ski under one arm, looked at it a moment in the light, dropped it to the asphalt, and dove back in again.

Skeevo was still going on about the not dump. "When they finally shut this thing down, it was taller than the Statue of Fucking Liberty. Back in the sixties, when the astronauts went up into orbit, the only man-made objects they could see from space were the Great Wall of China and *this*."

"That's . . . distressing," William said, although he didn't feel distressed at all, because Irene was pulling half a child's stroller out of the U-Haul with a quizzical look. She placed it in a pile to one side, which William took to mean she was considering it. "So what, um, what is going on with the landfill now? They've finally closed it?"

"They're turning it into a park," Skeevo announced proudly. "Going to be three times the size of Central Park."

William hummed. "And *Skeevo*—is that a . . . Polish name?"

He took his wallet out and thrust an ID in William's face. "Skeevington Monkeylips McBalzac the Third," he said. "I changed it when I left home. Got the idea from Reeny here, actually. I think everybody should be able to pick their own name, don't you?"

William looked nervously for "Reeny," but she was deep inside the trailer. How exactly did she know this very possibly insane person? And what did he mean he'd gotten the idea from her? Was Irene Richmond *not* her real name?

But then Irene began shrieking from the back of the U-Haul. William rushed over, imagining a collapsing wall of sharp objects and broken glass. Instead he found Irene straddling a segment of a large steel I-beam—running her hands wildly over its ridges and warps. Something had clearly happened to it, for the thing looked, William supposed, more like a T-beam now. The bottom edge was melted to nearly nothing. He wondered what could have done that.

"I knew you'd like it," Skeevo grinned.

"Help me get this into the light!" Irene cried.

It took the three of them shoving as hard as they could to get it closer to the open door of the U-Haul. William guessed it weighed over four hundred pounds. He sniffed his hands after pulling them away and recoiled at the harsh, burned-chemical odor. Irene was acting as if she had uncovered the Treasure of the Sierra Madre. What did she see in it? She was *so* happy—he hadn't seen her like this since they'd kissed at the hospital, not even when they were in bed together. She was like a child, overtaken by a joy far exceeding her total volume.

William closed his eyes a moment. He'd spent his whole life avoiding drinking or smoking cigarettes or pot, for fear of being addicted, and now here he was hooked on a drug that was in desperately short supply. He opened his eyes again and saw Irene and felt no doubts at all.

"We found it up in the northwest quadrant of the old landfill. They'd been relandscaping it, trying to do something about the grade for the spill-off. One of the bulldozers snagged this thing. They let me have it before anyone important figured out what it really was."

"What *is* it?" William asked.

"My guy there tipped me off. It's from one of the Twin Towers," Skeevo whispered. "Some of the rubble they cleared from there got dumped in the landfill before they closed it up again."

William found himself taking a quick step backward, but Irene was bending down closer so she could study it better. Then, without warning, she lifted the patch from her eye to reveal the red, puffy mess beneath it. Back in the apartment she kept the patch on, even when they slept together and even when she was actually sleeping. She took it off only in the bathroom to clean the black network of stitches. They ran around her eye socket like narrow railroad tracks.

"Jesus," Skeevo said, a crack in his voice as he looked away.

But William didn't mind. He was too busy watching her brilliant blue iris working behind the lid, nearly swollen over it. He watched as she studied its corners and edges, running her hands up and down its length.

"Can we get this back to the city?" she asked softly.

Skeevo agreed to give them a lift in his truck. Irene squeezed between him and William in the front seat, navigating them to the K Gallery, where she had access to Abeba's welding tools. As they drove out of the parking lot and back up through Staten Island, Skeevo and Irene caught up on old times while they shared a joint. He didn't ask about her eye. Instead, he wanted to know how she and William had met, and William liked how she relayed the story of meeting him at the Christmas party. The way she stroked his cheekbones as she described first seeing him. Maybe it was just the pot smoke getting to him, but it seemed like a hundred years ago.

William stared dreamily out the window as Skeevo told them all about his own fantastic-sounding life. He'd gotten married, had a child. He and Irene complained about traffic and global warming and capitalism as they drove up and over the glorious gray Verrazano-Narrows Bridge. Eventually Skeevo fished a cell phone out of his pocket and thumbed-up a video he wanted Irene to watch. It was of his wife—a pretty young Chinese woman—sitting in a plane seat somewhere, holding a baby boy with an enormous head. The head was so enormous, it seemed to be all this woman could do to support it in two hands. Skeevington Monkeylips McBalzac the Fourth—at least for now.

"Skeevs! He's adorable! William, did you look like that when you were a baby?"

"That baby is Chinese," William said. "I'm Korean."

"Technically he's *half* Chinese," Skeevo said.

Irene shook her head, and even without seeing her second eyelid droop, William knew that she was sad. "Babies aren't anything yet," she said. "You can't be one thing or the other until you get old enough to know what you are and what you aren't."

William wanted to argue, but she slumped into his shoulder.

He could feel her body tensing as she tried not to cry. Fortunately Skeevo was too busy dodging traffic to notice a tear leaking out from under her eye patch. William wiped it away. Then he caught the one falling from her good eye and wiped that one away too.

Infertility, Dr. Zarrani had said, was a likely long-term side effect of the chemo. So was ototoxicity (a sensitivity to high-pitched sounds), neuropathy (numbing of the fingers), heart damage, and most ironic of all, greater susceptibility to cancer in the future. Irene didn't seem to care about anything except losing the ability to have a child.

"How do you feel about adoption, William?" she asked. "I've always wanted to adopt a baby. I'm basically adopted myself, you know."

"I'm for it," William said. The video ended with Skeevo's son chewing merrily on his mother's hair. "That'd really drive my mother off the wall."

Irene sighed. "She's so sweet. You should be nicer to her."

William turned away and looked out the window at the dingy Brooklyn boulevard they were heading down. He took in a deep lungful of fresh air. It was difficult, but he needed to be ordinary again for a while. He needed to feel how he felt, late at night, while he lay awake next to her in bed, unable to sleep. In those dark hours with his eyes shut, he had been counting disappointments on a hundred imaginary fingers. Not things that he was disappointed *by* but disappointments of his own making. Things like having made more money than he deserved, doing mergers for companies with questionable ethics, being a terrible son—anything he felt the universe might be punishing him for by making the woman that he loved so sick.

He knew it was egotistical to believe it was somehow his fault, but this made more sense than trying to imagine it was her fault. All she ever did was turn ordinary things unordinary. Lying next to her, at home on the bed, or there on the truck seat, with her hair smelling burned and her arms feeling thin, with her skin red and her eye mutilated, he couldn't bring himself to imagine what she could've done to deserve this.

AUGUST

The steps of the Metropolitan Museum of Art burned through the seat of Jacob's pants as he stared out at Fifth Avenue, waiting for Irene. He'd arrived early and was annoyed because he didn't know exactly how early he was. He had given up wearing watches, and when his phone display broke, he'd refused to get a new one, because technically it still made calls—if he could remember the number to dial. Text messages were a lost cause, of course.

He had been wanting to call Irene all morning to insist that they bag this whole thing, but the only person's number he could ever remember was George's, and George had grown tired of Jacob calling him every ten minutes, asking him to look up someone else's number. It didn't matter. Jacob knew Irene would have insisted anyway. If he'd canceled on her, she'd have come by herself, just to prove she could.

It was their tradition to get dressed up and go to a museum on the second Sunday of every month. They had only missed one before, during a hurricane—but for God's sake, she was supposed to be taking it easy, not going around in hundred-degree heat, and not spending all week at the gallery learning to arc weld. How was she supposed to operate a blowtorch when she had trouble lifting her purse? One of these days she was going to set herself on fire.

Whatever admiration he'd felt back in July for her dedication and energy was now, in August, a distant hallucination. Now he just wished she'd ease up. Allegedly July's treatments had been much harsher than the previous rounds—*allegedly*, of course, because Jacob hadn't been informed about the previous round—but the others had filled him in on the pattern: she'd feel queasy during the days of treatment but not totally awful. And then, just when the inconvenience of the hospital visits was over and she began fantasizing about getting her life back, the aggregated chemo drugs and radiation side effects would hit all at once. She looked airless half the time, as if instead of putting something into her, they were siphoning something out.

Jacob peered over the shoulder of a man on the step below him and saw on his phone that it was 12:19, which meant Irene *was* a little late—they'd agreed to meet at 12:15. The man was reading a story on Gawker about some handsome actor that Jacob recognized but couldn't remember the name of, who had tried, and failed, to kill himself. The man kept looking up and making audible, dramatic gasping sounds, as if to make sure everyone nearby knew that he was *shocked*.

Several steps down from him were three orderly rows of squatting grade-school children, their teachers lazily circling them, looking up the avenue for their school bus. The rows of schoolkids began to get restless with the barber shop quartet busking on the corner, singing old standards like "I Got a Gal in Kalamazoo" and "You Make Me Feel So Young." At some point the teachers responded. "Let's do our song, kids. Come on!" Jacob eased back, curious if they'd be singing a little "Frère Jacques" or "The Farmer in the Dell"—but no, as he listened through the din of high-pitched voices, he could tell it wasn't any of those childhood classics. " 'Baby, baby, baby, oh!' " the kids sang, " 'Baby, baby, baby, oh . . .' " Jacob saw to his horror that the teachers were actually encouraging this atrocity—recording it on their cell phones. Surely it would be on YouTube before their bus arrived. Jacob thought he'd never live to see the day he missed Barney the Purple Dinosaur, but now here he was.

He was sore from the steps and could feel sweat over every inch of him. People rudely trampled by just inches from his spot, though there was plenty of room to go around. He couldn't stop wiping at his forehead and knew it was turning all red. Then, just when he thought he might actually implode from unexpressed venom, there around the corner, past the hot dog vendors, he saw Irene coming at last. She wore a long, flowing white dress, and her hair was pulled up in an elegant twist that hid how thin it had become after all the treatments. She was fully made up, as she usually was now that the eye patch had come off. She'd figured out how to cover the scars with foundation and eye shadow. She'd put on a bit of blush. Her cheeks, like the rest of her these days, were colorless.

"You look like a million bucks," he said eerily.

"Why didn't you wait for me inside? You look like hell."

They went up the steps and through the revolving doors into the crowded Great Hall. Irene tilted her head back to stare up at the vaulted ceiling, and Jacob noticed her lurch back. He moved quickly, as if to catch her, but she righted herself without a word. They got in line.

"One student," Jacob said, flashing his faded college ID.

"You need to get a sticker to show you're still enrolled," the old man said.

"Sticker?" Jacob feigned ignorance. "What are you talking about?"

Normally they went through a round or two of this, but Irene stepped in before it could escalate. "Twenty-five dollars is only a suggested price. Just say you want to pay twelve."

"They'll think I'm cheap!"

"You *are* cheap."

The old man began his spiel. "Sir, every dollar you spend goes directly to the museum's collection, which is unparalleled in the country in terms of its variety and excellent—"

"Where are the dinosaurs?" Jacob asked, peering around as he pushed his ten and two singles across the counter.

"Sir, that's at the Natural History Museum across the—"

"Honey pie," he whined to Irene, "I thought you said we were going to see the dinosaurs. We didn't come out here all the way from Tacoma just to see some *art*."

"You hush," Irene snapped, as she took a pair of little sky-blue M-buttons from the man. She clamped her hand around Jacob's wrist and jammed the button into his lapel.

"Ferme la bouche," she said, then marched off into the Egyptian Wing.

Jacob doffed an imaginary hat. "I *could* be from Tacoma," he said, mostly to himself, as he walked after her.

Normally, Irene liked to start by the mummies in the ancient Near Eastern art section, but this time she kept her back to them as she passed by the long, opposite wall, which displayed the scrolls for the Egyptian Book of the Dead.

"Can you read this?" she asked Jacob, pointing to the hieroglyphics.

He'd taken two semesters of Middle Egyptian in college, since he'd done Latin and Greek in high school and needed six "ancient language" credits for his classics major. He hardly remembered any of it, but usually Irene liked it when he ad-libbed.

"Ah yes," he said. "This here is a pilot script for an ancient Egyptian police procedural called . . . let's see here . . . yes. *CSI: Akhetaten.*"

Irene didn't smile but ran her fingers along the English text on the glass as if she were blind and it was Braille. " 'A spell to keep the heat within the body of the deceased until resurrection. Which must be recited over the figure of a heavenly cow.' "

Jacob scratched an invisible beard. "Never have a figure of a heavenly cow when you need one, though. That's the trouble."

The next panel described the Hereafter. "Each of the seven gates of Osiris is monitored by an attendant, a guardian, and an announcer."

"Well, sure. Under union rules, you can't attend, guard, and announce without three separate contracts."

Still no smile. "The Egyptians believed the dead lived in a Field of Peace, which they were taken to either on a ferryboat or aboard the solar bark of Ra."

"Solar *bark*?"

"It says 'solar bark.' "

"Like a dog bark or a tree bark?"

"Unclear. And here's a spell to—interesting—a spell to transform someone into a swallow that can travel freely between the real world and the Hereafter."

"Yeah, but then you're a swallow," Jacob sighed. "Ew. It says the guardian of the third gate is the Eater of His Own Excrement. That guy better at least be getting paid scale."

He was sure this was one of his better performances, but Irene was drifting silently into the next room. She breezed through groups of Asian tourists while Jacob found himself shuffling left, right, and left again, trying not to knock two Hasidim into the five-thousand year-old Kneeling Bull Holding a Spouted Vessel.

He caught up with her inside the enormous greenhouse that enclosed the Temple of Dendur. "Are we racing?" he asked as they crossed the moat.

"I'm looking for something," she said. "Sorry, I don't need the whole Jacob Show today."

She got like this when she was in the middle of a new piece in her studio. He liked it; he missed feeling that way himself, but he understood. She was the only other person he knew who had artistic impulses. Ordinarily this made her eager to pick his brain, seeking advice and context, but she had said nothing to him at all about her recent projects, not for months. Soon she was leaning into the archway where a nineteenth-century soldier had carved his name into its gray foot: LEONARDO 1820 PS GORDE o.

"You're looking for ancient graffiti?"

"I'm looking for something"—she sighed, then sighed again with the last bit of breath—"disappointing."

Extending his arms in mock-heroic pride, Jacob stood in front of her. "Behold! *Portrait of a Profound Disappointment*. Jewish-American in Origin. Circa 2009. Oil on Skin. Meat on Bone. Tweed on Meat."

Ignoring him, she stepped into the cool antechamber at the center of the temple. There two small children were fighting over a handful of playing cards with hieroglyphics on them and trying to match them to the ones on the walls.

"Careful! Don't trip on the wire!" Irene cautioned the kids, as they tried to climb over and under it at the same time. The little girl stamped her feet on the tile floor and looked up at Jacob, with an accusing finger pointed at her brother.

"He's taking all the cards!"

"Where are your parents?" Jacob asked.

"Here," Irene said, picking a card up off the floor that the girl's brother had dropped. "Jacob, what's this one?"

The little girl looked glumly down at the funny golden cross.

"That's an ankh," Jacob explained.

"Honk!" the girl shouted.

"Ankh," Jacob repeated. "Less *h*, more *ank*."

"Ankh!" she tried again. Her brother chimed in, eager to see what was going on.

"It was a symbol of eternal life."

"What's a symbol?" the boy asked.

"It's like a big brass disk."

"Whaaaaaat?" the boy asked nervously.

"Go find your parents," Jacob said, standing aside so the pair of them could rush off. "And hold on to that card. You'll live forever!"

The children bolted around his legs, back out to the main room, and when Jacob looked back, Irene was smiling, two tears on her cheeks. Other people were trying to get into the temple now, but Jacob held a big hand out toward them and shifted his frame to block the door again. "Sorry. Private party."

Irene turned back to the graffiti etched in the wall again: A L Corry RN 1817. She moved her hand over the carved letters, and a little dust came off on them.

"What's going on?" he said, stepping over to her.

"You're going to be such a good dad," she sniffed. "I want to be around to see that."

Don't be ridiculous, Jacob wanted to say. *In ten years we'll all be sitting around George and Sara's tacky living room somewhere, with their rug rats and yours all crawling up the goddamn walls, and we'll think back on this whole year, and we'll tell the older kids about how Aunt Irene had cancer once, and they'll never even believe it.* All this, he wanted to say.

Instead he said, "Ew. You know, procreative sex is against my religion."

"Just be serious for a minute, would you?"

Jacob stood silently, mouth open, no words coming.

Finally he said, "If you want to be disappointed, let's go look at the Warhols."

They made their way out of the Temple of Dendur, bypassing the American Wing altogether and squirming through the Medieval and Greek sections on their way to the second floor Contemporary galleries. As they walked, Jacob tried to tell her about the movie he'd gone to see with Oliver the week before.

"Which movie?"

"Some stupid thing. Title from an Elvis song."

"*Can't Help Falling in Love*? With Stone Culligan?" her eyes lit up. "You *know* he tried to kill himself yesterday."

"Who did?" Jacob asked.

"Stone Culligan! It was all over the news. He and that supermodel, Branca, broke up, and he slammed his Jet Ski into a bridge. They say he bruised his spine and he's lucky to be alive!"

"Lucky to . . . you're *damn* right he's lucky to be alive. He's got the face of the *David*, and he's worth a quajillion dollars. Doesn't even have any talent, not that *that* matters to this fucking planetful of philistines."

"Keep your voice down, okay? You're scaring people."

But Jacob didn't care about the gaggle of Floridian women pretending to appreciate some Monet painting they probably had hanging up in their pastel-painted bathrooms.

"How dare he? How *dare* he? How dare he try to fucking kill himself when there are—when there are people who are legitimately—"

Irene arched an eyebrow at him. "Dying?"

Jacob scratched his arms furiously. "That's not what I was going to say."

"Yes, it is," she hissed. "Yes, it is, Jacob, and you know what? That's—that's the worst thing you've ever said to me."

"It isn't what I was going to say," he insisted—but of course it was. "Fine, it *is* what I was going to say, but that's not how I meant it."

She crossed her arms, and her eyes went black.

"You're not dying, Irene. I don't believe that. Really, I—"

"Let's drop it," she snapped.

"If you'd just—"

"I said DROP IT!"

She was so furious that Jacob stayed several feet behind her the rest of the way across the museum. As hard as it was, he remained silent as they came up to the Contemporary Wing.

Then they came to the Warhols. In better times, they had sat for hours there on the floor, talking smack about Pop Art and Anti-Art and Anti-Anti-Art and *can't we for fuck's sake just make ART-ART?*—but now Irene wasn't interested when Jacob pretended not to be able to see the enormous camouflage-patterned self-portrait of Warhol.

"Where did he go? Isn't there supposed to be a painting here?"

She was transfixed by a huge painting at the end of the aisle—Anselm Kiefer's *Bohemia Lies by the Sea*. Twenty feet long and seven feet high, it showed a wild field of pink and orange poppies with a rutted road going up the center. It was one of their favorites—but this time it was familiar in a wholly different way.

"Looks just like Shelter Island," Irene said quietly.

As soon as she said it, it brought a hollow ache to Jacob's throat, and he knew why. He hadn't thought of the painting while they'd been out there—but now he saw that it did resemble the shoreline where she had first confessed to him that she'd been sick. Where they'd drunk the bottle of wine. Down in his gut he knew it was the last time he'd been happy—right there, after she'd told him, but before he'd really believed it.

"I've got to sit down a second," Irene said.

Jacob looked all around, but there were no benches. He couldn't stand the sight of her hunching down on the ground in her beautiful white dress—the sort of dress you could get married in, on a beach anyway. He looked around for a guard.

"Hold on. Maybe—maybe someone can get you a wheelchair or something?"

"Just let me catch my breath," she warned, as she stared at her reflection in the floor.

"Irene," he tried again. "For Christ's sake, you look like a ghost's ghost. You can't—"

She wrenched herself back up off the floor without a word. For the first time he wished she still had the eye patch on. Her gaze was Gorgon-like, petrifying, unbearable.

He stood rooted to the ground as she stalked off. In the white marble floor, he saw a miserable fuck staring up at him. What a pretentious prick he was. How could he ever have thought he could save anyone from anything? He turned and looked up at the gigantic self-portrait and knew, deep down, that he was nothing but a Warhol in his soul.

By the time he'd hurried after her into the dark room full of Josef Albers squares, lit only by the sickening Robert Irwin fluorescent bulbs on the far wall, she was nowhere to be found. He expected to find her sitting on the stairs that led down into the Modern galleries, but she wasn't there either. Nor was she by the Klees, nor by the Mirós, and then—fuck—not among the O'Keeffes (which she still nursed a little junior high crush on). He spat, swore, spun around, and backtracked a little—sure that he'd just missed her and that, as exhausted as she was, she couldn't have gone far—but she was nowhere.

He dashed into Arts of Africa and Oceania and the Americas, peering behind the Ethiopian totem poles and Filipino longboats and Eskimo death shrouds. He thought he spotted her studying a Korwar ancestor figure and then, a moment later, bending down to examine a Peruvian funerary mask—but no. Was she in a ladies' room somewhere? Was she hiding in with the European Furniture? Jacob knew that all those decorative armoires bored her to tears, but if she wanted to get away from him, where better to go? He searched high and low amid the gilt caskets and marble funerary portraits.

Never before had it occurred to him how much *death* there was in museums. Paintings of dead people. Sculptures of people who'd died forever and ever ago. Ornate vases and chairs and mirrors made by some dead guy who had sold them at some point to someone, who'd then gone and died and left them to someone else who'd died, and on and on until the great undying museum got its hands on these *remains*. And every wing, every bench, every window had some dead person's name on it. The dead Robert Lehman Collection. The dead Sackler Wing. The dead Grace Rainey Rogers Auditorium. The dead Thomas J. Watson Library. Oh, let's all grab a quick bite at the dead Petrie Court Café before heading down to the dead Ruth and dead Harold Uris Center for Education. It wasn't a museum so much as a mausoleum.

He rushed into the Branch Bank, with all that bland American furniture behind the facade, and then back out again on his way up to the Tiffany stained glass and then back down again toward Arms and Armor. Wall after wall of deathly instruments—swords and axes and crossbows and harquebuses. She wasn't by the fifth-century red-figured vases from Greece or the twelfth-century bronze spearheads from the Trojan War. He ventured back into the Medieval Wing. There was nothing left to do but cover ground he'd been through already, in case she'd circled back. Having been everywhere else, he came back to the Warhols, past *Bohemia Lies by the Sea*, and there, at the bottom of the stairs he'd first come down, was Irene.

She was just sitting there, staring out into the room. Had she been there the whole time? Had he blown right by her? She was looking at a pair of Klee paintings. On the left was a round-edged, purple and pink fantasy—little houses all in rows with fat little windows and doors. *Oriental Pleasure Garden*, it was called. Beside it, *Stricken City*. A brown and sooty monstrosity, a jagged bolt of death through its center.

"Jesus," he said, sitting down beside her. "I was running all over looking for you."

Her eyes peered up from behind the veil of her let-down hair, and he could see they were cloudy. Looking almost right through him. Her skin had turned so white and bloodless that it no longer blended with her makeup. She looked like someone wearing an Irene mask made in a knock-off factory.

"Fuck," he said. "Let's get you up. Come on, walk with me, okay? Can you?"

With his arm around Irene, Jacob was able to coax her to her feet and then slowly through the crowded aisles of the modern art exhibits and out through the atrium of marble Greeks. One step at a time he guided her toward the lobby and the exit beyond—hoping that everyone would just think they were two lovers unable to be an inch apart. He wanted, so badly, for her to exit under her own power.

"This was nice," she said as they came to the revolving doors. "I had a really nice time."

"You're delirious. You had a terrible time. I fucked it all up. But that's okay."

Jacob smiled as he eased past the security guards, trying to seem nonchalant. They stepped out into the blazing heat. Crowds milled down below them, pushed back from behind them. Traffic crawled along Fifth Avenue. He just had to get her into one of the cabs. He just had to get her down the steps.

"It's hot," she said, surprised.

"Hang on. I'm going to carry you," he said.

"The hell you are," she whispered, but he wasn't listening. He reached down with his free arm to the clammy space behind her knees and eased her up off the ground. She was lighter than a book bag. He could feel her bones through her legs and her white dress, which he was careful to make sure didn't ride up as he came toward the line of yellow cabs at the bottom. One at a time, slow and steady, he carried her down the steps.

"Hey!" someone yelled. "These two kids just got married!"

Jacob didn't have the wherewithal to answer, much less to explain.

"Look, he's bringing her to the car!" someone else shouted.

Just a few people at first, but then more and more, with each step they went down, turned and raised their phones to snap a picture of the young newlyweds. The barbershop quartet looked over and transitioned, sweetly, into a new tune. An old Elvis song.

" 'Wise men say . . .' " the four men sang in splendid harmony. " 'Only fools rush in . . .' "

Jacob looked down at his would-be bride, blond hair flowing over her face as her eyes locked onto his: afraid, exhausted, resigned, indignant, confused. She threw her head back and began laughing.

At the bottom of the sidewalk, the crowds parted and clapped. Irene reached up and kissed Jacob's sweaty, stubbled cheek. A cab pulled to a stop at the curb, and the driver rushed out and came around to open the door for them.

Jacob eased the beaming Irene onto the cool leather seats inside, the air-conditioning on sweet and loud. She clasped her hands over her sweating chest.

"Where to, lovebirds?" the driver asked.

"Mount Sinai Hospital," Jacob said, "and step on it."

SEPTEMBER

Sara hurried down the middle of a Duane Reade pharmacy, her empty *New York Journal* tote bag dangling from her right hand, the cheap gray linoleum squeaking beneath her worn ballet flats, and an Internet coupon folded in her left hand. *Hosiery, Shaving Needs, Incontinence. Greeting Cards, Tacky Crap, Well-Picked-Over Back-to-School Supplies. Fun-Size Bags of Candy Out Way Too Soon for Halloween.* Her shoes, like twin missiles, guided her to the same aisle that she went to every other day, just after giving Irene her afternoon dose of Prednicen-M at four o'clock. It knocked Irene out for one hour, allowing Sara this small window to pick up the supplies that she didn't trust William or George or Jacob to obtain properly.

Adult Diapers, Orthopedics, Dietary Supplements. As she came into aisle two, she saw immediately that the store had not gotten in a new shipment of Assure high-calorie meal-supplement milkshakes since her last visit. Dr. Zarrani had said Irene needed to keep gaining weight or she'd end up back in the hospital. Getting her released had been hard enough the first time. After Jacob had literally carried her to the emergency room, the nurses had treated her for dehydration and malnourishment as if she were just one more idiot off the street who had forgotten to drink water despite the heat wave.

"Didn't you tell them she's a patient here?" Sara had demanded of Jacob when she'd finally gotten there. When a nurse finally wandered over, Sara asked, "Doesn't it say in your system that she's got cancer?" The nurse stared down at the chart. "Who? *Her?*"

It had then taken two hours to get her charts sent down from oncology. Nobody could find the paperwork that said Sara was to be treated like family and allowed to know what was going on. Not that she didn't ask Irene to call her father twice a day. Then three more hours before Dr. Zarrani had been able to get her transferred upstairs to the twelfth floor east—not the nice, peaceful Zen garden part where they did the chemo treatments, but the other side of the building where there were beds for patients who needed to be admitted. *Admitted*. That was a joke.

Irene was still insisting none of this was at all serious. "Sara, relax. Jacob overreacted. I just keep forgetting to eat."

An RN had come to tell them that the doctors (invisible, apparently) wanted to run a litany of new scans. A nurse manager came by, listened gravely to Sara's concerns for less than three minutes, then disappeared. No one but the nurses came by all night, and Sara stayed, if only to make sure Irene didn't get up and walk out. Finally around seven a.m., five doctors all buzzed in at once while Sara was half conscious. They chirped about scan results and potassium levels and speaking to researchers in Georgia.

"When is Dr. Zarrani coming in?" Sara asked.

"He'll be here at ten a.m.," one said, and then they all vanished before Sara could explain that Dr. Zarrani was a she. It took five more hours to run the paperwork to clear and release Irene, on the condition that she stop the long walks and the heavy lifting and eat three square meals a day.

Irene had lost six pounds in the two weeks since the last chemo treatment. And it wasn't like she had that much weight to lose in the first place. She was five foot ten and 107 pounds. Sara had hoped she would be scared enough to not want to be carried to the curb again. She'd trusted that when William brought her back to his apartment, he'd make sure she ate something once in a while, even if the chemo nauseated her and nothing seemed to taste right anymore.

Well. Those were mistakes Sara wasn't about to make again.

Irene had made it exactly one week on her own recognizance. She'd promised William she'd stay in his apartment while he went out on interviews, relaxing and watching movies and eating takeout. Instead, she'd waited in her pajamas until William left, then changed into a T-shirt and jeans and gone to the gallery. She'd sculpted there until a half hour before William was due to return, then rush back, change into her PJs, and nuke the same three half-empty moo-shu pork containers that she fished back out of the trash every morning. What had she *thought* was going to happen?

One day Irene collapsed at the gallery. Of course, nearly ten minutes had passed before Abeba realized she wasn't meditating. "In a heap on the floor?" Sara had shouted, when she got to the ER again. "Please tell me someone told them this time that she's already a patient here?"

Different nurse, same story. "Cancer? This girl?"

Irene had lost eight more pounds. Sara couldn't recall the last time she herself had weighed only ninety-nine pounds—middle school? Dr. Zarrani's examination revealed that Irene's mouth and throat were peppered with stinging canker sores—a common side effect of the chemo and a likely reason Irene hadn't been eating. Why Irene hadn't mentioned that she was having trouble swallowing was entirely beyond Sara's comprehension. Probably a hundred times a day, Sara asked her how she was feeling, and every time all she would say was "Fine!" Why did she have to make it so difficult for everyone?

It was too much, Sara had said. They needed some backup. At least *one* real adult besides herself. Irene did claim to be *trying* to reach her father but said she wasn't getting through to him. Where the hell was he? Mongolia? Not as if they didn't have phones there. But no, of course, when Irene nodded off and Sara checked her phone log, it showed no outgoing calls to Mongolia or anywhere.

So it was still only Sara in charge when Dr. Zarrani insisted on inserting a "percutaneous endoscopic gastrostomy tube" into Irene's stomach—the only way to make sure she got vital nutrients. Four full days at the hospital this time, getting the surgery, recovering, while Sara learned how to rig an IV bag full of Assure milkshakes so that it would drip slowly through the PEG tube and into Irene's stomach. What else could she do? The boys were too obtuse to handle it, and Irene couldn't be trusted to do it herself.

The next day Sara had come to William's door with suitcases in hand. "You can go live with George if you want," she had told him, "but either way I'm staying here." William had not argued, smart boy, and within minutes had set up an air mattress for her in the dining nook. Sara had three weeks of unused vacation time saved up. She promised Luther that she'd edit five stories a day from home and answer the forwarded calls when the new intern was out or in meetings. She canceled appointments with caterers and bands and florists. She and George still hadn't picked a place, much less set a date. The apartment search was likewise forgotten. But none of that mattered now. She'd stay through Christmas if she had to, no matter how much Irene hated it, filling IV bags with the Assure she'd come to Duane Reade to buy.

She scoured the shelves, looking for Double Boost, which was always in short supply, since one Double gave you twice as many vitamins and minerals as a Regular. Why did they even make the regular? Who'd rather drink two of these instead of one?

The last set of scans had come back during the second hospital stay. The tumors still weren't shrinking. They weren't growing either, but they soon would be, now that the chemo and radiation treatments had ended. And the doctors couldn't just keep stepping up the treatments forever. It was time to try something experimental, like drug trials. Sara tried not to think about the estimated odds of success.

22 percent

16 percent

9.2 percent

Irene was like a child. She took every opportunity to stall in taking her medications—pretending to nap or to be busy in the bathroom. Saying, "Let's do it in a few minutes," when a few minutes rapidly became an hour, or two, even when these things had to be done strictly according to the color-coded Excel spreadsheet schedule that Sara had taped up in every room of the apartment.

The Prednicen-M had to be taken four times a day with an Assure. Irene had to apply a 1 percent hydrocortisone cream three times a day to the rash that was being caused by her denosumab injections. Actually, *Sara* had to apply the cream, because there were some spots on her middle back that Irene couldn't quite reach. Then every morning, thirty minutes before her first meal, Irene had to have one Fosimax pill with water, after which she had to stand upright for thirty minutes to prevent heartburn. For the canker sores, Irene had to rinse with a mouthwash of milk of magnesia and Benadryl liquid five times per day, and it had to be mixed fresh each time. Four times a day she had to take amphotericin B, for thrush. Zofran as needed for nausea; Vicoprofen as needed for pain.

Because it was hard for Irene to swallow, Sara had been quartering these pills every day, then grinding the pieces up with a mortar and pestle like some sort of apothecary. After a week of this, Sara had deep-red calluses all over her palm, so George went back to Sur la Table and bought a battery-powered spice mill that worked much better.

The milkshakes had to be poured into the IV bags, which could then be hung from the standing lamp by the couch, the cabinet knobs in the kitchen, the shower rod in the bathroom, and the coat hook in the bedroom. Jacob had affixed a 3M Command utensil hook behind every chair in every room that Irene might conceivably use. The hospital had given them only two IV bags, and these had to be washed after each use or the chalky residue clogged the opening.

William was there most of the time, but he was hopelessly disappointing at these tasks. George and Jacob came by nearly every day to help out for a few hours, and this gave Sara some time to do her editing and to sleep and to take anxious walks around Madison Square Park—but there were things the boys truly couldn't do: Irene's urine output had to be measured, so Dr. Zarrani could be sure that she was retaining enough fluids. This involved Irene putting a plastic measuring device on the toilet seat (which she forgot if Sara didn't remind her), peeing into it, and then calling the results out to Sara, who was keeping a record down to the milliliter. There were programmed cell phone alerts. There were laminated lists of hospital phone numbers for each of them to keep in their wallets in case there were questions. And still it felt like they were losing this fight.

Poor George had been on duty when Irene began having horrible cramps and had made a complete hash of everything while he tried to help without waking up Sara. Very sweet, but it meant three hours of agony for Irene while George tried to follow Internet instructions for a lower back massage that would ease her cramps. When Sara finally woke up, it had taken her ten minutes to get on the horn to three different people, who eventually concluded that, because of her all-liquid diet, Irene needed to have some senna tea twice a day to make sure she also had a regular bowel movement. That was another thing to log and another thing the boys didn't keep track of, along with cleaning the area around the PEG tube carefully with antibiotics and dealing with the mess that resulted that time when the cap came off Irene's tube in her sleep and the contents of her stomach dribbled out all over the couch.

"Why isn't she fighting this?" Sara had cried to Dr. Zarrani.

"She may be very depressed," Dr. Zarrani had said. "But she wants to get better."

Sara wasn't convinced. Irene seemed pissed off, not depressed.

"This is so goddamn demoralizing!" Irene shouted at least once a day, as if it were all Sara's fault. She was cranky not to have time to get to the studio anymore. She sketched in bed and on the couch while they watched endless reruns of *¡Vámonos, Muchachos!*, but half the time she fell asleep after drawing just a few lines. Then she'd wake up in an even fouler mood, as if she'd just been cheated out of valuable time.

"This is fucking torture!" she screamed, throwing her charcoals across the room.

Sara wanted to tell her that she'd get on the phone to the UN right away. File briefs under the Geneva Conventions. She'd throw one in for herself while she was at it. Because it was torture for Sara to see her best friend in this state. Torture to be barely sleeping, to be missing work, to hardly ever sleep in the same bed as George or have a meal that wasn't takeout. Her only social interactions, besides complaining to the boys and yelling at her interns over the phone, were during the brief times she walked to Duane Reade.

Lately she'd begun lingering, just to have the breathing room.

Sara stared at the cardboard sleeve that held the six individual Assure bottles together. It had a nice picture of an elderly woman on it, looking full of life and ready for a hot night down at the Old Folks' Home Ballroom, doing the Buffalo Shuffle with a nice half-blind Vietnam War veteran with some Viagra squirreled away among the cataract medications on the nightstand. Sara pushed pack after pack to the side, looking for the Double Boost, muttering to herself, *Good for you, Grandma. Go down swinging. Young at heart. Golden years and all that jazz. But if you could just leave a little Double Boost for my friend here, who is young at heart and young at body, still quite squarely in her Regular years, that'd be swell.*

At the pharmacy window, there was just one man in line, an older man wearing a ridiculous green spandex unitard, propping up a bicycle. Magnanimously, he gestured for Sara to go ahead of him to the counter—the pharmacist was somewhere in the back.

"She's getting my things already," he explained, as Sara thanked him. Setting her heavy bag down on the counter, she checked her wristwatch. Good. She would make it back by four-thirty.

"Aren't you a little young for those things?" the man said, gesturing to the Assures. Sara looked down at Grandma Golden Years, then back up at him. He looked a little as if he'd rolled right out of an Assure commercial: *Senior citizens, on the go!*

"Picking them up for my nana," Sara lied. She didn't quite know why she felt the need to lie—she didn't even call her grandmother nana, and she lived in Marblehead, two hundred miles away. "Don't ask me why, but she loves these things."

The man cringed, cutely. "There's a café near here that makes wheatgrass shakes. I'm totally addicted. I'm there three times a day. Drinking *grass,* for God's sake!"

Sara laughed because his teeth were tinged a faint wintergreen color, and his breath smelled faintly like a lawn mower.

"Picking up?" the pharmacist asked her, a round-faced Polynesian woman with black, unmoving, implacable eyes. BETTIE, said her ID badge.

Bettie, Sara thought miserably. "Bettie!" she said cheerfully, "Could you ring these up for me?"

Bettie's face was immovable, as it had been the Thursday before, as it had been the Thursday before that. "If you're not picking up a prescription, then you have to take your purchase to the front."

Sara spoke sweetly, though under her breath she cursed all the Betties that ever were. "They're a little backed up right now, and my—my nana, really needs these."

She wasn't beyond pulling out the cancer card when it might help in this type of situation—the cancer card had gotten her into it, after all. But she didn't want the nice bicycle man to know she'd lied about her nana.

"Doctor Von Hatter? Your total comes to thirty-four fifty with the Big Apple discount card."

But the bicycle man made no move to take his bag from Bettie. "Why don't you help this nice young lady first? There's no one else waiting."

Sara smiled appreciatively, but Bettie just stared at the doctor. "Thirty-four dollars and fifty cents."

"Charles *always* rings me up back here," Sara insisted.

"Charles isn't here on Thursdays."

"Yes, but—look. I pick up prescriptions here twice a week for Irene Richmond. You remember me? Prednicen-M? Zofran? Vicoprofen? The one percent hydrocortisone cream?"

Bettie stretched a hand toward her. "If you have an authorization to pick up for Richmond, I can check to see if she's due for a refill."

Sara knew Irene wasn't due for a refill on anything until Sunday.

"This is ridiculous," the old man said. "There's no one on line here but me. Zofran and Prednicen? Why don't you help this young lady so she can take care of her nana?"

Bettie shook her head. "She's not special. She can take her purchases to the front."

Even as the bicycler continued to try to reason with the pharmacist, those three words stuck in Sara's side like tiny prickers. For she was special, and had always believed it. She was more punctual, and she was better prepared. Driven harder and by purer purpose. Kinder to others and more loyal. Always recycling and never littering. Better behaved and never hypocritical. Harder working at the office, tipping more generously, and possessing of a thousand pardons.

And yet she couldn't save Irene just by trying hardest or being best. Because no one was immune to tragedy. No matter how respectfully Sara lived, death could not respect her in return. She, Irene, *all* of them were susceptible to collapse, regardless of preparations or punctuality or propriety. None of them were special.

Doctor bicycle man was getting angry now. He'd seemed so nice, and now here was this *rage* bubbling up. Even he was just another angry person in this claustrophobic fucking city—

Like her. She was furious all the time now. At Dr. Zarrani, who had seemed so on top of things initially but was now proving hard to reach and sounding hapless in the face of the usual treatments failing. At Luther, for allowing one of the city's greatest newspapers to become a purveyor of garbage, and at the people who preferred escaping into garbage to caring about real news. At herself, for editing said garbage as if it mattered how uncluttered its sentences were. At Jacob, for refusing to settle down and forever distracting himself from the beautiful poetry she knew he could write if he would allow even a sliver of joy into his worldview. And even at Irene, for her completely unacceptable, irrational, disrespectful, nonsensical, whatever-may-come attitude toward absolutely everything in her life, right down to dying—

And there, standing at the back of a Duane Reade while a spandex-clad septuagenarian argued with an apple-faced pharmacist, Sara first realized that Irene was going to die.

She wasn't getting better, no matter how many pills Sara crushed, no matter how rigidly she held to the color-coded schedule, no matter how she arranged the cells in the Excel spreadsheet. Their final tally was always the same: Irene was dying—and *fast*—and to Sara, knowing this was like seeing the line at the bottom of the bill. The balance, to be paid in full, for all the disappointments listed above.

"Never mind," Sara said, picking up her bag back again from the counter. The bicycle doctor looked as if he were going to try to convince her to stand her ground against this abuse of power—but Sara's ever-patient smile disarmed him, "Really, no problem."

For I am not special, she thought, as she turned her back on Bettie, who was again asking the doctor for the $34.50 he owed for the prescription co-pay. Sara passed back up the *Makeup, Travel Size Shampoo, Children's Toy* aisle toward the front of the store, and she even intended to do just as she'd said—wait in the line in the front like everybody else. But her feet guided her instead toward the door. She slipped the Internet coupon into the tote bag and pulled out her sunglasses. A stock boy paused as he dutifully unloaded tubes of toothpaste from a gray box onto the shelves. Did he know what she was about to do? She smiled at him and—so easy—he smiled back and stepped out of her way.

She walked directly out the front door, not pausing to look back when the little door alarm went off. The harried cashier in the front, dealing with the still-long line, didn't look up, and neither did the stock boy. Her heart pounded; she felt wonderfully dizzy. There was sidewalk beneath her feet, and she felt like herself again. At the corner she had to pause for the WALK signal to come on. She'd never stolen so much as a Chapstick in her entire life. The tote-bag straps strained against her clenched fingers, yet it seemed to weigh nothing at all.

It was only three more blocks to William's apartment, but something caught her eye: an M5 bus going downtown to South Street/Whitehall Station. Before she quite knew what they were doing, her feet angled away from their initial target and carried her to the bus doors just before they sighed shut. She pulled off her sunglasses so as not to seem rude when she smiled at the driver. She set the bag down on the ground and pulled her wallet out while he closed the doors and began accelerating out into the spotty traffic along Fifth Avenue.

"Oh!" she said, as she looked into the wrong pocket in the wallet. "Oh no! My card fell out!" And she looked up at the driver; it took him barely a heartbeat to reassure her. He handed her a little pamphlet from the side panel. "Go on in. It's okay, miss. If it was a monthly, you just call this number, and they'll replace it."

"Thank you *so* much." She felt a snug sensation, low in her throat. The driver was pleased to help a damsel in distress, and she was pleased to have pleased him, and also pleased not to have paid for the ride.

She sat down and looked out the window, past her reflection at the city rushing by. Windows reaching up into the stratosphere. Tunnels under the pavement, ferrying trains at breakneck speeds. And everywhere in between people walking every which way, wanting every which thing, all living and dying in some mysterious measure. Sara closed her eyes and shut the city out. Her phone buzzed in her pocket, but she didn't answer it. Either it was Irene, or George, wondering where she was. *I don't know,* Sara thought.

When she'd get back. *I don't know.* Where the medicine was. How to measure the urine or how to get the gunk out of the tube. *I don't know.* The phone stopped buzzing. Sara didn't check the message. Letting go of that last thing she thought was under her control was a high like no other. Realizing it never was. That nobody ever had control over anything.

Sara rode the bus all the way down to Whitehall Station. There, it went around the block and began to carry her back up again.

OCTOBER

George stared at his smooth white coffee cup, determined that, by the time he finished it, his life would be forever changed. Before this burned Starbucks coffee, he'd been George Murphy, jovial drinker, perhaps at times a little weak willed, not just with alcohol but with many things: sleeping past his alarm, eating at the McDonald's drive-through when he was in a hurry (and also when he wasn't), spending too much money on things he didn't need (at this he glanced guiltily toward the bulging Barnes & Noble bag on the seat beside him), and listening to the same rock music he liked in college, even though he *knew* it put him in an angry mood. Before this cup of burned coffee, yes, he'd been a man of bad, unbreakable habits. And yes, he, like the rest of them, had begun to go a little crazy with everything that was going on lately.

But *after* this cup, an entirely new George would emerge. A George more like these other productive and wholesome people at the bookstore café! A George who listened to peaceful, acoustic, harmonious songs like the one playing overhead, "Not Worth Fighting" by Envoy. This would be the soundtrack of the new, punctual, in-shape, fiscally responsible George.

Most important, the *sober* George. He wouldn't have another drink. These days it brought him little of the weightless joy it once had. More often than not, now, it just weighed him down more. It made him hazy and slow-witted. It was hard to admit it, even just to himself, but it had cost him a potential job at Harvard. He'd been lucky enough they'd called him, but now it had been weeks. Who was he kidding? He'd been so wretchedly nervous before the interview that he'd popped into a bar to calm down, thinking it might help to be around some people. He'd just had one beer. Full of confidence, he'd walked into the room where Drs. McManus and Schwartz from the physics department were waiting to interview him. Then, paralyzed by the certainty that the men could smell the suds on his breath, George had found himself barely able to answer even their simplest questions about the collapse of 237 Lyrae V.

Well, no more. That was the old George Murphy. Forever he would look back on *that* moment as the turning point—well, as a turning point that had then led to *this* turning point—to *this* cup of burned coffee, after which nothing would ever be the same.

Because now he had a reason to turn it all around. And screw his own well-being and his own future—those had been proven to be woefully inadequate to the task. That's why he'd been put between this rock and a hard place. Thank God it wasn't Sara.

"Thank you," he said out loud.

No one in the café even turned their head as he spoke to himself. They were all busily tapping away on their laptops, earbuds shoved halfway down their eustachian tubes. He heard no clinking of glasses or gurgling of taps, just the occasional bulldozer burping of the milk frother, and the jackhammer grinding of the Frappuccino machine. Otherwise, eerie silence prevailed throughout the café. When you said a prayer from a barstool, you could count on the guy two down from you to raise his glass and say "Amen." Drunks were just polite that way.

George's mother had always believed that a prayer had to be said out loud to really warrant heavenly attention. As a boy, he had said his nightly "Now I lay me down to sleep" at a normal volume, as if speaking to someone on the other side of the bed. The habit had stayed on at college. Jacob was a night showerer, and so George had been able to keep it up without him realizing. Once Jacob had come back for a forgotten razor blade and come quite close to catching him. "Talking to yourself, Georgie-boy? You know some people would say that's a bad sign, but I recommend you really *engage* with those voices in your head. It's important to listen. You really want to do exactly what they say."

What a bastard! But God, how George loved him. No one else made him laugh so hard. He and Irene were like the siblings George had never had. And now God was taking her away from him, from all of them, and George hated His ever-living guts for it.

But he had to do it. He had to give Him what He wanted. In the end, Jacob hadn't been the reason George stopped praying. Nor had he been at all persuaded by the "evil liberal atheist communist professors" Grandpa Earl had warned him about. No, when the professors spoke about the cosmos being big and him being infinitesimally small, it had only reassured George of his irrelevance before forces he could never hope to control or understand. First Darwin and then Nietzsche had failed to kill his God.

And then, during a seminar on Einstein and relativity, George had had a real epiphany: for every observable phenomenon, there were a million unobservable ones. So many things that his senses told him were true were only illusory: the straightness of time's arrow; the existence of only three dimensions; the solidity of rocks and the fluidity of water. Every simple, rational phenomenon was eventually unexplained by something wildly problematic and complex. He had no trouble believing that God and heaven could exist within the vastness that his brilliant professors couldn't define with formulas and hypotheses. And George believed in miracles and coincidences and mysterious ways. But he also believed that no matter how good a person he'd tried to be in every other respect, God had no mercy on he who'd begun having a nip of J&B each night while his roommate showered, instead of praying the Lord his soul to keep.

Now it was time to make a new bet. Now it was all on *his* shoulders. Irene needed him, and George had been stone-cold sober for three days. Not such a long time, but it was a start. He slapped his palm on the little café table. Then he said a quick Hail Mary, successfully spooking an old Chinese couple sitting at the table next to him. He polished off the last of his coffee and crushed the white paper cup in his hand. He lifted his shopping bag, and the plastic dug into his hand as he carried it across the street between the honking, blaring cars trying to get onto Queens Boulevard. By the time he got to the other side, he'd be a new man.

Across the street Irene and Mrs. Cho spoke amiably on the steps outside Super-Wellness Spa & Nails!, owned by one of William's aunts. George approached with a wave, hoping they hadn't been waiting long. Spiritual revelations were important and all, but Irene couldn't risk getting the flu, and September had ended with an unsparing cold front coming down from Canada, sending everyone scrambling for air-conditioner covers and pulling wool sweaters out of deep storage. Everyone George encountered seemed to be coming down with something, and Sara was Purell-ing everyone's hands every five seconds, so Irene wouldn't catch pneumonia.

Irene, at least, seemed to be glad about the sudden need for extra layers, as loose sweaters were gratefully *in* that fall—at least this was what she'd told George when he'd taken her to Anthropologie after her appointment last Saturday—and perfectly suited to covering the nub of the PEG tube that was taped flat against her stomach. She'd managed to keep her weight steady, and Dr. Zarrani had seen "positive signs" from the latest scans. The tumors seemed to be responding to these new experimental drugs. No one knew what tipped the scales for one person and not for the next. A PET scan could only see so much.

So there was cause for hope. George wasn't too proud to beg

God for help. Better men than him had done it, and plenty worse had seen mercy.

"How was the session?" he asked Irene.

"Good," she said, "I really think it's making a difference. I know you think it's stupid."

"I don't at all!" George protested.

Irene winked at Mrs. Cho, who shook her head as if to say there was nothing to be done about cynics like him.

George jogged a bit on the step, trying not to be annoyed. Why did everyone think he was so skeptical?

And yet he still couldn't stop himself from twinging, just a little, when Mrs. Cho took Irene's head firmly between her two hands and rubbed her temples in tight, concentric circles. She murmured in Korean and began to sweep her hands down Irene's neck.

"Good work today. Remember, feel the mysterious essence. The transcendental spirit. Everything has a vital life force: your body, your tumors, the ants on the pavement, the trees that the ants climb toward the light from the sun, which is alive, just like the moon."

George took a deep breath. Once a week, for three weeks now, Irene had been coming here, to a storage room full of bronze jars of GiGi bikini wax and crimson bottles of OPI Nail Lacquer, so that Mrs. Cho could perform this laying-on-hands ritual, lighting rose-hip candles and stretching Irene out on a folding table so that Mrs. Cho could throw powders in the air and mutter Korean incantations. Mrs. Cho had invited him to sit in on the first session, provided he could do something about all his negative energy. But as it turned out, his negative energy was persistent—and so George had begun excusing himself to the bar across the street. A nice place with a good atmosphere and—never mind. The nearby bookstore wasn't so bad.

Mrs. Cho moved her hands about a half an inch above Irene's body, not actually touching her. Her voice shook as she said, "Everything which is living radiates this essential force which animates all life throughout the universe. It is the electricity flowing in your nerve endings. It is the magnetism of your blood, which encircles your organs, and gushes throughout your veins and pumps inside of your heart."

George grimaced. True, the human body contained weak magnetic fields created by iron-bearing nanoparticles and the rotational states of protein molecules and free radical reactions. But it was on the order of one tenth of one *milli*tesla—perhaps enough to help homing pigeons and bats and sea turtles get around, but not enough to kill cancer cells. Mrs. Cho claimed this energy could be harnessed through chanting to create a healing warmth and realign the walls of Irene's cells. Well, who knows? Maybe it could.

"We can measure this great and powerful energy with the life within ourselves, within our hands and our breath. Your body holds everything of the earth and everything of the universe within it. This air that you are breathing contains the dust of distant stars collapsing. *Remember.* Doubt is only the denial of happiness." Was George imagining it, or was she staring at him? "Happiness must be invited. You must allow happiness to enter into you, for happiness is the cure for all disease."

George felt that happiness was kind of a tall order when the disease involved the total humiliation of the diseased. Unbearable headaches and constant nausea and aching joints and loss of bowel control and thinning hair and fingernails so soft that Irene had lost two of them just trying to sharpen a pencil. Still, maybe Mrs. Cho had a point, because fingernails or no, Irene still sketched happily for hours on end—beautiful, intricate designs that he studied when Irene inevitably conked out at some point. Were these finished pieces? It knotted George's throat to think of these pages and pages of plans that might never be executed.

Mrs. Cho was glaring at him again, so he faked a huge sunflower of a smile, lest his doubt emanate from his *chi* or something and deny Irene any curative happiness. He had to admit that, as Irene gave Mrs. Cho a parting hug, she did seem a lot happier.

"Remember," Mrs. Cho advised as she let go of Irene, "just for today, you will not be upset. You will not be afraid. You will be thankful and attentive. Kindness to all those around you, and whether you open your eyes or close them, clasp your fingers in prayer and contemplate with your whole heart. Say it out loud, and believe it, inside. Just for today."

George tried so hard not to laugh. They said goodbye to Mrs. Cho and went on their way, back toward the E train.

"How do you feel?" he asked.

"*Really* good," Irene said. She spoke softly, as usual these days. George strained to hear her over the sporadic honking of the backed-up cars. What sounded like a stadium's worth of voices echoed off the twin-level brick mall that lined the block. Ahead, at the corner, he could see a long stream of people crossing the road and heading toward the train.

George supposed it might be a store's grand opening, or perhaps they were protesting something. Maybe some celebrity was, inexplicably, dining at the Garcia's Mexican Restaurant on the corner. With a jolt he realized that Irene was still speaking.

". . . get incredibly *hot* all over whichever part of me she puts her hands over. Most of the time it's like a warm, soothing heat, like a bath or sunshine. I swear, it's weird, but when she moves over my eye or my elbow, it gets *very* intense. Almost to the point that I feel like I *am* actually burning up—like I have a *fever* or something."

Fifty years ago we'd have just given you sugar pills, George thought to himself as they followed the pack of people down into the subway station—where was everyone going? Irene went on, quietly, about the shaman ritual stuff, and how she was sleeping better and feeling more alert and less nauseous.

Down at the bottom of the stairs at last, he saw the problem.

MTA workers were cross-honoring people's Long Island Rail Road tickets because LIRR service to Manhattan was apparently disrupted—and so there was general bedlam and endless echoing down around the turnstiles, as people who had lost their tickets argued with transit employees. But still, *why* would so many people be coming into the city from Long Island on a Saturday afternoon in October? Ordinarily if there was a service disruption, passengers would be impatient, hurried, angry. But most of these people seemed downright exuberant. Giddy. Drunk, even. Had a Yankees or Mets game just let out? No, neither of the stadiums was on this line, and besides, practically everyone here was under thirty, and most looked under twenty. And not a foam finger in sight!

As they got through the turnstile onto the jam-packed subway platform, George noticed that many of the horde were wearing rock concert T-shirts. George had never heard of a single one of the bands.

He was worried that Irene was already looking completely exhausted when the E train finally arrived. They squeezed inside, but it was filled wall to wall with rock fans. A rather confused-looking older man in a gray suit and glasses offered his seat to Irene. George thanked him and hung somewhat oddly off the bar over her.

"Let me take your bag," she insisted.

"No, no," he urged. "It's really heavy."

She said something else, but very softly again, and George, distracted by the jostling of several loud concert fans behind him, didn't hear her at all. "What?"

"I said, what on earth did you buy?" Irene rubbed at her throat, which clearly was sore.

"Just some books for work," George lied. He was a bad liar, and what's more, he knew Irene knew it.

She arched a thin eyebrow at him, but he turned away to glare at the concert-shirted people behind him, who were shouting much, much louder now. The train was crawling through the tunnel.

George watched the dark wall sliding past behind Irene's head, the spray-paint rising and falling like an antic heartbeat. They could have walked to Manhattan faster!

Looking over his shoulder, George was soon able to size up the people making the most noise. Three high-school-age girls were hanging on the same pole as a humongous boy who was drinking directly from a bottle of Jack Daniel's. Each time he took a huge gulp from the bottle—God, George could *smell* it—he would release a roar like Simba at the end of *The Lion King*, and the pack of girls would collapse into hysterical giggling. George glared at them, but they were oblivious to everyone else in the train car. He could see immediately that the boy was very drunk—past a point that George knew, but only really by inference. Past the point where he wouldn't remember whatever things occurred between that point and the next morning.

Simba was wearing Birkenstocks, trendy skater shorts, and a North Face fleece. His hair was longer and more feathered than the hair of the girls surrounding him. These girls were rail thin and tanned, still, in mid-October. Instead of concert T-shirts, they were wearing tight dark jeans and the sort of wide-necked sweaters designed to show off carefully selected bra straps, which were, from left to right: fuschia, neon green, and black velvet.

George sniffed. Irene, with her white sweater and her golden scarf, looked like something out of another world. He tried smiling at her, but her eyes were shut tight against the sight of Simba, belching to the applause of the girls.

"What do these assholes think they're doing?" George whispered.

"Oh, they're probably going to that Envoy concert at Madison Square Garden," Irene said. "Don't you remember Sara was saying she wanted to go?"

George couldn't believe it. "An *Envoy* concert? Come on. Seriously? They're like a stoner pacifist love-in granola peace-sign band! This jerk's acting like he's going to Megadeth!"

Irene spoke out of the left half of her mouth. "We were young once too."

Jesus, what was he doing now? Swinging the bottle of Jack around and nearly clocking a scared-looking old lady in the head! George looked around furiously at all the other people on the subway—was no one going to do something? No, of course not. Everyone was just standing around rolling their eyes at one another. George gritted his teeth.

"Hey! Just ignore him, okay? We'll be at Fifty-ninth soon, and we'll transfer to the six anyway."

George watched Irene, sitting there choking down green sludge. He knew she was right.

"Just put your head back," George said softly. "I'll wake you when we get to the stop."

She shook her head, flinching as Mr. Jack Daniel's released yet another roar.

"HEY!" George found himself saying. "Come on. Keep it down!"

The boy staggered into the pole and bounced off again. This sent the three girls into fits of laughter, one of them backing up right into George.

"Hey, seriously, watch it!" he said, louder. The girl sneered at him, then looked away.

"Cut it out!" Irene kicked him gently with her foot. "You're just going to piss them off."

George was clenching his fists already but felt them go even tighter at Irene's soft-spoken implication that this guy would surely clobber mild-mannered George into next week.

"It's just you're here, trying to rest, and these assholes are—"

"George!"

Irene had a look on her face that he knew well. It was a get-your-shit-together face. He looked around for someone else who might intervene—where the hell was Jacob when you needed him? By this point, Jacob would be cramming the bottle of Jack down Simba's throat, and what's more, Irene would be clapping him on the back for it! Why did he get to rant and rave and fly off the handle all the time, but whenever George raised his voice even a little, Sara or Irene clucked at him?

The train made a sudden sideways move, and George watched the boy lurch forward and unwittingly spill his Jack. The splash hit George's arm, and then a fine constellation of brown dots appeared all over Irene's white sweater.

That's when George heard himself screaming.

"WHAT THE FUCK IS THE MATTER WITH YOU?"

Just like that there was silence in car. Outside, just the slow grinding on the tracks.

"IS YOUR BRAIN SO FUCKING SMALL THAT YOU ACTUALLY BELIEVE YOU ARE THE ONLY PERSON ON THE GODDAMN PLANET?"

The hulking kid stared, but it was impossible to tell if he really understood the words coming out of George's mouth.

"Hey, hey," one girl was saying, "don't freak out, okay? We're just having a good time."

George couldn't stand the offended expression on her face, as if she'd simply been behaving as anyone would. He felt cold all over.

"What about that old lady standing over there, who your friend almost hit with his whiskey bottle? That's somebody's grandmother. How would you like it if some clown like this guy walked up to your grandmother and hit her in the head? But you're having a *good time,* so who cares, right? My friend's got cancer, and this asshole gets to just spill booze all over her. But that's fair, right? That's totally fucking fair."

"Look, we're sorry, okay?" the third girl said. "Don't cry."

"I'm *not!*" George shouted, though he knew he was. He knew it was over, and he knew that Irene was crying too, and not because of them. The girls went back to ignoring George, and now so did Irene. When they finally got off at 59th Street and transferred to the

6, Irene wouldn't say a word to him. Finally, stepping out into the chilly air of Madison Square together, she walked, with George following, to a quiet corner of the park, and there she stopped.

"Sorry," George said. "I'm sorry." And he was. Sorry and sweating from all his pores. Sorry and wishing he could lock himself in a bathroom. Sorry and shaking like a leaf. "Don't tell Sara, okay?"

Irene put her hand on his and waited for him to calm down. It took a long time, and when he finally had himself together, they were both too cold and embarrassed to keep fighting.

"It's kind of nice to know you can't always keep it together."

Then before George quite realized what Irene was doing, she was tugging the overloaded bag of books from his throbbing hand.

"That's really heavy—" he tried to say, but it was too late. Irene tried to dead-lift the bag to her shoulder for more support but stumbled backward, and the bag fell to the pavement.

"FUCK!" George bellowed, so loudly that a second later he heard it echo back to him from across the park.

Irene was turned around on the ground and trying to say something, but he couldn't hear it until he bent down to help her up. "I fell down, George. It's not the end of the world. What is all this anyway?"

The Barnes & Noble bag had split open, and books had scattered across the walkway.

Irene read off the titles, one after the other. "The Dorling Kindersley *Complete & Illustrated Guide to Herbal Medicine . . . Healing the Soul: Optimize Your Mind with This Proven System! . . . Kicking Cancer's Ass: A Memoir.*"

"That's an authorized account by WWE champion Barbarous Bobby Blake."

"Oh, is it?" Irene laughed. "*Acids and Alkalines: A Chemical Guide to Cancer Curing.* And seriously, *Yoga, Yoghurt, and Yurts*?" She read from the back. " 'One woman's triumph over breast cancer while traveling the Serengeti in search of love, inner peace, and *bifidobac-*

teria.' George, there's got to be thirty books here! Did you buy out the whole Crackpot Cures section?"

He shrugged. It had been called Alternative Medicine, but yes, he had. He'd gone there looking for a juicing cookbook that Sara had mentioned—as a sign of his goodwill and his determination to support the whole wheatgrass-algae-pomegranate idiocy—and once he'd found it, he'd started looking at one book, and then another and another. What if the secret to curing Irene was there, inside one of them? What if he bought twenty of them, and the answer was in the twenty-first? Buying every single title seemed the only reasonable option. The girl at the register had looked at him in abject confusion.

He'd wanted to say, *Look, if you were in my shoes, you'd try anything too. What's $239.57 in exchange for Irene's life? What's a hundred or a thousand times as much? Is there any amount I shouldn't spend?* What he'd actually said was, "It's for a paper I'm writing."

Irene bent over and helped George pick the books up. She could grab only one at a time, using both hands. "You're so funny asking me not to tell Sara about your little flip-out. Like you won't tell her yourself the second she gets you alone."

George knew she was right.

When the books were all gathered, they slowly made their way to William's apartment.

"I'm going to haunt your wedding, you know that," Irene said.

"Come on, don't joke about that," George said.

"I'm not joking!" she said. "You can count on it, buster. I'm going to be up there hurling rice in the air whether you like it or not."

"I think Sara wants rose petals."

"She would."

"Rice is bad for the pigeons!"

"They have this pigeon-safe kind now."

"Pigeon-safe rice." George hummed to himself. "So glad someone spent time on that."

They kept talking as they rode the elevator up together, heavy stacks of useless books crooked under each arm, a half-empty bottle of green sludge sticking up above the mother-of-pearl handle of Irene's purse.

Sara must have heard them from all the way down the hall, because she flung the door to William's apartment open before they could even knock at it. "Where have you *been*?"

"We were waylaid by violent criminals!" Irene announced as she tottered in, transferring the armful of books into Sara's hands. She made a beeline for William's wide, white couch—where he and Jacob were drinking cocktails. "George had to beat them off with his fists!"

"Ha *ha*," Sara said flatly, as George planted a kiss on her cheek. He moved past her and dropped his armfuls of books onto William's end table.

"You are in serious trouble, mister!" Jacob shouted.

"For buying a bunch of nonsense books?" William asked, studying the titles.

"Fuck that. I mean he's in big trouble with *me*!"

George gave him a puzzled look, as he turned to Sara for explanation. "What's he—? Why's everyone drinking?"

Sara's eyes were brimming, and she was smiling widely. George was sure there must be some great news from Dr. Zarrani about Irene. After all this! After his panic attack at the bookstore, and his revelation, and his thunderstorm in the subway . . . but this was it! The sign he'd been waiting for! And now Irene was going to be *fine*. George felt a swell of gratitude in his chest; he would never, ever doubt again.

"Dr. mmmm and Dr. hmmmm called," she was saying. "They tried your cell and your office. They got Allen, and when they told him the news, Allen gave them my number, and they called me, thinking it might be our home number."

"Why . . . wait, why would the hospital tell Allen anything?"

Sara was confused. "Drs. *McManus* and Schwartz. From Harvard."

"WHICH IS IN FUCKING BOSTON IN CASE YOU FORGOT!" Jacob bellowed.

"Hush," Irene said, nuzzling her head into the itchy fabric of his tweed coat.

George still didn't understand. "What?"

"The lectureship," Sara said, beaming proudly. "They're offering you the job."

George didn't know if he ought to cry or faint or cheer. He settled on an extremely awkward mix of all four reactions, which sounded—Jacob would later tell him—like a dolphin choking on an orange. Then Sara was hugging him, and Irene was clapping as hard as she could—which wasn't hard—and William was heading over from the couch with his hand outstretched. In an instant, George forgot all about the subway ride and Mrs. Cho and the $239.56 and the books. He forgot who he was and where he came from.

"Cheers!" William raised his glass. "To Professor Murphy!"

George lifted his left hand instinctively—his hand knew what it was holding before his brain did. Before he could quite stop himself, George clinked the glass against William's and raised it to his lips. He took a deep gulp and swallowed. It burned every inch of the way down.

NOVEMBER

Irene liked that Dr. Zarrani delivered the bad news herself. For the first time in months, it was just the two of them sitting together again, no nurses popping in and out, and no friends hovering in the hallway. Irene was lying in a hospital bed, tubes running out of her arms and legs and torso. Only the IV machine made noise, beeping like a metronome on the stand. Dr. Zarrani had walked in looking tough, but barely a moment into the discussion, she'd had to sit down in the pink reclining chair in the corner. Irene appreciated this. What could be kinder, really, under the falling shadow of devastation, than for someone to pull up a chair?

The experimental treatment *was* having some impact, but only enough to stop the progress of the cancer. Upping the dosage might lead to some gains, but Irene was too weak to survive the side effects of such an increase, even with 24/7 care. Dr. Zarrani explained that this put them in a no-win situation. Either the cancer would kill her, or the treatment would.

Irene knew she was right. Already, she needed help getting in and out of the gigantic hospital bed. Her arms were as long and thin as kitchen tongs. Her hair was like pillow stuffing. The sores in her mouth and throat stung even through the perpetual morphine haze. Her body's natural defense for this was to generate biblical floods of mucus, which Irene had to spit into a beige plastic tub every two or three minutes. Nurses had to wake her every thirty minutes so she wouldn't choke in her sleep.

Meanwhile Irene could feel tumors everywhere now—bumps on her legs and shoulders, one behind her ear. The ones on her bones were weakening her skeleton such that a simple trip to the bathroom was alleged to be a grave risk for shattering a femur or a foot. There were others in places she couldn't feel, but the CAT scans could see them: one in her kidney, one in her small intestine, and worst of all, one the size of a baseball in her left lung, which made it hard to take a deep breath. They had her on an oxygen tank most of the time. All of this, in just under a month.

Dr. Zarrani went on to explain a few more details, but Irene wasn't really listening. She was watching as the woman raised her hands to support her heavy head. She was watching Dr. Zarrani begin to cry. She'd never done this before. The quickening of breath. The flush of cheeks. The shaking of jaw, and the slow filling up of the corners of each eye until, with a bursting, the drops couldn't hang there anymore. Each tear seemed to inspire ten more. Soon the doctor was weeping, full on.

"Shush," Irene said. "It's okay. Really. It's okay."

"You're smiling," Dr. Zarrani said after a minute. Mascara shot down like dark lightning from both her eyes.

"I'm glad you're crying," Irene said. "I'm glad—I don't know why I'm glad about that."

"Nothing wrong with crying," Dr. Zarrani sniffed, wiping her cheeks with tissues from Irene's bedside. The mascara came off in long, gorgeous smudges.

Neither of them said anything for a few minutes, and then finally Irene said, "Is it—is it weird that I'm kind of relieved? Like, just to know. You know?"

Dr. Zarrani shook her head. "You've been in a lot of pain for a long time. It's natural to feel relief."

Irene looked up at the cracked ceiling. "Should've run away when I had the chance."

"We'd like to get you well enough to go home for a little while before—well, before."

After a minute Irene said, "Do me one favor?"

"Anything."

"Tell Sara while I'm asleep."

Dr. Zarrani said she'd be glad to and to page the nurse when she gets here. Then she hugged Irene firmly, like an aunt, and excused herself.

When she was gone, Irene leaned over to the side table and scooped up the mascara-stained tissues. She slipped them into a Baggie and hid them deep down inside her overnight bag.

Irene wasn't disappointed. It reminded her of when she'd signed up to run a half marathon and was limping and staggering through the tenth mile alone when it had begun to pour torrentially, and an organizer pulled her aside to say that the race had been called off.

To not have to finish, in that moment, was more than Irene could have thanked him for.

When Sara arrived an hour later, Irene paged the nurse and then pretended to fall asleep. At some point she must have actually fallen asleep, or slipped into the haze of the morphine drip, for she awoke with a start to the sound of Sara's voice, demanding explanations. What had gone wrong? How could it have been avoided? What could they have done differently? Already conducting the postmortem. Irene knew that for herself, there were too many what-ifs to count. If she hadn't ignored it for so long. If she hadn't hidden the second tumor before the trip. If she had made more of an effort to keep her strength up. If, if, if, if . . .

Of course Sara still refused to give up the fight. "We'll see another doctor. We should have done that months ago. She's going to beat this. I know you think it's all bullshit, but we're in the middle of a very promising alternative therapy."

Irene nearly snorted. No way in hell was she still drinking that wheatgrass-algae juice. The week before, William had brought her another bottle of Bollinger Blanc under his coat (paid for, this time), but she hadn't been able to taste it at all. The same with the bowl of pasta George had brought, covered in Momma Murphy's marinara sauce (shipped on dry ice, special). That had actually scalded every sore in her esophagus. It all made her wish she'd known it was hopeless back in June. Then she might have really enjoyed those last, disappointing months instead of wasting them trying to make the inevitable evitable.

Irene waited until Sara finished a series of tearful phone calls to George, Jacob, and William before she pretended to wake up. She'd hoped that, maybe by that point, Sara would be cried out. But of course Sara started all over again when she saw Irene's eyes open. *Nice try*, Irene thought to herself, as she sat there, consoling her friend over the fact of her own death.

George came later and, like Sara, urged Irene not to give up. And so began the process of getting Irene well enough to go home for a little while before beginning the work of dying in earnest. Though she had more trouble moving or breathing with each passing day, George encouraged her to walk laps around the eleventh floor at seven a.m. It took twenty minutes to do one lap: about fifty yards up the hall and another fifty back. They could usually get two in before he had to kiss her goodbye and report to work. Only as the residual chemistry of the treatments left her system did Irene feel a bit better but also a little shorter of breath. Sara came every morning at eight and sat by Irene's bedside until eleven-thirty p.m. They watched TV, and mostly Irene tried to sleep or read William's copy of *The Iliad,* which she was still hoping to finish.

On that last, chilly Wednesday morning before Thanksgiving, William brought her a pumpkin latte. He had gotten up at five and gone all the way down to East Fourth Street to get one from Irene's old coffee shop there—because she had mentioned once how it was always the start of fall to her, and she liked to celebrate by taking the first cold day in November to put on her winter coat and buy a pumpkin latte and wander through the West Village looking for Christmas presents for everyone, always eventually getting hopelessly lost in one of those terrible diagonal intersections, where Sixth somehow crosses Bleecker and Downing and Minetta—or in the nexus between Seventh and Barrow and Commerce. It was her favorite part of the city, messy because it was original, made before the orderly grid above it had been imagined. Blocks of triangular madness in the otherwise rectangular city.

"I got lost for about ten minutes on Perry," William told her, putting the paper cup on a tray near her hand. "It's all loose ends down there."

He kissed her clammy forehead and held her hand. She felt a wave of sleep about to come over her, the likes of which no pumpkin latte could fend off, if she'd even been able to swallow anything in the first place.

"Where's my birdcage?" she asked him suddenly.

"Your . . . we put that in storage, remember?"

Her eyes would barely stay open. She had to think very hard about the shape her lips should take to form the words. She tried to say something else, but it was no good. A moment later she couldn't remember what she had wanted to say anyway.

"The nurses are saying that if you're up for it, they'll let you leave for a few hours so you can come over for Thanksgiving. Sara's doing a thing at my place."

For days Sara had been flipping through *Cook's Illustrated* and *Martha Stewart* and *The Joy of Cooking*, describing mouthwatering dishes to Irene to try to motivate her: a crown roast of lamb chops with whipped potatoes and slivered green beans. An icebox zebra cake for dessert. Irene didn't begrudge Sara this. She had been desperate to keep busy, now that Irene's needs were being met by the nurses at Mount Sinai, and she and George had officially given up thinking about the wedding until things "got settled." She'd given notice at the *Journal*, planning to look for a new job in Boston after the spring semester started and George became a genuine Harvard professor.

That day—the day before Thanksgiving—Sara had shown up at eight in the morning. She had to leave at noon, she told Irene. "But don't worry, George as always is coming for the whole afternoon. I need him out of the kitchen anyway."

"I don't need babysitting," Irene said. "He should help you carry bags at least."

"Oh, he'd only slow me down. And I'll be back by nine and stay until eleven. Don't worry."

Irene hadn't been worried. In fact, she wished that Sara would *not* come back at nine or stay until eleven. She wished they'd all go on with their own lives and not spend their own precious hours sitting there waiting for her to die.

It was while George was watching her that afternoon that Irene made up her mind to save them all from any more trouble. He'd been reading to her from the *Iliad,* getting pretty animated as he sipped contraband bourbon from a hospital Dixie cup. Irene promised not to tell Sara on the condition that he let her have a sip. It burned her throat like a forest fire, but it was a refreshing pinch against the sweet, steady stream of morphine that kept easing her further out.

As George read the final battle between Achilles and Hector, he got sweaty and loud. When it was over and Hector was defeated, Irene began to cry. She hadn't cried since well before Dr. Zarrani had told her the treatments were a bust. Somehow she found it far easier to weep over poor Hector, and the way Achilles was pulling his corpse around the camp with his chariot before leaving it facedown in the dust until he felt like dragging it around again. A better description of her own recent weeks Irene couldn't imagine.

George read about Apollo coming down and wrapping Hector in his golden shield so that his skin wouldn't rip . . . and then swearing at his fellow gods (and here George got up on his chair and shook his hand up at the drop ceiling), "'Hard-hearted you are, you gods, you live for cruelty! Did Hector never burn in your honor thighs of oxen and flawless, full-grown goats? Now you cannot bring yourselves to save him—even his corpse—'" and then George dropped the book when Nurse Darren came in and told him to get down or go the hell home. He resumed, more quietly, a moment later.

"'But murderous Achilles—you gods, you *choose* to help Achilles. That man without a shred of decency in his heart . . . his temper can never bend and change—like some lion going his own barbaric way.'" There Irene lost the words for what felt like just a moment in the river of morphine. "At last when young Dawn with her rose-red fingers shone once more, the people massed around illustrious Hector's pyre . . . they collected the white bones of Hector . . . shrouding them round and round in soft purple cloths. They quickly lowered the chest in a deep, hollow grave and over it piled a cope of huge stones closely set." And then George was closing the book, and Irene knew sleepily that he had reached the end. With a great sigh he sipped from his cup and said, "'And so the Trojans buried Hector breaker of horses.'"

Irene tried to say thank you, but it came out as just a slurred sob. George seemed to get the idea, though, and he gave her a warm kiss on her forehead. Then he set the book on her nightstand and went to use the restroom.

She dozed off and woke up, it was dark outside, and Sara was there too, flipping through a magazine article about festive votive centerpieces made out of branches of yellow and orange bittersweet.

"Am I going to get buried?" Irene asked.

Sara looked up at her quickly, then looked out the window.

"Let's not worry about that right now," George said to her.

"When am I supposed to worry about it?"

Tears in her eyes, Sara said, "After Thanksgiving. Let's talk about it then."

Irene left it alone. She coughed up some more mucus and drifted off. She woke up again at eleven-thirty as Sara and George were leaving.

"We'll be back again at eight. And the nurses said that if your numbers are good in the morning, they'll arrange for you to come back with us for dinner."

Irene nodded, even though she felt sure that her numbers would *not* be good in the morning. She couldn't say why exactly—nothing hurt more than it had the day before, but it was slightly harder to take a breath, even with the oxygen mask. Slightly harder to lift herself up off the pillow to receive George's hug goodbye. She felt her heart pumping just a quarter-beat slower.

She closed her eyes for a minute, knowing that Jacob would be there soon. He had been telling everyone that he had to work double shifts at the asylum, but Irene knew he was just angry with

George for moving to Boston. He arrived at Irene's bedside just minutes after the others left.

"Do you just hang around on the street until you see them leave?" she asked.

Jacob rolled his eyes and said nothing.

"Just go to Boston with them then. Nothing's keeping you here."

Jacob flinched. "Don't be absurd."

It occurred to Irene that she'd never get to see the end of it.

"He finished the book today," she said. "The Hector part."

" 'So now I meet my doom.' " Jacob closed his eyes, speaking softly so as not to bring the nurses over. " 'Well let me die—but not without struggle, not without glory, no, in some great clash of arms that even men to come will hear of down the years!' "

"Do they still bury people?" Irene asked.

Jacob thought about it. "I think you have to have bought a plot somewhere. I don't know if you can just do it last minute. There must not be a lot of space left in the city. It'd be all the way out in *Queens* somewhere. Cemeteries are always in terrible neighborhoods."

"So I'll be cremated?" she sighed.

Jacob spoke softly. "That's how I'd want to do it. Cleansed by fire and all that. Plus I hear it's very eco-friendly."

"And then what?" she asked. "Sara keeps me on her mantel in an urn? In Boston?"

Jacob lightly pounded the arm of the chair. "Not on my watch! I'll make sure you're scattered."

Irene purred. "I never did get to France."

So many things she never got to do or see. It seemed impossible, even now that she knew.

Jacob patted her hand. "Then to France you shall go."

"I'm trusting you then."

"Well, that was always your first mistake. Now get some rest, or those nurses will never let you out tomorrow, and Sara will have a meltdown."

Jacob leaned down, and Irene kissed him goodbye. She watched his frame fill the hospital doorway and recede down the hall. It had always been his first mistake too. For Irene had no designs on making it to Thanksgiving, for a crown roast she couldn't chew and an icebox cake that she couldn't taste. No, she had only one wish left—and that was not to die in a hospital room with pink walls and teal plastic trim. If she was going to go, then she was going to *go*. All week she'd been working on the plan.

Around two a.m. Nurse Moira began her rounds, beginning with the rooms down the hall, and Nurse Darren entered prescriptions into the computer at the main desk. Nurse Bethany would still be changing into her scrubs. Irene had been watching, carefully, as they adjusted the IV pumps and monitors all day, to learn how they could be switched off without sounding any alarms. It took about thirty seconds to get free, including plugging up the PEG tube and locking it down flat with some medical tape. Then she put on her red coat and some booties that Sara had knit for her. They had been in the closet covering a large pile of medical supplies that Irene had been gathering that week, in preparation for a final art project. She wouldn't get the chance to finish it, but there was a detailed sketch on top of the pile so Juliette and Abeba could assemble it after she'd gone.

Irene smoothed her hair in the reflection of the elevator door. When the elevator came, it was empty. The doors shut, and she began to descend through the hospital. *What gives out first?* she wondered. Heart, lungs, or legs? She didn't particularly care so long as it happened before they dragged her back to that plastic room. She wouldn't die on 11 East. She simply would not.

"'Night," she said pleasantly as she breezed by the guard at the front. He looked up at her for a moment, and then she was past him.

Cold, fresh air blasted her face like a frozen kiss. She crossed the slippery street, and from there it was just a few steps to Central Park. Soon she was in a dark, open meadow, the individual icicles of grass pushing up through the loose weave of the booties and crunching under her heels. On the far side of the meadow was an oval patch of dirt, still reddish beneath the gray frost. She went a little farther and then paused under a tree, taking time to watch the shadows dancing there in the dark, unlit heart of the city.

Trudging into the chilly valley between two baseball diamonds, she thought back on the years she'd lived with her grandmother Fiona—the only time she'd ever really felt at home as a girl. An inveterate smoker, Gramma Fee had developed emphysema (to no one's surprise) just after Irene turned fifteen.

For a year Irene had watched her grandmother dying, bird thin and wisp haired, an oxygen tube hooked beneath her nose. Each time she saw the doctor she'd swear to them she'd never smoke another cigarette, so help her God . . . but by the next day she'd be puffing away, tugging the little wheeled oxygen tank behind her like an impolite puppy. Irene remembered the big diamond-shaped warning sticker on the side of the tank: WARNING: HIGHLY FLAMMABLE. DO NOT OPERATE THIS TANK NEAR ANY OPEN FLAME. Every day she'd watch the cigarette burn slowly down until it was barely an inch from the little nozzles that stuck up into her Grandmother's nostrils. It was like living next to a bomb that might go off any second.

It had been good practice, Irene thought, as she came up the other side of the valley and toward a grove of dark trees, feeling all the while as if Gramma Fee were just beside her. She could almost hear the creak of the little wheels on her tank. Smell the sweet, forbidden smoke. See the outline of white hair and white nightgown at the edge of the dark.

Nurse Moira stood at the main nurses' station with Irene Richmond's forms in front of her. The emergency contact number was for Sara Sherman. She punched the numbers into the phone and checked her watch again, hoping she could wrap up the call in time to do her rounds before her boyfriend called. Someone half-asleep answered. "Ms. Sherman?" she asked. "I'm very sorry to wake you, but Irene has slipped into a deep sleep. She's only breathing now with the help of a respirator." They could keep her on it and she would remain alive, but she wouldn't wake up. "My advice is to go back to bed," the nurse said. "She'll be the same in the morning."

Sara hung up without saying goodbye. Go back to sleep? Her whole body was shaking as she got up and threw her clothes on. She was already half dressed by the time George realized what was going on. "It's happening?" he asked her. She didn't respond, but he knew it was. He was still getting his shoes on when he saw her running out the door. It took him a moment to realize that she wasn't waiting for him. He made it down to the street just in time to see her get into a cab. She was gone before he could shout for her.

Irene wandered up and down the hills of the park. In the winter wind that whistled by her ears, she heard whispering. In the gusts that came this way and that, she felt a firm hand on her back. In the city, the wind usually blew in an easterly direction, out to sea, but strange cross-currents were pushing her west, to the far edge of the park. Maybe the dead became winds, just areas of pressure, moving this way or that. Sometimes a breeze, sometimes a whole continental front or a wicked storm. Sometimes a great and sticky stillness. Traveling the globe by indiscernible patterns. Clumping into clouds and vanishing through the ozone layer. Maybe heaven was just the air all around. Maybe this cold wind around her was her grandmother. Maybe it was some other ghostly presence. Maybe it was Achilles, though she hoped it was Hector. The city was so alive that simply walking around in it was a life-support system. Its pulsing avenues flooded her veins; its streets flushed her arteries; its people burst this way and that like the valves of her heart. On the other side of Broadway, the road sloped sharply downward, and it became even easier to go on. She felt as she had wanted to feel all along. As if she were falling, steadily, toward the wide, dark river.

George caught a second cab, and from there he called William, and William called Jacob. Afterwards, with nothing else to do he stared out the window at Central Park, its paths and lawns shadowed and quiet. Then, just as he was thinking of trying Sara, he saw, bobbing above the treeline, the outline of Spiderman, and—he wasn't sure if he was dreaming—Ronald McDonald. It took him several minutes to piece together that these must be for tomorrow's big parade. They arrived at the hospital just a few minutes apart, sometime past three-thirty. Sara had already set Nurse Moira straight. They wouldn't be waiting until morning. They wanted to go to the ICU immediately, where Irene had been taken for closer monitoring. Nurse Moira said she'd get it figured out and then disappeared. They waited a long time. George found some coffee. William and Jacob watched an infomercial about a new device that ensured your socks would never again be separated in the wash. Eventually Nurse Moira came back with forms for Sara to sign, and a doctor had to sign off, and though they'd been through it already six or seven times before, there was the usual confusion over why Sara, no relation to Irene, was the one listed on all the forms.

Finally, someone named Dr. Ramos took them to see Irene in the ICU. She was laid out under some white sheets, fast asleep, mouth stretched open around a plastic breathing tube as thick as a tennis ball. Sara began crying immediately, and George barely registered that Dr. Ramos was quietly explaining to him that they would need to wait a bit longer. He couldn't actually take her off the respirator. He was Catholic, and while he in no way judged them, he couldn't morally take a living woman off life support.

Sara and Jacob and George all yelled at him at once. William watched, silently, as their raised voices registered no movement whatsoever on Irene's still face. Dr. Ramos left, and everyone cooled down. They waited almost another hour until the second doctor could be found. Dr. Hanks came around five a.m. to begin the proceedings.

Irene entered the long, thin park along the river, not sure exactly how to get across the West Side Highway on the far side. There the Hudson coursed mightily, its purpled surface forever lit by the coast of New Jersey. *Near* the river, the winds began to push in different all directions. Up toward the distant spire of a cathedral by Columbia. Back toward Broadway. Deeper into the park. Then up on the hill, she spotted something. Tall, white Greek columns reached up through the night, supporting a great marble dome on the top. It looked like some kind of lighthouse, or a tomb. Had she been here before? A long time ago, maybe? She thought she'd have remembered it better if she had. Though it was only fifty or so feet up in the air, it looked like Mount Olympus with the Pantheon on top. All the winds now seemed to be pushing her this way, as if they too wanted to have a word with the gods.

She wasn't alone. Not far away, on the ring of benches around the memorial, a man lay buried beneath a mass of unfolded cardboard boxes. He wasn't moving, and Irene knew well that this night was too cold to sleep in, no matter the number of boxes you made into blankets. Her red coat was a muddy, stained mess now. If she couldn't get up, then she too would freeze to death before morning. It seemed fitting, she guessed. To die in the cold like a homeless person, which was what she had always been, in a way. One of the thousands of people who were everywhere and nowhere all the time. To die here would seal it. And at the foot of this beautiful monument, in this stolen coat, in these soggy excuses for shoes—it seemed like an honorable place to lie down.

Nurse Moira stayed with them the whole time, but William couldn't take it. He said his goodbyes and left just as they were about to begin removing her breathing tube. George and Sara went up together, hugging and squeezing and kissing her, but she barely moved. It was only when Jacob went up and whispered something in Irene's ear that they all saw her smile slightly, around the sides of the tube. George and Sara demanded to know what he'd said, but he wouldn't tell. Eventually Nurse Moira helped Dr. Hanks remove the tube from Irene's throat. They all watched to see if she'd open her eyes again. If she did, they wanted her to see them there, stationed by her side.

Except death didn't come. She tried to slow her breath and just let it happen, but it didn't. She found herself staring up at the tarnished plaque embedded in the stone wall of the monument, which read:

ERECTED BY THE CITY OF NEW YORK
TO COMMEMORATE THE VALOR
OF THE SOLDIERS AND SAILORS
WHO IN THE CIVIL WAR
FOUGHT IN DEFENSE OF THE UNION

Suddenly it seemed all wrong. She was no sailor; she was no soldier. She wasn't Hector, and this was no war that she'd been fighting. On each side of her stood a marble plinth, carved with the names of fathers and sons who'd sunk along with their ships. Boys and men who'd drowned in icy waters, far from home. *Must be nice,* she thought, *to die next to your brothers.* What did they always say? Born alone, die alone? But who was ever really born alone? And why die alone if you didn't have to?

She had caught her breath again. She got up and began to walk back across the street, past an idling truck dropping off stacks of the morning's newspapers. The sky above was just turning to faintest blue. The family who had been there at her birth was now far away, but her other family, her real family, was there inside the warm heart of the city, asleep in an apartment that looked like a catalog page, with the table already set for Thanksgiving dinner.

Her chest rose and fell as she tried to breathe, but her eyes never opened. Little by little she changed. Her breaths became shorter until they could barely tell if she was breathing at all. It was like seeing a person walking away on a wide city street. Becoming smaller, and finally not disappearing so much as becoming the horizon. In the end none of them could put their finger on the exact moment it happened. But afterward they knew they'd all seen it happen together.

II

This is just the way of mortals when we die.
Sinews no longer bind the flesh and bones together—
the fire in all its fury burns the body down to ashes
once life slips from the white bones, and the spirit,
rustling, flitters away . . . flown like a dream.

—Homer, *The Odyssey* (trans. Robert Fagles)

Everything takes longer than you expect.

—Murphy's Second Law

WHY WE LEFT THE CITY

We left the city for good reasons, or at least they seemed good at the time. We had more lives to live and couldn't spare another hour waiting for the G train. We couldn't keep paying more and more for the same square inches. We couldn't keep asking the landlord to fix the same refrigerator. We couldn't move into a twelfth apartment. We left over bridges and through tunnels, still hoping for our security deposits. Be gone, oboe practicer in the next apartment! Be gone, old couple across the street without curtains or clothes. Anywhere else we could own property. Anywhere else we could own cars! Anywhere else we might be anyone else, or maybe our long lost best selves were only a U-Haul ride away. We lay up at night, wondering, *What sorts of people would we be if we were no longer nervous and frayed?*

Some of us tried to fight it, desperately ordering more drinks past last call. We divided and subdivided, putting up drywall to turn one bedroom into two. Taking second jobs and thirds. We pushed farther out. Greenpoint was the new Lower East Side, until Bushwick became the new Greenpoint and BedStuy became the new Bushwick. All the people we'd displaced on our way out there looked up to find us coming for them again. *When does it end?* they asked. *We're sorry,* we answered. *We don't know how to stop.* Then we looked back over our own shoulders and said, *Already?*

We spoke knowingly about interest rates. We asked no one in particular what the value of our time was. Anywhere else, it seemed, it would be more. Other cities, other towns promised us benefits, made better offers. We could always come back, couldn't we? We'd had everything we wanted here, once. Hadn't we been told that now we'd made it here, we could make it anywhere? Only none of us could say, exactly, what it was we'd made.

So desperate to succeed and in such hasty enterprises! Once we knew someone who worked at the same place for nine years. Another had nine jobs in one year. We dreamed of being fired. *Let us go!* we cried. There were so many things that we would do differently next time. We began to hurt each other and insult everyone else. Black clouds moved with us wherever we went, and friends recommended a new yoga studio, less gluten, window-box gardening. Doctors prescribed things to help us sleep, smile, function. We were afraid to go on vacation because we didn't know if we could take coming back.

It was time. Time when our bartender knew our turtles' names. Time when a girl on Franklin Avenue threw up kale tacos on our shoes. Time when a panel of tin fell from the bar ceiling and smashed our pitcher of Negronis. Time when we recognized the opening act's lead guitarist from where he panhandled by the Met Foods. Time when that eighteenth stroller pinned us in at brunch and refused to let us out. They were finding bloody sheep's heads in the park. In Midtown there was a place where a burger cost twenty-nine dollars. Now we knew our flood zones. Our boss had joined CrossFit. There was another new old museum and another new Disney musical and another convention for home picklers. The L train wouldn't be running for the next nine weekends. The price of a MetroCard was going up again. We hardly noticed, and that scared us more than anything.

It was remarkable how easily and insensibly we'd fallen into routines, beating the same track from apartment door to office elevator, stopping midway only for the same *pain au chocolat* and coffee and the same café with an ever-rotating staff. For lunch there were the same endless salad bars and armies of chilled sandwiches. Now we ordered our dinners with the click of a button. The same button, the same dinners. No need to speak to anyone. The bars were the same, the drinks were the same, even the new ones (especially the new ones), and afterward we took cabs home and didn't even look out the window.

There were parts of the city we hadn't seen in years. They reminded us of people who had left us, and we excised them from our maps before they could spread. *It's not the same,* we said, *it's just not the same. It's not like it was, before.* We never said before what, but it was understood. We resented those who left almost as much as we hated those who stayed, because they weren't enough. Like old wood, we splintered apart at the slightest touch until we were nothing but slivers stuck in each other's fingertips.

How worn and dusty were the places we had been holding on to. Deep in the ruts where everything settled. We wanted to rise up and out. See the moonlight amid the mountains. Breathe dry air and drink soft water. We began to build our castles in the air, hoping sooner or later they'd carry us off. New days came like clockwork without becoming tomorrows. We slept less and less, dipped in darkness through the daytime and heated by burning light in the endless evening. And only when we finally got up, threw on our clothes and walked away, did we realize that we had all been gone for years already.

ZUGZWANG, WARD III, 2010

JANUARY

During his first year working at Anchorage House, Jacob had stepped off the bus each day in front of Winston, the daytime guard, with satisfaction. While others rode on to their frictionless white office towers, he had but to give Winston a quick sarcastic salute to make the imposing wrought-iron gates creak open. Up and up the gravel driveway he'd climbed, past semicollapsed stables and yawning gray oaks. In a former life it had been a convent to the Bonnes Sœurs de la Grande Miséricorde with a giant statue of Jesus on the front lawn. Now it was a 125-bed private psychiatric facility accepting Blue Cross/Blue Shield, United Healthcare, and Medicaid, for adolescents who were persistently suffering from a host of mental ailments or required rapid stabilization in a "secure twenty-four-hour therapeutic sphere." Jesus had been hauled around to the back, near where the nuns were still buried.

That first year Jacob had come in early just to spend an hour outside under the big willow tree by the duck pond, feeling like Keats, gazing up at the haunted spires and the patched, leaky roofs that were home to hunchbacks and gargoyles of his mind. At night he'd ducked out during moonless evening shifts and paced the snowy graveyard that still claimed the bodies of three dozen Wives of Christ, his heart stinging in his ribcage as the shadows whispered poems in his freezing ears.

But now the great gray fortress stood indifferent to Jacob's return. He kept his eyes downcast on the slush-eaten driveway, wary of slipping and breaking his neck. The ducks had all gone south, and the iced-over pond was an opaque prison to last year's leaves and the trash that had blown over from the Chinese Boys Academy across the way. Jacob paused beside it, trying not to feel cold and trying to think how exactly it had all come to this.

He'd gotten the job mainly because of his size—of that he was certain—and he'd accepted because being a poet wasn't exactly lucrative. He remembered a professor, the hoary poet Penn Hazelwood, once telling their class, "Stop any guy on the street and ask him for the name of any living poet. Nine out of ten of them will say 'Robert Frost' or 'Shakespeare' or someone who's been dead for decades or centuries. The other one will say 'Billy Collins.' And that's the ball game, chowderheads. Sorry to drag you into this mess."

From his spot beside the pond, Jacob closed his eyes and with no effort at all, summoned an image of Irene just seconds after she'd died. He'd never seen that kind of pale before. What skin looks like without any blood left beneath it. Easy to remember, hard to think about. But from this memory he could rewind to the moments just before she'd died, when he had, true to form, gotten the last word in. He'd sneaked up to her bedside while the nurses were increasing her morphine drip and preparing to remove the breathing tube, and he'd whispered in her ear before "they" eased him out of the way again. He swore he'd seen the corners of her lips creak up.

To Sara, he reported that he'd told Irene that, in her hospital gown, she was the spitting image of Grace Kelly in *Rear Window*. To George, he'd said that he had finally confessed to completely forgetting to water her plants when she'd gone upstate three summers earlier. But these had both been lies. As far as he was concerned, only two people needed to know what he'd actually said, and he was the only one left.

Inside, at least, Anchorage House was warm, and the combination wheel to his locker felt familiar under his fingertips: 3–8–25. Orderly whites had been hanging there since November. Still a faint smell of bleach. In the men's room, the same old graffiti—a three-inch hirsute penis, a misspelled Young Jeezy lyric, an offer for a good time if bibjguy4you@msn.com was contacted. In his clean white uniform, he felt like a new person, freshly born, rather than someone who had, forty days ago, watched his friend die.

The door to Ward III was keycard-locked, but just past it the door to Oliver's office was always open to both patients and staff. Because no one at work knew they were dating, Jacob fired off a casual "Hey, Dr. B," while barely tapping the door frame. Inside, Oliver was chatting with Sissy Coltrane, head of art therapy, but instead of repeating Jacob's "Hey!" Oliver froze as if he'd seen a ghost. Sissy turned, eyes wide. Jacob had spent enough time talking crap behind other people's backs to see he'd just caught them speaking about him.

"You're back!" Sissy chirped, rushing to the door, her arms extended inside a scratchy, sleeveless wool sweater. It was like being hugged by a bird's nest.

"We've missed you! Oliver said you were with your poor friend in the hospital! That can be *so tough*. My mother had this operation on her rotator cuff once, and she was in bed for six weeks. I mean, I'm *still* reliving it. Terrible. Anyway, I hope everything worked out okay—"

She kept talking, but Jacob was more intent on glaring at Oliver than listening. He had told Sissy about Irene, this much was clear. But had he *not* then also told her that Irene had died?

Oliver mouthed a helpless apology behind Sissy's back, making that look he always made. *For how would he know that kind of personal information?*

Jacob didn't know what to say. Sara had been the one to call people, afterward. Then she'd posted this kind of creepy announcement onto Irene's Facebook wall, prompting distraught replies from "friends" who hadn't actually spoken to her in half a decade. Long, memorial messages filled with frowny faces and little hearts. Jacob had read every entry, waiting to be really nailed. Why not? Everyone else was crying all over the place. Even George was sniffling as he'd helped him snip obituaries out of all the newspapers Sara had notified. But Jacob had just sat there scissoring, quietly inhuman, as he stood now in Oliver's doorway, Sissy's eyes already beginning to leak.

"Yeah. It wasn't—it didn't—she didn't end up making it."

At least Sissy released him from her hug, as she turned to Oliver, horrified.

Oliver looked worried, as if Jacob were a giant mess of wires and plastic explosives that he'd just deliberately kicked. But Jacob had been getting this look from nearly everyone since it happened. They expected him, of *all* people, to lose his ever-loving shit. It was, after all, what Jacob Blaumann always did. But they didn't see—there was no "always" anymore. Sara, George, Oliver, his own mother—everyone had told him once or a dozen times to just *let it out. It's okay to be upset! Pitch a fit, pound some walls, you'll feel better.* But surely he owed Irene more than that. He could hold on to this thing for however many years he had left. Long, long after everyone else had forgotten, he would remain Irene's cold, stone memorial. So all he did was say thank you politely—and, he hoped, not crazily—before walking away.

FEBRUARY

Jacob was assigned to monitor Dr. Feingold's eight-thirty a.m. group, which met in the common area—a few worn couches facing each other, a couple of easy chairs facing the windows. Jacob sat in the corner by the board games as the assembled patients named their greatest fears.

"Being alone," said Jane with the Seconal-dead eyes.

"Polka dots," called Annabeth, bulimic, at one point down to a mere eighty-seven pounds.

Jamal coughed and said, "Falling? Like off of a really high building or something?"

Dr. Feingold nodded in amicable fascination at each offering, as if it were both astute and deeply informative. He pointed his pen tip at a girl with glasses so thick they looked as if they could melt pennies in strong sunlight. Dr. Feingold always went around the circle in group therapy counterclockwise. Yet her hand was raised—five bitten fingernails confidently aimed at the ceiling. Jacob didn't recognize her, but that didn't mean she was new.

Corporate policy advised against fraternizing with the patients. A patient might try to use personal information. They were always wheeling and dealing for better food, private rooms, supervised trips outside. He couldn't be bonding with them over their favorite films one minute and the next tackling them to the floor when they became gripped in a delusion that gorillas sent by their stepfathers had come to sell their kidneys on the black market.

But this girl didn't seem *that* crazy. With seriousness that Jacob didn't doubt, she said, "My greatest fear is dying without accomplishing anything important at all."

Others in the group rolled their eyes quietly. "Thank you, Ella. That's very brave," the doctor said kindly.

Ella lowered her hand and folded it in her lap calmly. She turned politely toward the boy next to her, as he began speaking about his fear of scorpions.

Something about the girl bothered Jacob. Normally it was easy to pinpoint, as everyone in Anchorage House was off in some fairly obvious way: train-track scars on their wrists, vomit-stained yellow teeth, hair patchier in places where it had once been pulled out. Jacob knew whose tired eyes came from the morning's dose of Xanax and which type of arm itching was a bad reaction to Ativan. But he couldn't see anything obviously broken about this girl—Ella

Yorke, according to his roster. She was sitting up straight, while everyone else slumped. She was smiling patiently, but not with the halcyon glistening of antianxiety drugs or the defensive smirking of the sarcastically imprisoned. As she nodded her head in empathy with the scorpion boy, the realization rolled slowly toward Jacob like a Tiananmen tank: hers was an actual smile. It felt like years since he had seen one.

Just before she turned to catch Jacob's eye, he looked down, studying a chessboard, which had been abandoned midgame. He tried to work out who was winning. Black's king was in a much safer position, but White was outflanking along the left side. He studied the board a little longer, trying to see what moves were coming up, but became stuck. He didn't know whose turn it actually was. If it was White's move, then White was in trouble, as both bishops were being threatened. But if it was Black's turn, even if he did take either of the bishops, there was no move that wouldn't leave his queen exposed to the White knight . . . Jacob felt his phone buzz twice.

Sara texted him now three or four times a week. *When are you coming up to Boston? Write me a poem! Are you still dating that doctor? Why don't you quit that stupid job and come up here to be a lobsterman?* His responses were absolutely minimal. *Where? No. Yes. Gross.* She was very excited about the U.S. team's chances for gold in Vancouver, wasn't he? He'd typed a reply about how he'd been boycotting the Olympics since A.D. 393 when Emperor Theodosius had kicked out the pagans, but then he deleted it. How could she be bubbly? How could she be watching sports?

He was still annoyed that Sara had flipped out at him for not showing up at Irene's wake last month (even though he'd *said* he wouldn't come several times). Jacob hadn't seen the point in getting drunk with a lot of arty scenesters who didn't even know Irene except as the girl who took their coats at events. Jacob imagined them all standing around with their cocktails, sweating under layers of wool, wondering *where is the damn coat-check girl*? When the pictures went up on Facebook the next day, he was glad he hadn't gone. How dare everyone be smiling? How dare they stand around in their Louboutin shoes, clutching their Michael Kors clutches with fucking lipstick smears on the rims of their goddamn plastic cups, playing a bunch of upbeat songs off Irene's iPod?

Who *were* all these people? If these were her friends, where had they been all year? How dare they enjoy themselves while what was left of Irene sat on a back wall shelf in that monstrous, tacky metal urn that George had picked out from the funeral home catalog? A room full of artists, and nobody could sculpt a goddamn urn to put her in? Knowing that crowd, it was probably lucky her ashes weren't suspended ironically in a bottle of urine. What a seismic waste of time, money, talent, and life.

Now Sara was talking about working with Juliette and Abeba to open a big show of all the artwork that Irene had left behind. To Jacob, this was the most unbearable. Not that he would expect them to understand. She'd made these things because she loved making them. For her, it had never been about getting recognition or selling pieces to collectors. Her work belonged in a museum. In its *own* museum. He ought to do it himself. Hang it all up somewhere in perfect spotlighting and then padlock the door before any else could ever see it.

Sara just wanted to let it all go. Paste it into scrapbooks and move on. Start a new life in Boston as Mrs. George Murphy, a woman unpained. She kept bugging him about meeting her to go through the storage units and Irene's old books to figure out which should be kept and which should be donated. She kept asking if he'd reach out to William, who hadn't been heard from since the wake. At least in the photos he had the decency to look as if he hadn't eaten all month. Sara and George, on the other hand, had been radiant—and Sara, with her new haircut! An edgy flapper bob to go along with her new job as social media director for *The New Bostonian*.

George with his stupid *Harvard Crimson* bowtie. Jacob couldn't stand it. They, of all people, ought to understand. *Irene cuts our hair!* he'd wanted to write in the comments section. *George, what'd you do with the suit Irene hemmed?* But he wouldn't snap. Let them wonder why.

"Wouldn't have pegged you as a chess fan, Jacob," Dr. Feingold said. "You any good?"

Jacob looked up and realized that he was alone in the room with the doctor.

"I'm actually Bobby Fischer in disguise," he said. "Don't tell anybody."

"I think Bobby Fischer died."

Jacob held his finger to his lips.

Dr. Feingold stroked his bald spot for a moment. "Listen. You're Jewish, aren't you?"

"Jacob Blaumann?" he laughed. "Irish Catholic, through and through."

He grinned. "Hey. Sissy mentioned what happened to your friend."

"Did she?"

"She sort of brought it up in our last doctor's meeting."

"I thought Sissy just had like an MFA in knitting or whatever."

Dr. Feingold smirked. "Look, I was just wondering if you'd been to synagogue. I thought you might not know of a good one up here."

"Thanks, but I'm not a templegoer, really."

Still, Dr. Feingold looked quite serious. "You should go. Be with other people. Say the Mourner's Kaddish and all that. Sure it's all a little dusty, but they wouldn't be traditions if they didn't do something for the people who say them. My father passed away a few years ago. Pancreatic cancer. Brutally painful, but at least it's fast, since there's nothing you can do for it."

"Sure," Jacob said, fishing his phone out of his pocket as if it had just buzzed. The text message he'd received was indeed from Sara.

I'm sending out Save the Date cards . . . He jammed the phone back into his pocket. It buzzed again, but he already knew what the second message would say: *What's your address?*

Jacob hadn't even been to his apartment under the church since December, nor to the city at all. He didn't know anybody there anymore.

"Anyway, after my father passed, my rabbi told me I should take the year off. No big life decisions. No changing jobs, no starting new relationships, no moving to a new city."

"Sure. That seems smart. Wait for everything to settle. Well, that seems—sure."

But the last thing Jacob wanted to do was stay in this dead-end job. It was long past time to move on. Ever since Irene, he'd entertained a thousand escape routes. Heading up to Boston to be closer to George and Sara. Backpacking the Appalachian Trail. Joining a cult in Costa Mesa. Dusting off his old thesis and reapplying to Yale. Like crying, it seemed nice in theory, he was just out of practice.

"So?" Jacob asked.

"So what?"

"So how'd it go?"

Dr. Feingold thought about it. Finally he said, "Well, I'm still here."

MARCH

Ward III was where patients came after being at Anchorage House for more than thirty days. Most kids were in and out in under a week, referred via psych consults and crisis managers and social workers and court orders. Oftentimes they just needed a break: an orderly schedule, a little counseling, an empathetic group session, and the usual medications. Lots of kids came in on stuff; lots had stopped taking whatever they were meant to be on. A couple of days, a week, and most had their heads screwed back on again. In Ward II, they could chill for twenty-one additional days. There the docs did what they could for the kids and then either released them, transferred them to special clinics, or moved them up to Dr. Boujedra's group on Ward III. Long-term parking.

The Ward III kids were neither well enough to go home nor sick enough to be shipped out. Languid, world-weary, they sat wistfully in psychiatric purgatory while others came and went. A few kids had been there for over a year, their parents happy to foot the bill and keep them safe, not to mention out of their own hair. Some had even come to feel at home, waiting for their Godots while trained professionals took a daily interest in their thoughts and feelings. Not like the real world was so fantastic anyway. Jacob sometimes saw the appeal; who wouldn't want to be constantly around people who were always hoping you'd soon be well?

He suspected that Ella Yorke was in this last camp. She seemed almost happy to be there, raising her hand in group sessions, standing around by the sorry excuse for a library, earnestly staring out windows, always annoyingly smiling and *meaning* it. Jacob found himself passing the hours imagining how she'd ended up there: bad breakup, penned some dramatic Plath-esque ode to sharp cutlery in an English class somewhere, meeting with perplexed teacher, misfired hysterics, a call to campus security . . . et cetera, et cetera? Or was she more the shut-in type? Cutting class to watch SOAP Network, first a few hours a day, then eight, then twelve, then twenty? Who knew? She could be utterly batshit. Secretly collecting the tabs off soda cans to trade with the Plutonians when they came to harvest everyone's earlobes for fuel.

But Jacob had a hard time believing it was anything like that. Her biggest aberration was that she seemed so damn sincere about everything. He kept expecting to come in to find she had been released, but every time she was still there. And it began to be a strange reminder that *he* was still there, too. He hadn't exactly decided to take Dr. Feingold's advice to take the year off and *avoid* major life changes, yet every time the idea arose of actively pursuing something, he'd beg off.

"Why don't you go back and get your master's degree?" Oliver asked him one weekend as he lay in bed beside Jacob. "Don't you think Irene would have wanted you to?"

Jacob stared up at the clean white carpet of Connecticut sky. What Irene would have wanted for him—he could answer ten different ways at ten different hours of the day.

"Or try something new, if you want. Jacob Blaumann," he said dreamily, "*master* of law! You could do your own television serial."

"We just call them shows here," Jacob said. "Cereal's for eating."

Jacob had actually grown fond of the schoolboy Briticisms. He liked to imagine Oliver as a young boarding-school student, lounging around like this on Saturdays and enjoying the occasional company of men. During the week he was hardly ever in the mood, but on Saturdays he was like a giggly teenager who'd stumbled onto this new, secret activity.

"I'll be Jacob Blaumann, Master and Commander!" Jacob said, stretching his arms to frame the opening titles.

"A master . . . piece!" Oliver clapped and Jacob left to take a shower. Minutes later he tried hard not to hear Oliver whispering on the phone to someone through the tiled wall. "No, he's seeming better, I think."

Toward the end of March, Jacob was reassigned to afternoons, and this involved watching over Sissy Coltrane's group in the art therapy "laboratory" (her term). Sissy led the group through middle-school-level exercises: sketching their shoes, sculpting little bowls, banging out campfire songs on tambourines. Ordinarily it was the sort of rotation that Jacob would have begged Oliver to get him out of, but Jacob didn't complain. Through a haze of clay dust drifting up from misshapen pottery, he kept half an eye on Ella Yorke.

It wasn't as if he was seeking out information on her, just taking note when something appeared. Paul, one of the other orderlies, told him she was seventeen and had been in and out of Anchorage House four times over the past two years. This time she'd been admitted during the Christmas rush and after her thirty-day evaluation had been cleared to stay. She was supposedly so smart that, despite having missed portions of her junior and senior years, she had graduated in the top 5 percent of her class and been accepted at Columbia. But after one semester she was back on medical leave.

This week Sissy had them work on self-portraits in acrylic paint. Everyone was given a little two-by-one-foot canvas and a hand mirror to work with. Ella had worked on her self-portrait, spending two whole days endlessly erasing lines and redrawing them, walking a few paces away to see how it looked from a distance, then rushing back to make some tiny adjustment. Once she spent the entire hour just mixing brown paint, adding a little more umber, a little more ochre, a little jet black, to get the shade right. She'd hold the brush up to her own hair for comparison.

Jane and Annabeth snickered. They had plastic garbage bags over their smocks and held their brushes far away, as if they were CDC agents and the paint were a deadly pathogen. Jacob had a terrible urge to paint polka dots all over Annabeth's picture. The boys made slapdash efforts: cartoonish versions of themselves with stick-figure arms, carrying hockey sticks or driving race cars. There was an epic game of paper football flicking they were always trying to resume.

When everyone else was washing out their paintbrushes in the sink, Ella sat at the table, daubing paint onto the canvas, then stabbing it repeatedly into the jar of milky brown-black water. Then she took a final, displeased look at her painting and slumped forward, mashing her cheek silently into the moonscape of dried paint that covered the table.

Sissy was occupied by the girls at the sink, so Jacob went over to see if she was all right. "It doesn't have to end up in the Met," he said.

"It's all out of proportion," she replied. "These stupid plastic mirrors are so warped."

Indeed, the cheap hand mirrors were rippled like puddles frozen in midbreeze.

"They won't give us glass ones," Ella muttered. "Somebody might, you know—"

Jacob nodded knowingly. "Try to find out who's the fairest of them all?"

Ella laughed so loudly she seemed to even surprise herself. She lifted her head up and clamped one hand over her mouth, but Sissy wasn't even looking.

Jacob leaned forward to examine the portrait more closely. The warping wasn't the problem so much as the hollow grin—teeth gritted and lips pursed, as if the girl in the picture had just sucked a Warhead.

"Here's your problem. *This* is not what a smile looks like. This is what it looks like when someone is being operated on without anesthesia."

Ella's smile grew so large that it overpowered her face, launching her cheeks up so high that they all but hid her dark brown eyes.

"See, there you go. Draw that."

Ella froze, picked up her mirror quickly and looked into it. "I look like a . . . like a . . ."

"What?"

"Like a mental patient."

Jacob laughed so fast that he had to cover his mouth. He couldn't remember the last time he had laughed like that at work, or even alone with Oliver.

But Ella didn't seem to see the humor in it. She dropped her head back onto the table. "No wonder my love life's such a drag."

"Well, you really can't judge a smile in captivity like that," Jacob said. "They're much nicer in the wild. See, there. Like that."

Ella stared into the mirror again. "It's a vicious cycle. I look in the mirror, hate what I see, then paint what I see, hate what I paint, look back in the mirror at myself hating what I painted. It's actually a perfect analogue for the major depressive experience."

"The major depressive experience? You make it sound like a semester in Spain."

"This basically *is* my study abroad."

Jacob looked over at Sissy, who was now showing someone the proper way to Saran Wrap a paint palette to keep it fresh for the next day.

"I had a friend who was an artist," he said, immediately annoyed at himself for using the past tense, "and she told me self-portraits aren't really about faces but what's going on behind the faces."

Ella considered this. "If I painted *that*, they'd seriously freak."

"So?"

"So then they'll think I'm still depressed, and I won't be able to start school again in the summer session so I can catch up on all the bullshit that I'm missing every stupid awful second that I'm stuck in here trying to get myself to be fucking *normal*."

And with that Ella grabbed the jar of painty water and dumped its bilious contents directly over her self-portrait. The murky black water tidal-waved in all directions, mostly back onto her own lap, and she jumped up, as startled as if it hadn't been she who'd poured it out. Shadows leaked into the paper, thick drops running down the length of the self-portrait and off the edge. Already it was pooling heavily under her stool on the floor.

"What *happened*?" Sissy shouted, rushing over.

Ella gently lifted the soggy edges of the portrait. Its agonized smile now peered out from behind a thick gray fog, but the smile on Ella's own face was nothing short of spectacular—cheeks rising so high that they fully engulfed her eyes.

"Darling, what happened?" Sissy asked again.

"Clumsy me," Jacob said quickly. "My fault."

Which, he supposed, in a way, it was.

APRIL

After that, Jacob began noticing Ella almost everywhere. She seemed to have only one friend—Maura, a mousy girl with greasy hair who wedged herself across from Ella during mealtimes. Ella seemed to politely tolerate her presence, though something told Jacob that she'd be far happier sitting alone with her book than discussing the weather, the ABC primetime lineup, and what nail polish they'd wear again when they finally got home. But steadily Jacob noticed that Ella (and often Maura) was looking at him, then quickly away.

During group sessions with Dr. Feingold, Ella began to sit in the chair closest to the chessboard where Jacob stationed himself. When he led the patients down the hall after sessions, she invariably walked at the front of the line. In the common room, he would rotate positions periodically, to try to keep an eye on the rowdiest groups of patients. Slowly he became aware that whenever he moved locations, she followed, orbiting him like a moon. During meals Jacob would sit with the other orderlies at a long table near the side of the room, and wherever he sat, whichever direction he faced, Ella would sit one table over, no more than a few feet away.

"Someone's got a little crush on you," remarked Paul.

"What?" Jacob asked. "A what?"

Paul smirked and made rapping motions with his hands. "A little infatuation with your situation. A yen for your zen, man. Some uncomplicated admiration. Some pokey little puppy love. A hankering for your—"

Jacob didn't want to know how he'd finish that rhyme.

"Die in a fire, Paul." He stood to leave despite Paul's assurances he'd only been kidding.

It was pouring outside, and Jacob didn't feel much like a walk anyway, so he spent the rest of the break in his bathroom stall, quiet except for the echoes of his sandwich being eaten.

Not that she didn't seem, well, *better* since he'd spoken to her in the art lab that day. Her "Portrait of Ella in Gray" was now hanging up in the common room to everyone's frank admiration. And he hadn't done anything wrong. He'd never laid a finger on her, even when she'd jumped up from spilling the jar—and this was more than he could say for some of the actual doctors. Little Dr. Rutherford, with his gross mustache, had allegedly had a three-year affair with a former patient, a gifted trombonist with a drinking problem, yet he was still working down on Ward II as if nothing had ever happened. Dr. Parker, a behaviorist with a husband and kids at home, had last year started sleeping with a janitor in the little-used fourth-floor library. And Dr. Harrison, who still *ran* Ward I, had actually married a former patient of his from another hospital where he'd worked in the early 1970s. Everybody knew about it. They had an annual Christmas party at their house in Greenwich; Oliver had gone many times.

It always seemed to Jacob that Oliver lived vicariously through these stories at the same time that he lived in constant terror of them—a good lawsuit being all that stood between Anchorage House and total collapse. In honest moments, Jacob even wondered if Oliver didn't enjoy sleeping with him so much as doing so beneath a Sword of Damocles.

For the hundredth time, Jacob thought about walking out on the job, on Oliver, on this life. Of decking Paul in the mouth before he did. Of calling Sara, only he had no idea where to begin. She was still after him about his address for the Save the Date card. She wanted to know if she could mail it to Oliver's place, or to Anchorage House—did he have a mailbox there? Jacob just said he was looking into it.

As he passed by the art room, he checked to see that Sissy wasn't inside, then walked slowly around the room, pausing in the far corner by the bowls, pencil cups, and coffee mugs that the patients had made last month. They couldn't keep them in their rooms, now that they'd been fired, because they might shatter them and harm themselves with the jagged bits, so these eminently functional artworks sat here, functionless, until their makers headed home. Jacob casually inspected Ella's mug. He smiled proudly. What a perfectly sane mug! A golden pattern was carved around the top edge—no, not a pattern but some kind of incoherent lettering. At first he thought maybe she was insane after all, but upon closer inspection, he realized that it wasn't merely Greek to him. It *was* Greek, Ὀλυσσεύ, repeated all the way around.

Jacob hadn't read those ancient letters in years, but he knew the name of the epic hero of the *Odyssey* when he saw it. Odysseus. There had been a time in his life when he'd been able to recite whole sections of it from memory (*Sing to me of the man, Muse, the man of twists and turns driven time and again off course*), usually while quite drunk at the sort of jugular parties that nobody ever threw anymore. Four semesters of Attic Greek, studying crumbling dusty books in forgotten corners of the library, translating words that had been translated a million times before. Words that were meaningless claptrap to everyone else in his universe, as if poetry alone weren't a dead-enough, lost-enough language. Sometimes it seemed as if he'd spent twenty-some years working his ass off to ensure he'd have practically nothing in common with anyone.

"Jacob?" The lights came buzzing on as Sissy Coltrane blew into the room.

"Hey there," he said with a forced wave, well aware that he was holding Ella's mug awkwardly in his other hand.

"Looking for something?"

"Pencils," Jacob blurted out. "We're all out. Over in the lounge. Dr. Boujedra said I should come in here to see if you had any extra."

Sissy fished around in a drawer until she produced a fistful of pencils. "Oliver's usually so good at keeping the supplies on order," she said. "That's Ella's mug there. She's got quite an eye. Smart, too. Oliver told me she got some kind of Presidential Scholarship last year, right before she came back."

She had called Oliver "Oliver" twice now.

"What's her deal?" Jacob asked, while Sissy crossed to a refrigerator in the corner where she kept open paint jars. She pulled out a brown paper bag with a greasy spot on one side. "She's so smiley most of the time. You sure she's not kind of coo-coo?"

Sissy pulled out a fat, cold egg roll. "Jacob, you know I can't discuss that kind of thing."

Jacob rolled his eyes. As if she and "Oliver" and Paul and everyone else didn't spend half their lives gossiping about which patients saw chartreuse elephants and which had been arrested for pulling the emergency brakes on the subway and which had been found naked on the roof, covered in glue and feathers torn from pillows, trying to fly to Mars.

"Not such a strange case. We've tried all kinds of medications, but she still becomes severely depressed by the strangest things. Oliver described it really well the other day—what did he call it? Oh yes, he said it's like a hypersensitivity. An 'extreme adjustment disorder.' Like an acute stress disorder, only the stressors aren't unreasonable or unidentifiable things."

"So they're just—*actually* stressful?" He hated the way she kept saying "we."

"Yes, but not stressful to the extent that she experiences them. For instance, going into a deep depressive funk for weeks because—I don't know, a houseplant dies. Or she saw a Christian Children's Fund commercial on TV. Those ones with Sally Struthers?"

"Finding Sally Struthers depressing is cause for rehabilitation?"

Sissy eyed him warily. "Well, yes. If you can't get out of bed for three days afterward. You or me, we'd feel bad for a minute, maybe two, and we'd move on. With Ella? Well, you know what brought her back here this time, after doing terrifically for six months without trouble? She saw one of those St. Jude's posters on a bus. You know, with the little bald chemo children? Apparently she just lost it. Began weeping and didn't stop for two days, even after her boyfriend drove her back up here."

Jacob hoped his eyes hadn't widened too much on the word *boyfriend.*

"So how long before she goes home?"

Sissy set her egg roll down and pulled out a white carton full of lo mein. Then she snapped apart a pair of chopsticks, and then to get the stray splinters of wood off, she rubbed them against each other like a Cub Scout trying to start a fire.

"You know how it works. She can stay here until someone stops paying for it. Or until she's ready for the world, I guess."

"Who's ever *ready* for it?"

Sissy looked exasperated, its own reward. "Why are you so interested?"

"I'm not really. Just, she talked to me the other day, and she seemed—I don't know—she seemed fine. Made me wonder what she's doing here is all. Hey, where'd you order from?"

"Pardon?"

"Is that from Szechuan Garden, in Stamford?"

She looked down at her half-chewed roll. Jacob glanced at the colorful assortment of cabbage and carrot inside, and the smooth brown spiraling of the wrapper.

"Stamford? No. Of course not. I live in Katonah," she said. "I don't know. I just order off the menu on my fridge. Hunan Palace? Dynasty Pagoda? I can't remember."

MAY

Then one day Ella was gone. Not in Feingold's group and not in art therapy. Not lining up for decaf coffee at seven on the dot. Jacob overheard a despondent Maura mumbling to another girl that Ella's parents had come over the weekend to pick her up and take her on a Wonderland Cruise for two weeks before going back to start the summer session at Columbia. Her mug was gone from the rack, though "Self-Portrait in Gray" still hung on the wall in the common room—left behind, perhaps overlooked in her rush to get back to her real life. He liked to think she'd left it there for him. A way of saying thank you. Goodbye.

"There, there," Paul said, when he saw Jacob moping over his roast beef sandwich, "plenty of other crazy fish in the sea."

Jacob wanted to lay into him—tell him that for one thing he was gay, and for another not everything always had to be about sex, despite what *The Real World: San Diego* and the CW's *Vampire Hookups* might suggest. Not everyone was so lonely and desperate that they leaped into bed with the first willing partner. Sometimes a cigar was just a cigar, and sometimes a skyscraper was just an efficient way of arranging offices given limited surface area. But Jacob barely mustered a good eye roll before heading off to eat his lunch in the bathroom again.

He hadn't meant to look Ella up on Facebook. He didn't even have a Facebook *account*. He felt this was important to stress. When he had to—when he really *had* to—he used Irene's account, which she had hardly used herself, never even bothering to upload a profile picture, so that now it displayed just a ghostly outline of a woman's head. She had given him her password, and he used it only in cases of emergency. As he looked at messages for her, he wondered who else might have been there. Then he thought of Ella and couldn't remember—was it York or Yorke? So he'd tried typing it out, there in the little search bar—*Ella York* . . . no, no . . . *Ella Yorke*. Yes. That was it. And without thinking, he emphatically hit the enter key.

And there she was. Smiling like a girl in a toothpaste commercial, in a blue high school graduation gown. Eating tacos in a college cafeteria with a couple other girls. Unwrapping a present in front of a fake Christmas tree. Eating mozzarella sticks in Washington Square Park with a girlfriend, wearing churchgoing hats at a Salvation Army. He realized what a difference just a few years made. Facebook, the Internet, all this had been a part of her youth, while for him, now, it hardly existed. He paused on a picture of her wearing a cranberry prom dress and pinning a corsage onto the tuxedo lapel of an earnest-looking young man—when he hovered the pointer over the boy's face, his name popped up, unrequested. Francis U. Williams. *Francis and Ella*. Then Jacob signed off, almost immediately. It had been only a tiny, accidental lapse in professionalism.

This was how Jacob planned on explaining it all to Oliver, as he walked quickly through the halls of Anchorage House to Oliver's office, where he had been abruptly summoned over the PA system, midway through his shift in Dr. Feingold's group. He knew he was in deep shit even before he saw that the door to Oliver's office was, unusually, closed.

"Dr. Boujedra?" he said, knocking quickly on his way in. "You wanted me to come—"

Inside the office, Jacob saw Oliver's elbows on his desk, his hands gripping the sides of his balding head. A police officer stood a few feet behind the door, fiddling with the dispatch radio on his belt. Jacob froze. Surely not because of him?

"Thanks for coming in. Unfortunately, my father just had a stroke behind the wheel of a car. He's been killed. This officer needs me to go and identify his body."

Jacob didn't understand. "What? All the way to *India*?"

The police officer looked confused.

"Jake—you know—" Oliver paused to collect himself. "My father has been in a senior citizens' community in Mount Kisco for a few months. Before that he lived in New Jersey."

Jacob *had* known this. It was just the way Oliver spoke about his father—always reminiscing, always in the past tense, made it seem like Dr. Boujedra, Sr., still lived far away. But yes, now that he thought about it, he remembered that the man had been widowed six years ago and had then retired to the United States.

He began remembering snippets of conversations with Oliver—anecdotes of how Dr. B. Sr. had been behaving erratically. The diagnosis was Alzheimer's, and Oliver had gone down to Jersey to bring him up to the Glendale Retirement Center.

Jacob thought of something. "Where'd he get a *car*?"

Oliver looked embarrassed.

The officer spoke up. "He pocketed a set of keys belonging to the assistant director of the facility. Nice little blue Porsche. Cayenne model?"

"Yes," Oliver said bitterly. "Which he totaled. Drove it into a water hazard at the Sunningdale Country Club."

Jacob tried to cover his snort of amusement with a fake sneeze.

Oliver didn't seem overly convinced. He sighed. "I suppose I should be happy he didn't kill anybody. Anybody else."

All Jacob wanted to do was throw his arms around Oliver, but he kept pretending that he was just a dutiful employee. "How can I help?"

Dr. Boujedra cleared his throat. "Officer Himmel is giving me a ride to the morgue. I was hoping you could drop my truck off by my flat later this evening on your way home from work. If it isn't too far out of your way. I don't think I'm in any condition to drive, and I'd—I'd leave it here but the Glendale people have asked me to come by in the morning to pick up his things."

Jacob could barely hear himself saying, "Sure, sure. Of course."

Oliver was standing, arms folded against himself, his face turned away. Coldly, he sorted papers into his bag to take home. Then he handed Jacob the keys to the truck and walked off with Officer Himmel.

Jacob went into the bathroom to stick his face under the tap, slurping coppery water until his mouth was numb and his stomach was full and sick. He fumbled his way into the stall. It was like being hung over—or still drunk from a week ago. Fuzzy sheet over his eyes, cotton in his mouth and ears. He'd never had a panic attack before. He'd always figured it would be like being out of breath, but he was breathing fine, even though his nostrils stung as if he'd been huffing Sriracha. He ground the heels of his palms against his eyeballs, which felt as if they'd been turned to marbles inside their sockets. When he felt like he could walk again, he went straight to Oliver's parking spot and jumped into the truck.

At first he intended to just head back to Oliver's early—maybe lie down for a while and flip through one of the pretentious little green leather-bound Poetry Classics volumes that he kept way up on the top shelf in his study, so no one could see they'd come through some Time-Life subscription service back in the 1980s. But as Jacob went out the back way and got onto the Hutchinson River Parkway, he began to dread the idea of lying there alone in the *flat*. Waiting for the sound of keys in the door and knowing it would be Oliver, all sad and depressed, or maybe still aloof and despondent as he'd been in the office.

Steadily, Jacob accelerated. The trees along the parkway were brilliant green and moving lightly in the breeze. He rolled the window down a little and set the radio dial to seek. He'd never even met the elder Dr. B. Probably Oliver had known this was coming. He was probably more annoyed about having to pay for the Porsche.

Jacob wondered what he'd do if his own father died. Probably drink heavily. Certainly be extra rude to people like Oliver. And he didn't even *like* his father—Oliver and his dad had been quite close. Well, no, not that close. The real problem was that Jacob was dating a man in his late fifties who was still basically in the closet. The old man had gone to his grave believing that his son was straight. Still asking when he and his ex-wife would finally get back together. Now Jacob wondered if, somewhere deep down, Oliver wasn't relieved: both his parents had died without knowing their son slept with men.

Jacob remembered coming out to his own parents at age fifteen to Royal Shakespeare Company–level hysterics. His father had sworn solemn oaths, and his mother had literally beat her breast. Oliver had never lived through such a scene. True, post-fallout had been better—he got a rare apology from his father and had gotten to watch him reading, in extreme discomfort, self-help books with titles like *Love Is All: Accepting Your Gay Son*. That had been pretty priceless; there had been illustrations. Plus, he'd got to check out men at the mall with his mother after school.

Jacob hardly called his parents now and only visited on his birthday. He wondered how it would feel to be an orphan.

The radio came onto a classic rock station, and Jacob punched the button to hold it there on the tail end of "Paradise City." He cranked it as high as it would go, rolling both the windows down so that the wind roared back and forth across the bench seat. " 'Oh won't you please oh take me hoooooome . . .' " He recalled nights in dark Ithaca basements, lost in the strobing of jury-rigged lights, voices all around him shouting this anthem from before their time.

Jacob sped up, sailing around each bend, tacking between lanes around sad little Hondas and Kias and Scions. His heart thundered, and cool air pummeled his face with tiny fists. The music crescendoed and crashed into silence, and Jacob felt as if his whole body might burst. Just then a little prerecorded promo came on: *Two for. Two for. Two for Tuesday.* Jacob remembered loving this as a kid, when they'd play a second song by the same artist, right after the first. And softly, the rising return of Axl's moan, knock knock knocking on heaven's door and Jacob pounded his fists against the steering wheel, lost in a joy greater than he'd felt in over a year, ecstatic—filled up like this by not just one song but a second, just when it ought to be over.

Like a multiple orgasm—a subject of intense debate once between himself and George—whether guys could ever have one. Sting claimed it was possible. Back at school Jacob had wanted to sign up for a course in "orgasmic mastery" taught by a Dr. Koolhaus downtown. Sara had said it was God's way of making it up to women for childbirth. Then Irene told stories about nights she'd spent with a woman in Detroit who could wrap her tongue around a Coke can. He could remember how George squirmed, trying not to lose his mind thinking about that—hopeless. Even Jacob had taken a cold shower.

He noticed that he'd gone past the exit that cut over to Stamford. Way past it. He was seeing signs for Meriden, still heading north toward Hartford.

From there, he vaguely knew, he must be able to take something else east toward Boston.

It all seemed so simple, he didn't know why he hadn't seriously considered it before. He'd crash on the couch at George's for a week or two. It would be good to see them again. It had been petty of him, not uncharacteristically so, but now it had gone on long enough. Of course George should go to Boston and work at fucking *Harvard* if he got the chance—and just because he looked happy in Facebook photos didn't mean he actually was. George was just unflappable—that was what everyone liked so much about him.

Jacob wondered how he would get Oliver his truck back. Probably stealing it wasn't the nicest thing to do to someone who'd just lost his father. Now the classic rock station had on some Joni Mitchell bullshit. He wanted something angry. Less Bob Dylan, more Dylan Thomas. To Dr. Sr.!—Jacob raised an imaginary glass to the windshield. Driving around a Westchester Country Club golf course in a stolen Porsche. He had to hand it to Dr. B.—at least he'd gone out on his own terms. *Rage, rage against the dying of the light.* Maybe that was why it had been so brutal, at the end, to see Irene lying there in the bed all morphined and breathing on a machine and, well, going gentle. If old age ought to burn and rave, then youth ought to be downright atomic. There shouldn't have been anything spared for miles after Irene went out. She should have decimated the entire city, with no one left standing.

Soon Jacob grew tired of driving, tired of the trees, and tired of the second Joni Mitchell song on the radio. "Two for Tuesday" could cut both ways. He was tired of never knowing how he'd be feeling next: panicked, annoyed, orgasmic, weepy, worn out. Traffic had slowed to a crawl in the right lane and was barely faster in the left. He inched along, following a red snake of brakelights around the winding curves, until at last he saw the cause of the holdup. About ten cars with their flashers on, moving slowly as one through the right lane, and the left clogged with people trying to get around. One by one Jacob passed the cars in the right lane line until at last he pulled up ahead of the chain, to the black hearse with purple zinnias ornamenting the hood. PAULSON & PETERSON FUNERAL HOMES was written discreetly along the side. Just as he was about to pass it, the traffic ahead of them slowed down, then stopped.

Jacob tried not to look over at the hearse through the passenger-side window. He pictured Oliver down in some hospital basement, like where they must have kept Irene, afterward. Some creep balding doctor opening a metal drawer in a refrigerated wall. Inside, at first, just a pile of white sheets, as if someone had forgotten to make the bed. Just have a look, and we'll be all done here. Underneath, a life-size-doll version of the man who raised him. Made of something cold and white that isn't skin. How hard it would be to believe it—to say, *Yes, this is my father*—when you didn't see it happen.

Jacob took the first exit and looped around on an overpass, getting back on the parkway heading south again, the way he'd come. He turned the radio off and rolled up the windows. Again, he blew right by Stamford. By the time he got back to Anchorage House and parked in the director's spot, he'd been gone just over one hour, and there were only two left in his shift. Dr. Givens and Dr. Berg were down by the little trash-filled pond, smoking cigarettes. They definitely noticed Jacob climbing out of Oliver's truck, but he was finished caring. Life was too fucking short. He wasn't going to give two fucks about what everyone else thought.

Inside, he walked back into the bathroom stall and sat down on the closed toilet seat. He lifted the truck keys to the cold metal wall and scratched lightly, a little surprised how easy it was to leave a mark. Back in high school he'd done it all the time, leaving cryptic poetry, but he didn't quite feel up to that yet. He would go to Boston in a few weeks, once Oliver was feeling better. His feet were steady on the tiled ground. His legs didn't shake on the edge of the seat. His hand scraped at the paint. A little less-than sign and the number three beside it: <3. It made a little heart, just like the ones people had written on Irene's Facebook wall.

Then he got up and went straight to his assignment in the common area. The patients were playing board games and doing puzzles and watching *Judge Judy* on the TV.

Paul patted his palm against the wall, as if to coolly invite him over. "Hey la, hey la, your girlfriend's back. I just saw Jorge from Ward One sneaking a cigarette in the back stairway. Said they readmitted Ella Yorke this morning."

Jacob wanted to just throttle him. "Fuck. Is she all right?"

"Said she looked kind of sunburned."

"No, I mean what the hell happened?"

"Guess you'll have to ask her. Even money she'll be up here again in thirty days."

"Shit."

"Well, you know what they say," Paul grinned. "Fourth time's the charm."

JUNE

The Ward III library was set into an old linen closet off the common area, which had been fitted with shelves and the sort of partly shredded paperbacks found on the racks outside bookshops for a dollar, or for free in a laundry room. A collection of castaways, curated only to the extent that anything vaguely interesting had been chucked. There were a handful of feminine empowerment books for teens and a few pop-psychology favorites: *The Road Less Traveled* and *In Search of Self.* The sprawling oeuvre of Dr. Phil. Jacob had noticed that Ella, during her previous stay, had been working through the odd classics, Charles Dickens and Jane Austen, but the library mainly carried the B-side stuff. *Pickwick Papers. Northanger Abbey.* She had plowed through these in the span of a few days. It had taken Jacob a year in college to trudge through *Middlemarch,* but Ella had it back on the shelf in under a week. There was really nothing much written after 1890, and when he asked Oliver why they'd omitted anything written after Freud bought his first couch, Oliver had answered that the selection hadn't been updated since before his arrival, ten years earlier, but that he had once spoken to Dr. Dorothy about it. She was on the committee that oversaw purchasing of books, games, DVDs, etc. Basically everything had to be assuredly harmless. Nothing too scary or too bleak. This explained a lot. After the Industrial Age things got a bit dicey, didn't they? But most kids wouldn't slit their wrists after reading *Mansfield Park.* Jacob argued they might, when faced with the prospect of reading it over and over again all summer.

There was no poetry of any era, which Jacob took as a compliment. Nonstandard line breaks were mighty suspicious. Enjambment, slant rhyme, lack of punctuation? They could easily send anyone over the edge. Keats died young, Shelley drowned. Sylvia Plath, obviously, was strictly *verboten.* How many girls came in there saying *The Bell Jar* (practically a suicide manual!) was their favorite book? Jacob had always wanted to give them a copy of "The Colossus" and say "there, there." And good old Frost had never killed anyone, had he? Why not at least give them the sort of stuff that made the days worth passing? Finally he volunteered his services to Oliver, saying he'd be happy to sift through the anthologies for life-affirming poetry, but he got the answer he'd expected. Safer not to. Anchorage House couldn't afford to be sued just because some patient had a bad reaction to *Les Fleurs du mal.*

Oliver seemed to be doing okay. Distracted more than anything else. Jumpy sometimes. What was more bothersome was how eager he was to use his newfound grief to reach into Jacob's. "Now that my father's gone," he'd said once, as they showered together one Sunday, "I feel like I have the chance to really sum up what we meant to each other. You must know what I'm talking about." Or the night after, going through the magazines for recycling, Oliver had fondled a bit of the rough twine and said, "The funniest things remind me of him. What is it for you?"

Jacob supposed he could have answered truthfully: girls in red coats, Spanish-language television, hot tubs, almond croissants, that stupid Plain White T's song, the entire Metropolitan Museum of Art (which he hadn't been back to). Jacob resented the implication that these things were equivalent to Oliver's twine. Fine if he legitimately missed his father, but it wasn't the same. Like when Oliver recalled little racist things his dad had said when he was a boy. "Well, he wasn't perfect! Makes it worse, in a way, remembering all his flaws. *You* know what I mean."

Jacob thought of Irene's compulsion for girls who treated her like shit. How she'd loved getting wasted on champagne and spending Midas amounts of money on vintage clothes and how she'd been notoriously bad about paying people back what they'd loaned her. She'd been fierce about her secrets, as if believing that without them they'd have long ago gotten bored with her. None of them even knew where she'd come from or how she'd ended up in Ithaca. It felt like a lack of faith in *them*, when you came right down to it. But everyone had dumb flaws when they were twenty-six years old. Oliver's father had had *fifty years* to climb beyond those early shortcomings. He'd had decades to regret his bad choices and outgrow his habits.

And what would Jacob regret if his bus were to sail over a guardrail the next day? He didn't think more time watching Oliver "processing" would be on the list. No, what he'd regret was not being there when Ella's thirty days were up. Oliver he couldn't help, but Ella—well, he had begun to formulate a plan. If she couldn't get to her summer session, then he could bring it to her. After work he holed himself up in Oliver's study, ostensibly working on some new poems but actually quietly climbing up and down the swanky bookshelf ladder, digging through his green Time-Life poetry volumes. Working carefully, using a ruler and half a scissor, he sliced out one poem after another.

Once, he'd gone up looking for Elizabeth Bishop. "The Fish" was one of those poems he'd remembered reading, around Ella's age, that had just turned his blood cold. *While his gills were breathing in / the terrible oxygen.* Who knew you could rhyme things like that? Slice went that page, and he watched it flutter down to the floor. Then he'd spotted Blake just after it. (Oliver's books were alphabetized within an inch of their lives.) He guessed that Ella had probably read "The Tyger" in high school, in some tissue-paper-paged Norton Anthology, but had she ever read "London"? Probably not. Had she ever been to London? he wondered. Jacob had done Europe in high school on a class trip: the Jewish quarters of Rome, Paris, London, Madrid—with bonus stops in Dachau, Auschwitz, and Buchenwald. He'd always meant to go back without chaperones, but what poet could afford the jet fuel these days to cross the ocean? Ooh! Wordsworth. "Daffodils" was good stuff, but was it the right thing? It was tricky.

On the day Ella finally came up to Ward III, Jacob was all set. Barely acknowledging her presence in the group sessions or the art room, each morning he would find his way over to the closet library and slip one poem into the middle of whichever book he'd seen her reading the day before. Then in the afternoon, when she went over to reclaim her book, he'd watch from the windowsill as she found the poem tucked inside. Anne Sexton one day, Keats the next. He tried to avoid any chronology. "Is there a W theme?" she wrote on the inside cover of one book after the first few days, when she'd gotten William Carlos Williams, Wislawa Szymborska, and Wallace Stevens. The next day she got Wang Wei and a note that said, "Theme = Poems That Do Not Suck."

At first he'd been wary of writing on the poems, because anyone who found one lying around her room was bound to get the wrong idea. But then he realized it wasn't like anyone would recognize his handwriting, except maybe Oliver, and what was he going to do about it? Anyone else would just assume it was a by-product of some interpatient romance (which were just about always going on). Teenagers were teenagers, especially crazy ones.

After one week, Ella wrote a poem back. He found it folded up under the edge of the chessboard during Dr. Feingold's group. While the patients went around discussing their relationships with their parents in advance of that afternoon's visitation, Jacob quietly unfolded the neatly hand-printed page. "The Whole Ball of Wax" described a ten-year-old girl who eats every crayon in a box of sixty-four, vividly imagining the flavors of Brick Red ("too salty by a mile") and Caribbean Green ("like pea soup turned up the dial") and "Outer Space" which "vanishes between my teeth / refusing to exist in me." After the final crayon, a Yellow Orange, sets her "intestines roiling" (not bad, for a rhyme with orange), the girl eases her own belly button open with two fingers and extracts the titular ball of wax—"a lump / indigestible and indefensible. / A Crayola cortex / slick with slime / my parents shriek / and jam it down the disposal / with two ounces of vegetable oil. // They hit the switch. / Colors fly into the air / settling like snowflakes / in their shirt collars / and hair."

He could feel her eyes on him, searching for approval. Without supplying any visual cues, he took his pen and began circling weaker words, underlining a few tremendously good ones. There needed to be another syllable here, one removed there. Rhymes weren't really in vogue anymore, but they were tolerable until you turned into Dr. Seuss. He noted this in the margin and slipped the poem back beside the chessboard and listened to the group's discussion again.

"My parents are both so in love with themselves, it's disgusting," Anne Marie was saying. "When they look at me, they're just seeing themselves, and if I'm not doing a good job with their half, they get pissed."

"Mine are divorced," John agreed. "So they each just see the shit they can't stand about the other."

Dr. Feingold nodded. "There is a mirror effect there, yes, but it goes two ways. Parents see their own faults in us. We see our own fears in them."

Jacob didn't think this was particularly true, as a rule, at least not in his case.

A prim girl, Karen, announced, "My parents think the president was born in Kenya."

Dr. Feingold was trying hard not to smile as she continued.

"Last Christmas my dad bought everyone in the family guns. Mine and my brother's they're going to keep in the attic until we're older, but he said he can't wait until because by then the government will have outlawed the Second Commandment."

Jacob listened as the group described mothers who lived at Bed Bath & Beyond, racking up credit card bills with purchases of window treatments, pod coffeemakers, and slow cookers that were never even unboxed. Fathers who drank a six-pack a night while watching *Three Stooges* reruns. Some loved too much, others not enough. They had stuck them in here, though no one gave any sign they were happy to be away from these alleged monsters, who embarrassed them in public, didn't understand, had no idea what it was like to be a kid these days. They were overbearing, underbearing, and bared too much skin at summer swim parties. They slept with teachers, secretaries, neighbors, or the parents of friends, or else they desperately needed to get laid. They had gotten divorced too fast or had stayed together too long. They had married too young or too late. They had irresponsible numbers of children, or they had focused all their energy and attention on just one. They were untrusting, unsupportive, manic, drunk, cheap, anal, bullying, balding, varicose veined, miserable, fucked-up, saggy-armed, Botoxed. The list was endless.

Jacob waited to hear what Ella would say, if anything. What had happened to make her this way? Why did she need to be kept safe here, like him? Had her parents raised her in some kind of protective bubble? Was she, like some zoo-born animal, incapable of reentering the jungle? He heard the other kids talking about their big plans. All eager to get out and join some startup. Or marketing their own lines of purses or building an Etsy empire. But Ella never seemed interested.

"Ella. You've been very quiet," Dr. Feingold pressed.

"My parents are—" She took her glasses off as if to clean them, then set them back. Jacob realized he had both feet wrapped around the legs of his chair.

"My parents are such . . . stupid—" Ella began.

Dr. Feingold gestured for her to continue.

"Such stupidly happy people."

Jacob spotted them later at the family visitation, held biweekly in the sanctuary of the former chapel. The stained-glass windows here were the last real building features that remained from the convent days, deemed too beautiful to be torn out, even if they did depict horn-tooting angels and sword-wielding saints. Jacob couldn't actually get close enough to hear how the visit was going, but he watched: mother just like Ella but with hair up in a twist, chin doubled, and cheeks red with capillaries; father pudgy with a street-sweeper mustache, spiffy spectacles, and a Livestrong bracelet. Still? Jacob wondered if his own parents looked this way to other people. Like better-padded versions of their offspring. They were both beaming vacuously. Not that they appeared unintelligent, just that their enthusiasm didn't seem to be merited by the circumstances.

Other parents had the decency to seem uncomfortable, worried, or even put out by their journeys. Lots of them spent the majority of the hour looking around, trying to get Oliver's attention so they could discuss his sense of their child's progress, rather than actually visiting said child. Mr. Yorke was looking around all right, but not for a consult—seemingly, he was admiring the stained glass, squinting up at a depiction of the Lamb of God on a purple hillside. Jacob thought at first, maybe he was a religious nut of some kind, but then Mr. Yorke scrunched his face up in an imitation of the lamb's and made a little *baaaaaaaaaah* noise to get Ella to laugh. She didn't, but Jacob did.

He watched them say their goodbyes and wrap her in bear hugs before they left.

"What's so funny?" Paul asked.

"Your *mom's* so funny," Jacob replied. "Hey, I gotta take a leak."

Paul was always happy to uphold the sacred brotherhood of pee breaks. "I'll cover you."

So while Oliver was busy with Karen's parents (who indeed wore matching PALADINO FOR GOVERNOR buttons on their shirts), Jacob ducked out the main doors a little ahead of Ella, then pretended to be just coming back from the restroom when she came through.

"Where are you headed?" he asked.

"Back to the common."

"Let's go the long way." Without really thinking about it, he held the doors open to the outside.

Ella looked warily at him and then, just as he was about to apologize and explain he'd only wanted to get some air, she walked boldly past him and out into the world. They walked quickly, neither saying anything about the fact that they were hurrying to avoid being seen, and they didn't slow down until they were back by the relocated Christ statue.

"Your folks left early?"

"They got us all tickets to a movie, but I told them I couldn't—"

She glanced at him sideways, knowing that he knew she'd been cleared for an afternoon outing. That he'd know that it wasn't what she'd meant by *couldn't.*

Jacob thought about it a moment. "What movie?"

"That new one with Stone Culligan."

She noticed his scowling. Jacob wished he could explain why the star annoyed him, and the argument he'd forever be reminded of by him, but bringing up Irene at all felt wildly inappropriate. It might even send Ella into a tailspin. He couldn't reconcile it all himself. How could he explain what had happened to a girl who found telethons depressing?

"Check the *DSM*, but I think not wanting to see a Stone Culligan movie is proof of sanity."

She sighed. "They were so disappointed! They never show it, but I know they were."

"Why didn't you want to go?"

"It looks *sad.*"

Jacob had seen a few commercials for it over Oliver's shoulder, and there had been a review in the latest *New Yorker.* Fresh from rehab and now dating a different Israeli supermodel, Culligan was taking on substantial material for the first time. Playing one of four brothers uniting for their mother's funeral, Culligan arrives sexily disfigured from a recent ATV accident, which in a fit of art-imitating-life turns out to be *not an accident at all, oh my god!*

"I take it you're not a fan."

"He's not my type." It was hard to tell if his implication had landed. Ella did get very quiet and remained so as they stepped around a half-dozen headstones.

"I don't get it," she said. "Why do people pay fifteen bucks to sit in a dark room with a bunch of strangers so they can watch actors pretend to be miserable for two hours when they can see it for free if they just open their eyes? And anyway, how do they get up afterward and just go across the mall and buy sensible shoes at Ann Taylor Loft?"

"Why do you like poetry then? At least in movies sometimes things explode."

"Poetry makes things look more beautiful. That's okay."

Jacob checked his watch but made no effort to turn back. It would take them a few more minutes to realize Ella wasn't where she was supposed to be.

"Shitty movies can make things more beautiful too. If Stone Culligan felt how you feel once and turned that into something, then that's one less thing to keep to yourself all the time."

Ella looked at him through fogged glasses, then removed them as if to wipe them clean but instead just waved them around. "I wasn't going to jump. Off the cruise ship. I don't know what you heard, but I wasn't."

Jacob shook his head. "I hadn't heard anything. Who thought you were going to jump?"

She crossed her arms over her chest and walked ahead.

"My parents. The stupid deckhand guy who saw me on the railing. The asshole ship doctor—who becomes a doctor on a goddamn cruise ship? That's what I want to know. That's not a reputable career, you know? That's not, like, a sign of excellence in doctoring, to spend your life bandaging kids' skinned knees and—and—"

"Worrying a lot about Legionnaires' disease, I imagine."

"Exactly. Who would choose to do that? Who would work on one of those floating prisons all year long? Someone like that shouldn't be taken seriously, is all I mean."

Jacob didn't say anything, though he was thinking that at least if he'd signed up for a year on a cruise ship, he could practice his backstroke once in a while.

Ella was stepping widely to avoid the ground in front of the nun's headstones. "'Here Lies Sister Mary Sullivan.' 'Here Lies Sister Alice McNally,'" she read as she leaped over the graves.

Jacob decided to try one too. "'Here Lies *Sister, Sister*, American TV sitcom.'"

She laughed, and he wondered if she even got the joke. But then she said, "TGIF," as she crossed herself and went along to the next.

"'Here Lies Twisted Sister, who really aren't going to take it anymore.'"

"You're too young to know about them."

"My dad still has all his old records."

"And terrible taste, apparently."

"Hey, speaking of taste, what'd you really think about my poem?"

Jacob had been wondering if she'd have the nerve to ask him face to face. He felt another small swell of pride that she had. "Just what I wrote."

"But what do you *really* think? Like, do you think I've got what it takes? To be a poet?"

Jacob examined her closely. "You're going to need a *thing*. Like white-person dreadlocks. Or a ponytail that goes down to your shins. Or wear a lot of rings maybe. Like an insane, abnormal number of rings."

Ella frowned. "I was thinking about getting a tattoo."

"You don't have a *tattoo* yet? Oh, God. I'm not sure I can be seen with you, actually."

Ella looked around perfunctorily to see if the coast was clear. "Do you have one?"

"I have the Chinese symbol for love tattooed on my left ankle."

"You do not."

"I can't show it to you though, because these socks are really complicated."

"Be serious."

Jacob quietly used a headstone to scrape a bit of mud off his shoe. There was a poem engraved on it that he had never seen before, though he had been out in the graveyard a number of times and had, in his boredom, looked at all the sisters' headstones plenty of times before. Somehow he must have missed this one. Or rather he felt as if he had read it before, ages ago in some anthology, for he half-remembered it even as he scanned the simple lines.

> It is a fearful thing
> to love what death can touch.
> A fearful thing
> to love, hope, dream:
> to be—
> to be,
> And oh! to lose.
> A thing for fools, this,
> and
> a holy thing,
> a holy thing
> to love.

At some point as he looked at the inscription, Ella had come over and begun reading it too. She waited for him to say something. He thought about simply saying that he had no way of knowing if she'd be a great poet or not, and that the odds were heavily stacked in the "or not" column, and that even if she managed to find her way to the other side, it meant doing a lot of work for nearly no compensation or recognition whatsoever. But standing there, reading those words on the headstone, he found himself unable to give his usual answer.

"I'll tell you if you answer one thing for me first. In all seriousness. Why were you on the railing if you weren't going to jump?"

Ella took a sudden interest in the twigs around her feet, kicking them this way and that.

"It was like being a little kid again. Like not being afraid, at all, of anything. I don't know if you've ever been way out in the ocean like that. I never had been before. But when you're out there far enough that you can't see land from any side? It's just incredible. Like being on a new planet. There's nothing man-made, just the sun setting and these clouds that are just on *fire*. Every color imaginable. The whole crayon box. And when the wind picked up, I couldn't even hear the engines going, or the kids crying down by the pool, or the birds shrieking down by the snack bar . . . it was just all gone, and I felt like I was in heaven. I wasn't afraid of anything. It was like I was weightless. But I swear to God, I didn't want to jump."

Jacob wanted to hug her, or at least pat her shoulder or rub her head. He settled for holding a hand out and helping her to her feet.

"Did you try telling Dr. McDisney on the boat about it? Or anyone here?"

Ella shrugged. "I didn't know how to describe it."

Jacob motioned for her to follow him back. "It is one of the hardest things there is to describe, in my experience."

"What is?"

"Happiness. All these poems I'm digging up. That's the theme—that's what they are."

Ella spoke slowly, as if worried about mispronouncing something. "I was happy."

They walked back, slower this time, not afraid of being seen, right up to the side door. Jacob deposited Ella safely back in the common area without a single raised eyebrow (except from Paul, and who cared?). She went and played a game of backgammon with

Maura, and the two of them spoke about daytime TV, and while Paul was distracted by a boy attempting to watercolor the windows, Jacob made his way over to the bookshelf and pulled out *Tess of the D'Urbervilles*.

He felt Ella's eyes on him as he wrote on a blank page in the back. "Okay, chowderhead, you're a poet. Write me a poem. 'Orange Peels.' Five stanzas. Free verse. Due Friday."

JULY

Dr. Dorothy Zelig was in charge of the widely advertised new pet therapy program at Anchorage House, which involved taking exceptionally high-strung patients (like Maura) and helping them to relax by playing with dogs. Children who had suffered various abuses at the hands of grown-ups learned to accept love and to care for living creatures. Even if it sounded like hippie-dippy hogwash to him, Jacob had never had any issue with Dr. Dorothy personally until he was once again summoned to Oliver's office in the middle of the day—this time for exactly the reasons he'd feared. He didn't know how he'd missed spotting her, and he suspected she'd been hiding down behind some shrubbery on the far end of the graveyard and not at all walking one of the therapy dogs and minding her own business, as she claimed during the meeting in Oliver's office.

"Gosford had to take a tinkle," Dr. Dorothy declared, "and that's when I saw Mr. Blaumann here and the patient Ella Yorke talking suspiciously out by the old statue."

She spoke as if she were a witness in an episode of *Law & Order: Pedantic Bullshit Unit*.

"I wasn't aware," Jacob said, "that I was talking in an especially suspicious manner."

Oliver, sitting behind his desk in full-on, serious Dr. Boujedra mode, eyed Jacob wearily. "So you don't deny that you were with the patient outside the building?"

Jacob considered that it was essentially Dr. Dorothy's word against his, and that Ella would probably deny everything if they spoke to her about it. But he didn't *want* them talking to her about their chat, and giving her the impression that she had committed some sin just by having a conversation. And for another thing, fuck Dr. Dorothy.

"Yeah, no. I don't deny it. Ella was clearly upset, and it was a nice day, and I thought some fresh air would put things in perspective. Legend has it that nice weather has a calming effect on human beings, but I'm just an orderly so I couldn't say for sure. Obviously I'd have to do a longitudinal study with multiple placebo groups and write a seven-hundred-page dissertation to be qualified to say so in an official capacity."

Oliver was upset, but Dr. Dorothy beat him to it. "*This* is what I'm talking about. A real lack of respect among the staff for the hard work and expertise represented by the doctors, and it is undermining the authority that we have among the patients."

Jacob rolled his eyes. "Oh, please. You got a D.O. from the University of Barbados, and you teach kids how to pet dogs."

"Mr. Blaumann, I won't tolerate disrespect toward the doctors here," snapped Oliver. "Clearly you *are* aware that the code of conduct expressly forbids venturing outside the building in the company of a patient. So why did you feel it was within your rights to do so?"

Jacob had never heard him shout before—it gave him chills, how much it sounded like his father.

He knew he had no chance here. Despite the fact that he hadn't said anything inappropriate to Ella, and certainly hadn't *done* anything, he had legitimately broken the rules in letting her outside without permission. It was definitely a fireable offense, and it wasn't like his record was sterling otherwise. For years he'd worn his contempt for this place on his sleeve—talking back to the doctors, calling in sick, cutting corners, arriving late, leaving early. He'd been daring them to fire him almost since he started working there. Losing the job now wouldn't keep him up at night exactly, but if he told Dr. Dorothy to shove it, then he'd be gone and Ella would be on her own. On the other hand if he promised to give Ella a wide berth from here on out, there wasn't much point either.

"Ella Yorke," he began, much more flushed than he felt he had any reason to be, "is a very bright girl. We had a conversation one afternoon in Sissy Coltrane's art room—"

"*Dr.* Coltrane," Dr. Dorothy stressed.

"Okay, but she's *not* a doctor though, she's—"

"Mr. Blaumann, please," Oliver urged.

"I've just got to say, all this doctor this, doctor that crap is getting kind of Second Commandment. 'I am the Lord your doctor, thou shalt have no other doctors before me!' "

Dr. Dorothy nearly spit on the carpet. "Is he serious? He's really out of his mind. Oliver, he's—this kid needs help."

"He's not a kid, Dorothy, he's twenty-eight years old. And as I understand it he's having a difficult year, but *Jacob*, as a sign of respect in *this* workplace, you will refer to the doctors by their proper title, and that is final. Am I understood?"

"Does that mean I'm not fired then?"

There was a little flirtatious hint in Oliver's eye as he said, finally, "You have to promise me that you will not engage Ms. Yorke any further without guidance from professionals. From *doctors.* My door is always open."

Jacob reluctantly promised, and Oliver called the meeting to a close.

But as they were all standing up, Jacob turned to them both. "Can I just ask? Have you seen any kind of improvement, therapeutically speaking, in Ella Yorke since she came back?"

Dr. Dorothy gave him a dirty look. "That's not something we can discuss with you."

"Oh, come on. You tell us all the time which patients are doing worse, so we can keep a closer eye on them. What's wrong with saying if one is doing better?"

Oliver, surprisingly, accepted this logic. "Ella's actually been improving a lot since she came back. Her dosage of Prozac has been reduced. Dr. Feingold notes that she's been participating more in her group work, and Dr. Coltrane has nothing but good things to report. In our sessions she is . . . optimistic. It's a big improvement. In fact, if things stay positive, we all think she's going to be ready to leave by the end of the summer so she can start school again."

At this, Jacob smiled widely, and it seemed to confuse both psychiatrists—and even himself. Was he smiling smugly? Cryptically, sarcastically, menacingly? No. It was just an actual smile. A natural reaction to hearing something he'd been hoping to hear.

"Is there something—Jacob? Is there something we should be aware of?"

No end of things, he thought.

As punishment for the incident, he was put onto night shifts for the remainder of July, beginning the very next evening. After riding in on a bus packed with people heading home after a long day at work, Jacob arrived at Anchorage House just as the sun was setting behind the main gates. He'd been up since morning, spending the day alone in Oliver's flat, watching television in his underwear. It was vaguely boring but hardly a punishment. More like a punishment for Oliver, for now Jacob would hardly ever see him except on weekends.

He was still in a fine mood when he went to the bathroom to change. He had been eyeing a few of the longer novels in the common area library. *Anna Karenina*? Did they assume the kids would simply never finish it? Not like there were *trains* around, but still. Either way he was rather looking forward to the solitude. Only as he stood up, about to leave, did he notice something on the stall a few inches above his head where he'd etched his heart a month ago.

Someone had turned it into the top of the letter R, in the word PRAY.

Whatever. Probably one of the visitors had done it. No big deal. He left the bathroom.

By midnight he'd abandoned the Tolstoy with barely ten pages read. Anchorage House was practically silent with all the patients in their beds. After another hour he was desperate for *some* kind of incident: nightmares or insomnia were common, but only rarely did they erupt into anything that required an orderly's help. The doctor on staff was Patrick Limon, a slow-moving man in his seventies whose white hair burst Koosh-like from his skull and flowed seamlessly from his nostrils to his mustache and beard. In his white lab coat he glided from room to room, administering the odd night dosage and then sliding off again.

Jacob walked the length of every hallway. Then he walked them all backward. Then he tried the stairs backward and nearly broke his neck. Finally he marched back to the bathroom, looked again at the defacement of his graffiti. PRAY. So imperative! He took out his keys and scratched a response beneath it, in gigantic letters: WHAT FOR? But he didn't feel better. He checked his watch again. Four in the morning, and nothing left to do but tackle Dr. Limon and demand to be given a sedative. Something—anything—to stop the running commentary in his own head.

Once he'd heard beautiful whispering, poems begging him to write them down. He still heard whispering, only now it was considerably nastier. *All you've done is get her hopes up. Why? So she can head on back out into the world only to find that it is exactly as twisted and black and sick and fucked up as she thought it was? She isn't depressed, she's just thinking fucking clearly. Mind your own business. Haven't you learned anything? You can't save her. You are not special.*

He couldn't handle another hour, let alone another month, of this solitary confinement—which is what it was. How did these kids do it? Two hours left to go. There was no way. He was never going to make it. After another twenty minutes he'd decided to just leave. It was long overdue. He could probably walk to the bus station in an hour and then just go right on up to Boston. He sure as hell couldn't stay here. He went to his locker and took his real clothes—not even bothering to change into them—and then went back to the common area and grabbed *Anna Karenina*, thinking that if he got picked up by some creepy trucker, he could at least club the guy with it if he tried to get fresh.

As he shoved it into his bag, he spotted Ella's portrait still hanging, gray, on the wall in the dark. She'd be back at school soon, and not even too far behind schedule. He worried, though, that she might get depressed again when she found out he'd quit. He figured he had better leave some kind of goodbye, so he tore a page out of the back of the Tolstoy and went over to the chessboard, thinking he'd write something and leave it there for Ella to find the next day.

Only when he sat down he found there was already a piece of paper wedged under there. He'd sworn he'd checked earlier, and there was no way Ella had left her room, but there it was—not a poem this time, but a letter, which read:

> *Hope you get back on your old schedule soon! Paul was up here watching group as usual. Did you know he picks his nose? There was a guy in here last year with OCD who picked his nose so much that they had to actually put mittens on his hands. I asked Dr. Wilkins about it. Rhinotillexomania. It's a real thing! Before Maura, I had a roommate with OCD, and when she got nervous, she would pluck out her eyebrow hairs. The doctors warned her that it wasn't like when you shave your leg hair. It doesn't just grow back, but she couldn't help it. After a week she didn't have any eyebrows left! She tried to draw them back on with eyeliner, but it looked totally deranged,*

so I found a pen and shaded them a little, and that looked a little better, but then it came off in the shower a few days later. I told her we could just do it again . . . it wasn't like I had anything better to do, but she said it was pointless. I heard they sent her someplace down in Florida that specializes in OCD. I kept thinking, "She's right. It is pointless." Was she going to spend her whole life drawing her eyebrows back on every time she showered? Someone told me they can tattoo them back on again, but that's got to be pretty obvious. And if they ever did grow back, wouldn't she pluck them out again? It wasn't like walking around eyebrow-less was making her less anxious. So it was doubly pointless. Pointless squared. Just a pointlessness spiral, and then I got stuck in it. That's how I get about things. That's why I'm here. That's what my parents don't see. For them it's easy to just say, "Well, it could be worse! She could have plucked out her eyelashes too!" and they'll actually laugh about it and then go eat soup. I mean, hypothetically. They don't eat, like, odd amounts of soup. It's just that they do soup things. They do normal everyday soup things instead of, I don't know, caring. You're the first person I've met here, or really anywhere, who doesn't just go eat soup. I hope that's not weird to say. That day you talked to me about my picture was the first time anybody in this whole place ever asked me about something like that. Nobody looks closely. Not the other kids here. Not even doctors whose job it is to look. Everybody's just got their nose in their own soup. They say they care, but they don't put poems in books for me to read. They don't tell me I can be a poet or call me chowderhead. They talk to me about "adjusting my expectations for the world." And how I need to be realistic and just accept that this is how things work and that life is unfair and some people just don't get to have eyebrows, which is at least better than being a baby who is born starving and sick which is at least better than being raped and

> *murdered and I ought to be happy that I am smart and well-fed and have loving parents and clothes and a house and all that means I won't have to think about those other things which aren't in my control anyway so that's why I've just got to "work on me" and stop worrying so much so I can get better and get out of here and do something with my life, which is a precious gift I never asked for. I know, I know, I know. Anyways, I hope you get back to your old shift again soon because Paul is the worst.*

Jacob sat there a long time, reading the note twice more in the dark. He stared down at the pieces on the chessboard, both sides still trapped in their zugzwang, equally poised to lose. But then what was so bad about losing? he wondered. At least then you could start a new game. Worse to stand there forever. Idly by. Taking time off when there was so little time in the first place.

On the page from the book he'd ripped out, he wrote first in huge letters, "MAKE THE WORLD ADJUST ITS EXPECTATIONS OF YOU." Then he added, in smaller letters, "Assignment: Write me a sestina about soup for Tuesday. And a sonnet about eyebrows for Sunday." Then he folded it up and placed it back under the chessboard.

AUGUST

Solitude, it turned out, was something you could get used to, like anything else. Jacob finished *Anna Karenina* in two weeks and came up with a complete lesson plan for Ella. He continued to communicate with her via the chessboard, discussing poems along with whatever was going on during the daylight hours: Maura had a crush on one of the new patients named Roy, Paul's nose-picking was continuing, and Sissy was teaching them all to crochet, though they had to use cumbersome plastic hooks that nobody could hurt themselves with and they were forbidden from making scarves or anything with long sleeves. There were a lot of potholders happening. Ella was attempting a beret. Also word must have somehow gotten out that Dr. Dorothy was the one who had ratted on Jacob, because someone (Maura) had apparently stolen her glasses during a dog-petting session (not even at Ella's behest) and dropped the pieces into a vent.

Oliver had promised to get Jacob back on days just as soon as things quieted down (i.e., when Ella went back to school). Jacob didn't hold it against him, but he worried that their time apart didn't seem to be doing Oliver much good. He was increasingly despondent even on weekends. They still had sex in the morning on Saturday, and after that he seemed interested only in the television. Jacob sat through some political chatter about the Chelsea Clinton wedding. Oliver got a little choked up at the "candid" photos of old family moments: Bill and Chelsea and Socks watching a movie at the White House, Chelsea walking through an African village with her mother and making funny fish faces at her father.

"They're so sweet together," Oliver said.

"I guess," Jacob replied. He wasn't really paying much attention, flipping openly through the collected Keats, trying to choose which poem to excise when Oliver next went to the bathroom.

"I always wanted to have a daughter," Oliver said, searching the cracks in the ceiling.

"Hmmm," Jacob said, temporarily distracted by a commercial for the Stone Culligan movie. Had they really named it "Death Be Not Proud"? There ought to be a law.

Oliver trimmed his toenails, which he knew Jacob disliked witnessing, then changed the channel to BBC America, where an episode of *Coupling* was on.

Jacob watched as much as he could stand of the perilous minutiae of modern quirky relationships—about ten minutes—before he complained. "Can we watch something else?"

"I like this show."

"You're not even laughing!"

"I don't laugh at everything I like."

"It's a situation comedy. You're supposed to laugh at the *hilarious* situations they're in."

"I'm laughing on the inside."

"Hilarity isn't a cerebral thing, Oliver. You can't wryly observe hilarity."

"*I* can," he said simply. Someone on the show walked out of a closet without clothes on.

"HA HA HA HA HA," Oliver said.

Jacob smacked him with a pillow, and Oliver pinned him against the mattress, and they ended up having sex again. Afterward Oliver changed the channel to a nature show—a peace offering that kept Jacob in bed through lunchtime (cold cereal and half a banana, still in bed)—and they talked for a while about the oceans. Stunning, alien creatures that inhabited the depths. The British documentarian explained the reproductive cycle of the common Sydney, or gloomy, octopus. A little baby octopus floated there on the screen, about the size of a quarter, with pinkish flesh so translucent that a red lump of a brain was visible, floating behind its eyes.

Oliver began sniffling.

"It looks like a Martian from some crap B movie! Why on earth are you crying?"

"Look how *small* it is. You can literally see the big black ocean right through it! And the parents don't stick around to teach them how to survive out there. They just *know*."

"It's an arthropod, Oliver. You are projecting onto an arthropod."

"Octopuses," Oliver sniffed, "are *ceph*alopods. And they are highly intelligent creatures. They are one of the only other creatures with the ability to empathize."

Jacob had to agree that, by this logic, octopuses were above a lot of humans he could think of. Paul, for one. Still, he thought crying over them was excessive.

"They have what are called episodic personalities," Oliver added.

"What's that?"

"They behave consistently over the span of a few hours or even a day, but inconsistently over longer time frames."

"Is that why they call them gloomy octopuses?"

"No, that's because when they're mature, they turn gray colored. He's going to explain it in just a minute. Wait."

"Hang on. You've *seen* this before?"

Oliver didn't reply. He always got this way after he'd been caught crying. Jacob knew he probably could respond more kindly or at least bite his tongue but—an octopus?

"Are we just going to stay in bed all day?"

"You can go out if you want to."

Jacob went. He took the keys to the truck and drove out into Stamford, knowing that a good boyfriend would have talked it all out with Oliver. Listened to him pontificate about cephalopods and empathy and episodic personalities and how his dead father had sometimes been gloomy—and a good boyfriend would have loved him for all of it. Jacob didn't know how Oliver did it—sat around listening to people being sad all the time. He wished to hell that Oliver and all the others would just *do* something with all that disillusionment, as he'd done with Ella. You didn't have to limit it to poetry. Maybe the world wouldn't be so depressing if depressed people were more productive. There should be a whole Works Progress Administration for the clinically depressed. The DPA! Rise up, ye who are down and out! Tear up the rusting bridges and rip out the cracking highways and build new cities out of the rubble!

He drove to Borders, fifteen minutes down the road. When he got to the store, he ambled through the current releases, the magazines, and the café and eventually located the poetry section—half of one shelf. Paranormal Teen Romance had four. But no matter. He ran his fingers along the spines, searching for the one he'd been thinking about breaking his "no epics" rule for—one that he felt would tell Ella everything he needed to tell her himself but couldn't begin to say. He'd been debating translations in his mind—hoping there might be an edition available with the original Greek on the alternating pages. But all this proved to be grossly premature, for the store didn't seem to have a single copy of any edition of *The Odyssey*.

"Excuse me," he asked the clerk behind the information counter, a teenage girl who seemed as bored as any six Anchorage House patients. "I'm looking for *The Odyssey*. Is there maybe a classics section somewhere?"

She shook her head. "Author's name?"

"Homer," Jacob said.

"Homer what?"

"Just Homer."

"Like Madonna?"

"Yes, exactly."

Her black-polished nails clacked at her keyboard, and she looked up, puzzled. "Nothing under 'Homer.' You sure you don't mean like the guy on *The Simpsons*?"

"No, I don't mean like the guy on *The Simpsons*."

"Because then I could look it up under Simpsons."

Jacob sighed, wanting so badly to go off his rails, but for the first time in his life he wasn't sure of his ability to get back onto them again afterward.

He settled on taking a deep breath and spelling the title out for her, slowly. After a minute she shook her head. "I can put it on order for you if you want."

"Do you have it at another store?"

She checked and after consulting a manager was able to give Jacob directions to the other store where they had a copy. But when he got there, it turned out they didn't actually have one. A middle-aged man, as bored as his younger counterpart at the first store, was happy to redirect Jacob to a third store, and there, finally, Jacob did find a copy of the Fagles translation. As he paid for it at the front, he joked to the cashier that he had driven nearly four hours now trying to find the book.

"Sounds like you've had quite an odyssey," the cashier said with a smirk.

Jacob could have kissed him on the mouth. But he settled for asking if he might know how to get back to Stamford.

When he finally returned to the flat, it was already getting dark.

"What happened to you?" Oliver called. "Dinner got here an hour ago!"

"Let me *tell* you—" Jacob began, thrusting his hard-won copy of *The Odyssey* out in front of him like a trophy. But he stopped, mid-sentence, when he came to the coffee table. Oliver was back to watching the BBC America channel. And there on the screen was Sally Struthers herself, in grainy 1980s VHS quality, surrounded by tiny, emaciated African children, chewing on their thumbnails and staring wide-eyed into the camera, through the decades, out into the living room where Oliver was far more attentive to the huge spread of Chinese food that he had ordered.

Jacob had the fleeting feeling that those pale little shrouds of children were actually looking *at* the Chinese food—waiting for their moment to reach through the glass and steal a wonton. He forgot all about the book in his hand for a minute as the commercial continued—the 800 number flashing on the bottom. *Should I call?* he wondered. He had always thought these things were scams, or fronts for religious organizations. The sane, human thing to do was to change the channel. To take up club-league kickball. To read all the cartoons in the *New Yorker* and stuff the rest. To sit down and have some lo mein and talk about his epic journey to find an epic poem about an epic journey. In other words, to live.

"It's cold, but you can heat it up," Oliver said, turning back to the television screen just long enough to confirm that his show wasn't back on yet.

Jacob carried the book everywhere: under his arm up and down the Stamford antiques district as he and Oliver searched for new light fixtures; on the seat beside him on the bus, underlining passages during red lights; just inside his duffel bag with an Attic Greek dictionary so that he could retranslate stanzas late at night in the common room. He worked on it so obsessively that he nearly forgot that he had promised to fly home to see his parents for his birthday the week before Ella would be leaving. He'd have missed the flight entirely if Oliver hadn't noticed it on the schedule—months ago Oliver had requested that Friday off so that he could catch a less crowded midday flight and get down to Florida before night fell. (His parents now refused to drive after dark.)

"I need a day off anyway," Oliver said. "Let me drive you to the airport."

Jacob didn't need to pack. They kept a drawer full of warm weather clothes for him down there, and his mother always had a new toothbrush waiting in the holder in the guest bathroom. So he carried the book with him out to Oliver's truck, slid in beside it, and immediately resumed underlining. After several weeks he was still only on Book 15, where the goddess Athena is urging Odysseus's son, Telemachus, to hurry home before his mother, Penelope, weds one of her many suitors, and there were still *nine* books, plus a lot of conclusions he meant to draw at the end. If he was going to get it to Ella before she left Anchorage House, he'd have to really dig deep.

"It's good to see you studying again," Oliver commented as they drove over the Whitestone Bridge. Out the passenger-side window, Jacob could see Queens rising up across the river, and somewhere beyond it, he knew, was Manhattan. His old apartment and his old notes and his old life, all waiting there for him to return.

"Are you thinking about going back for your doctorate?"

"Is there something like art therapy but with poetry and books? Is that a thing?"

It had been some time since he'd seen Oliver look pleasantly surprised. "Bibliotherapy! Yes, there have been some good articles written about it. I could pull a few together for you if you'd like."

"Thanks. I've been thinking I'd like to try it."

"You mean start therapy?" He actually shouted this, utterly delighted, as if he'd been waiting ages for Jacob to say it.

Annoyed, Jacob explained, "No, I want to *give* therapy. I mean, I minored in psychology. I think I'd be good at it. If Sissy Coltrane can do it, I can too."

They rolled on past the *New York Times* building, and soon Jacob could just spot the remnants of the old World's Fair.

"Sissy has a certification in art therapy," Oliver said after a while.

Jacob snorted. "What Sissy has is an alpaca muumuu and a sense of entitlement."

Oliver groaned. "This is about Ella Yorke, isn't it?"

Jacob didn't answer but went back to annotating the book until soon they were winding along the terminals of Kennedy Airport, heading for Delta.

When they finally got to the curb where all the bag handlers were waiting, Oliver forced a smile. "Well," he said, handing Jacob a small silver case, "if you want to get certified in bibliotherapy, I think it'd be brilliant. But in the meantime, maybe you can use these."

Inside the silver case were twenty or thirty business cards that in gilt letters read, JACOB BLAUMANN. MASTER AND COMMANDER OF POETRY. SPECIALIZING IN EPIC WORKS. Jacob turned one over in his hands once or twice and then slid the case into his breast pocket. They were beautiful.

"These are perfect," he said. "Oliver, really. Thank you."

He couldn't think of the last time he'd bought Oliver a present, and certainly not out of the blue, and he considered apologizing until he realized that Oliver was trying to segue into something else.

"Jacob," he began, "I understand how rough this past year's been on you, but honestly, we might need to face the fact that this isn't . . . I mean perhaps we ought to—"

But Jacob hurriedly kissed him on the lips and pushed the side door open. Once he was out, he tried to close the door, only it got stuck, and he had to stop and open it again.

"It's jammed on the seat belt there," Oliver said.

"I can see that."

"Just push it back inside."

"I'm—" He bit his tongue and knocked the belt back inside. Then he closed the door again and waved goodbye. Oliver drove the truck off past the police officers, who were directing everyone away. The door was still wobbling. Way down near the very end of the lane, he watched as Oliver stopped, got out, came around, and with a firm hand this time, convinced the door to stay shut.

Jacob kept notating while he was standing in the security line. When the time came, he placed the book into the little gray bucket, set the notepad on top, and sent it off into the X-ray machine. The business card case he placed, with his keys, belt, three pens, shoes, and cell phone, in a separate bucket.

"Excuse me, sir?" the security guard asked him on the other side, as he reassembled himself. The guard looked at the book and thumbed through the notepad at the scribbled foreign lettering and sketched boat diagrams and maps of routes, as if they might contain secret codes or be some kind of blueprint for a bomb. "Is this everything?"

"Yes," Jacob affirmed. "This is all I have."

Progress. One whole book finished between boarding and taxiing, and Telemachus and his father were reunited at last, but then about an hour into the plane ride, the pen that Jacob was using to mark up the book began to leak. Cursing, he tried to mop up the spill with the back side of one of Oliver's business cards.

"Do you need to borrow a pen?" asked the woman next to him. Jacob looked at her for the first time since she'd sat down beside him. With long red nails, she dog-eared her place in *Heaven Exists!*, a book about a boy who allegedly died, went to heaven, and returned to report about it.

Jacob thanked the lady for the offer. She fished in her purse a moment, until she pulled out a ballpoint BIC.

"Oh," he said, hesitating, "it's blue."

"Sorry?"

"It's a blue pen. I've been writing all my notes in black. Does that sound crazy?"

The woman didn't say but looked a little nervous as she tucked her pen back away.

"How is that?" Jacob asked, thumbing toward her book.

She made an unmistakable *eh* face before asking, "What's that about?"

"This jerk who gets lost at sea for thirty years."

"Do you have a big test on it coming up?" she pointed to his notebook, which Jacob then covered slightly with his hand.

"No. It's a gift for someone."

"Lucky someone," the woman said.

Jacob went back to his work. By alternating his leaky pens every five minutes, and mopping up the ink spills in between with the backs of the business cards, he made it through the rest of the section just before the wheels touched down in Tampa.

SEPTEMBER

He hardly recognized his parents. It was like *Close Encounters* down there in Tampa, as if aliens had abducted the weary, grumpy people who had raised him, leaving behind these revitalized, reprogrammed retirees. His father and mother had once sleepwalked through the first half of the day. Now they woke up every morning at five a.m. and ran three miles together. They split a grapefruit for breakfast, and to cool down they swam laps. And they weren't alone. The predawn world of Tampa was alive with octogenarians in DayGlo tracksuits, power walking down the little fake streets. Their retirement community was twenty acres lost in time, polished Cadillacs and Oldsmobiles parked in every driveway. Men wearing hats. Women stopping to chat on the corner. In the afternoons his father had tennis lessons with a coach who had formerly trained Tennessee teens for the pro circuit. "He's got trophies in a case in his living room," Jacob's mother exclaimed when he joined her for a cucumber peel in the spa. "He thinks he's Mr. Big Shot."

His mother had befriended a woman named Lydia in the condo next to theirs, who had been a chef in Chicago for many years and was now showing his mother how to make cheese soufflés and teaching her about wine. "We're taking a trip out to the Loire Valley next year. Have you ever been to a real vineyard before?" Jacob found himself saying he hadn't, already mourning a whole childhood of nonexistent soufflés.

Weirdest yet was how they'd both become more Jewish. They'd stopped going to synagogue when he was a kid, thanks to Gene Blaumann's compulsion to debate the rabbi every Shabbat before they'd even consecrated the challah. When you were too argumentative for Westchester Jews, you were in pathological territory. But now Gene Blaumann was going to Saturday-morning services? His mother was involved in an outreach program, focused on what she called the "next generation crisis." The problem was no longer that good Jewish boys (like Gene Blaumann) married shiksa women but that even children of two natural-born Jews were less often devout, to the extent that fewer and fewer were bar or bat mitzvahed.

"Better not let them meet your gay son then," Jacob said.

But his mother shook her head. "Oh, who cares? They all watch

Will and Grace now. Nobody cares you're gay. Just do me a favor and tell them you go to services for Shabbat."

Fortunately between the exercising, the culinary lessons, the services, and the card games, his parents were almost too busy to notice he was there. He indexed *The Odyssey* by the pool most of the day before they dragged him out to Amici's, the local Italian place that "everybody" went to, for dinner. Nobody was interested in his complaint that it seemed ludicrous to use an English possessive with a plural Italian noun.

"We got you an iPhone," his father said as antipasto came. "Give it to him, Anjelica."

His mother dropped her knife on the fried artichoke. "Let him open it and find out!"

"What's the surprise?" his dad said. "That's what everybody gets now. Coach told me the 3GS is really good. I got one for me too."

And before Jacob's very eyes, his own father produced an iPhone from his pocket.

"You can put all your songs on here. Books too! Don't have to lug that huge thing around with you all the time. You're going to mess up your back. Take it from me."

Jacob clutched the book on the bench beside him as if it were a life vest and Amici's Family Restaurant were about to get hit with a tidal wave. "Thanks so much," he said, taking the gift without unwrapping it.

"And you can get Facebook on it too," his mother said. "Are you on Facebook?"

"No, I am not on Facebook. Tell me you aren't."

"Oh, you have to see. Gene, show him how you put all your people in it."

And Jacob watched as his father held the phone up over the bowl of calamari and scrolled, slowly, through a list of contacts with his thumb. Jacob watched as his mother craned her neck to see who was coming into the restaurant and if it was anyone she needed to wave at. Maybe they were still his parents after all.

"So are you meeting any nice men up there?" she asked.

Not that Jacob was going to answer, but for fear that he might, his father quickly changed the subject. "Why don't you quit that stupid job and call Phil Jalasko's son at Sony Records? Poetry's kind of like music, and I bet you they could use someone smart like you to fix up some of those lyrics. 'You and me could write a bad romance'—is that English?"

"Please tell me you don't have Lady Gaga on that thing."

His father sighed and mashed some buttons. "Phil's son put some stuff on there. I don't—I can't tell how to take things off."

"Here," Jacob said, "let me show you." The next morning they drove him back to the airport and dropped him off at the curb, his father waving his phone in the air, smiling, and his mother crying as she did every time they did this.

"When you get there, if you don't mind, just let us know you made it, all right?" she asked as she hugged him by the curb.

Begrudgingly, Jacob had to admit that it was somewhat pleasant to listen to *West Side Story* and Fleetwood Mac's *Rumours* over and over again on the flight back (the only two withstandable CDs of his mother's that he could find). And with a fresh set of pens and a pack of Kleenex, he managed to get all the way through Book 24 before they touched down in New York. That night, after Oliver fell asleep watching another nature program, Jacob got up and finished the concluding notes in the study. He worked all night without sleeping, and during the ride to Anchorage House, he read and reread the notes. It was the hardest he'd worked on anything since *Shitstorm,* and he wasn't even a little sad to be giving it away.

That morning, before the wake-up rounds began, Jacob slipped the annotated copy of *The Odyssey* onto the bookshelf in Ward III. By lunchtime, it was gone. As he patrolled the outer hallway, he saw Ella in the cafeteria in deep-reading mode. Maura's chatter from the other end of the table wasn't causing even the slightest distraction. Ella's eyes flew between the book and the notebook. In Feingold's group, everything about her demeanor suggested that she was no longer present, besides bodily, in this universe. And as Sissy tried to get everyone to make hand puppets out of paper bags that afternoon, Ella glued on eyes and ribbons idly, her smile stretching and collapsing like the bellows of an accordion playing inaudible notes.

At last, in the afternoon Jacob had the chance to talk with her briefly in the common room. Paul was watching, he could tell, and so were Dr. Dorothy and Dr. Wilkens, from where they were conferencing next door, but Jacob had no reason left to care. Whatever happened, this thing was hers.

Ella clutched the book as if it might run away. "You did this?"

"That?" Jacob looked carefully. "Appears to be the work of a fellow named 'Ho-mer.'"

Ella looked at the ceiling, as if the right words might be up there. "Well. Thank you. I mean. I don't know how to thank you."

"You did already. Just before there . . . when you said 'thank you.'"

She got a look as if contemplating many, many things that she couldn't possibly find the time to say. At last she settled on "Okay, this time you have to explain though. Why?"

"Just something to take with you when you go."

"No, I mean, why *this* book? Not that I'm—not that I don't love it. I *love* it."

Jacob wanted to tell her that it was something he'd needed to reclaim; something someone else hadn't been able to finish; a journey he'd needed to take, vicariously. He wished there was time to sit and explain it all. But she was due to be picked up just after his shift.

"A while ago I saw your mug in the art room. You wrote 'Odysseus' around the rim."

"Uh, yeah. In *Greek,*" Ella said. She could hardly keep from laughing. "My boyfriend—" She had to try again. "My ex. I don't know what he is. Anyway, his middle name is Ulysses."

Jacob felt himself blush and wondered if this was the guy he'd seen in her prom photos.

"Ulysses? What, is he from Brooklyn or something?"

She danced backward a little. "No, his parents are big Civil War nuts. They do those re-creations and things? He *hates* it. But I always thought it was kind of sweet. I was going to get it tattooed on my wrist. Anyway, I learned to write it in Greek like that so nobody would figure it out."

Then, moving up onto the window ledge for a moment, she lowered her voice. "We were still dating the first time I was here, and I was kind of obsessed, talking about him all the time and doing stupid stuff like weaving his initials into these Native American dream catchers that Sissy was having us make. She told me I had to knock it off. Said it wasn't healthy."

He was sure his face was red now. "Sorry. I guess I thought it was your favorite book."

"Well. It is now," she said.

Jacob, who hadn't been nervous talking to a girl since around the third grade, found himself at a loss. "You always looked as if you were trying so hard at everything here. You're a smart kid, and you're going to do great things with your life, and I guess it sucks that it's always going to be a little harder for you than for other people, and you'll have to stay on your medication, and sometimes you're still going to see a homeless guy on the street or something and it's going to break your heart, and you'll want to crawl under a rock somewhere and hide everything good that you've got to offer from the world because it's going to seem like the world doesn't deserve it, but I promise it does—"

Jacob was talking so fast and gesticulating so wildly that he was running out of breath. Paul was staring at him now like he had three ears. He was glad that he couldn't see Dr. Dorothy out in the hallway, and he hoped she couldn't see him. His lungs felt like rocks in his chest, and it was as if a great swarm of bees were building a honeycombed hive inside his skull. He felt the whole room wobble like the door to Oliver's pickup truck, and then Ella was grabbing something—it looked like a paper bag for him to breathe into. He snatched it and held it up to his mouth, forcing out a deep breath that inflated the bag before either of them realized that it was, in fact, her hand-puppet from art therapy. Its googly eyes rattled as he inhaled, and the green pom-pom that had been its nose fell silently onto the rug.

Ella laughed first—a shocked and delighted giggle that she seemed unable to settle—and as Jacob mimed a little defensive stamping on the offending clown-puppet, that set her off even more. The other patients were all cracking up, and in a moment he felt Dr. Wilkens's hand on his shoulder, coaxing him to head over to the nurse to get checked out.

Jacob tried to say he was fine, but it didn't come out. He gave Ella a farewell salute, and she clutched the book to her chest again, mouthing the words *thank you* as he took shaky steps, backward, out of the room. After getting a little orange juice into his system, the nurse said she thought he'd be all right, but Oliver sent him home early just to be sure. It was only as he rode the bus back that he remembered the other thing he'd meant to write in the front of the book—that he'd signed up for Facebook, using his new phone. But in his haste to leave he'd left it in his locker. He thought, maybe in the morning, then, he'd send her an invitation, so they could be friends.

Sometime later that night, with no book to annotate, cold ginger beef in a takeout container at the foot of the bed, and more hilarity on the television, Jacob decided he'd wait another day or two. Tomorrow he'd get up and go through those gates again to Anchorage House. And she'd be off in her real life, and maybe it was all just better if he left it that way.

OCTOBER

October arrived, and with it the golden leaves around Anchorage House began to fall into the duck pond where Jacob, once again, resumed his daily vigil. Under the willow tree he would stand and think about what he'd said to Irene in the hospital, her smile, their conversation the night before about Hector, and the way Irene had felt in his arms when he carried her down the steps of the Met. He thought about the way she'd bent down before the pyramid walls and how she'd looked standing in front of the painted field of poppies. He remembered her on Shelter Island and how, out of everyone, she'd told him last because she'd known that of all of them, he was the one it would break. He'd always thought that being a cynic would prepare him for something like this, but she'd known that only made it worse, because it made you think you wouldn't care, and yet of course you would. He thought even further back, to the way she'd looked in the hot tub that night on the roof of the Waldorf Astoria, opaque bra against the snow-blown skyline of Manhattan. He hadn't gone to her wake, wasn't planning on going to see the show Sara was organizing, of all the things Irene had been working on that year—not because she'd wasted herself on them but because he didn't see how any of them could be more powerful than her simple being.

Jacob waited for the old routines at Anchorage House to resume their comfort, but week after week he found no trace of the numbness he'd known before Ella. There were more hellos at Oliver's office door and the same old snide remarks from Paul, this time about the new behavioral therapist—Dr. Patricia Cain, whose bosom seemed to occupy Paul's every waking thought. Jacob was ready to find him a pacifier to suck on.

About the only real change was with Sissy Coltrane. She'd gone from being oddly friendly around him to being downright chummy—acting as if they were old buddies, asking if he was thinking about getting some different job soon. At the height of it, she even handed him an assortment of brochures to continuing education programs that she claimed to have stumbled upon one day in a public library somewhere. The programs ranged from nursing to publishing to information technology.

"Oliver told me you were thinking about going back to school. You know, I just feel like you can't ever underestimate the value of a nice change. I lived out in the Midwest for a while after college. I worked on a ranch. Can you believe it?"

"I can, actually, believe that," Jacob said.

"You'd love it."

"I wouldn't."

"Oh, come on," she said. "Just think about the poetry you could write in the mountains, the prairies. You know there are still places in this country that no human feet have ever touched? I miss the horses. Fishing in an icy stream on a summer's day, blackbirds and locusts and all that. I'm telling you, the poems will practically write themselves."

Jacob gagged. "That's good, because I sure wouldn't want to write them."

Instead of getting annoyed, she slapped his shoulder, as if this were just typical Jacob. It *was*, but there wasn't any typical anything between them, so why would she be acting like it?

"Where *would* you go, if you could go anywhere?" she asked.

After a little thought he said, "Think I'd really like to be a goatherd."

"Brilliant!" Sissy clapped her hands as if he'd correctly identified a shape in a kindergartner's lineup.

"I'd live way up on the side of a mountain with a long winding path down to the bottom. There'd be a river there, full of nymphs and woods nearby haunted by panpipes. And people from the town on the other side of the valley would cross the river and hike up the path and buy my goats whenever they needed to make sacrifices to the gods. I'd be known, mountain-wide, for having the best goats for currying godly favor."

He could tell Sissy was mentally fitting him for a straitjacket. He just didn't care.

"And there'd be this little cave on the far side of the mountain, at the right edge of the known world, where some horrific monster was rumored to dwell. The kind that spits acid and devours children whole. And anytime something went wrong, we'd all blame it on the monster. Bad weather, dead crops, sick relatives. Can you imagine? If evil was just this thing that lived down the road? Not some North Korean Napoleon or Afghani fundamentalist fanatic. Not some—some all-pervading uneasiness. Not some malignant cell on a mission. Imagine if you could point to a spot on a map and say, *There—that's where bad things come from.*"

The phone rang on Sissy's desk. Dropping her pencils in a pile onto the table, she swooshed over to pick it up. "Sissy Coltrane? . . . Oh *hi,* Oliver! You're— . . . Oh yes, he's here. Would you like me to send him over? . . . Oh. Sure. All right. Okay, bye now! Talk to you later."

"Whither shall I wander?" Jacob asked, raising his arms to the ceiling.

"He says you've got a surprise visitor waiting out by the gates!"

Jacob felt the sudden weightlessness, the vanishing of all walls and floors and tables, the fresh new world of the top deck of a cruise liner. Had Ella really come back to visit him?

Wasting no time at all, he charged back to his locker, threw his jacket on over his work clothes, and marched outside and down the gravel driveway. A little green Prius was idling on the other side, its driver half hidden behind an enormous and fashionable pair of rounded orange sunglasses, hair trimmed short. He wondered what Ella could be saying to Winston that was cracking him up so much that he could hear him laughing all the way up by the old, disused, and slouching stables. But then she whipped the sunglasses off and Jacob saw her face.

It was Sara. He'd never seen her behind the wheel of a car before—back in college, George had driven them everywhere in his old beat-up station wagon. Now he recognized the haircut, and the glasses, from the Facebook photos of her and George at fancy cocktail gatherings in Boston, at the mahogany Harvard Faculty Club, at Tresca in the North End, in *The New Bostonian*'s corporate suite at Fenway Park.

Wishing the nuns had thought to dig a moat around the place, he waved as Winston opened the gates so Sara could drive in. She jumped out of the puttering car and ran to him—some feat in the cream-colored heels she was wearing. Mud splashed all over the old-lace bows on the toes as she tackled him in a slender-armed bear hug. He remembered the shoes had been Irene's once—she'd blown almost two hundred dollars on them at Mel's.

"Jacob!" she shouted, melting into his shoulders as she hugged him. Then, straightening herself up, she pulled a gold-embossed envelope from an orange ostrich-skin handbag that matched her sunglasses. "So *this* is where you work? Wait. I have to move my car before this nice man gets in trouble."

He followed her back to the green Prius and climbed in. He was about to ask what she was doing here when she threw the gear into reverse. A black-and-white screen flickered on in the dashboard to show that the driveway behind them was clear, and a sensor went off when she got too close to one of the brick walls as she K-turned around.

"Um, my shift isn't over for another hour, crazy."

Sara flashed her eyes at him mischievously. "You're being kidnapped! I'm sorry, but it was the only way. This morning I called Oliver, and he agreed wholeheartedly that you needed to be taken down to the city for a belated birthday bacchanal."

"He said that?"

"Well, no, he said you'd become a 'first-class mope,' and I said you always *were* a first-class mope but that if you'd recently reached platinum mope status, something had to be done."

They were speeding down the street toward the southbound Hutchinson River Parkway. Jacob knew that the more he resisted, the more Sara would insist.

"Could we make a quick stop at Oliver's? I'm still in my uniform."

Sara appeared delighted. "I get to see the *flat*?"

It took Jacob a moment to remember that he had told Irene all about "the flat" last year and that, as with everything in their circle, it had soon been repeated.

"How would you like to see *the* Szechuan Garden?"

Even after all this time, he knew her far too well.

Before long they were seated across from each other in his usual spot, just back from the side window. Jacob had changed his clothes at Oliver's and now looked "dashing" according to Sara, in a blue striped shirt and dark wool pants. As they had their first round of Tsingtaos, she outlined the epic evening that she had planned for them: they were to eat nothing *too* filling here at the old Szechuan Garden, because she had a seven-thirty appointment with a caterer at Seventeen Madison, which meant they'd feast on free samples of passed hors d'oeuvres (including the chef's famous pickled radishes), minted lamb lollipops, rock shrimp served on Himalayan salt blocks, and of course the signature sirloin Sriracha sliders.

After that there would be a cake tasting at Happy Puppy Wonder Cakes, down in SoHo, which had *the* best lavender buttercream frosting and the infamous "crack" cookie pie filling that had been deemed the "city's crackiest" by *New York* magazine that summer. After that, dancing was possible, depending on the crowd at Niagara, to be followed by drinks at an Oscar Wilde–themed speakeasy called Dorian Gray's, which was "secretly" located behind a full-length portrait of a French cavalier in an otherwise excellent *crêperie* on Allen Street. You had to pull on one of the light fixtures next to the painting and then tell the painting how many in your party, and if there was room, the picture would slide over to let you in. If not, you wrote your cell-phone number on a piece of paper and slipped it through a small crack in the wall, and someone would text you when there was a booth available.

Jacob didn't know where to begin: perhaps that there'd never been prohibition on alcohol in Ireland, where Oscar Wilde had been born, or in London or France where he'd later lived, and that he'd died more than twenty years before there was any need for speakeasies here in America. But he listened to Sara gush about these places she'd been *dying* to go ever since leaving the city. It was as if nothing had changed for her. She thought she could walk back in, and it would all be the same. She told him he was welcome to crash that night in her hotel room, where George would meet them in the morning.

Jacob didn't see the point in arguing, seeing as he had absolutely no intention of doing any of this. They were on their second round of Tsingtaos, and it wasn't quite five o'clock. He'd never seen Sara have more than three before needing to curl up and take a nap somewhere. Already he was planning on persuading her to come back to Oliver's. He found himself only half listening to her as she spoke. Scarlet leaves scattered as the bus rolled up and sighed to a stop outside the window. Needlessly, he ran his eyes down the familiar columns of misspelled food items and pointed out his favorites to Sara.

She reached across the table and took his hand in hers. "I'm so glad to see you're okay, Jake. We've all been worried about you."

Her eyes were red underneath heavier-than-usual mascara. *We all?* Who did she mean, besides herself and George? Was she still talking to William, even? He thought about telling her that he'd nearly driven up last month, after Oliver's dad died, but instead he asked, "How is Georgina doing?"

She let her eyelids flutter shut as if she couldn't bear to look at him as she said it. "He's hanging in there. He's—you know. I think of all of us, he was probably the least ready for what happened."

Jacob paused, surprised to hear her say this.

"He's been distracted," she concluded, and began braiding the wrapper from her chopsticks, tapping her toe on the linoleum, looking about four inches from him when she spoke. Unlike George, as Sara got more anxious, she drank less. *Happy families are all alike; every unhappy family is unhappy in its own way.* Damn, that was a good line. He had never liked it before, mainly because he felt that his own family was unhappy in a generic kind of way. But Gene and Anjelica Blaumann weren't his only family. Now it seemed undeniable to him that, whereas his New York family had indeed been happy in the way that all groups of young dreamers are happy before they've given up, they were all quite unhappy now, each in their own special ways. That was what made it all the more miserable: they couldn't even be unhappy together.

"Speaking of the wedding!" Sara said abruptly, though they hadn't been speaking of it at all. She dug around in her purse and produced a lovely cream-colored envelope.

He read it out loud. " 'Mr. Jacob A. Blaumann. Of question mark street. Apartment number question mark. NYC, NY. Question mark, question mark, question mark, question mark, question mark, dash, four more question marks.' "

"I take my postal codes very seriously," Sara said. "Open it already!"

He did. " 'Please save the date of March 20, 2011, for the wedding of' "— he paused and then shouted her name across the room— " 'MS. SARA SHERMAN AMPERSAND MR. GEORGE MURPHY'— that's a commendably bold font choice there—'New York, New York. Invitation to follow.' Don't you need to tell people where it is?" Jacob asked, flipping the card over. "Where's the place I check off chicken or fish?"

"That comes on the invitation."

"This isn't an invitation?"

"No, this is a save-the-date card. The invitation comes—well, soon now actually, but I've been trying to get this to you since June."

"I've been swamped."

"I know. It's hard to—I know it isn't the same. Look. George and I wanted to ask you—we were wondering if you'd read something at the wedding. You pick. Something from *The Bridge* if you want. Of course, an original Blaumann would be fantastic, but—"

Before Jacob could refuse, the little jingle bells on the front door sounded. He glanced around just in time to see Sissy Coltrane walking in, her bony arm hooked around Oliver's. They were laughing and paused to punctuate their happiness with a soft kiss. Even the servers seemed to realize this was awkward, as in midconversation Oliver began strolling directly to his usual table, which was apparently also *their* usual table, and where Jacob and Sara were already sitting.

"Oh! Jacob!" he shouted, loud enough to scare the fish in the tank in the back. "Funny to find you here! Sissy and I were just having a meeting. Sorry. You must be Sara. We spoke on the phone? I thought—I thought you two were heading for a big night out in the city."

Jacob watched as deep red shame soaked through the baggy skin of Sissy's cheeks, and she looked as if she wanted to bolt out of Szechuan Garden and the entire state of Connecticut. Oliver did a very nice job of looking vaguely off at the window, as if the situation might disappear if he didn't acknowledge it. Fortunately Sara wasn't as ambivalent.

She pulled Jacob to his feet, and they were out the door before anyone realized they were dining and dashing. It was like a scene in a movie—too exciting to be real. Or to be part of *his* life, at any rate. But the longer he sat there, mute, in the passenger's seat of the

Prius, the more sense it made. His secret, older boyfriend had a secret, older girlfriend. Sara, on the other hand, was fuming. She sped down the parkway ranting, like the Jacob of old. *How dare he* this and *how dare he* that. Jacob didn't argue. She had a valid point. But what shocked Jacob the most wasn't Sissy's age or gender, or even the fact that Oliver was sleeping with another of his subordinates, but that he'd *dared*, period. How could someone who only ever ate at one restaurant juggle two love lives at once? Jacob was almost impressed.

As the skyscrapers emerged on the horizon, and the city noises grew in his ears, and the world outside the car filled up with people, rushing around with such purpose, Jacob felt like no part of it at all. He couldn't shake the feeling all through the night as Sara dragged him through the streets, outraged and leery the whole time, to the caterer and the cupcakes (they skipped the dancing) and to the speakeasy, where they really did pass through a secret passage to sit at a narrow bar and sip twenty-dollar cocktails made with Carpano Antica and house-made ginger syrup and yellow chartreuse. He let the night happen to him, moving through it all like a ghost. At the end of the night, he stood at the foot of the hotel escalators and kissed Sara goodbye on both cheeks and said he had to get back home. He promised to meet her and George for brunch in the morning, though he already knew he would not go. She promised him it was going to get better, that he didn't need Oliver—and Jacob knew that that was true. He wasn't feeling like this because of Oliver. This was how he'd felt all along, but Oliver, Anchorage House, and even Ella had been distracting him from it. He was absolutely lost.

Jacob walked all the way to Columbus Circle. He'd been gone so long, the old MetroCard in his wallet had expired. He bought a new one and went down to the 1 train, waiting at the very end of the platform, trying to get as far as he could from the fiddler and the guy with a washboard who were playing something intolerably cheerful. He closed his eyes and waited to feel the faint breeze—the front end of the gust of wind before the train—the first signal to every real New Yorker that a train was coming, before you could lean out and see the headlights on the tracks or hear any noise at all. He still knew just where to stand to have the doors open right in front of him. When they did, he stepped into the back of the train and for the first time in his life found himself in a car that was completely empty. His heart pounded as he studied the vacant yellow and orange seats. He stood, in the very center, as the doors closed, and he began to fly along beneath the ground. He shut his eyes and tried to feel as if he were weightless, on a new planet, lost in the sound of the tunnels. Instead he felt himself underwater, unable to breathe, as if the car were packed with a thousand people.

And then, with no one there to see, Jacob wept for the first time since Irene had died. And he kept weeping, even after he transferred to a 2 train at 72nd Street. Nobody minded much. It wasn't so odd, in the city, to see a grown man crying in the middle of a whole lot of people. He got off at 110th, with the dark void of Central Park at his back, and walked the rest of the way to his old apartment—some thirty blocks through Harlem, lurid and alive, all brassy horns and endless green lights arching above the avenues. Everyone seemed younger than they had been a year ago; everything felt bigger. It was always the same city, only more so, and this was why he'd had to subtract himself from it. He couldn't stand to see it not being less so: the bums and the bridges and the bodegas and the bottles that overflowed the trash cans on the corner. She wasn't there, and it seemed impossible that all this could still be going on.

NOVEMBER

Either Oliver felt guilty enough or Jacob's cold shoulder wore him down, because at the beginning of November the paperwork was completed to have Jacob join the staff part time as an assistant art therapist. This meant he'd work an extra shift per week, which barely helped cover his train ride each day up and back from Harlem, but he didn't mind. Under the auspices of this "special pilot program," he was even able to get permission to walk with patients around the property. He had a budget to buy books (one copy of *The Odyssey*, which had to be shared) and an hour a week to meet with patients to discuss readings on an individual basis. Maura signed up, and then so did Roy (they were "dating" now, whatever that meant when you were both stuck in a mental institution), and then Jane and Annabeth joined.

It was slow going. A lot of them protested the choice of material. Many seemed to be hoping they'd talk about *The Hunger Games*, but Jacob encouraged them to read slowly and out loud if a passage didn't make sense at first. They discussed history and geography as they hiked around in the crisp, late autumn fog. Around the overgrown foundations of the original manor house, they dissected the Lotus Eaters, and down in the graveyard they went over the cannibalistic Laestrygonians. Under the drip of mossy overgrown trees, Jacob began to recall some of the Gothic creepiness that had appealed to him about this place not so long ago. They walked to the farthest north side of the property, past the stables with the collapsed roof, where they could stand amid the rubble and read from "Nausicaa" while the clean-suited men and women of Discover Card waited for the bus across the highway. Down by the duck pond they watched the Chinese Academy boys soccer team practicing their goal kicks. Jacob and Maura spoke about the Cyclops.

"Odysseus is kind of obnoxious," Maura observed. "He manages to get away from Polyphemus and instead of being, I don't know, *grateful*, he's got to stand on his ship and call him a 'shameless cannibal' and a 'coward.' No wonder the poor thing decides to hurl half a mountain at him. And then Poseidon makes him get lost for another ten years or whatever?"

"Hubris," Jacob said. "Arrogance. Pride. Everybody's got a bit of it in them somewhere."

Maura looked as if she might prefer to just jump into the duck pond. Jacob had never paid much attention to her before, but she was a sweet kid, shyer than Ella and twice as anxious.

"Well, think about it this way," he said. "If Odysseus hadn't been so high on his own superior intelligence, he'd have gotten home to Ithaca in weeks, not years. He wouldn't have lived with the sorceress Circe or seen the land of the dead or bested Scylla and Charybdis. That's half the story, and the better half too. Literature is really just the documentation of human struggling."

This seemed to perk her spirits up more than a little. Jacob was happy to be outside, talking about poetry. The ducks hadn't yet flown south, and the boys across the way were running comically in place, cotton socks pulled up to their knees. Thanksgiving was coming up. He couldn't believe it had been a year already.

"I wish we still had gods," Maura said eventually.

"I've never been very religious myself," Jacob admitted.

"No, I mean *gods*, plural. What I love about this book is that there's all these monsters just sort of going about their evil business. And there are *twelve* gods running around up there on Mount Olympus, fighting, getting in each other's way, hopping down to mess with the mortals whenever the mood strikes them. It all just makes a lot more sense to me. None of them are all-powerful or all-knowing, not even Zeus. They're constantly getting stuff wrong. It explains all the evil stuff that gets missed, like these monsters on their islands. Makes more sense than there being just this one God up there, supposedly completely understanding everything and *intending* everything—even, like, plagues and assault rifles and starvation and AIDS and homeless veterans and just plain old sadness."

Jacob tried to step in, but Maura wasn't nearly finished.

"And, like, everyone seems to think that this must be proof that there is no God. Or that if there ever *was* a guy up there smiting sinners and sending angels off to grace the faithful, He's packed his bags and headed off for greener pastures. But what if the Greeks had it right, and there are just too *many* of them. Bumping around up there, trying to get things right and not always doing such a great job—forgetting monsters, getting too drunk, and running off with the wives of other gods, but still coming through with a nice miracle now and then? I think we need *more* gods. That's what I think. One isn't enough."

Jacob clapped. It was a rant he'd be proud to call his own.

Maura grinned. "Oh, by the way, I got a letter from Ella last week! She's making the dean's list at school and dating some new guy named Fred. Seems nice, if you like guys named Fred. Everything's going really well. She asked about you."

Jacob looked off at the lake. He wondered how a diaper had managed to get in there, and he watched as the bloated, grimy thing floated back and forth in the breeze. "You know, before *The Odyssey*, before the Trojan War even started, Odysseus didn't want to go?"

Maura shook her head.

"He didn't want to be a hero or get into a huge war over Helen of Troy, even though he'd sworn an oath to Menelaus that he would. The poor guy just wanted to stay home. So he pretended he'd gone insane, thinking it would get him excused from military service. He ran around plowing his fields, day and night, with salt instead of grain and, I imagine, ranting and raving like a lunatic for any and all to see. And everybody bought it—he almost got away with it. But then Agamemnon came by and decided to test Odysseus to see if he was truly crazy. He put Odysseus's infant son down in the field in front of the plow. He reasoned that if Odysseus were really insane, or *really* wanted to stay safe at home, he'd plow right over his son. But of course, he didn't."

"What a jerk," she said. "The other guy, I mean."

"Oh, well. He gets hacked to death later on," Jacob grinned.

This didn't seem to comfort her as much as it did him.

"My point is that Odysseus knew he had to choose," he said. "He knew that even though the gods favored him, they weren't going to get him out of the jam. He knew he was going to have to stop pretending and get out there and *fight*, not just because he loved his son but because he had made an oath and was bound to keep it. And so he went off to the longest, bloodiest, most absurd war that had been fought in the history of mankind. And *he* was the one who cleverly dreamed up the Trojan horse and finally ended it.

"If he had never gone—if he had stayed home with his son as any sane man would want to do—well, who knows? For sure, Homer wouldn't have written one book about him, let alone two, and half of Western literature wouldn't have been based on the trials and tribulations of this crafty, arrogant guy and all the good and all the evil he saw. This guy who won a war and spoke to gods. This guy who dined at distant palaces and sailed to corners of the globe that no one had yet set foot on. This guy who crossed over into the land of the dead and returned to tell about it. There wasn't a man alive then who'd seen so much of the world as Odysseus, good and bad, and *that* is the point.

"You've got to entrust yourself to the waves, lash yourself to the mast, pray the gods are on your side, and rely on cunning to survive the rest. The seas are full of forgotten monsters, yes, but they're full of forgotten glories too. And the people who stay home and sit out the war never get to see them. That's what I think, anyway."

Maura beamed up at the clouds rolling busily across the wide gray sky. And for a little while, until the November chill won out, they both believed there was a heaven out beyond them where a pantheon of gods and goddesses still did their occasional best to keep tabs on a world that had only gotten larger since everyone in it had stopped believing in them.

DECEMBER

It wasn't clear who found out about Oliver and Sissy. Certainly Jacob hadn't told anyone. But the rumor spread overnight, until everyone had heard the news. Allegedly the board was upset. Sissy was Oliver's direct report, and one or the other of them would have to go. Word was that Sissy was taking this as her chance to leave and go out West, with icy streams in summer and horseflies and grand plateaus and blackbirds and whatnot.

Oliver called Jacob into his office that afternoon. He kept the door shut and spoke in whispers, as if he might somehow get in more trouble. "Jacob, I don't know what you've heard, but obviously—"

Jacob stood back and raised his arms dramatically. "I'm shocked—*shocked!*—to find out that there is gambling going on in this establishment."

"Is that supposed to be funny?"

"It's pretty funny in *Casablanca* at least," Jacob said. "Look, I don't care if you want to try to be straight. I don't think it's going to work, but hey, I get it. After your father and everything."

"Jacob, I don't want to talk about that. I'm trying to—damn it, I'm trying to apologize to you here. I tried for months to make it clear that our relationship just wasn't working."

"Hell, Oliver, I knew that."

"Then why didn't you just end things with me and move on, if you knew?" Oliver looked as if he might cry.

Jacob felt terrible. What a way to treat his gloomy octopus. "I think I was sort of taking the year off. I didn't want to make any decisions I'd regret."

Oliver's eyes were wet. "You thought you might regret leaving me?"

It sounded a lot sweeter than he'd meant it, but Jacob was willing to let him have it. "It was a dumb idea."

Oliver looked out his window. "Sissy has agreed to leave. The board will give her a severance for keeping quiet. She's going to move out to Montana and start a community art program there."

Jacob whistled. "Well, if I'd known there were payoffs involved . . . you and I shouldn't have been so discreet."

But Oliver wasn't laughing. "She has a daughter. Did you know that? She'll be eleven next month. We get along, she and I. Her name's Virginia. I thought maybe it wasn't too late for me to be a father to her."

Jacob snorted. "Trying to take a positive role in a young girl's life? I don't know, Oliver. That sounds unhealthy to me."

But Oliver didn't laugh. "You must think I'm a fool."

"Look, go with her then. Round up cows with Sissy if that's what you want to do. Nothing's stopping you, Oliver. Really. Nothing."

Oliver seemed unconvinced, so Jacob clapped his hands and struck a mock-triumphant pose: " 'Therefore, take me and bind me to the crosspiece half way up the mast; bind me as I stand upright, with a bond so fast that I cannot possibly break away, and lash the rope's ends to the mast itself. If I beg and pray you to set me free, then bind me more tightly still.' "

Oliver seemed torn between laughing and rolling his eyes. Laughing won out in the end. "You seriously need some help, my love."

Jacob shrugged. "I don't want to know anyone who doesn't."

They shared one last embrace of the old kind.

JANUARY

The year had passed, and Jacob went to Manhattan and walked into a synagogue. He took a yarmulke from the wicker basket. He put it on his head as he had, as a boy, on countless torturous Friday evenings, which stretched a dotted line back to some of his earliest resentments. He took a prayer book from the woman, and in minutes he was in the back of a big blue chamber, singing along to the same songs his Hebrew school days had tattooed onto his brain stem. The Jews of the Upper West Side were assembled around him—Jacob had expected them all to be old. He was surprised how many people his own age were there, and how many children, some dozing and some stretching and some turned around in their seats to stare at him with their big dinner-plate eyes. And, too, there were old men and ladies who could hardly heave themselves up when the time came to rise.

Jacob only mouthed along at first, not sure he wanted to pray, not to this God who'd taken Irene, and who'd taken over for all those other gods. But if once there was a god of the sun and a goddess of harvest and a god of war and a goddess of wisdom, then maybe this Consolidated Entity was still all those many things. Within this One Him, capital-G God, all the lowercase ones still existed. There was still a grim god of the underworld in there, and a tempestuous god of thunder. A sprightly messenger god and a raucous god of wine. Maybe He was still squabbling amongst Himself, still getting drunk and cheating on Himself (with Himself) and messing a thing or two up. So maybe He didn't always wind up rewarding the best or punishing the wickedest. So maybe sometimes He took the wrong ones and let the right ones stay long past their due. Jacob could forgive Him for that. After all, it was a humongous world, and there used to be twelve of Him. Even then it hadn't ever gone smoothly.

The rabbi and the cantor stood up in the front of the room and led the congregation in songs written nearly as long ago as the epics of Homer. They stood in front of the lighted closet that held the ark. Jacob remembered how much he liked that—the centrality of this document, the most sacred thing in the building, adorned with gold and readable only read by those who'd mastered the long-forgotten languages. It was what tied them all together.

When they read the Mourner's Kaddish and called on those who knew someone who was seriously ill, or who had lost someone in the previous week, a dozen or more people stood up all around the crowd and spoke the names of their departed or their departing. Then the rabbi called out the list of congregants' names who had passed away in that week in years past, and as their loved ones heard the names, they stood for a moment and then sat down again. There were so many.

"Are there any names that anyone would like to add?"

Jacob stood up, and he wasn't alone. Three people came up on his left and four to his right. He said Irene's name out loud, and the others spoke their names, and the rabbi asked them all to sit down again. Jacob felt scared and warm all over. He was both emptier and more satisfied. More alone and less, as if he'd just said goodbye and hello in the same breath.

The service ended, and various board members began making announcements about food drives and outreach programs, and Jacob found himself thinking about an article Ella had recently posted to his Facebook wall. A scientist had a semiridiculous theory that as clay was being shaped on a wheel, it absorbed the sound waves of the people speaking around it, and these vibrations were then trapped within the earth and air and water. And this terrific madman thought he could figure out how to play this record back again, even through ancient ceramic vases and urns, and hear the conversations of people who had been dead and gone and forgotten for *five thousand years*. Perhaps, Jacob thought, the scientist would find a way. He wished there had been a potter making a vase in Irene's hospital room, so the vibrations of his last words to her would have been caught in its wet clay, and that this scientist someday would queue up his machines and point them at the little vase. Years from now someone else would hear him whispering the words that had made Irene smile in that last minute.

When you get there, just let me know you made it, all right?

WILLIAM ON THE BRIDGE

1

Exiting the gallery doors, William saw the Brooklyn Bridge: two mammoth trunks straddling the East River, water blacker than the sky above. Over the surface a second, silver river of reflected light flowed the opposite way. Pale yellow headlights crossed the bridge's span, departing Manhattan at the end of a long, cold Tuesday, while Brooklyn issued her own red taillights back against the tide. From where he stood, they were all just little points of light, proceeding and receding toward friends, meals, televisions, sins, solitude, sleep.

The bridge appeared to dwarf the skyscrapers on the far shore. Aortal and ventral, a pair of vaulting, twinned cathedral arches, roped together by a drape of cables. Slow troughs and sharp peaks, like a heartbeat on a monitor. True, William didn't know much about architecture, couldn't tell a keystone from a cornerstone. But he knew it was extraordinary. Particularly after what he'd seen inside the gallery, and after having just finished the second half of a joint he'd begun before arriving.

Particularly with the little piece of Irene he now carried in his jacket pocket. After a year in her wake, he felt her close again, hovering over his shoulder, two or three steps behind. Everything was louder and brighter, as if some knob on his dashboard had been cranked up after countless months on low. Living back at home, in his same old bedroom, smoking in the same old bathroom with the same old shower on, having the same old dinners and listening to his parents have the same old arguments. But now all the lights burned brighter, and he loosened his favorite red scarf, despite the chill in the air.

Hearing a sudden whoosh, William wheeled around to see a passing tour bus. The sightseers leaned over the railing to photograph the bridge, their flashes firing off uselessly in the dark, the glowing of their phone screens glowing back onto their smiling faces. He was glad to have someone to share the moment with, but even after the bus rolled away, he didn't feel alone. Who was out there?

Sara and George and everyone else were still at the opening. *Irene Richmond: The Disappointments.* It was an awful title—she had never decided on one herself. But no matter. *BOMB* and *Artforum* were calling it one of the biggest shows of 2011 (even though it was only February), and thanks to them it was a mob scene. Juliette and Abeba had organized it with Sara, who was treating it like a rehearsal for the upcoming wedding. The same lighting designers, the same printer for the programs, the same caterers, who were now bringing around chocolate mousse served in marzipan-speckled eggs. Special Ethiopian coffee had been roasted. George had selected five North Fork wines.

The soon-to-be-married couple were the only people William had really known inside, and they were circling around like guppies, too quick to be caught. George was asking everyone if they'd seen Jacob, unclear if he was simply late (as always) or not showing up. The ironic thing was that William had actually mistaken George for Jacob at first. He didn't look well. Heavier set, hairline receding. All the wedding planning, George had joked, fully aware of the looks he was getting. Sara, too, looked altered. Impatient. Missing twenty pounds she hadn't needed to lose in the first place.

Everyone was giving toasts and making a big show of looking at the show. William didn't see anyone else looking as he was looking. For the past two hours, he had religiously documented every sculpture, painting, and sketch, using his phone to record every inch from every angle. Already private dealers were bidding through back channels (or so Juliette and Abeba claimed). By week's end, the pieces would be dispersed across America, maybe the world. Stationed in collectors' foyers and bedrooms and on mantels above fireplaces. Tying rooms together. Creating atmosphere. Disappointment everywhere!

The proceeds were going to the Richmond Memorial Fund—an art school scholarship that Sara had organized. (Never mind that Irene had gotten her education gratis, sitting in the backs of lecture halls.) She was talking about getting into nonprofit work full time if this got enough attention from the right sorts of people. Certainly there had been a few photographers, snapping away. William had deliberately avoided their flashes and, once he could, ducked away before Sara or George could introduce him to anyone. They hadn't spoken to him more than a few times all year, and he was surprised to have even gotten an invitation to the show. When he'd called Sara to accept, she'd acted as if they'd always been old friends, but he knew they hadn't been and soon wouldn't be again. Quietly he was editing himself out of their story.

He hated everything about it. He hated that Irene wasn't at her own show. He hated that he kept thinking she was around the party somewhere, trying to pretend she wasn't nervous about the coming reviews. Certainly there was buzz—possibly too much. Abeba seemed to fear there could be a backlash because people tended to think anything they'd been hearing a lot about was overrated. Better to be the underdog, to be plucked from obscurity. No, Juliette argued, because then why had you been so plucked and not them? They'd hate you worse for that. It was all a big catch-22. No way to win. Sell too little, and nobody cared. Sell too much, and you were a sellout. Unless you made selling out part of your shtick. But it didn't really matter, William supposed. Irene's show was a one-shot affair. First and last. By a dead girl, about dying. It was both unusual and confusing, two things that typically sent buyers reaching for checkbooks. But William didn't care about that. As far as he was concerned, the work was perfect in and of itself.

Who else could have come up with something like *Patient R5691414510*? Irene's last known sculpture, a life-sized effigy constructed out of the clear plastic bags the hospital gave out to hold personal items. Irene had entrusted the assembly instructions and sketches (all scribbled down during her last good days at Mount Sinai) to Sara, along with an inventory of the parts she had piled up under her red coat in that tiny closet, so that the cleaning staff wouldn't discard them: bags stuffed with used gauze from her surgical dressings, tissues covered in other unidentifiable fluids, empty IV bags, balled-up pamphlets that the nurses left behind to advise on wound care and whatnot. She'd even salvaged an old PEG tube, and there it was in the gallery, running right into the "torso" and off toward an IV stand that Juliette and Abeba had set up alongside the piece. (The bag had been filled with neon-pink acrylic paint, meant to resemble a strawberry-flavored Assure milkshake.)

By Irene's instructions, Juliette and Abeba had suspended *Patient R5691414510* in the air with a series of clear fishing wires, so that she appeared to be levitating or maybe lying in an invisible hospital bed, her left arm dangling off the side, with Irene's actual patient ID bracelet delicately looped around the "wrist" of an inflated rubber glove. Abeba was running around telling everyone what a challenge it had all been to preserve, and the headaches Irene had caused them all with the permits needed to present these potentially unsanitary items in public. William wondered who the new assistant was, who'd *actually* had to deal with all that, as Irene once had. The real purpose of the little narrative was, of course, all about stirring up some controversy and tacking another zero onto the price tag. Irene had never cared about that, and neither would he.

What he cared about was that she'd made a dozen intricate pieces in the year following the diagnosis. It was remarkable what she'd been able to do with the little she'd had on hand. Sculptures made out of glued-together orange prescription bottles and empty Assure bottles and Chinese food containers studded with little colored pills. There were several sketches she'd done after moving in with William, when she didn't have access to her supplies. *Stricken City II* was the view out of his old apartment's window, done in sumptuous simple charcoal. As in briquettes from a bag in his hall closet. "Stark and serene," the critic at *BOMB* had written. The *Times* had preferred the three-dimensional *Portrait of a Profound Disappointment*—fashioned from chicken drumsticks (courtesy of Hill Country delivery), which Irene had Mod Podged and which did look eerily human when draped in a tweed that was clearly meant to resemble Jacob's coat, though it was actually fabric taken from an old hat of William's that he had only just then realized was missing. *Artforum* had deemed it "hauntingly decayed" and complimented the "blooms of rich, saturated pigments" in *West of Eden*, with its unreal landscape of seashells and vineyards and trash. Someone at *Salon* had felt this piece was "anodyne and dogged" and that the whole show was a "sheer visual confusion" full of "mundane flotsam and jetsam," which was "erratic to the point of solipsism." To each their own, he thought.

William remembered how Irene and her friends had made fun of the "so-called art" at the Christmas party the night they met. He wondered if, to someone else, the moldy yam had meant as much as all this did to him. Maybe. But he wanted to believe that there was something here that would carry these feckless people inside Irene's heart and guts. That it would be—how had Jacob put it?—metamorphic. Not just fucking television.

There was a crowd around *Ms. Daphne*, a painting of a transvestite reclining on a waterbed *à la* Modigliani, with startlingly hideous wallpaper in the background. This hung beside *Man in Crooked*

Necktie, a portrait of George in a suit, holding a vanilla cupcake in one hand. And of course William recognized his Christmas gift to her (formerly his own Christmas gift to his mother), now unraveled and carefully molded into the stunning *Kimono Cocoon.*

Certainly the most popular piece in the show was the I-beam from the World Trade Center. *The Iron Queen.* She had done nothing whatsoever to the steel itself, leaving every bit of rust and dirt that had accumulated along its length, but through some alchemy William didn't quite understand, she had affixed seventy-seven nude Barbie dolls to it. Beige plastic crawled, climbed, and sprawled all across the girder, in places so twisted up on top of one another that you could barely see the metal underneath. Something about seeing that same, painted-on smile over and over was tremendously unsettling. From certain angles William thought it was some kind of Elysian orgy. From others it seemed like a hellscape worthy of Hieronymus Bosch. This had been, apparently, the piece that she'd been sneaking off to work on at the gallery right up to her collapse at the museum last summer. As far as he, or anyone, seemed to be able to tell, it was finished. Every strand of fake hair harmoniously and horribly in place.

William kept thinking about that last day. The day before the end. She had been pretty drugged-up. But she had asked about the birdcage. And she had tried to say something else after that, but it hadn't been clear—these, her last words to him. He told himself that they had just been nonsense, pointless pain-killer koans. But he couldn't shake the thought that maybe she had been asking him to do something for her. He wasn't sure at first, but the more he'd thought about it, he was convinced that she'd said the words "Tell my father." William had been thinking of how to find him, and now he had finally come up with an idea.

William looked up as Sara called the crowd over to *Patient R5691414510* so that she and Juliette and Abeba could thank them all for coming. He had quietly headed the other way, toward the "piece" that he had been eyeing all night. *Jewelry Box, Bird Cage.* It was hanging in the corner exactly as it had hung in Irene's apartment. Had she intended it to be sold as a piece of art? Unclear, and possibly irrelevant. As Sara began to retell a story about meeting Irene while they'd been interns at the university press (Sara had been charged with finding out if Irene was stealing toner—she was), William got up on his tiptoes and reached his slender fingers toward the thin bars of the birdcage. This time he found the hidden door that he'd seen Irene open to retrieve a necklace before leaving for William's apartment. He opened the cage and grabbed the little black address book that he'd first seen there more than two years earlier. Then he'd shoved it into his breast pocket and stepped out into the night, where, after lighting the other half of the joint, he'd caught sight of the bridge.

He knew the fastest way home was on the subway. But instead he trudged up the icy lanes to the foot of the Brooklyn Bridge and thought back to the morning, a year ago, when he'd left Irene's hospital room. Typical William. Early exit. He just couldn't handle the very end. He'd needed to walk up that corridor toward the elevators knowing she was still alive. Out on the street, and later on the bus, he hadn't been sure one way or the other. By the time he got back to his apartment, he reasoned that it was probably over. But he still didn't know. He'd felt so numb and yet not nearly numb enough.

That was when he'd dug out the shoebox where she'd been keeping the last half ounce of Northern Lights premium indica that she'd bought from Skeevo. He'd never tried it before, but now he did, in the same careful way she'd taught him to roll it for her. With each hour that passed, he figured the likelihood was a little less that she was still alive. The probability approached zero, but even the next day and the day after, it didn't reach the asymptote. It felt instead like those months when they'd been broken up. Weeks went by, and then months. In the rational gray matter of his brain, William knew she was gone, but there was no convincing the irrational spaces inside it. Little sparks flew from synapse to synapse carrying the words *She Is Dead* across the gaps that kept insisting *She Is Here.*

The pathway over the bridge was steeped in soft tea-brown light. He felt Irene as a gambler feels his luck at a certain seat at the table. The way a sculptor feels something besides her own will moving her hands. It was like seeing out of a second set of eyes and hearing with another pair of ears. Walking a hundred feet above the water, between two worlds that were also one. He didn't know how else to describe it, except to say it felt as if she were walking just behind him.

2

At eight the next morning, he stood in front of a glass wall, the smell of fresh bread coming from the bakery behind him. He stared out at the traffic circumnavigating Columbus Circle, from inside the Time Warner Center. He'd spent half the night at a back table at Veselka, studying the address book, where he'd found Skeevo's number scribbled down and had sent him a text message: *Hi, this is William Cho, Irene's friend. We met in Staten Island that day.* To his amazement, there had been a reply after only moments. *Cool. How are you?* And after a few quick pleasantries they had agreed to meet the following morning at the bakery, where Skeevo was washing dishes part time and learning the mysterious art of bread making. William hadn't seen much point in going home, and he'd been afraid to sleep, for fear he'd wake up and find the feeling had gone. He'd spent the rest of the night wandering around, and it had left him with quite an appetite, so he was glad to see Skeevo bring over a few fresh loaves of something called *pan de horno*, which was heavenly.

"People think it's all about the starters, or the yeast," Skeevo explained. "But just as with a lot of things, there's an art to it. You form a relationship with the dough as you knead it. Too much or too little, and you get flat, dead crap. Not enough air in there. It's a living thing, bread."

Steam rose off the bread as William ripped into it. Light glinted off the ever-rising escalator steps. A red sunburst of fabric was being hung in the window of a store across the way. He kept thinking he might see Irene stepping out of the entrance to the Mandarin Oriental Hotel, on the arm of some man in a better suit than he'd ever own.

Skeevo wore an ADVENTURE TIME T-shirt, ripped jeans, and a pair of sneakers with silhouettes of Questlove on the tongues. His cheeks were reddish and rough.

"I guess you heard what happened with Irene," Skeevo said.

William nodded. "I was with her at the hospital when it happened," he lied.

Skeevo didn't say anything but sipped his double espresso and scratched his cheek.

"How did you hear?" William asked.

"Facebook," Skeevo replied. "Fucking shame."

William cleared his throat. "How well would you say you knew her?"

Skeevo shrugged. "Better than most customers. Which isn't to say very well. But you learn a lot about people when you smoke with them enough."

"Like what?"

This earned him a suspicious look, and William stared at his bread, flushed.

"I'm—I'm just trying to find her father. She asked me to—I think she asked me to make sure he knew what happened."

Skeevo toyed with the neck of his T-shirt and laughed. "Wow. I guess dying really changes people. She told me she never wanted to see or hear from that piece of flyshit again."

William frowned. "What about her mother?"

"Left when Reeny was little. Ran off with some other woman and left her with the dad and the soon-to-be wicked stepmother.

Guess they were pretty much a treat in and of themselves, but it wasn't until Daddy Dearest pissed away her college fund at the track that she actually took off."

With that, they sipped in silence again. William checked his phone and saw there was a voicemail from his mother, which he deleted unheard, and a text from Sara, inviting him to brunch at the Harbor Grand Hotel. William saw Skeevo was staring up at the snow-capped statue of Christopher Columbus in the center of the circle.

Remembering a random fact he'd learned about it at school, he said, "Did you know that every official distance in New York City is measured from that statue? It's the center of the center of the universe."

Skeevo laughed. "I've learned in my travels, William, that the universe has no center. No center, no limits. We live in the midst of infinity."

Just as William was about to agree and thank Skeevo for his time, he caught sight of something—someone—familiar out of the corner of his eye. A streak of blond hair and a red coat passing the Sunglass Hut.

"Irene?" William shouted, and jumped up so quickly that he slammed his knee into the flimsy table. Whirling as he tried to stop it from tipping, he wound up instead sending espresso and *pan de horno* everywhere, landing on his back on the marble, his eyes fixed on a crown of lights high above.

"Whoa, whoa, whoa!" Skeevo moved to help. "You okay, man?"

Blood rushed back into William's cheeks as he felt clear air fill his lungs. When he looked up again, the woman in red was gone.

"Sorry." William breathed deep. "I—it's like I keep forgetting."

Skeevo grabbed some napkins and helped mop up the mess. "Hey, no sweat. Happens to me too. Last week I saw her standing on the F platform heading uptown when I was heading down. A week before that it was twice in the same day."

"It's crazy," William apologized. "I'm so sorry."

"Don't be. Listen. This is *love*. It's far more powerful than death. It's like I was saying. In an infinite universe, in an infinite number of infinite universes, all things exist simultaneously. Anything that can be, is."

William got up and stood by the glass. "Are you saying you believe in ghosts?"

Skeevo folded his fingers. "I once saw three ghosts in a single afternoon."

Stifling a groan, William pressed his hot forehead against the cool glass of the window. He felt faint vibrations from a bus downshifting in the circle. It eased around the southern curve and curled around to head north along the park. An endless river of traffic wound counterclockwise around Columbus Circle, all roads leading away from this point, like the cross of two axes on a piece of graph paper. *This is love.* He drew two zeroes in the condensation, with a comma between. 0, 0. Then he traced a cartoon ghost around it.

"I didn't even know her," William sighed. "It's so stupid."

Two one-night stands. An awkward Christmas dinner at his parents'. A few months of silence. And then what? A couple of awful summer months when she'd been either ducking out to the studio, stuck in the hospital, or forcibly convalescing in his apartment. A year later and William still didn't have the faintest idea what Irene had been doing with him.

3

Before leaving the mall, William showed Skeevo the address book, but he didn't recognize any of the names or places in it. He seemed only moderately surprised when, afterward, William awkwardly asked if he could buy an eighth ounce of the same stuff Irene used to get, which he'd been increasingly nostalgic for, especially after the awful weed he'd been buying off a neighbor's teenaged son. Skeevo met him in the men's room ten minutes later with a small, pillowy paper bag that smelled like what he remembered. He told William to call anytime and to punch Irene's dad in the throat if he ever did track him down. Then he went off to resume kneading.

William tied his scarf back on and caught an E train to the Harbor Grand Hotel, which was down near Wall Street, but on the opposite end from where he used to work and not anywhere he knew well. He had to plug the address into his phone, the new Cobalt 7 with TrueVoice technology; his brother had bought it for him for Christmas, and thankfully it had a supercharged battery. As soon as he sat down on the train, he took the address book out again and flipped through it one more time. Each name, street, state, and zip code brought him an ounce of peace. They were like elements in an epic equation, in which X equaled Irene. Who she'd been, before anyone had known her.

There was no entry for "Mom and Dad," but that didn't mean they weren't in there. One hundred and twelve names in fifteen states. All night he had been ruling out the ones he recognized. This had narrowed the list down to just a dozen people. They could be clients or friends or weirdos she'd met on the subway. But maybe one of them was her family.

William got off the train at Church Street, where he noticed a new voicemail from his own mother and decided to ignore it until after he'd gotten a chance to smoke, which he'd found considerably helpful in dealing with her general lack of sanity. He walked past the eternal construction around the World Trade Center site to the Harbor Grand: a gorgeous hotel built above an old colonial inn that supposedly had been there since shortly after the natives had sold Manhattan to Peter Minuit for sixty guilders and some loose beads. Inside, he found less of a restaurant, more of a tavern, furnished with antique chairs and silver gaslights.

He didn't see Sara anywhere but did spot George, sitting at the head of a long table, regaling people from the opening the night before.

"Mr. Cho!" George said, standing up with a mimosa in each hand. William could see that he hadn't slept either, and after a congenial hug, George sat back down somewhat absentmindedly, still with both drinks. "Sara had to duck out. Thanks for coming by last night. You really should have stayed! You missed all the drama."

"There was drama?"

George practically licked his lips. "One of Irene's exes showed up right after the toasts."

William considered he might remind George that *he* was one of Irene's exes as well, but there was no chance for a word in edgewise.

"Yeah. You probably never met her. She used to come visit sometimes up in Ithaca. She's the *worst.* When Sara saw her come into the gallery, she nearly lost her mind, I swear to God. The last time she came around, she ran off with Irene in what turned out to be a stolen pickup truck. One minute the two of them were doing it on Sara's roommate's chaise longue, and the next minute the cops were calling from *Pittsburgh,* and the two of them were gone, along with all the Percocet I had left over from getting my wisdom teeth out."

William tried to look both impressed and concerned. "What was her name?"

"Alisanne. Alisanne Des Rochers."

William tugged awkwardly at the end of his scarf, a strange heat creeping up the small of his back. He had looked last night for Alisanne in the book and not found her, but now he recalled some jagged evidence of pages torn out in the D section.

"What did she want?"

"Who knows? She's a maniac, I'm telling you. Sara caught her poking around Irene's birdcage piece and totally flipped. She had Abeba make her leave. It was intense."

After two mimosas, William excused himself to the bathroom

where he went to the sink to splash some water on his face. He came out and sat down on an old Windsor bench in the reception area that creaked miserably under his weight. He took the address book out of his suit pocket and thumbed to the back, where there were a few loose photographs. There were the naughty Polaroids, of course, but also several PG-rated pictures taken in college days. George and Jacob dancing with Irene in the student center under a disco ball. Sara and Irene collapsed under shopping bags at a food court, sharing a root beer float the size of their heads. Irene standing ankle deep in a creek, arms stretched to a brilliant sun just out of the frame. Her face in the glow of twenty birthday candles on what appeared to be a penis cake honoring Jacob's birthday. In another she and Sara and George were covered in white paint, and Irene was sticking her tongue out. Her shirt said I GOT RIPPED AT VAN WINKLE'S—NYC, NY. They all looked younger and happier.

Just then George stopped in from his own trip to the bathroom. "Thought we lost you," he said. With a loud thump, George landed on the bench beside him, which complained but didn't break. William tried to tuck the photos away, but George had already seen them. "Looks like sophomore year maybe? Habitat for Humanity."

"You should probably have these," William said, pushing them toward George.

He only pushed them back. "No, that's all right. I've had enough nostalgia for a week. Sara just finally finished going through everything from her stuff we put into storage. Photos, dishes, jewelry, books . . . all those clothes. God. We took most of it back to that secondhand shop she liked so much with the vintage shoes. Mel's? I guess now it's thirdhand."

He seemed to regret this observation almost right away, and William ignored it.

"I've been thinking—well, right before she— . . . I think she wanted me to get in touch with her father and stepmother. I think someone should, you know? It doesn't have to be me, but . . . I just want to know who she was. Where she came from. You know, I don't even know why she—why she liked me."

George sighed and raised his hands into the air as if offering something to the heavens. After a moment William wondered if he hadn't begun calculating field equations in his head, but then he finished with a stretch and a loud yawn.

"There's a kind of apocryphal physics story," George said finally. "Someone's giving a cosmology lecture about how the sun is just one star in three hundred billion in the Milky Way galaxy, which is just one galaxy in two hundred billion in the universe, which is just one universe in the whatever-it-all-is—and this woman stands up and says something like 'That's crazy! Everyone knows the Earth is flat and rides around on the back of a giant tortoise.' And the lecturer says, 'Well, ma'am, in that case, what is the tortoise standing on?' and she replies, 'Another tortoise, of course!' and he says, 'Well, so what is *that* tortoise standing on?' and she says, 'Another tortoise, of course!' and he says—"

"George!"

"Right. Sorry. So he says—he says, 'And what is *that* tortoise standing on?' and she says, 'Sir, I'm telling you, it's tortoises all the way down!' "

William got the sense that this was the punch line, and he gave George a perfunctory laugh before saying, "I don't understand."

"That's Irene. She's just tortoises all the way down. Mysteries on top of mysteries, however far down you go."

William felt something seizing up in his chest and hurriedly tried to pay George for the mimosas, which he refused, of course. He looked about ready to fall asleep on the bench.

"My love to Sara," William said quickly, before walking off to the men's room. There he locked the door and rolled a joint on the counter by the sink, carefully, just the way she had taught him. Then he stepped outside and walked down into the Battery, where he could smoke it in relative peace and quiet. He stared out across the gray skies toward the Statue of Liberty, cold and alone in the open harbor, and thought about calling his mother.

They hadn't exactly been getting along lately. Shortly after Irene died, she had asked him to join her for a *Seoul Jinogwigut*—a ceremony to usher the last of Irene's seven souls to paradise. He didn't expect her to understand that he didn't *want* Irene's seventh soul ushered to paradise, just as he didn't want to hear her theories about how Irene's cancer had been caused by *jabkwi*, wandering malicious spirits, who had nestled into the psychic hole Irene had created by turning her back on her family—her ancestors were pissed, in other words, and misfortune was sure to befall those who pissed off the ancestors. Whatever. Let her stand around shaking jujube sticks and burning paper effigies of horses and invoking the spirits. But now it had been a year, and his mother was still trying to come up with ways to help Irene's soul reach the next world.

When the tightness in his chest finally dulled to a weak throb and he felt sleepy, he walked to the street and hailed a cab. It was only when he sat down in the backseat that he realized he had absolutely no idea where he wanted to go.

"You know a bar called Van Winkle's?" William asked.

The driver nodded. "Up on Avenue B."

William said that was the place, even though he didn't have the faintest idea. He clutched Irene's address book in his hand like a holy book as they headed uptown. Pressing one cheek against the cold window, he listened to the other cars. Their sounds began to overlap, repeat, and blur together. The foggy voice of the radio tuned to sports. A faint, charred coffee smell came from the front seat. The door hummed and the road sang, and soon everything was lost in a white wall of shrouded air slipping past the window.

Ice was quickly covering the windowpane. Strange—though not as strange as the warm hand he felt on his. Without looking, he knew it was Irene's hand. It just *was*. And she just *was there*, as if she had always been. Not ghostly, not cold, nothing spectral or apparitional at all. Her hand on his arm and on the back of his neck. Her head pressed onto his shoulder. Fat snowflakes were falling outside the window. William could feel her fingers sliding between his, looking for a comfortable grip, as she sighed lightly and kissed the side of his neck and then a slightly firmer one, pecking at a spot she always liked. He was afraid to look directly at her.

Are you a ghost? he asked.

No. She giggled. *I'm a bird. A very special, rare type of seagull.*

What makes you so special and rare, Madame Seagull?

I hate the sea, she said.

That's pretty inconvenient.

A long sigh that tickled his neck. *I'll admit, it's a problem.*

So where do you live then?

She jabbed her nose into his neck a half dozen times as he squirmed. *I'm practicing to be a William-pecker. So I can make my nest inside Williams.*

Outside a beam of blond sunlight fell onto the frosty window, and William watched as a million fine, symmetrical crystals of ice melted and condensed into steam, filling the backseat of the cab. He turned to try to kiss Irene, but she pressed his cheek the other way. He could almost see her hair out of the corner of his eye, falling down over the white shoulder of his shirt, spilling thick and golden. Then he pushed her hand away, turning the rest of the way—and woke up alone.

4

Van Winkle's turned out to be a seedy dive bar, covered from ceiling to floor in stickers for punk rock bands, half of which, William imagined, had long ago ceased to exist. There was a stage in the very back, and as he sat at the bar sipping a cup of burned coffee, he tried to imagine a teenage Irene, pink streaks in her hair, diving the stage.

He imagined her there with a group of forgotten friends, on whose couches she'd once crashed, making the pilgrimage from wherever they'd come from originally to the anonymous Lower East Side, doing what she had to do to forget the home she'd left behind.

Not exactly eager to go back home (having now received a third message from his mother), William pulled out the address book and, feeling invigorated, began to dial.

First he tried someone named Geoffrey Irving, in Tarrytown, but he wasn't available. According to his half brother, who answered the phone, Geoffrey was serving ten years in Sing Sing. Maybe he had known an Irene or a "Reeny" once, but William would have to go up there to ask him. He thought he probably would not. Instead he ordered a fresh coffee and asked the Cobalt 7 to look up Geoffrey Irving's record, which seemed to involve stolen cars and an arrest in 2002, which was at least a year after Irene had ended up in Ithaca. In any case, he was their age and thus too young to be Irene's father.

William moved on to Ed Simpson of St. Louis, Missouri, a retired train engineer who was happy to pause *The Price Is Right* to talk a moment. Mr. Simpson remembered a girl named Renee who had once dated his son, Ed Simpson, Jr., now Colonel Ed Simpson, Jr., presently off completing his third tour in Afghanistan. William thanked the man and asked him to thank his son for his service before moving on to the next name in the book.

No one picked up the phone at the home of Sally Paulson of Rochester, but when he looked her up on the Cobalt 7, he found a picture on the staff page of the Maquokeeta Farm in New Hope. He remembered Irene mentioning once working on a farm there. But Sally was African American and so probably not likely to be Irene's mother.

He couldn't get through to anyone at the number listed for Anthony Lemon, of Antwerp, Ohio. Then he had three more dead ends in a row with Evelyn Cross of Key West; Mary Winter of Mary Winter's Garden Center in Houston; and finally Poppy Daniels (gender unknown) of West Virginia.

William was just about to give up and surrender to the fourth call from his mother, when he tried Mr. Bernard Wyckoff, of the Pruder Pools and Aquatic Center in nearby Brighton Beach, who picked up the phone and said that, yes, he had an outstanding order for someone named Irene Richmond, but he was going to need to come down and pick it up himself.

With no other leads, William gladly got into another cab by the bottom of Tompkins Square Park and headed for Brooklyn. On the way he, more reluctantly, decided to call his mother back to let her know he wasn't dead, lest she start trying to send his own soul abroad.

She sounded strange when she answered. "William, I have to go. Something happened."

"What is it? Is Dad okay?"

"Your father is fine." There was a short silence. "Do you remember Chongso Kim?"

William vaguely recalled a pudgy eight-year-old from his father's congregation, who had thrown up a metric ton of yellow cake at the Annunciation potluck luncheon.

"This morning he snuck out of his room to buy a comic book and was killed by a car crossing Northern Boulevard. Hit and run. Everyone here is very upset. I made *sam gae tang* to bring over to Mrs. Kim's."

William closed his eyes, feeling suddenly sick and trying not to imagine what it would be like to be out on the road in front of the cab he was in, hitting the front fender.

"God. That's awful. I'm—so sorry. Please tell her I'm sorry."

He knew his mother would be in a rush now, on her way to a room full of weeping women, carrying her big bowl of stew: Cornish hens stuffed with rice and chestnuts, in a ginseng and garlic broth. She'd add it to the mounting pile of Tupperware in the kitchen and then do what she could, perform the rituals that might comfort the grieving mother, finding the shadow of her son in the haze of incense.

"You didn't come home last night?"

"Yeah, sorry. I'm—staying with friends in Manhattan. You remember George and Sara?"

Then his mother spoke softly. "She is lost on the road from This World to That World."

"Who? Sara? No, she's in the financial district."

But his mother only said, "You call me back later," and hung up.

5

William was a little surprised to find the Pruder Pools and Aquatic Center still open in February. Half the other stores along the seaside stretch that he'd walked down had been shuttered for the season. There were only three customers inside when William entered, under a thick yellow haze of cigarette smoke, which not even the chlorine in the air could mask. He approached the only person he could positively identify as an employee, a man whose face was hidden behind a massive, wiry white beard. He was sitting in a deck chair in the back sipping from an orange plastic mug that said LIFE'S A BEACH on the side and reading a historical thriller about the Civil War. When William introduced himself as a friend of Irene Richmond's, the man extended his hand, then barked, "Aqualad?"

"Sorry?"

With a huge heave, the man rose up out of the deck chair—his giant hand setting down his book so as not to lose his place—and then shifted gears with a flickering smile.

"He's in the original packaging. Near mint condition. I was going to just ship him, separate from the other stuff, but then her first check bounced and I never heard anything."

Confused, William followed the man to a door on the side wall by the pool floats, marked PRIVATE, and opened it. Inside, the only light came from eerie, dim halogen spotlights above a long row of display cases. Neatly arranged inside were action figures and dolls of all sorts and sizes, still entombed in original packaging. Maybe a thousand caped, muscular superheroes. Lithe, peach-skinned Barbies. Original Raggedy Anns and Andys. Babies with porcelain faces and glass eyes behind lids that seemed to flutter. The six original American Girls in their boxes. *Let us out*, their tiny trapped faces seemed to implore.

Mr. Wyckoff tapped a heavy knuckle into one of the cases, at a figure of a boy wearing a tight orange shirt and impossibly tiny green swim trunks. Just like in the comics William had read as a child, he had deep, purple eyes. *Aqualad*, the packaging announced, *Prince of Atlantis*. In the background was a wide white beach, spotted with futuristic crystal towers and huge cliffs of diamond. "You'll never destroy Hidden Valley, Garn Daanuth!" he declared in a flat white speech bubble. *Endowed with the Martian power of the Metagene!* the corny, 1970s-era packaging promised. What Martians had to do with Atlantis, William could not remember anymore.

"Like I told her, there's a small crease on the corner of the package."

William squinted but he barely saw this tiny imperfection. Before he could say anything, Bernard took the boxed figurine out of the case and handed it to him. William turned it over in his hands a moment before he realized it was for him. Right after they'd gotten back together he'd told her the whole story about the kimono and Mi-cha.

He noticed Bernard's face was practically glowing, now that he was standing so close to the halogen lights. Cheeks, nose, forehead—all were blazing. Long jaggy capillaries branched like rivers. What'd they call that? Gin Blossoms. Like the band. He recalled the blotches Irene had sometimes gotten in harsh sun, or after a second drink, and once upon eating a strong vegetable curry. It started to get especially noticeable after the chemo. "Rosacea," she had said. "Runs in the family."

William took a deep breath and, keeping his eyes on the action figure, found the courage to ask, "What was the rest of the order? You said you sent Irene the rest already."

"Yeah," he said, "seventy-seven identical, unboxed Barbie dolls. Don't know what the hell she wanted to *do* with them."

William's heart pounded. He knew exactly what she had done with them. Slowly he thought he was beginning to understand. He turned to the man's desk and saw a framed photo. There was the enormous, smiling Bernard with an arm around a tiny woman with dark short hair. They were in the stands at the racetrack, pointing excitedly to a picture of a chestnut-colored horse under a blanket of white carnations. They appeared to be celebrating a happy moment with a bottle of champagne.

"That's my wife, Maggie," Bernard said proudly, "just after I won five grand at the 2009 Belmont Stakes."

William tried to look impressed. Beneath this were two school photographs, each taken against a familiar blue Sears background.

Mr. Wyckoff tapped the edge of the photo of a heavyset girl, maybe ten years old, with braces, hair back in a ponytail. "That's Lorraine, my youngest. And here's Greg. He's three-A most outstanding wrestler, 2010 eighth-grade individual champion."

William looked for any resemblance in Greg, whose buzzed hair did seem to be blond, but whose heavy jaw and high forehead looked nothing like Irene's.

"Nice. Just the two kids?" William asked.

Did he detect a slight hesitation as Mr. Wyckoff turned to lock the display again?

"Well, Greg eats enough for three. And Lorraine's sweet as a dozen daughters."

"They must have had a good time, growing up with all these great toys."

Now William saw clear displeasure in the man's eyes. "These are not *toys*," he said. "These are *not* to be played with. These are collectible figurines, for serious hobbyists only."

William looked back up at the man. If he was Irene's father, then in her final weeks of life, she'd conned him out of seventy-seven Barbie dolls, which she'd then melted onto a two-foot-section of an I-beam from the World Trade Center site. William thought, with all respect due to Skeevo, he would rather not punch him in the neck.

"So look. Let's not have any trouble. You can pay me the full amount now, and we'll be done with it. Like I said, the check she wrote bounced. I am this close to calling my lawyer."

Maybe Irene had, in fact, been taunting Wyckoff. Hoping even that he or some lawyer would someday stumble upon the truth: that Irene was his daughter, and that she'd had the last laugh. William almost laughed himself. Talk about unfinished business. No wonder her soul wasn't moving on! Then he remembered that this, of course, was totally insane.

And yet somehow he felt compelled to say what he said next: "Actually, she died."

Bernard's eyes widened, and then he groaned. "Just perfect."

William took another deep breath, terrified but suddenly sure that this was why Irene had asked him to find her father. Just one second, and it would all be over.

"I think—sir, I'm sorry. But I think—I think she might have been your daughter."

Bernard glanced at the photograph of Lorraine, then back at William, confused. "The hell are you talking about?"

"Did you—sorry, but did you ever have another daughter?"

The man's red-veined face went white, and his lips seemed to move without orders. "Carrie Ann?"

"Carrie Ann?" William echoed.

And that was when he saw every red line on Bernard's face tighten. William's eyes shut in fear, and he tried to lurch toward the door. Then he felt a stone fist crushing into his temple, and his whole body twisted around. One foot lost contact with the floor, then the other. His uninjured eye opened to see the dolls in their glass prisons lurch and spin around until they were below him and the ground was above. His legs still kicked toward the door. There was a flash of white, blinding light, and then darkness everywhere, like deep, deep water.

6

William's head ached, just above his eye, and his jaw was in agony. Had he actually been punched in the face? He had never been in a fight before, but he realized, slowly, that this was what had happened. And that now he was lying in the damp sand of a very cold beach. There was dried blood on his lip and all down his shirt. He vaguely recalled staggering out of the store, trying to get away from Mr. Wyckoff and then blacking out. Carrie Ann Wyckoff? He couldn't seem to reconcile this. It couldn't be her name. Faintly he could hear the voice of the Cobalt 7 inside his pocket, and he pulled it out to find its screen badly cracked.

Hello. Where can I guide you today? it asked, over and over in a woman's pleasant voice.

For a while William cried without getting up or moving. Everything hurt, and worse, he couldn't feel her anywhere anymore. What was there left to do now but go home? Allow this defeat to mark the beginning of the rest of the long defeat of his life. Alone and in ten kinds of pain.

Then he noticed he wasn't exactly alone. He had, apparently, escaped the store still clutching the Aqualad package, which now lay a few feet away in the damp sand. He studied bright blocky colors of another age, the vaguely homoerotic outfitting, and the cheesy fists-on-hips posture of a teenage superhero. In one violent motion, he reached out, grabbed it, and tore the plastic housing from the cardboard—feeling some pleasure at the separation of the long-sealed glue. He took the little boy out and studied him closely.

Hello. Where can I guide you today? his phone asked again.

William stared at the caped figure and had no answer.

Hello. Where can I guide you today?

Something in him snapped.

"WHERE IS SHE?" he howled. "WHERE'S IRENE?"

He saw a burst of purple behind his eyelids. He thought he might throw up. And then—

Then the phone replied, in the same stiff but agreeable tone, *Finding Irene.*

William set the doll down and studied the spider-webbed screen of his phone. He watched a map forming behind the cracked glass. For a moment he almost believed that it might actually locate her. Eventually a picture of her old East Fourth Street apartment emerged, the address still stored in his contacts list somewhere.

He lay there cradling Aqualad in one hand, the phone in the other, thinking about the day he'd broken into that apartment. How he had felt an odd peace there among her things—pasta strainer on a hook near the kitchen, overgrown spider plant on the windowsill, a stack of magazines stolen out of the downstairs recycling bin, a blanket from the Met with a Monet print on it. Her things, without her. At first he'd thought it was just the adrenaline of being where he wasn't supposed to be, but soon he'd realized it was something else. He was with her, without her. What did it say, that he'd always felt closest to her when she wasn't there? In her apartment, by himself. By her side as she slept. In the hospital while the morphine carried her off in a Stygian stream. Looking at a picture of her, taken by somebody else—

Of course. He slowly got up and brushed himself off. As head-aching blots of pink stopped moving in front of his eyes, he turned to the phone and asked for the person that he knew he should have started with.

"Cobalt. Find Alisanne Des Rochers."

It turned out that Alisanne Des Rochers, owner of a Web design company based in Paris, was prompt on e-mail. Before William had even fully pulled himself together, thrown the action figure into his pocket with the weed and the address book, she'd responded to his query, saying she was still in town and could meet him at her hotel, The Quaker, in Long Island City.

The driver who picked William up expressed mild concern for him with a perfunctory "Are you okay, sir?" before returning to his phone call in some West African–sounding language. William said nothing. He closed his eyes and did not open them again until they'd arrived.

When William stepped into the glass and steel lobby of the hotel every eye was on him. How bad did he really look? Fortunately, before the porters could swoop in on him, a woman approached him from the bar area.

"You are William Cho?"

She wasn't what he expected. Since he'd first seen her name written on the back of Irene's dirty Polaroids, he'd been envisioning a regal French beauty. Leslie Caron from *An American in Paris* or María Casares from *Les Enfants du paradis*. In his mind she'd existed in black and white.

But here was Alisanne, in the somewhat-acned flesh. Thick eyebrows. Greasy, dark hair cut in a childish bob. Lips wide, flat, and pink, parted slightly, as if she were about to chew something. Her hands were blue and veiny, her nails polished black. Her nose looked as if it had been broken and then rebroken a few times for good measure. She had a wart on her neck the size of a pencil eraser with thick black hairs springing out of it. The black hood she was wearing was part of a denim coat and her black boots were laced up to her knees.

The porters looked displeased as he trudged inside, leaving sand behind on the dark carpet. He apologized, but Alisanne didn't appear to care. The hotel seemed to be constructed of different-sized panels of glass in interlocking square frames. Some were frosted to the point of complete opacity and others were crystal clear. Behind the desk was a waterfall, flowing somehow up and not down. An enormous sculpture of a spider eating a wasp sat in the middle of an otherwise pleasant-looking garden. There were four oversize gnome statues in the mailroom. Were they part of the building decor? Or had someone ordered them? William tried not to stare into the adjacent yoga studio, where people were bending themselves into holistic pretzels.

They went wordlessly to the sixth floor, where Alisanne opened her door with a keycard and invited him to remove his wet clothes. "Take a shower. I'll find you dry clothes. And some tea."

William hesitated, seeing that the shower was divided from the main room only by a pane of frosted glass that didn't reach the black-tiled floor.

"You are—not my type," she said flatly.

Reluctantly he removed his wet pants and shirt. Alisanne dropped them into a plastic bag and ordered some tea while he showered and washed what felt like an entire sandbar from his hair. Clean and warm at last, he stepped out in a towel, and Alisanne handed him a pair of ripped black jeans and a T-shirt for a band called MALADROIT. He was a little embarrassed to find that they were almost exactly the same size.

She poured him a cup of tea. William sat with it on the edge of the bed, thinking he should let her have the chair, but she sat down cross-legged on the floor.

"Your eye will be very swollen by tomorrow," she said.

William nodded. It hurt like hell, but he wasn't about to let her see that. "So you live in Paris?"

"Sometimes," she said.

"And you came all the way here for the show?"

She stared at him, almost curiously. "I came to get something that belonged to me."

"Oh," William said. "Me too."

She laughed and spat something from her teacup onto the floor. "No. You want to know who she was."

William frowned. "I guess."

Alisanne smiled, cryptically. "Who did this to you?"

"Her father."

She seemed almost impressed. "Horrible little man."

"Not so little," William winced. "I thought she wanted me to tell him what happened. She asked me, I think, before she died."

But now suddenly he wondered if what she'd meant was that he should make sure her father *didn't* find out. If she had, in the final hours, regretted her plan. If it had even been her plan. William felt utterly foolish. He didn't know what he'd been thinking. He didn't know why he'd thought he knew anything about her at all.

"And you called me because . . . ?"

"You knew Irene better than me. I was hoping you could—shed some light?"

Alisanne considered this a moment. "Why?"

"Why what?"

"Why would you want me to 'shed light'?"

"Look," he said, "we should—we should help each other out. I've been—Christ, just look at my face, okay? I've been through a lot already, so please just *tell* me."

"Tell you what?"

William realized he didn't know what he wanted to know. Who she was? Where she'd been? What she'd done? "How about where you met?" he said finally.

"We met in San Francisco."

"And?"

"And she was a terribly stupid girl. Away from home one week and already broke. Sleeping in the park, selling all the things she took from her nice grandmother. Trying to buy a sandwich. She fainted on the sidewalk in front of me. So I brought her home and let her stay with me. And what does she do? Reads all my Camus and messes up my sheets and kills my balsamine plant and makes me fall in love with her. So then one day I go out. I come home. She is gone. Stole an expensive first-edition book that my father bought me. Does that—how did you say it—shed light?"

William rubbed his head. It didn't. "I keep thinking if I knew who she *was*, I could . . ."

But after all this time he didn't know what he wanted to do. Let her go? Keep her close? Somehow do both things at once. Be free, and haunted, forever. If only he could keep her inside a box, safely stashed away in a closet or a drawer, to be taken out only when he wanted. In the pit of his stomach he knew that Irene would have hated this more than anything.

"I just want to know if she really loved me," he said.

Alisanne shrugged. "She loved everyone."

"I want to know that she loved me best."

"She loved you last."

"But not on purpose."

"Yes, on purpose."

William considered this. "She would have left me eventually."

"Yes," Alisanne agreed, "sooner or later."

William sighed. "I wanted it to be later."

"You think later you would have said, 'Okay, this was good. I've had enough. Please die now. Excellent loving you.'"

He supposed she had a point. Whatever might have happened between him and Irene in the long run—had there been a long run—if, at ninety-nine years old, he'd seen her slipping away on that hospital bed, something told him that he'd still have looked away before the last moment. He'd still have wound up lying next to a mound of sheets wishing she were underneath. He'd still be feeling her cool breath on his wrinkled neck.

"Maybe there are people who live together eighty years who don't love each other as much as you two did in one year. Maybe others spend a single night together and love each other more than you'll ever love anyone. But what does that matter now?"

William glared at her. Then he picked up his still-damp coat and said, "Come on. I bet I know what happened to your book."

7

Alisanne had a rental car, so she drove him back into Manhattan through the Midtown Tunnel. On the way, she told him what little she knew about Irene's mother. Her name was Mary, and she'd come from Texas, where her first husband had worked on an oil rig in the Gulf of Mexico. There'd been some sort of accident—a fire, she thought—and he'd died and Mary had gotten some insurance money out of it. She met Bernard Wyckoff somewhere outside New Orleans and got knocked up and married him. Irene, or Carrie Ann, had been born somewhere in the Florida panhandle, where Bernard's family was from. The Wyckoffs operated several local strip clubs, including one where Mary wound up waitressing part time while Bernard gambled away what was left of the insurance money and his parents raised little Carrie Ann.

It was there that Mary met a dancer named Izzy, whose real name turned out to be Mary as well. At some point one of the Marys seduced the other, and they ran away together. Irene was never entirely clear on why they left her behind. Possibly they thought she'd be better off with Grandma and Grandpa Wyckoff. Possibly they worried that Bernard, or his gambling buddies, would come after them if they took her along. Maybe there was a calculation: no judge in the Florida panhandle in the late 1980s was going to grant custody to an exotic dancer and her lesbian lover.

Alisanne didn't know, because Irene had never known. Bernard wound up marrying a woman he worked with, Maggie Pruder, and moving them all up to Brighton Beach to take over her family's pool supply store. Mary and Mary had ended up in Virginia where now, both middle-aged, they worked for the department of public utilities in—and Alisanne seemed smug to have figured this out before William—a little town called "Irene."

Locked in a line of bumper-to-bumper traffic, somewhere down under the river, as the fluorescent green light of the tunnel cast a pallor over everything, William felt another piece go into the puzzle. Irene. Of course. And yet it didn't feel finished. The puzzle didn't match any image on any jigsaw box. No cityscape or field of sunflowers. No kittens with balls of yarn. Just another tortoise under the one above it, and on and on.

William said nothing, focusing instead on rolling another joint without spilling weed all over the car. Alisanne watched him wordlessly as she drove them toward Mel's Secondhand Shop, where Sara had taken the last of Irene's things from the storage unit earlier that week. Alisanne parked just off Washington Square Park. They walked through together, sharing the joint as they avoided tourists holding bags from boutique shops, and stepped quickly past dreadlocked students on benches.

It struck William suddenly that it was the first part of the city he'd been in all day that he recognized. A girl played the violin in hopes of spare change. A pair of bearded middle-aged men smoked cigarettes while playing chess. A trio of heavyset Germans stood under the great Arch and made peace signs with their fingers, while a man in an orange ski cap changed his pants a few feet from them. William couldn't stop looking for Irene behind every lowered hood and winter cap. But he didn't feel her anywhere.

"You roll these like her," Alisanne said, passing the last of the joint back to him.

William took the last tiny hit and tossed it to the sidewalk. "Well, she taught me."

"Me too."

Mel's was hot and crowded. Australian women walked up and

down a maze of cramped aisles, examining denim jackets and mod-patterned dresses. Paisley and flowers burst everywhere like fireworks. Technicolor angle-striped dresses and jumpsuits with bell-bottoms. Pictures of Twiggy and Audrey Hepburn, torn from old *Vogues*, now framed on the walls. Two men were having a contentious debate over a pair of silk pajamas. A fourteen-year-old girl was trying on a pair of pale mint-green shoes, yelling at her mother that she *needed* them. They were *only* three hundred and nineteen dollars. They were from the *sixties*! The mother, who didn't look old enough to have owned shoes in the sixties, was ignoring her, checking an e-mail on her phone as the girl pitched a fit.

"Excuse me?" William asked a harried-looking man in bubble-gum-pink pants who seemed to work there. His cheeks were sunken like those of a corpse and made his eyes bug out. "We're looking for an old book that someone might have sold you recently."

The man was already shaking his head. "No returns, no refunds."

"Oh that's not—no problem. We'll pay for it."

The man sighed and tapped the sides of his alligator shoes together, his hands still busy tugging things uselessly into temporary order, soon to be undone by the browsing customers. He looked at Alisanne, then back at William, and registered a fair amount of concern.

"Before we get to books, sweetheart, you need a hat worse than anyone I've ever met."

William blinked. "I do?"

The man balled his hands and looked William in the eye. "Your forehead looks like an eggplant. Come here. When I'm done people will think you're Don Draper."

The man climbed a small ladder to retrieve a man's hat from a high shelf, up above a rack of kipper ties. He pulled down a charcoal-gray one and pointed William toward a mirror. Not only did it hide the lump above his eye, but it also looked awfully good. More Sam Spade than Don Draper, but he liked it. And he couldn't explain why, but he had the strangest feeling that Irene would have liked it too.

"Can you wear a hat to a wedding?" he asked Alisanne.

"Is it outside?" she asked.

"I don't know," William said.

"Just take it off during the ceremony. Don't be vulgar."

William promised, and the man pointed them back toward the used books. There were hundreds, all piled up and in no particular order. Alisanne began sifting through the stacks. William didn't even know what they were looking for. He opened books at random looking for handwriting or doodles that looked like Irene's, but it was tough to tell. Was that her *7* in the phone number scrawled in the margin of *The Count of Monte Cristo*? Was that her lazy spiral on the back page of *The Little House on the Prairie*? Just then William's finger paused on a green volume that seemed familiar.

The Iliad. Homer. He picked it up and opened it slowly. Its pages were covered in familiar handwriting. His own. But also in hers. He'd forgotten all about the book. He'd last seen it in her hospital room, before she was moved to the ICU. Afterward it had been the last thing on his mind. Sara had surely brought it home and put it into storage with the rest of her things. And now it was here.

"Aha!" he heard Alisanne shouting from just around the corner. She emerged with a plain, if somewhat beaten-up white book by Albert Camus. In plain red lettering, it said *L'Etranger* and beneath that, simply, *Roman*. The shop, apparently unaware that it was a rare first edition, was selling it for $1.50, which Alisanne paid gladly.

"I have to go now," she said. "Thank you, William."

He moved in, suddenly, to hug her. She tried to jump back. Then, having failed to escape the embrace, she surrendered.

"Who knows," she said, "what she ever saw in either of us."

But now that they had met, William, somehow, thought he did know. There was something about Alisanne that felt familiar. She was too blunt where he was too polite, but underneath was a kindness so strange that they both usually hid it away. And he supposed that must have been what it was. What Irene alone had been able to see. The thing she'd loved.

After paying for his new hat and his own former book, he stepped outside and returned to the park, where he sat down on the icy bench not far from the silent fountain. He opened the book carefully. He remembered that first night, how she'd defended, in a way, his preferred translation when Jacob had tried to mock it. Lattimore. *Richmond* Lattimore. She had underlined his first name in blue ink, on the title page. William smiled. He wondered how many more of these moments he might have in his lifetime.

Suddenly he hoped that he'd never find all the pieces. He was glad there was nothing but tortoises all the way down. The air smelled of vegetable curry, and there was a frenzy of branches up in the trees above him. Only then did he remember he was still wearing Alisanne's clothes. Sitting there in them, and in his new hat and the scarf from Irene, he felt almost like another person entirely. So this was what it was like. This was what Irene had learned. How to be someone new.

Just then he saw a hint of color on the edge in the back of the book. Carefully he turned to find a beautiful scene on the back leaf done in watercolors. Grays. Purples. Yellows. Blues. A busy street. Cars moving around a traffic circle while tall buildings gleam in the sunlight. White towers rising up into the blue heaven of a new day. The red neon on a Chinatown restaurant, still lit in the daytime. Sunlight gleaming off a water tower. The hushed, holy green that crept into the brown skeletons of city trees. Asphalt meridians curving through. Far away, the line of towers forming a horizon at the river. And rising up behind it all—the Brooklyn Bridge. No doubt it was hers. Her colors, her lines, her trembling wavelength. It was titled only "View from 4R," but there on the opposite page was a note, in her handwriting.

> *William—Thank you for the book. I hope Sara gets it back to you! And I hope you don't mind I did a picture on the other page, back when we were broken up and I thought I'd probably never see you again. I should explain, I guess, since you'll want it back now. That's the view from my bedroom at my grandmother Fiona's apartment, 12 Spruce Street, where I went away to live when I was a girl and, let's just say, not the most darling granddaughter ever. I loved it there, but then she got sick and passed away. I took some money and ran off because I didn't want to have to go back home again. Once I told you how I was born into the wrong family. For a long time I looked for my right one, and now I know I found it. Sorry I stole your mother's kimono. We should have been friends a long time ago, William. I would have liked that. Since we met, I've been wondering if this is fate, you know? Not in a cheesy way, but what if, no matter what I did all these years, I'd still be dying, just somewhere else? But then I think that maybe the where is what's important. If the gods bother, then man must have free will. Je suis toujours sur le point de te quitter. All my love, Irene.*

William sat there a long time. So she was from—well, just where he was from. He studied the picture again. Irene's childhood kingdom. Like him, she'd stared out at this at night and fallen asleep in the same womb of street noises. Who knew? Maybe they had passed each other on field trips, or crawled under the same turnstiles. Surely they'd both gotten up early on snow days to watch NY1 to check for school closings, and on the Fourth of July they'd both watched the same fireworks in the same sky. They had skinned their knees on the same sidewalks and answered the same essay questions on the same Regents Exam. And when everyone else had left home to come here, they had been leaving there to come home.

8

After a while William left and started walking toward the closest train that would take him home. He called his mother on the way, but she didn't pick up, and then he remembered she would still be with Chongso's mother, wearing red *mudang* robes in their living room, with all the shades down and curtains drawn, while the assembled members of the Kim family sat on the couches and watched her do a dance that their grandparents' grandparents had done. There would be howling and shouting and crying. The ghostly ancestors, lacking the proper equipment for speech, would be invited to borrow her vocal cords and tongue and lips. And the Kims would gradually allow themselves to believe what they needed to believe. That Chongso was fine. Locatable. Watching over them in the company of a hundred generations of Kims. William wanted to believe in this too; he was so tired of pretending that he didn't.

He picked up his phone and, through its cracked screen, sent a text message to Sung-Lee, the girl he had gone out with twice while he and Irene had been broken up.

Did you hear about Chongso?

I kno! So sad! How r u?

I'm good. How are you?

Really good. Drink sometime?

His thumb hovered over the screen. Staring down at the penumbra of green light, he felt an odd sensation running up his arm. He moved his thumb gently to the keyboard and replied.

Now?

They met near South Street Seaport, where she knew a place that had good drinks and wasn't too noisy. William soon found himself walking down Fulton Street, staring up at the Brooklyn Bridge again, which from this side seemed almost made of light. He felt the shadow of something close behind him. He passed dark window displays full of faceless mannequins. A saxophone cried out from the footsteps of the church. Everyone, everywhere was drunk.

William moved through crowd after crowd, seeking her silhouette. As he crossed under the FDR Drive, he heard Sung-Lee calling his name from the opposite corner. It took him a moment to spot her: in a navy blue coat with white trim, stepping out of a cab. She expertly navigated the cobblestones in stiletto ankle boots. She kissed him lightly on the cheek when he got close.

"I almost didn't recognize you," she said. "*Love* what you're wearing."

"You do?"

William knew he was blushing. Sung-Lee looked far more beautiful than he'd remembered, at least in the soft light of the street. She wore a glittering necklace of silver sharks' teeth. Her eyes were shadowed by a soft green.

"I hear your mother's looking for you."

William tried to explain. "Oh. Well. I was just—"

"Bad boy," she teased. "Call your mother."

Did she wink at him? Yes. He tried to laugh, as if it had been a joke, but something in her tone seemed off. She'd been so shy the last time they'd gone out. She'd worn flats. She hadn't kissed his cheek unprompted or said anything along the lines of "bad boy." He wondered if she was already drunk. The last time they'd gotten together, she'd had half a glass of wine and almost fallen asleep. Nothing like this.

"So they're searching, like, the whole tristate area to find the guy who hit Chongso. Once they do, I hope they run *him* over." Then she rolled her shoulders. "Anyways, how's life?"

"Life's . . . life," he said. "How's yours?"

"*Really* great," she said. "I'm having a lot of fun."

"Fun. I think I had that once," he joked.

She laughed. A lot. And grabbed his hand and said, "I'll remind you. Come on."

She led him down the street like a puppy dog to the Cutty Sark. A jaunty little ironwork clipper ship dangled from the sign at the entrance. Windows were festooned with ropes as thick as his wrists and aged canvas sails. A chandelier made from a ship's wheel hung from a rusty block and tackle in the center of the room. At the many wooden tables along the decking sat men and women drinking beer and eating fish and chips. William and Sung-Lee took a seat at a table beside a man in a red wool cap, who was splitting a bowl of chowder with a man with sideburns and a porkpie hat.

She flagged down a passing waitress and ordered two Manhattans, one with five brandied cherries. "They rinse the glass with absinthe," she explained. "Really makes the flavors pop."

"Yeah, but doesn't it eat holes in your brain?" William asked.

"Buzzzzzzzzz," she lifted a pointer finger to the side of William's skull. Then she ran a hand over the lump on his head.

"So, what, did you get into a fight?"

William smiled. "Actually, yes."

She seemed—surprised? No. Impressed. He kept looking around, as if someone might see him with her. Not like he was cheating, even if that was how it felt.

"I can't be out *too* late," she announced, withdrawing her hand. "I've got a six a.m. flight to Istanbul for a conference."

Some very loud song thumped its beat on the speakers across the way. She was sort of singing along and shifting her hips. At the chorus she sang along, "'O . . . oh . . . oh. Dreams weave the rose . . .' Have you seen this music video? It's *so* awful. But I love the song." She shrugged as if this were one more of life's unresolvable little mysteries.

"What kind of conference?" William asked. The drinks arrived, and he wondered how fast he could finish his and get the hell out of there. She fished one of her five cherries out and began to nibble on it. "Mifamurtide. It's this new drug that just finished a phase three trial. They're approving it soon in Europe. It's *got* to go well because we really fucking blew it last month in Copenhagen. It wasn't *my* fault, of course. It was this idiot, Parker, who screwed up the goddamn time zones or hit his snooze button or something and didn't show up, and of course we left all the materials with him. I had to get up there with *nothing* and do the presentation from memory. I mean, it was the worst thing ever to happen to anyone. You don't even know."

William nodded agreeably. He couldn't decide if he was being polite or pathetic, but either way he sensed he'd regret it.

"I just hate it when people waste my time, you know?"

He couldn't decide if this was a veiled dig at him, or if she was just too obtuse to realize how it could come across.

"Thank *god* it all worked out. And my boss was so impressed, he took me on his jet to stay at his villa in Panama. It's, like, on the top of a private mountain that used to be a volcano. The only way to get there is to, like, take a helicopter? And the whole thing is, like, fucking glass walls so we'd be just, like, sitting in the kitchen, and you can see whales out in the ocean, like, blowing water a hundred feet in the air. Out of those blowholes?"

William tried his hardest to seem impressed and jealous, which he assumed was the point.

" 'Atlantis ROSE,' " she burst out, singing along to the same song. " 'Drums wreathe . . .' "

"Sounds like things are great then," William said.

"*So* great," she replied, again doing a little dance in her seat to the song as it ended.

"Are things . . . serious between you and your boss?"

Sung-Lee burst out laughing. "Him? No. He's, like, married or whatever. It's not even a thing. And—" Then as if it were a big secret, she leaned in to say, "He's got the grossest back hair? I had to just tell him at some point—keep your shirt on, you know?"

Last time they'd gone out, she'd been insufferably demure. Now she was like her own evil twin sister, and it was no improvement, except that, he supposed, she did seem much happier. He couldn't stop watching her fingers fiddling with the edge of her navy lapel.

"You seem different," he said at last. "I mean, in a good way. I mean, I guess, I'm impressed when people can do that. Just take on a whole new attitude."

Sung-Lee again leaned in. "I started doing *Entrance.* Have you heard of it?"

"No. Is it some kind of drug?"

She shook her head and then stared up at the ceiling as if searching there for the words to explain it. "It's like—*so* incredible. It's all about the radical reinvention of your brain's whole structure through hypnosis. Well, it's *not* hypnosis. It's a semiconscious state induced by rhythmic motion and chanting. At first it's sort of like yoga almost, but then you go into this full-on trance state. That's why they call it that. En-Trance. Right? And while you're in the trance state, you can just *unlock* all these things. It's all about realizing what you're doing to hold yourself back, like through hatred or fear or nihilism or eating gluten. You identify the things you want, and you finally allow yourself to take them—"

William lost the end of her diatribe as a garbage truck rolled by outside, thudding and crashing and beeping and flashing its lights as men in neon vests hopped off to collect black bags of trash that gleamed in the streetlights. He looked back up at Sung-Lee, coaxing the last of the cherries between her lips. Was he a thing that she had decided to allow herself to take? Or was he something to unlock? Some kind of shackle; the gluten of her love life. He watched the men outside throwing bags of trash as if they were nothing but black air. He could see Sung-Lee following his gaze to the door. What did *he* want?

"Let's go up onto the bridge," William said.

On the very edge he stood with Sung-Lee under a wash of golden light, watching boats cutting through the darkness hundreds of feet below their feet. Her hair blew up into his face, and her arm pressed against his as she pointed excitedly at a pair of helicopters going wing and wing, only feet from each other. Surely it was no accident that she was crushing her butt into his thigh. His hands seemed to remember, as he pressed one against the small of her back. This was what a real body felt like. When he turned to kiss her, she didn't disappear. Her lips opened, even greedily, at his touch. Tongue behind savage little teeth. Her chest heaving up, and her hands weaving, rising, up his spine. A powerful wind enveloped them, pushing downriver. She smelled like poppies and Earl Grey—had she just bitten his tongue? Yes. He tasted pennies. His hands whipped around her waist and down the back of her skirt. Her hips swayed, danced a little, as she had in the bar. *O . . . oh . . . oh. Dreams weave the rose.*

Her cheekbones were glowing. He stopped, not sure of himself now. Her dark, heavy lashes lifted, and the soft brown pupils beneath studied him, twitching. He'd forgotten, almost, what it was like to really *see* a person. And to see someone seeing you. She traced a finger along the horn of his nose and the line of his lips.

She shouted over a passing UPS truck, "When the fuck did you learn to kiss like that?"

William watched the corners of her lips rise up into the folds of her cheeks. A smile like a perfect parabola. The tips of her fingers ranging . . .

"Did she teach you? The girl you left me for. Last time."

"I'm so sorry about that," William yelled back. "I know I should have called."

But she grabbed him and kissed him even harder. There was a lull in the traffic as she whispered now, right into his ear, "Don't hold grudges. That's fear and hate, William. And besides I definitely don't stand in the way of true fucking love."

"I mean, I don't know if I'd—" Except he would. It was. Or had been. True fucking love.

She looked in his eyes. "You're still in love with her."

"She—died," William said. He knew she knew this; their mothers talked.

"Like that matters," she said. Then very seriously, she asked him, "Have you kissed anyone else since she died?"

"I don't want to talk about it," he said. Then he added, "No."

This seemed to be the right answer. She began kissing his neck, and he could feel her hands on him again. He turned away and looked at the other people on the walkway. Families. Couples. Faces, waists, feet. Hair on shoulders. But none were the ones he wanted.

"Let's go back to your apartment," she said.

"I can't," he said.

"Why not?"

He paused, pretty sure he didn't want to tell her he'd moved back home with his mother a year ago. He was surprised, actually, that she didn't already know, which meant that his mother hadn't been telling people about it.

"They're spraying it actually. Pill flies."

She kissed him again, almost angrily, "Then let's go to my place."

William whispered okay, and she melted against him, and he gripped her tightly, knuckles white. They didn't speak again about Irene as they walked back to Manhattan and caught a cab to the Upper East Side. Instead she talked to him about her annoying coworkers, her ex-boyfriend Jeremy. William felt himself sweating. He wondered why he was doing this. Because he was scared of her? Yes, but there was something else. The more she touched him and the more he touched her back, the more he felt something else. Someone else.

Inside her apartment, Sung-Lee was tearing William's coat off before the door had shut behind them. He liked the way her hands felt against his sore jaw. The way her teeth nipped at his ear. His tongue throbbed a little where she'd bitten it, but this pain, along with the familiar ache above his eye, was lost in the whole ache of his body now. It was dark in the room, and he couldn't see her very well, only shadows and the warm feel of her skin against his. She pulled her dress up and off, and beneath there was only cinnamon flesh and pink underwear, no bra, the silver sharks' teeth falling down between her breasts. He buried his head there and filled his lungs. Poppies and Earl Grey. Her hands were tussling with his belt buckle, fingers hooking through the loops, steering him into the room.

Her black hair whipped around her head like something self-possessed, and she demanded, "On the couch." William looked longingly over toward the other side of the room, at her bed, but there was no reaching it. She almost hurled him onto the couch. Increasingly it was all William could do to simply hang on and do as he was being told—loudly and repeatedly—not sparing on the *fucks* and the *shits* and other things. She was purposefully screaming. There was no way he was *that* good. Not that it wasn't kind of incredible, though. Even if it felt a bit like he was being used. Even if it was a relief on several levels when it was over. "That was nice," she said, though little about it had been anything like nice at all.

He woke up a few hours later to the sound of her in the bathroom, and watched through slit eyelids as she came out, fully dressed, and quietly left the room. Six a.m. flight to Istanbul. Business class, nonstop. William walked over to the bed, finally, and pressed his face into the cool pillows. Just as he began to slip back to sleep, he felt a warm hand on his back, and the tip of a nose on his neck. Had she come back? Changed her mind or gotten a later flight?

How was that? came a whisper in his ear. *What was that like?*

William started up and began to roll over, but just as before, he felt a hand press against his cheek as if to stop him. He felt a flood of guilt, of stomach sick. As if she'd seen the whole thing.

Oh please, she said. *Don't be ridiculous. It's just sex. And if I thought you'd fall in love with Sung-Lee and forget all about me, I'd say go for it.*

William felt his face go hot. He wouldn't cry in front of her, whether or not she was really there.

She was quiet a moment, and he thought maybe she'd gone. *I have to say, I really miss sex.*

Ghosts can't have sex?

No bodies, no nerve endings.

No fair.

You don't know the half of it.

William felt her hand lift from his back, and he reached around to grab it but found only air and his own warm skin. *I'll find you,* he promised.

As he fell asleep, he thought he heard her saying, *I'm not lost.*

9

Twelve Spruce was a prewar building made of clean white brick. William located the dusty buzzer near the door and tentatively pressed 4R. He knew it was crazy, but he wanted to try. If no one was home, then fine. But to his surprise, the door shook and unlocked. Across a dark lobby, he climbed into a creaking old elevator that took him slowly to the fourth floor. There he soon found 4R, with a mat out front that said WELCOME.

William knocked at the door and waited. A few moments later someone answered. An old Hispanic woman with wide wrinkled circles around her eyes. For a brief moment, though he knew she was long dead, William imagined it was Grandma Fiona. Behind her the sound of rapid gunfire and shouting in Arabic came from the television, followed by a trumpeting of transition music and the opinions of an unseen news anchor.

He took off his hat. "Hi. I'm sorry. You don't know me, but a friend of mine used to live here in your apartment. And I was wondering. Could I come in for just a minute?"

There was, he knew, no earthly reason this woman should allow him, a total stranger in a slightly disturbing French punk rock T-shirt, to enter her home, but to his surprise she moved away from the door without a word.

"My name is William. Um . . . *Mi nombre es* William?"

She nodded and walked back over to the big white couch in front of her TV. The floor was covered in scattered trucks and balls and other children's toys. There were religious paintings on the wall, a Madonna and Child and a few Christs on crosses. Everything seemed to have been recently remodeled. The floorboards were new and fitted together. The walls were white and bumpy, in the way of all New York apartment walls, painted over with each new tenant. If only he could peel it back and see underneath. Would there be smudges and tea stains and fingerprints and stray flecks of oil paint that had once been Irene's? William moved lightly into the apartment, wondering which of the rooms had been her bedroom. He passed a sideboard table that was being used as an altar. There were photographs of children and grandchildren to be prayed for, and in front of those an arrangement of candles and little statues. A bowl for holy water, and a smaller one with something grainy inside like salt. There was a very nice set of rosary beads carved from a red wood, just next to a little incense burner covered in ash marks.

William stood there and thought about his mother, who would be back at home by now, putting away the tools of her ancient trade: apples and rice cakes and money and tiny paper figures. Iron chains and small boats that she'd waved in the air. Drums and pieces of paper drawn now with letters and symbols. Science and medicine were good things, his mother had told him, growing up. To heal diseases, to mend bones, to tend to the sick, the elderly, and the newly born. To do research on AIDS, as Charles did, and to peddle pills and vaccines like Sung-Lee—these were noble things. And lucrative, not to forget that.

But a *mudang* treated something else. Something that couldn't be reached with chemicals or seen on X-rays. The thing that causes illness, the thing that comes before viruses and bacteria, even DNA. *Uhwan.* What she called "misfortune" and others might think of as simple "bad luck," though it was far worse than that when *uhwan* began to creep into your life. Just a few things would go wrong at first, but well within the realm of expectations. A setback here, a letdown there, but you keep up, mostly. Bad things happen, but don't they happen to everyone sometimes? Only like in an undertow at the beach, you are being pulled gradually in the wrong direction. You correct, but you overcorrect. You flail, but this makes it worse. Things fall apart, and you hurriedly glue the pieces back together and cannot ignore the resulting cracks. There isn't time to do more because other, larger things are going wrong already. Medicine cannot cure the problem. Psychology cannot resolve it. One day you wake up to discover that where once there was one thing wrong, there are now hundreds. Far more is wrong than right. Because misfortune is a plague that begets plagues. What starts as a tiny imbalance creates a ripple effect that can take down empires.

What string of ever-worsening misfortunes preceded Chongso's accident? What had made Mrs. Kim decide to punish him that morning? What had led him to dare to sneak out on his own to buy the comic book? What had the driver been doing instead of watching the road? No disaster is a singular incident. It is the tsunami that follows the swelling tide. It is the nuclear meltdown that begins when a dozen fail-safes have failed. Before the chemo, before the cancer, before the cell mutation, there is the misfortune. *Uhwan.*

William felt for the small lump in his back pocket, beneath the address book, and fished out the little Aqualad figurine. One final time he studied. He liked to think it was part of some thirteenth art piece that she'd never gotten to make. He liked to think it would have had something to do with him. Only then he thought that, really, as much as all the pieces had to do with death and disappointment and her friends, they also had something to do with him, her last love. Gently, he set the little superhero down on the altar beside the candles, and said a quiet prayer for Chongso Kim.

William moved through the apartment, half expecting some dog or husband to appear and kill him. He had hoped—he didn't know. That he'd walk in and find Irene there, sitting on the couch beside Grandma Fiona, book on her lap, twirling her hair, paint on her arms. That she would ease her body around his as he lay down and touch his hair. That he would call her No Ears and they would talk about Yesterday and Today, with no mention of that foul uninvited guest Tomorrow. If he could have just one more day, he thought, like the first one. Before she'd heard back from the doctors and begun dying. If he could just have one more day when nothing was wrong, when time could be wasted, because there had still been so, so much of it out there.

And then he saw, through the window in what was now a room filled with old boxes. It was the exact view painted in the back of his old book. The Brooklyn Bridge. Cables arching up like the frame of a great harp, vibrating with the whispered secrets of its crossers. This was the window she'd looked out of each night as she fell asleep and each morning when she'd woken up. As he lay there, he imagined he could hear voices traveling up the strings and through the steel, flickering between the cars and in the thump of the bicycle wheels against the wood. He saw the roadway rising and falling, like a wave out on the sea.

It took him a moment to remember that he hadn't smoked anything all morning. This wasn't that. All those voices, all those wheels and feet were coming together into a harmony. A simple, perfect note that resonated with the bridge itself and the churning river beneath. Echoing with the cries of the captains of the great wooden ships, just setting sail from South Street, casting off for the seven oceans, to journey in dreams. William watched in awe as the notes moved through the roadway like a sine curve, an octave that caused bricks to detach one at a time from the towers, a flat foot on each shore.

Into the blue sky, cars and people flew like a peppering of seagulls, up and up and never down. Up into the crystal cotton of the clouds. Light gleamed off their wristwatches and hubcaps and handlebars. They became fins in the ocean of sky. Brick by brick, the bridge rose into the air, pulling the river with it, drop by drop. Atlantis rose. Land of tomorrows and yesteryears. Once there was a continent that sank into the sea. *Farewell!* he cried to the people as they vanished. Trillions of them, it seemed, as the entire bridge fell into the sky.

THE WEDDING OF SARA SHERMAN AND GEORGE MURPHY

Sara Sherman ran between the rooms of the bridal suite, lifting her dress so it wouldn't sweep the Waldorf's tapestry rugs. The dress was still an eighth of an inch too long, even after she'd told the lady at Nelson's to shorten it at both the six-week and the one-month fittings. So now the lace along the edge had accumulated a faint grayness as she rushed from the front door—where she'd just received an update from Zacharie, the hotel's event coordinator, about the situation with the chairs—back into the bedroom where her sisters, Adeline and Eddy, were converging on George's mother, intent on taking down the hair that the stylist, Erikah, had spent two hours putting up that morning.

Barely had that been handled when she caught her own mother plucking "excess" baby's breath from the bouquets. Sara redirected her into checking on whether the Krazy Glue was setting properly on George's Grandma Pertie's snapped heel. And did anyone have an approximate GPS location on his older brother, Clarence? Who, despite having strict orders to stay in Midtown, had sneaked off that morning to visit the Cloisters near Fort Tryon Park, only to wind up getting stuck in a cab on the West Side Highway behind some kind of gubernatorial motorcade? For all Sara cared, Clarence could rot on the asphalt overlooking the Boat Basin, but of course, this actual Mensa member had decided it would be a good idea to take the two wedding bands with him.

She was interrupted by George's little niece, Beth, the seven-year-old daughter of George's younger brother, Franklin (who at sixteen had been absentminded about protection at a post-prom party). Sara liked Beth immensely, for she was apparently the only other responsible human being in the entire bridal suite. Beth had been fully set in her flower-girl dress, with hair done and shoes on, for over two hours now. Now she held Sara's phone in the air calmly and said, "It's ringing." Beth was in charge of fielding calls and beating level twenty in *Plants vs. Zombies*.

Sara looked at the phone: it was Minister Thaw, who had already left two messages that morning. He had conducted their required premarital counseling sessions, where they'd had plenty of time to delve into the minutiae of Episcopalian dogma and how it differed from George's Catholicism and "What about the children?"—and *now* he was bringing up reordering all the readings, even though the programs had already been printed and the whole thing had been successfully rehearsed the night before. *Stay the course!* she wanted to yell into his fuzzy little ears. *We're almost through this!* Instead she rejected the call, handed the phone back to Beth, and called out to the bridal suite, "Does anyone have the chalk?" Again, only Beth knew the location of the Crayola box and began helpfully whitening the gray hem of the wedding dress.

"Thank you, sweetie. And do you know where Adeline is?"

Beth didn't. No one nearby knew. Perfect. Not only had their mother guilted Sara into asking her uptight older sister to fill the maid of honor post, and not only had Adeline then thrown a spectacularly dull bachelorette party (appletinis and feather boas), but she had already abandoned Sara and the day's proceedings.

As unhappy as Adeline was to leave the safety of Gloucester for even one weekend, their younger sister Eddy (short, since always, for Edwina) was being no better about being away from her ashram. Eddy had come to town with the uninvited George-Harrison Zimmerman (first name, legally, "George-Harrison"), whose hair was both longer and shinier than Sara's had been at any point in her life and who had brought his guitar "just in case."

Sara had a hard time not fixating on how much easier all this would have been with Irene at her side. She didn't trust anyone else's opinions on jewelry, decorations, or invitations. At every turn in the planning, she'd wanted to call up Irene about the wisdom of champagne-colored heels, or get her input on calligraphers. And of course, here she had two perfectly good sisters, only the two of them combined couldn't begin to fill the opening left by her absent best friend. "I hope you don't think you're wearing Grandma's pearls" was Adeline's only contribution, while Eddy wanted only to remind Sara that the tuna on the reception menu was being dangerously overfished. Sara had found herself talking, half to herself, half to the absence of Irene, all throughout the planning process—and now that it was over, and the wedding was happening, it seemed inconceivable that Irene wasn't there to see it all through.

Irene's aesthetic was the driving force behind the whole event. In going through her things, Sara had found a few of the old guidebooks they'd bought in college when first planning their trip to the Côte d'Azur. Boom—here was the color scheme: the turquoise waters off St. Tropez, and the rose rooftops of Monaco. Bam—there was the font: a vintage script used by the Hotel Negresco on its dinner menu.

Sara found it impossible to believe that she and George would be there, for real, in just twenty-four hours: reading under the bold-blue-striped beach umbrellas at Cannes, climbing the spiral stairs of the elegant fairytale castles of Antibes, tossing a pair of dice at a craps table in Monte Carlo. All of the Shermans had chipped in to send them first class. Sara tried hard to remember this, and to let her gratitude balance out Irene's absence. She had already planned out every detail of the trip, from what she would order for dinner at Le Chantecler in Nice, to where she could rent a sun umbrella in Théoule-sur-Mer, and the rules for baccarat when they visited the

Place du Casino in Monte Carlo. And up on the very top of a mountain, in a sun-drenched spot called Pointe Sublime, she and George would scatter Irene's ashes as she'd asked them to, and it would be done at last. Sara couldn't stop dreaming about it.

Adeline called from the next room, "The photographer says he's ready for you!"

"Is George up there already?" Sara shouted back.

"He didn't say!"

"Has anyone heard from him yet?"

Silence.

Sara gathered her gown and moved slowly toward the front door, with the sisters and mothers all rushing over to send her off enthusiastically, to tell her she looked beautiful, to remind her how lucky she was. Sara made sure Beth had the folder with the marriage license in it and headed to the freight elevator (the only one with roof access). She was sure her sisters were already pulling bobby pins out of Mrs. Murphy's hair and her mother was back to editing the bouquets. She turned back to the crowd of turquoise-satin bridesmaids at the door. "I need everyone else up there in *ten minutes*. Moms, aunts, cousins, brothers, *sisters*. *Both* families. Bouquets and boutonnières. *Shoes* on." That one was for Eddy, who seemed to feel that wearing closed-toed heels somehow made her a party to systemic gender marginalization.

"Aye-aye, captain!" Eddy saluted back. "Go, go, go!"

Sara did a last check of her hair and makeup in the reflection of the closed elevator doors. Who *was* this girl in the cold steel with the cupid's bow lips and the Clara Bow eyebrows? It was all wrong. Why had she let the lady do it that way?

The elevator doors opened. Inside, a small Hispanic woman hid behind a cart filled with fresh towels and cleaning products. A little radio was blaring some sort of sermon on a tinny Spanish station. "¿Dónde está, oh muerte, tu aguijón? ¿Dónde, oh sepulcro, tu victoria?"

"Oh!" the maid screeched happily, covering her mouth with both hands, in the universal language of bride excitement. "¡Eres tan bella!"

"Gracias," Sara managed.

In just an hour Sara would be standing up there, holding George's hands in front of Minister Thaw and listening to him read from First Corinthians. *Love is patient, love is kind.* And she would nod mindfully as Thaw rattled off his list, of all the things that Love Was Not: envious, boastful, proud. And with her wearing the most beautiful dress she'd ever worn, on the most expensive single afternoon of her entire life. The rest of the verse was practically a checklist of how Sara had been feeling all year. Love was not: dishonoring others, being self-seeking, or angering easily. Check, check, and check. Love keeps no record of wrongs? Sara had a whole spreadsheet of them. Who hadn't sent a gift, and who had brought a plus-one without asking, and who had demanded that they be married in a church in the first place, and which cousin wasn't coming despite living less than three hours away, and which aunt had to be cut off after two by the bartender and . . . Love doesn't delight in evil but rejoices with the truth. It always protects, always trusts, always hopes, always perseveres.

Love never fails.

The radio piece ended, and soon a commercial began. Sara recognized it from the first somber piano chord. She had been hearing it everywhere all week: in cabs, at her dentist's office, at the gym. At this point she could practically recite it from memory. "At Mount Sinai Cancer Center . . . the patient is the center of our universe. Like Sue, who thought it was all over when her liver cancer came back. 'I came to Mount Sinai, and right away I was working with a team of specialists in *my* type of cancer. Providing the very latest options, including personalized therapies, just for *me*.' Today Sue is cancer-free, thanks to specialists like Dr. Atoosa Zarrani . . . 'We live for the chance to help people like Sue. My colleagues and I worked hard and together . . . we cured her.' "

Well, good for fucking Sue. Sara wanted to snap the antenna off the piece-of-crap radio and drive it through the speakers.

Then there was a hand on hers. "No cry," the maid was saying. "You look so beautiful! *Happy* day!"

Sara coughed as the elevator came to the twentieth floor at last, and the maid pushed the cart away, smiling and crossing herself and wishing her well in Spanish. The doors closed, and as Sara went alone up the last few floors, she tried to fix her mascara in the reflection of the emergency call box. Steadily she felt the elevator easing its ascent, and she looked up expectantly at the sound of its cheerful ding. The doors stayed shut as things settled. She held her breath. Crazy how, after almost ten years together, just a day away from George, and she was as excited to see him again as she had been that first day, waiting for him to come down from his dorm to pick her up for the movies.

At last the doors opened onto the roof of the Waldorf Astoria Hotel. For the first time all morning, she smiled, as she scanned the wide blue cloudless sky and all the rooftops of midtown Manhattan for George.

In George's dreams he saw a spinning wheel of hydrogen gas, thirty-six billion miles across, beginning to collapse under its own immense weight. Though it had been spinning for over one hundred thousand years, its end had come. Seismic shocks ripped through the icy disk, just ten degrees above absolute zero. He watched it radiating microwaves and great streams of plasma—solar winds that emanated in all directions at once. Ninety-nine point ninety-nine percent of these rays traveled on through emptiness forever, reflecting off no other planets or asteroids or matter of any kind, being sucked into no black holes or other gravitational fields, crossing paths with no other particle. Turbulent storms moved along the circumference at speeds greater than sound, as the wheel contracted like a great iris in space, years passing in moments, the core becoming hotter and brighter as it shrank. Faster and faster, the humongous orbit of gaseous molecules, ten times larger than our whole solar system, caving further and further in on itself—until in one spectacular and sudden stabilizing moment, it all stopped. And everything became still in the space around this new, glorious star. And then George woke up alone on an unfamiliar couch, vaguely aware of being completely naked.

Feathers of all colors drifted through the air. Hot pinks, neon greens, and bruised purples danced a lazy *pas de trois* around the martini glasses on the coffee table, sticky with the day-old residue of sour apple Pucker. The television was on, but muted. George's arms were wrapped around a gray lamp that seemed to belong on the side table. He'd heard of waking up with lampshades on your head but never cuddling with the lamp itself. Slowly he remembered that he was in the hotel room that Sara and her sisters had used the night of the bachelorette party. After their spa day, they had come back here to throw on their slinky dresses and high heels and feather boas before the big bar crawl. The boys had thrown George's bachelor party that same night down in Atlantic City and had been so late getting back the next day that they had gone directly to the rehearsal dinner without stopping into the room to see that it had, clearly, never been cleaned.

George set the lamp down on the ground and looked around the room, to the extent that he could without moving his head. Clarence and Franklin, his two brothers, weren't in view—presumably they'd taken the bed in the next room. And Sara's sister's boyfriend George-Harrison, whose idea it had been to go out for a few more after the rehearsal dinner, had his own room down the hall.

Which left only Jacob. Had he gone home, or was he around somewhere? George still couldn't shake the feeling that Jacob was only acting as if nothing were wrong, but maybe nothing *was* wrong. Supposedly he was turning over a lot of new leaves. He was taking night courses at Pratt on Tuesdays and Thursdays to earn his master's in art therapy. Sara claimed he was writing again; she had been badgering him to read something at the wedding, but he insisted he had nothing new.

Taking a deep breath, George lurched up from the couch—just like ripping off a Band-Aid, he thought. As with a Band-Aid, he immediately felt a searing pain. It was behind his eyes, in his ears, and climbing up his brain stem. The entire room pulsed and blurred. It took almost everything he had to keep himself from lying back down again—but no, he had to get up. This was his *wedding day*. Everything would finally change. Sara would ease up on the interval training. He'd be able to focus his energies on the future—their real future—and make mornings like this (was it morning?) a distant memory. Tomorrow they would be on their honeymoon, and afterward these yesterdays would be well behind him.

Yesterday. What an odd kind of hell that had been, to return from three sweaty hours in traffic on the Garden State Parkway, smelling vaguely of the baby powder that the strippers (apparently) used to keep themselves from sweating on the poles, finding glitter that had once been attached to the nipple of a woman named Roxxxy and was now somehow (he knew how) *in*side his left nostril. Man truly was a disgusting animal. He'd never felt more so than he had that afternoon, changing in the moving car in front of George-Harrison and walking directly into a Michelin-starred restaurant to dine with his parents, for whom a racy evening was watching a Robert Redford movie on cable, and all his soon-to-be in-laws, and to look the woman he loved right in her lovely, dark eyes as she asked with a knowing smirk just what exactly he'd gotten up to. Bless her. Absent any shred of doubt that the debauchery would mean anything to him. Knowing that whatever occurred couldn't touch what they shared.

He watched a purple feather creep along the ceiling and get caught in a downdraft near the balcony and go surfing down the drawn shade toward a corner on the floor. He took a deep breath and tried to walk. Amazingly, he didn't fall over. Now he could see the clock in the kitchenette—and that he had just under forty minutes to clean himself off and get to the roof for the photographers. He grimaced. Not a lot of time—but he just needed to put one foot in front of the other. Sip some of the ginger ale from the minibar. Maybe eat a cracker if he could. Keep a couple of aspirin down. Get to a shower.

As he set about these tasks, he felt sick in every conceivable way. He was used to hangovers, of course, but lately they had been different. Now the hangovers started during the fun. It used to be that only with the coming of the morning did he have any regrets. But steadily the distance between the during and the after had collapsed. Now he regretted things even as they were happening or even *before*—knowing that they would happen, because he lacked the will to stop himself.

George hunted for the remote control but couldn't find it, so he eventually walked over to the TV and turned it off by hand. No mystery as to what he'd been trying to watch, drunk and butt-naked in the middle of the night, cuddling with a lamp. He'd left it on Televisión Española, which aired three reruns of *¡Vámonos, Muchachos!* every night beginning at one a.m. The girls had discovered the show on their own, years ago, though back then he had never really understood the appeal. It was a multicamera sitcom featuring a group of six twentysomething friends in downtown Mexico City. Nobody else he knew seemed to have ever heard of the show. It didn't even broadcast in HD, further contributing to George's sensation that he was traveling back in time by watching it. It felt unmistakably like a 1990s show, in the vein of classic NBC Must See TV. Mostly the *Muchachos* characters seemed to have no jobs to prevent them bantering at the spacious Torrefacto café, with its pink and blue mod-style couches and patterned orange walls.

The muchachos were Santiago, a nerdy orthopedic surgeon

who had trouble talking to women, despite being a born romantic; his handsome roommate, Tomás, who worked at Torrefacto (though he was rarely seen actually working); the beautiful Constanza, a high-maintenance TV weathergirl who was in a tumultuous relationship with Tomás; Isidora, the architecture graduate student who shared Constanza's loft, an utter and charming mess of a girl, perpetually disorganized and overwhelmed by life; her brother Aarón, who played guitar with a struggling band called La Palabra that was always about to get its big break; and Renata, by far the quirkiest of the gang, a speech therapist with her own sporadic practice, though she was so childish at heart that George wondered how she stayed in business. She and Santiago had a will-they-or-won't-they tension that couldn't really be characterized as sexual. The humor was all very PG: gags involving talking parrots and lost purses and cases of mistaken identity and sinks overflowing and letters being misaddressed. Someone was always getting locked out of an apartment while wearing nearly nothing. They were all always running out of minutes on their cell phones at *just* the wrong time. There had to be hundreds of episodes, and from what little George could find online about it, the show was still being made, airing in Mexico a year before rerunning in America.

George had first come across it while trying to clean up the DVR. Sara had left the series on the record list, and over the course of the first six months, they'd amassed *fifty hours* of episodes. She couldn't bring herself to watch it anymore and had asked him to delete them all, but George found himself unable to. Instead he began watching them, late at night, alone. He guessed he was sleeping only three or four hours a night, most times. He didn't see how it was possible to still be alive on so little sleep, but he managed to get through the day, bleary and exhausted, only to get into bed and find himself wide awake. He would lie there in the dark until sound-sleeper Sara was out, and then get up and wash dishes, make himself an Old-Fashioned, reorganize the books and DVDs, water the houseplants, and watch an episode of *¡Vámonos, Muchachos!* while drinking a second Old-Fashioned.

Trying to settle his stomach, George chewed some stale crackers he'd found in the hotel kitchenette. His phone was ringing on the counter. A miracle he had drunkenly managed to plug in his charger. Allen's face appeared on the screen, and George rejected the call. He couldn't believe Sara had insisted on inviting him. Not only that, but she'd also made Rob bring him to the bachelor party!

It was during that evening, when George had drunkenly done all the things that passed for bonding—playing blackjack together, stopping at Gary's SuperLiquor to buy enough Pabst to drown a team of oxen—that Allen had asked him point-blank if he'd ever been with a woman other than Sara. (Where was Jacob when you needed someone to throw a little cold water on the situation?) George had been too obliterated by cheap beer and the relentless throb of the synthesizers to lie. Knowing it was all over his face, he shook his head.

"That's so *fifties*, yo!" Allen had screamed. "Shit, you're like my fucking *grandparents*."

Like George's fucking grandparents, too, he supposed, or even like his sleeping-in-separate-bedrooms-for-the-last-twenty-years parents.

Allen didn't seem likely to drop it. "What if there's something weird down there, and you don't even know it because you've never seen any other ones?"

George made a face. "I took AP Biology, Allen. I have an Internet connection." Then he gestured up to the stage at the current dancer, who was bottomless, just as advertised. "I know what a—I know what one's supposed to look like."

After briefly clutching his head in his hands, Allen threw an arm around George. "That's craziness. I mean, I just couldn't. It's—evolutionarily counterproductive!"

"Oh, you're a biologist now?"

"Look. The male of the species is naturally drawn to polyamorous behavior, and the female is *structurally* inclined toward birthing and child care . . ."

George didn't hear much after that, partly because of the bass coming off the stage and partly because he had heard this all before from Allen, who was fond of sharing stories of his conquests, late at night when they were up editing grants, or poring over thousands of data points in the lab, sometimes even in the middle of the day just walking down the halls at the institute. Allen was an aficionado of all the new online dating sites: Match.com, OKCupid, Chemistry .com, ScienceConnect. He even had an app for his phone that let him scroll through the profiles of nearby available women and indicate with a swipe of his finger if he was interested in them, as if he were seated at some sort of sex buffet. Sara said she couldn't figure what on earth these women saw in him, but according to his locker-room talk, Allen was getting laid left, right, and center.

George suddenly felt a profound desire to know: "Is it really so great sleeping with all these different people?"

Allen paused as if, for an instant, he couldn't comprehend the question. Then, incredulous, he responded. "Man, it's *awesome.* I—George . . . you're making me sad. I'm sorry. This is your night, and I'm happy for you and Sara and all but—what a question!"

George stopped listening. Jumping into bed with some woman he'd only just met seemed pleasant in theory but awful in practice. Not just being naked in front of a stranger, not just having his anatomy and performance evaluated by someone whose standards were unknown, not even the awkwardness of what to do with all that you'd used up in one another afterward, but mainly just the idea of being that close to someone he didn't know crucial things about: Middle name. Best friend's name in middle school. County of birth. Number of siblings. Feelings about Elvis. Preference for or against nuts in brownies. Ability to ride a bicycle. Major allergies. Burial locations of childhood pets. Most embarrassing moment of adulthood. Approximate number of pairs of shoes owned. Use of contact lenses. Song to be played at their funeral.

George supposed he had always been a monogamist. Even back in kindergarten he had gotten in trouble. A meeting had been called with his mother and Mrs. Remington. Young George had been systematically working his way through the girls in the class, asking them each to marry him under the swing set, with a ring made out of a twisted juice-box straw. And as an adult, now, when he did spot a beautiful stranger, riding home on the T at night, he never fantasized about jumping into the empty conductor's cab for eleven anonymous minutes in heaven. No, he'd imagine beginning some awkward conversation: she'd drop something, or he'd trip over someone else's umbrella, and they'd chat amiably for a few stops about something in the news. They'd discover some shared love of something—the fresh berry crème brûlée at Finale, or how the Gardner Museum still left blank spaces on the walls where a half dozen paintings had been stolen in the 1990s, or the six-story fish tank at the New England Aquarium. And then the fantasy would fast-forward. Some weeks or months would go by and, by chance, George would find himself alone one rainy afternoon, walking by Finale, or the Gardner, or the Aquarium. And there she'd be. They'd see each other by accident. Remember. Laugh. Act like old friends. Go to grab a cup of coffee. But this wasn't the weirdest part of the fantasy. Not in the least.

The weirdest part was that always, he'd imagine that somewhere in those intervening weeks or months, something would have happened to Sara. She'd have left him or been in a terrible accident. It was usually nothing specific, just that she was gone, and he was sad. The whole thing was awful—but it was the only way he could clear his conscience so the fantasy could continue. Even in his wildest dreams, he couldn't fathom cheating.

George tried to forget all this as he climbed into the hot shower. Fifteen minutes left to go. Shampoo. Conditioner. He couldn't find his toothbrush, so he used a fingertip to scrub his teeth. He knew

Sara would tell him to just throw up. He considered jabbing his finger back a little farther and seeing what happened, but the thought of it was somehow even worse than the thought of his belly remaining full of last night's post-rehearsal tequila shots. If she'd been there, he would have done it. To show her that, despite his poor decision making the night before, he was now, that morning, 100 percent committed to getting things back on track.

But without her there, he couldn't manage it. There was so much he couldn't manage without her. He bent down right there under the stream of water and prayed that he would never have to. Sick unto death, he thanked God that he was going to marry Sara in just a couple of hours. Through the fog in the bathroom, he could see the clock on the wall. Ten minutes left. He closed his eyes, let the hot water run over him, and tried to picture her body—they had been so busy in the lead-up to the wedding that it had been a few weeks since they'd slept together. She'd been working so hard to fit into her dress that he'd begun to almost not recognize her.

Truth be told, in the past two years things had slowed down considerably in that department. Which was his fault, not hers. Just as he couldn't bring himself to relax and enjoy a cold drink or a long walk or a night out, he had been struggling to keep his head in the room when he was alone with Sara as well. Clothes off or on, really. When they were having dinner or watching TV, he was aware of always being halfway somewhere else. It used to be the other way around—whenever he was away from her, she was all he thought about. Of course he knew that these things changed over time. People went from being lovers to companions over the course of a relationship. He just didn't think that would start to happen before he turned thirty, before they'd even said, "I do."

But after what they'd been through—essentially managing a hospice out of William's living room—he felt as if his twenties were already far behind him. What still felt right on top of him was the loss. Irene's absence. At night, while *¡Vámonos, Muchachos!* was on commercial breaks, he would sometimes stumble over to her urn on the mantelpiece and clink his drink against the curved metal handles as if to say hello. Occasionally he'd lift it off the fireplace and carry it over to the couch so it could watch with him. Sara had *not* been happy, the first morning she'd found him there like that.

Soon after this incident, they'd agreed it was time to scatter the ashes. Jacob had told Sara how Irene had asked to be scattered in France, and she'd agreed they ought to do it on the honeymoon. There was a spot in the mountains nearby where the cliffs rose two thousand feet above the most beautiful turquoise water. Sara knew that one of Irene's greatest regrets was never having left the country, and here was their chance to rectify that. George didn't know if it was really the right move, but he wanted to make Sara happy, and he wanted to get things back on track. There would be the wedding night, in the bridal suite, and there would be ten more beautiful days in a French seaside paradise, where absolutely nothing could go wrong.

He turned the shower off and stepped out, getting his breath back, beginning to feel again, the top layers of his sickness lifting, leaving only the deeper part behind for him to live with. Towel around his waist, he sneaked into the bedroom, only to find that his brothers weren't there. The bed was made. Their tuxedos were gone from the closet, and there was a note on the dresser saying that they were going to find some breakfast and would meet him on the roof. The note ended with *Where's Jacob?*

George grabbed his tuxedo out of the bag and began to assemble everything. He had seven minutes. He slipped on the boxer shorts with hearts on them that he'd bought for the wedding, followed by a pair of thin black socks, and then he got his arms into the starched white shirt. As he did the buttons, he roamed around the hotel room, watching the molted boa feathers dancing. It was as if a whole cast of *Sesame Street* characters had disintegrated in there.

George wafted his arm in the thin space, sending a flurry of colors up into the air again. They fell like confetti.

He slipped on the tuxedo jacket and looked at himself in the mirror. It was perfect. As if nothing had ever happened. He walked to the shade that he'd drawn over the balcony doors, wanting to let some light in before he left. There was an explosion of reds, purples, yellows, greens, and blues as the shade pushed the air away. And there, on the other side of the glass, he saw Jacob, sitting at the patio table, already groomed and fully dressed in his tuxedo. He looked vaguely miserable, tapping the tip of his pen at the corner of a piece of hotel stationery like a crazed woodpecker.

He looked up at George and mouthed, "What time is it?"

George slid the door open. "Five minutes to one."

"You're supposed to go up for photos."

"Yeah, I know," George said, standing back and turning around for Jacob to admire.

Jacob tapped the pen again. "I was supposed to wake you up an hour ago."

"It's okay. I got up."

"Sorry."

"What?" George couldn't remember ever hearing Jacob say that word before.

"Sorry," Jacob repeated, looking down at the paper. "I got caught up in this."

There on the paper, he could see a poem—or the rough guts of a poem at least—covered in cross-outs and inserts and arrows shifting things from here to there.

Jacob looked at the page in annoyance. "What's a word that rhymes with *fellatio*?"

George grinned and, before taking off for the elevators, reminded Jacob to be up on the roof in fifteen minutes for the group photos. He had three minutes to spare. Sara would be coming up just behind him. He hadn't felt this happy all year, knowing he wouldn't disappoint her.

Everything came together just as it was supposed to. The rooftop of the Waldorf was wide and clear, and the views of the city in all directions were nothing short of jaw-dropping. It wasn't too windy or too cold. One of the first warm breezes of the year blew through the assembled Murphys and Shermans that day. Everyone behaved. Brothers and sisters fell in line; mothers hugged each other; everyone smiled. Whatever problems and dramas and concerns had existed before were forgotten.

Later the photos would show George holding a glowing Sara in his arms and she looking up at him with absolute, pure adoration. They kissed with a sea of high rise towers behind them. They danced to invisible music; she spun weightlessly. Hand in hand they walked away, smiling back over their shoulders. Her dress was white all the way down to the hem, where it appeared to float just above the ground, as if by magic. She buried her nose in the bouquet of white roses, the shadow on her eyelids echoing the turquoise in the peony buds.

In the group photographs, all six bow ties were straight, and every heel and hem was the right height, and everyone's hair stayed where it was meant to stay. The photographer told jokes like "How many tickles does it take to make an octopus laugh?" ("Ten tickles"), which were so terrible, they actually were funny. And when it was all over, they crowded into the elevators and went down to the front of the lobby, where two white limousines were waiting for them. Every parent, aunt, sister, brother, grandparent, and friend was ferried to the church in under two minutes.

Enormous, majestic flags rippled over the church entrance as everyone piled out of the limousines and moved to their stations. The guests, who had been arriving for the past half hour, were being ushered in smooth rotation, each oohing and aahing over the programs, especially the floral trellis detailing that Sara had created with the designer, based on a 1920s Heiligenstein vase. The lettering on the inside wasn't, as George had feared, unreadable in the dimmer light inside the church. In fact, it exactly matched the brick face inside the sanctuary—and the Oldenburg font choice was a real winner.

And there was Clarence! Made it with ten minutes to spare. He'd actually climbed out of the cab he'd been stuck in on the southbound lanes of the West Side Highway, crossed the northbound lanes on foot, and scaled the six-foot retaining wall along the park so he could catch another cab going south along Riverside Drive. He arrived with both wedding bands in his pocket, as safe as could be, and when the organ began to play the processional, he walked calmly up the aisle with Adeline on his arm, followed by the rest of the wedding party.

St. Bartholomew's organ pipes—the oldest in the city—were imperious and soft at the same time. George could feel their vibrations in the air around him. His mother looked lovely, not unlike Audrey Hepburn, with her hair still up in its twist, as she walked him to the altar. There George felt something overhead that he hadn't felt in some time, hard to describe as anything but a not-aloneness. As if the George beneath the George that everyone could see were in good company. It was like tasting that bottle of wine on Shelter Island, or even like seeing that dead body for the first time. A flicker of something beyond what was known and measurable in the universe. But soon all thought of it was gone, as he saw Sara coming down the aisle with her father.

Warm sunlight washed across her face, the stained glass glinting up above her. Her father was crying a little, just the right amount. She willed herself not to look over again, knowing she would immediately begin crying also. She fixed her gaze on George, who looked magnificent at the end of the aisle, towering over the hunched and sleepy-eyed Minister Thaw.

Minister Thaw had some things to say. Sara could barely hear them. Something about there being this small village in Italy somewhere that had a silver statue of Saint Bartholomew. During his feast they routinely carried the statue around the village. One day it became mysteriously heavy and the villagers were forced to set it down. Just then the rocks ahead of them collapsed into the valley. The very ground they had been about to pass over completely disappeared. Had it not been for the sudden miracle of the statue's weight, everyone in the village would have died. Then many years later, the village was captured by enemy raiders who sought to pillage anything of value. When they came to the statue, however, they found it was light as a feather. Thinking it was a fake, they let it be. This, according to the minister, was a perfect metaphor for the miracles of marriage. It could sometimes be surprisingly heavy, keeping the couple grounded—and yet at other times it could be as light as air—invisible, unfettering, even uplifting. And just as God had protected the faithful villagers, so would He protect his faithfully wed.

Sara could *see* George almost wanting to argue with the man right then and there—how could he claim that God, with any great consistency, protected true believers? You couldn't cherry-pick miracles when they made for a nice homily. That was just bad methodology. But no, he was letting it go—just a cute little eye roll to Sara, as if to say *they* knew better, and nothing else mattered. She squeezed his hands.

This was happening. This was really happening. Her sister was standing up and reading the passage from *The Velveteen Rabbit*: " 'Real isn't how you are made,' said the Skin Horse. 'It's a thing that happens to you. When a child loves you for a long, long time, not just to play with, but REALLY loves you, then you become Real.' 'Does it hurt?' asked the Rabbit. 'Sometimes,' said the Skin Horse, for he was always truthful. 'When you are Real you don't mind being hurt.' "

Franklin was next, with good old Psalm 121. "I will lift up mine eyes unto the hills, from whence cometh my help. My help cometh from the LORD, which made heaven and earth. He will not suffer thy foot to be moved: He that keepeth thee will not slumber. Behold, He that keepeth Israel shall neither slumber nor sleep. The LORD is thy keeper: the LORD is thy shade upon thy right hand . . ."

Now Minister Thaw was recounting Christ's first miracle, performed at a wedding in Galilee. That word always made George think of the song, "Puff the Magic Dragon" who had "frolicked in an autumn mist in a land called 'Honah Lee' "—but as a boy he had misheard it and had for some time believed that Puff was from northern Israel. He looked up at Sara, and he could see her lips were moving, mouthing the words to the song she *knew* was in his head in that moment. They smiled, and Sara wished, a little, that they could recite the song instead of the vows that the church required, and she hoped this wasn't as sacrilegious a wish as it felt. George's eyes bugged a little, as if to ask if she could believe this was all really happening, and hers bugged back as if to say that she couldn't, but it was, and that through everything that had happened, over all the years, they had made it here.

Of course none of the guests could see any of this happening. They fanned themselves with programs, strained to hear, and subtly adjusted their clothing. Grandma Pertie unwrapped a lozenge midway through the vows, irritating more than a few people nearby, but it was quickly forgotten. There was an audible buzz when Franklin Murphy got a text message from American Express, concerned about that morning's suspicious $103.22 breakfast charge—he hadn't notified them that he would be traveling out of the Midwest. Beth forgot herself at one point and could be heard softly humming the theme to *SpongeBob*. Jacob, standing to one side in the front with the other groomsmen, was mentally rewriting his poem and wondering what the hell William was doing wearing a fedora in the back row.

Then there was a sudden blasting on the organ pipes, and a cheer that rose through the pews, with people flying to their feet in applause, for Minister Thaw had just told George that he could kiss his bride, and (with gusto) he was doing so. Beaming, proud, resilient: they came then down the aisle arm in arm, waving and smiling at everyone. Both of them had assumed that since they had known each other so long and had lived together for years already, the moment would feel no different, really, than a million prior moments—but it did. They both were a little surprised, but there it was. A strange sense of having expanded. As if they had been, until now, living in two neighboring apartments and finally had knocked down the wall between them.

They had no receiving line—no time! It was right on back to the limousines, where the first round of champagne awaited them. Sara had arranged for four bottles of the more expensive Krug NV Grande Cuvée Brut, to be shared by the wedding party members only, then stepping down to the more reasonably priced Moët. They went around the corner and up the three blocks and back around to the gorgeous Palm Ballroom at the Waldorf Astoria. The crème marble floors were polished, and the mahogany wood was gleaming in the chandelier light. The band was playing something light and jazzy that everyone could talk over.

The cocktail hour flew by, with people steadily arriving from the church, met by a steady revolution of servers with hors d'oeuvres: crostini with duck confit and rhubarb marmalade, green tomatoes with balsamic and crispy serrano ham, elegant mini mac-and-brie cheeses, a festive French play on pigs-in-a-blanket that involved tiny croissants wrapped around an authentic andoulliette, and the coup de grâce, a gloriously orange spoon made out of Mimolette cheese that contained a single scoop of Prishibeyev caviar topped with crème fraiche. These were passed out with shots of Gray Goose, but there were also blood orange gin and tonics, a ginger bourbon lemonade, and George's newly refined blackberry sages. There were thick lines at both bars at first, probably because of the hand-carved ice cubes, but within fifteen minutes, at the most, everyone had a glass in hand.

They were young but once. For one night and one night only, let there be no heartburn, no traffic, no bedtime, no chafing, no fears. George and Sara wanted to create not just a moment but a memory—a moment that lives beyond its borders—and the usual shrimp cocktail and steely Chardonnay wouldn't cut it. There would be nights ahead (oh yes, there would be) as there had been nights before, where nothing would go right, where the memory of a tulip and sea grass centerpiece on a perfectly set table would be needed. Where a turmeric-flavored butter would be remembered. Where a spring vegetable salad could be recalled, along with the way the dressing perfectly prepared the tongue for the truffle in the wild mushroom soup that followed. The earthy quality of which was then met and cleansed from the palate by the perfect purple scoop of beet sorbet that followed. And the steam released from the phyllo-dough parcel containing juicy red lamb loin encrusted with macadamia nuts and a swirl of potatoes mashed with Roquefort . . .

Father danced with daughter; mother danced with son. Sisters made tearful speeches in which they both spoke the truth and lied through their teeth in wishing the happily couple nothing but the very best. Brothers told what light-blue stories they could of George's love life before Sara (the story of his serial kindergarten proposals came up in both their speeches).

And then Jacob unfolded his hotel stationery and smoothed the wrinkles out against his sleeve. A big cough, a steadying look in George's direction, and a good throat-clearing.

"This is just something—Sara asked if I'd read something brief. A poem. Anyway. This is part one, of, I think, three parts, about what was maybe the greatest thing that ever happened to me. Which was meeting these two people and following them here. Anyway."

And he began to read, " 'We came to the city because we wished to live haphazardly, to reach for only the least realistic of our desires, and to see if we could not learn what our failures had to teach, and not, when we came to live, discover that we had never died . . .' "

He went on and on. George had never heard anything like it from Jacob before. Was it technically even poetry? It wasn't exactly brief. His mother was looking around as if someone were supposed to flash the lights, but others were laughing, and Sara was crying for the first time all night—oh well, she'd almost made it. The poem (if it was a poem) was about them (all of them) as they had been before. She could hardly remember when it had been like that.

When Jacob finished, no one quite seemed to know what to do, so George stood up and loudly cheered and clapped, and it being his day, everyone else followed his lead. Jacob took a bow, and then a drink, and dessert was served.

Six tiers of alternating Opera and St. Honoré Cakes with a vintage topper from the 1920s, obtained on eBay after a vicious auction in which Sara had left several competitors eBleeding on the virtual floor. The cake was served with the special-roasted coffee (with a shot of Napoleon brandy added by those in the know) and then a series of passed postdessert munchies: champagne wine gelée, a sour cherry-filled soufflé, and a perfect madeleine stamped with an *M*.

Dancing late into the night, for hours without slowing down, as the older folks steadily said their goodbyes and returned to their rooms, the young folks felt more and more free. All past time seemed to disappear, and friends who had long ago dated and ended things awkwardly were seen boogying to the band's cover of Sisqo's "Thong Song" in utter violation of all normal rules of engagement. At one point Jacob somehow successfully swung Sara between his legs during "Take the A Train," and he and George got up and did their old air guitar routine to "Paradise City," and when the lights, finally, blasphemously, came up after Zacharie's fifth warning that they were past their contracted usage of the space, there were cries from all around to keep the party moving—to grab their wedding favors (custom-monogrammed shot glasses) and take the action down the road to the Turtle Bay Saloon or the new Midtown 3015 nightclub.

But George and Sara knew it was time for them to call it a night and let the others go on without them. She got out her bouquet, and all the single women crowded around to play catch, but Sara expertly rocketed the flowers right where she wanted them to go: over Eddy's head and into Beth's waiting hands. Bull's-eye.

Then Sara grabbed George's hand, and they left: barraged in their exit by catcalls, cheers, well-wishes, and charmingly lewd comments. Someone (top suspect: Jacob) threw a condom at George, which missed and got lost in a chandelier. It was up there with William's hat, flung excitely during "Under Pressure." Zacharie was on it already. Sara had already made both Jacob and William agree they'd all get together soon after the honeymoon so she could give them their souvenirs. There was talk of brunch, and George knew she would make it happen.

Then alone together at last in the elevator, George and Sara fell into each other's arms, kissing rhapsodic and hungry, chasing the tail end of the evening's high, fumbling with the cuff links and hairpins that still restrained them. They managed to find their way blindly into the bridal suite, which had been cleaned and filled with fruit baskets and flowers and chocolates and two more bottles of champagne in ice buckets. They bypassed these and found, finally, the enormously wide bed; the last hook on her gown; the buckle on his vest; the wedding night underwear, so carefully picked out by Sara's sisters—soon removed and flung far in their flurry. Grasping, giddy, they pawed at each other's bodies as if they were brand-new. Floating on an ocean of down comfort and the scent of lilacs and the wide constellation of city lights outside their flagrantly opened curtains, George and Sara made love as they hadn't in months—or honestly, years—love like neither of them could specifically recall having made in the early days of their relationship but that they were equally certain they had made. And as they pressed their heads together on the pillow and closed their eyes and lost sight of the other for the first time since the morning, they both felt that things were right and good, and that everything they'd been through had led them to this place at last.

It was still dark in the room when Sara woke up. Lights from the neighboring buildings shone through the open curtains and made gray shapes upon the bed. Which was empty, except for her. She rose slowly and walked to the door, which had been carefully closed just to the point where the latch didn't spring into the hole and make a noise that might wake her. She eased it slowly open. A flickering light cast on her bare toes and the rug beneath them. She looked up, knowing what she was about to see because she had seen it before so many times. The television was on, volume down low to a commercial for dish soap in Spanish. There on the couch, completely naked, empty bottle of complimentary champagne beside him, was George—her husband, George—sound asleep. And on the couch beside him, under one of his arms, was the dull metal urn containing Irene's ashes. Just as she did most nights, Sara tiptoed into the room, willing herself not to cry, and gently lifted George's arm from the urn. In the morning he wouldn't remember taking it out of the bowling ball bag, just as most mornings he didn't remember taking it off the mantel and putting it on the couch cushion beside him, as if she were somehow watching.

From his blue beach towel, George spent hours watching the yachts and cruise ships moving back and forth across the glassy surface of the Golfe de la Napoule. Every fifteen minutes Sara's cell phone would vibrate, and over on her own adjacent blue towel, she would rotate. Once an hour she would sit up and apply a fresh coat of lotion to her arms and legs, wordlessly leaning over toward George so that he could do her back. That morning she had gone for a five-mile run on the beach, except she'd gotten caught up in it and done seven. After a quick dip she'd eaten half a sandwich for lunch and plopped down onto the towel to rest and try to get some color. George tried not to stare at the topless French women just down the beach. The white sand was almost polka-dotted with rosy little nipples. You sort of got used to it, after a while. Sara wondered how many more lavender lemonade spritzers the waiter boy would have to bring before she'd unhook her bikini top. "I don't see the problem," George had said an hour earlier, maybe two, as he'd reapplied her lotion. "Personally I like a nice tan line."

"Oh you do, do you?"

"Yes," he said decisively. "Like a frame around a painting. Makes them look official."

"I think I might take my top off," Sara said.

"Okay." George reached to the hook.

"Not yet," she said, batting his hand away. "I meant later."

"Okay," George said, capping the lotion and watching Sara flop down again.

Up and down the beach, George saw other couples sitting just as he and Sara were, some talking, some not talking. It was early in the travel season, and the beach wasn't crowded. Little tables sat empty, with umbrellas open to shade the vacancies beneath them. Everyone was quiet, except once in a while a group of students would pass by, at least five or six speaking loudly in Czech or Swedish or Polish. Sara thought it was probably Europe's spring break. There had been a lot more of them around last night, wearing cheap wristbands and neon-banded sunglasses and sneakers without socks or laces.

Suddenly Sara sat up, businesslike, a good ten minutes before her timer would go off.

"Hi," George said quickly. "This is nice, isn't it?"

"I think we should take our hike to scatter Irene's ashes tomorrow."

He was surprised. "I thought—we had it planned for the, um, end of the week, after Monte Carlo and all that."

"I think we need to get it out of the way. Don't you feel like it's sort of hanging over us? As nice as this all is, I can't quite relax."

She could tell that George was annoyed, possibly even a little upset. Which was just as she'd suspected all along—he really didn't *want* to scatter her ashes. Maybe even he was hoping that by the end of their ten days in France, he'd be able to persuade Sara to abandon the plan. Here he was, trying to wallow in the waist-deep water, and she was going to make him go right ahead and cannonball into the deep end of the pool? But she couldn't take it anymore. The sulking, the despondency, the pondering. He was a born problem solver, a doer of puzzles. And she believed in him. She believed he would comb through the data on 237 Lyrae V and correctly identify the variables and reengineer his hypotheses until they were tested and proven. He would discover great things, but this—this couldn't be solved. The answer to grief didn't lie in the appendix of a philosophy book or even in Ecclesiastes. He would never be able to drink enough scotch, or stay up late enough on the couch, to unravel it. *X* equaled nothing. Not zero, nothing. *X* equaled a waste of time. But what could make him see that? What could make him let it—her—go? Day by day she tried to make their love the greater problem to be solved.

"Let's do it," George agreed. "Tomorrow first thing."

Sara leaned her back against his chest and felt his arms wrap tight around her and his chin rest firmly on top of her head. Together, at last, they stared out at the waves at the shoreline. One of the bands of roving students was passing by. Someone with green streaks in her hair did a cartwheel and fell backward into the water, laughing. Another grabbed a cigarette from the hand of a third, and a game of keep-away began, with the red-hot ember flying around like a sparkler. George wondered if they had ever been that young; Sara remembered that they had been.

Slipping one of her arms behind her back, in the space between it and George's chest, she thought for the first time that even if being married meant that she would spend every day from here forward watching George grow older (as he would watch her), then she was extremely lucky that the two of them *had* known each other when they were young. No matter how they changed from here on, they would still have that between them. She'd be able to see behind the bags under George's eyes and find that spark of still-twenty because she'd seen it before. They could always save that for each other.

Gingerly, she unhooked the top of her bikini and let the straps fall down. George's hands instinctively rose to cover her up, but she gently nudged them higher to her shoulders. In her whole life she'd never been naked in public. There were so many first times left to come.

That evening they took a cab into Cannes to dine at the famous La Palme d'Or, and between Michelin-starred courses, they strategized the next day's hike. On the way, Sara had contacted their tour operators and made arrangements. The group they'd originally planned to hike with wouldn't start out until the end of the week, and there was nothing scheduled for the upcoming day. But they could make their own way to the Chalet Castellane and pick up some basic supplies and a map of the national preserve. They spent the entire meal talking about the things they expected to see on the hike, getting more excited with each delicious course and each paired wine.

They were just coming to the last of three desserts when George looked up and noticed someone familiar sitting across the restaurant from them. "It's Santiago!" he said, a little too loudly. "From *¡Vámonos, Muchachos!*"

Sara squinted and saw George was right. "Wow. He looks *much* handsomer in person."

"We should say hello," he said. "Just that we're fans. You know?"

"Do you know his name? You can't go over there unless you know his real name."

"It's Victor. Something."

And before she could stop him, George was crossing the room with almost frightening speed. She watched, afraid that he would say or do something very drunk and they'd be asked to leave. But to her surprise, with each step, she could see him pulling himself back together. There was her old George! The consummate and confident host. Had he been capable of this all this time? Santiago—Victor—seemed polite and friendly, not at all put out by the intrusion. He gestured to the gorgeous woman next to him, introducing her to George, who in turn, pointed back at Sara, who waved excitedly in their direction. They spoke for a minute or two, and George shook his hand again and returned to the table.

"Well?" she squealed. "What did he say?"

George stared at his dessert plate and played with his fork. "He said the show's over. He's here celebrating with his wife."

"George! What a great story! I can't—"

And she had been about to say she couldn't wait to tell everyone, when she remembered that the only someone who cared besides them was back at the hotel in an urn. Which explained the gloomy look she now saw on George's face.

"The last episode aired in Mexico a week ago. It won't air in America until next year."

She tried to cheer him up. "Well, did he tell you what happens? How does it end?"

"Oh, yeah. He gets Renata, and there's a big wedding."

Sara clutched her heart. "I knew it!"

Neither of them said anything for a minute, and finally Sara said, "Well, I can't wait to watch it!"

George took her hand. "Let's get the check. Big day tomorrow."

Leaving the restaurant, both of them waved cheerfully at Santiago's table, and then they were quiet all the way back to the hotel, just watching the city lights going by and playing with each other's hands. They were both so full and tired that they went straight to bed. Sara fell asleep almost right away, but George lay awake. He couldn't quite figure out why it made him so sad to know the show was over. Renata and Santiago would be together, married, out there in TV land, forever. It was stupid. Just fucking television. But it bothered him that Irene, who had watched every episode from the beginning, would never know the ending.

They left in the morning with everything mapped out: where to find the Styx (the local name for a series of lovely natural bathing pools), as well as spots suitable for kayaking, fly-fishing, or rock climbing if they were interested. They had a tight schedule to keep if they were to get back to their hotel in Antibes by dark and then travel up the coast to Nice as planned. They'd go nine miles through the rocks along the turquoise riverbank to reach Point Sublime, an elevated spot at the far end of the canyon that offered breathtaking views of sheer cliffs and the pristine water, with miles of untouched woodland all around—the perfect spot to scatter Irene's ashes. Carried off by the mountain winds, they would dissipate into a scene of natural and epic beauty that, they agreed, would be beautifully fitting.

The skies were clear the next morning after they finished provisioning at the château. The owner, Raif, a Flemish man in loose overalls, said bad weather was expected overnight, lasting probably the rest of the week, so it was good they'd set out early. George couldn't help but feel that this was, in some way, fate. The moment he stepped out there into the fresh air, he felt young again, as if he were still discovering what his body could do. When was the last time he'd worn hiking boots? He'd been a Boy Scout once upon a time, out there in the Senecaville Lake campground. It all came back to him, during the first two hours of the hike. Cutting up worms for a day of failed ice fishing. Canteen at his hip. Flimsy little compass in one hand, a nice hiking stick in the other. Only now instead of his father he had Sara at his side, with a bottle of Côtes de Thongue and an assortment of cheeses wrapped up in her pack for lunchtime. In his own pack he had a bottle of J&B from the hotel, which he thought he'd save to celebrate with after emptying the heavy urn he was carrying. The weight had hardly bothered him at first, but the pack felt heavier and heavier in the third hour. George looked forward to their return to the château, eight pounds lighter and warm with scotch.

They were still creeping carefully down into the gorge, advancing toward the little curving line of water at the bottom. There were well-placed footholds in the rock and cables bolted in to grab for safety. For a while Sara was aware of the occasional white and red markings along the trail, but there were so many other hikers making the same trek that day that she hardly noticed when she stopped seeing other people ahead of or behind them. George had brought a map from the chalet, but they hadn't needed to look at it even once. It was simple to follow the trail and the river, which got wider and more powerful, the closer they came. At first they'd been chilly, well shaded by the giant cliffs, but as the sun rose higher in the sky, it became very hot, very quickly. When in the fourth hour they came at last to a little pebble beach by the water's edge, they decided they definitely deserved a break for lunch.

George wanted to cool the wine down a little, so he undid one of his bootlaces and made a sort of noose around the neck of the bottle, tying the other end to a branch that had fallen by the bank. While they waited for the wine to cool, he and Sara strolled barefoot through the stream, letting the freezing water soothe their blisters. Light danced down through the leaves. It was like something out of a fairy tale—for the first time, George felt good about their choice for Irene's final resting place. It had that same quality as the shores of Shelter Island. What had she called them? Mythic.

"We never do things like this," Sara said.

"Back in Ithaca we used to go hiking all the time," he replied.

She remembered going hiking exactly once, for about fifteen minutes, before Jacob ran into a spiderweb on the trail and refused to continue. The farther they got from those times, the less she idealized them and the more George seemed to. He didn't remember how often they'd fought and argued.

"The wine should be cold enough by now," he said. They'd walked a lot farther than he'd intended. "I say we drink half now and save the rest for the next stop."

Sara agreed, and they turned to walk back to where they'd left the bottle cooling. After a few minutes she began to wonder how they'd gotten so far upstream, because they should be back at the pebble beach by now. George was sure it was just a little farther, so they kept going, but still there was no sign of it.

"That's crazy. How could we have missed it?" she asked.

They decided to walk back a little ways and double-check. So they turned around, and now everything seemed different yet again from what they had seen before.

"Did you see any kind of fork in the stream?" George asked for the eighth time.

There was no sign of the beach, the wine bottle tied to the branch, or their backpacks, or Irene. Sara wasn't especially worried, sure that if they didn't find it soon, they were bound to find some other hikers who could point them on their way. But as the minutes ticked by, they saw no one and heard no one, and she became aware of something even more distressing.

"It's getting kind of dark."

"Kind of," George agreed, just as they felt wet drops fall onto their faces. He looked up through the leaves above, thinking maybe this was just some mist or dew from the morning, dripping off of the treetops, but the powerful sound of rain in the distance was unmistakable, and soon it began to pour.

"Let's get over by that cliff." George tried not to sound worried. "This will pass by us pretty quickly. You get all kinds of weird weather patterns in canyons. Lots of very fast changes in air pressure when you have altitudes like this."

Sara could hear thunder and tried to remember how to count the interval between thunder and lightning to see how far away it was. The trees were swaying wildly as the wind picked up. She couldn't help but worry about their packs, and Irene, out there somewhere.

They got their boots back on, though George moved a bit awkwardly with only one of his laces, and they hurried over to a rocky ledge. In an indentation deep enough to slide into and out of the rain, they got out of what clothes they could, shivering, and tried to wring everything out, their wet bodies pressing clumsily against each other in the narrow space. They made jokes to pass the time; they thought back to the dinner of the night before and lying out on the Riviera beach; they imagined what Jacob would say if he were with them. George could just see him, shouting lines from *The Tempest* or something.

But the minutes worryingly ran into an hour, and one hour into two, and the rain only got more intense. They had no flashlights or phones, no blankets or shoes or food. George realized that his watch had stopped and he didn't have his compass. He remembered Raif at the château assuring him that the bad weather wasn't due until nighttime but was likely to last for a while. George prayed—that the rain would stop, that they would find their way back to the pebble beach where their things lay. He hadn't prayed in a long time.

Terrifyingly fast and brilliant lightning sparked blue-white down a tree and out along the branches. At first George thought the incredible crackling sound was the earth itself coming apart underneath their feet. By the time he had realized what had happened, it was over—just a burned acid smell in the air and darkness. Sara was scared that it was getting darker, and they were pretty soaked, so finally George agreed that they should move out along the bank of the stream. They went carefully, looking out for bushes, rocks, tree roots, and other hikers as they walked through the storm.

The rain pounded around them like bullets; branches slammed their bodies from both sides; the wind twisted in all directions. At first George kept talking, trying to stay upbeat, but before long Sara couldn't hear him. In fact, he couldn't even hear himself, so they fell into a silence. It lasted a long time. Another hour, maybe more. They held hands so tightly that their knuckles began to ache, and their wet palms began wrinkling against each other, so that when they did have to briefly detach—to get a better grip on a rock or to push a branch out of the way—it felt like Velcro wrenching apart.

Finally, the rain softened and slowed to a drip. George guessed it was now maybe late afternoon, but the clouds above the trees were still black and heavy. Sara knew they ought to keep searching while they had the chance, but beyond exhausted, she lay down in the first clear area and wondered how they'd survived.

"We're going to be fine," George said. "The important thing is we're not hurt."

Sara tried to take comfort in this, but to her the important thing seemed more to be that they were still very lost. She couldn't imagine getting up now and starting to look for the trail. If they were missing for a long time, she imagined, it might be in the news. At least locally, back home—which meant 7News Boston now, not NBC 4 New York. She looked over at George, lying on the wet ground beside her, staring up at the edge of the great, gauzy sun, now beginning to beat through the clouds. She could tell it was soon going to be brutally hot. George looked completely shot. And she was sure he hadn't the faintest clue where they were now.

"For fuck's sake," she heard him saying. "Irene!"

Sara looked over, in the half-hope that Irene was actually *there*, that she had appeared in the midst of all this madness to lead them out. But George was pointing not to some ghost but to his backpack. It was up ahead, half sticking out of a bush, nowhere near where they had left it. There was no pebble beach or stream anywhere nearby. Someone had found it and tried to walk off with it, then realized it was much too heavy and tossed it into the bush. George's dry clothes, the liquor bottles, and all his other supplies were gone, but Irene, or her urn at any rate, was still there. Sara dug around in the pack and found two granola bars that had fallen to the bottom. They ate them without speaking. The thief had also—thank God—left behind the guidebook, the little gift shop compass and the very soggy map from the chalet. As she shook these carefully to dry them out, George smacked at the compass, which had gotten water inside and was now cloudy. Inside, the needle seemed to spin freely. He paced around as if he were looking for cell reception, then gave up and began studying the map.

"Any idea where we've gotten to?" she asked.

George laid a finger down on a small bend in the river marked "Bettes," a little ways off the marked path. "This was where we left our stuff. On the pebbly beach. Then we walked this way a little while and came back along here . . ." He traced the path with his thumbnail.

"What time is it?" Sara asked.

"I have no idea. How long were we walking?"

"We couldn't have been going that long," she repeated, looking again at the map.

They peered around at the rocky cliffside, hoping to spot one of the red and white trail markers.

"Let's say at most we were walking around for an hour. Moving maybe two or three miles an hour, given the conditions?"

As Sara watched, he cautiously spread his fingers out to measure three miles. Then he set his thumb down on the pebble beach and rotated his hand around this point. It was a huge area, filled with all kinds of strange squiggles and shapes that she couldn't identify on the map key.

"So . . . basically, we could be anywhere in here?" Sara said.

"Basically."

George climbed up on some nearby rocks to get a better view, but he couldn't make out any significant features. The sun had come out from the clouds between two barren cliffs along the horizon, but neither had any houses or roads that he could see—only some old, falling-down link fences along the white rock shores and the occasional cluster of sun-baked trash.

"I think this way is the best option," George said. "Where there's litter, there's bound to be a path, or people."

But there were no people, and there was no path. By the third cliff, Sara was beginning to doubt they could even find their way back to the stream. The next set of rocks turned out to be an extension of the previous one, and still there were no signs of civilization.

"I don't understand," she cried. "There were dozens of hikers out here with us this morning. Now nobody?"

George took out the map again, and scrutinized it. "None of this adds up at all," he shouted.

He tried tracing little circles on the map representing the distance to the horizon, as far as the eye could see before the earth curved away. Wherever he saw a clump of rocks, he traced a circle, until it was covered with possibilities. He began to feel dizzy. They had not had their lunch and he could only assume their cheese, the wine, and Sara's pack were all long gone.

"Sara, what's left in the canteen?" he shouted.

"It's about half full," she said. "Goddammit. We should have refilled it at the stream."

George shook his head. "I think we're cursed." He was dying for a real drink. Usually by now he'd have had at least his first of the day, and this had been a far more stressful day than most. He kissed Sara on her sunburned forehead and continued studying the map.

There was no key, and he wondered what any of it meant. The small purple triangles marked what he presumed were mountains: la Blache and Clau and Mandarom, with numbers next to them. 1725, 1549, 1667. At first he thought these were dates, but no, more likely altitudes. Only standing where they were, all the mountains loomed equally huge. And there were dozens of them! Some had no names at all, only numbers.

"What are you *doing*?" Sara called from where she was resting.

"This goddamn map doesn't make sense! Nothing's where it should be."

"How can things not be where they should be?"

"They can't. But they aren't."

Then Sara was screaming. She had spotted someone in a white shirt, moving through the woods down below them, maybe a mile away. George joined her as she hurtled down the slope, trying to get to the only person she'd seen in an hour before they somehow disappeared. It was a person—she was sure of it—a pale, angry man with a voluminous white beard, who as he became aware that they were bearing down on him, rushed quickly in the other direction.

George called out to him to "stop, slow down, wait!" When at last they got within a hundred yards of the old man, Sara waved her floppy white hat at him. "Sir! Sir! *S'il vous plaît*. Please! Could you help us? Help . . . um. George, what's the French word for 'help'? How do I say, Which way is it to"—she paused, not sure where they even wanted to get to anymore—"town. *La ville!* Am I saying that right? Is it 'vil' or 'veal'?"

George had no idea, and the little man was yammering in French so quickly that she couldn't even tell when one word ended and the next began. From the way his face pinched up at them, she could guess that he was in no mood to help them. He continued to duck around the trees and scowl.

"Allez-vous en!" he shouted, terrified. *"Je veux être laissé seul."*

"Help!" George yelled at him, waving both hands. "We're . . . WE ARE LOST!"

"He doesn't understand," Sara shouted. "George! The guidebook has travel phrases. On the back cover. Back cover."

As George dug inside the pack to find the guidebook, Sara tried to beg the little man, who shouted at her in French as he tried to get away.

"Please. We're Americans. We're lost! Americans? Lost!"

The man picked up a rock and hurled it at her, and it fell halfway between them.

She screamed and hid behind a tree. "We don't want to hurt you!" she shouted. "We need to find Point Sublime!"

"What's that in French?" George shouted.

"That is French! Sublime *is* a French word. Maybe it's 'Pont'? Sub-lime? Subleeem? Suble-me? George, what's 'lost'? How do you say 'We are lost'?"

Sara called again to the little man, but it was no use. He was rushing away, flinging rocks at them as he went.

"George, hurry up!" she screamed.

"I'm looking!" he screamed back.

The little man made it to the cliffside and nimbly climbed up the face, turning back occasionally to shout and make obscene and angry gestures. Desperate, Sara tried to climb after him, but it was no use. The tiny man was pulling up onto a ledge that led around to a higher part of the canyon.

"Perdus! Perdus! Perdus!" cried George as he rushed over to the cliff, clutching the guidebook in front of him. *"Nous sommes perdus!"*

But as he ran, holding the book up in the air like a flag, he stubbed his toe on a rock, and the book dropped onto the dirt behind him. The man was gone, and the sun beat down on them as they sat there exhausted and miserable, more *perdus* than ever.

"How could you let him get away?" Sara sobbed.

"Me?" George yelled. "You were scaring the hell out of him."

Neither of them could even look at the other. They were still panting from the climb, shaking with both fear and adrenaline. George wordlessly got out the compass and began his ritual of smacking it and spinning in circles, trying to get the needle to land somewhere. Sara looked for any sign of the little man but saw nothing but wide expanses of woods in front of them, with no paths or mountains.

"There's got to be something somewhere, right?" George said after another several hours of walking. "I mean, at some point we'll end up in Italy or Spain or something."

Sara didn't answer him—she'd fallen into a dark silence, which put George into his usual jittery-talking mood, which only further fueled her irritation.

"We're going north, right?" he said.

She didn't reply. She didn't care which way they walked.

He peered at the cheap little compass. "It *says* we're going north," he said, "but then why is the sun setting behind us?" They hadn't been able to see the sun behind the rocks for some time, but now it was visible, dipping below the clouds, big and red.

"How can the sun set in the south?" he asked, whacking at the compass.

It was then that she snapped. "How in the *hell* should I know?"

"Don't blame me for this, okay? You're the one who was so eager to do this today. If we had waited and gone with the group, this never would have happened. I'm doing the best I can here!"

Sara shot him a deadly look. "If we'd waited, you'd have come up with some excuse not to do it! I can't wake up one more time to find you drunk on the couch hugging her ashes."

"Well, excuse me if I'd rather go to bed with something that isn't running to the gym every time I turn around. You're always anywhere but next to me!"

He gave the compass another heavy whack, but the needle continued to declare they were heading north, when all logic and physics would dictate that they were heading *east*, away from the setting sun.

"My skin is peeling off," Sara sobbed. "I'm starving. And we're going to die out here."

"We're not going to die," he insisted, though he was beginning to fear the same.

"Forget where the sun is, and think about what we do when it goes *down*," she shouted. "We'll be out in the middle of the woods, with no lights, and no food—"

He smacked the compass again even harder, but it didn't budge.

"Would you cut that out?" she screeched, angrily clawing at his arm. "You're going to break the damn thing, and *then* what?"

"It's already broken!" he shouted. "That's not south!"

"Who gives a shit?" she shouted back at him. They hadn't fought like this in—ever. Normally they fought about reasonable things, like what movie to see or whether to have Christmas with his family or hers. One of them would inevitably give in (usually George), and they'd move on without animus. He didn't know how to hold a grudge, and if she did, well, she didn't when it came to him. But here there was no giving in, no moving on. They couldn't escape this.

It seemed to her that as furious as she was with him now, it was, in a sense, nothing new. She'd felt this way for a long time now, since he'd stopped being the George she'd always known. She wondered if he knew how much he'd changed, and if he thought she was different now. They'd been together such a long time, and partly they had managed it because they had never demanded very much of each other. Love, faithfulness, kindness: these had all come easily. It had never been very hard to make things easy for each other. But these past few years they had begun to lean harder. When Irene got sick, they had begun needing more from each other. They'd both changed, little by little, and she hadn't minded it because she'd assumed that when it was all over, they'd return to the way they'd been before.

But what if there was no way back to before? Now it was as if he couldn't stand unless she were propping him up. Drinking, moping, miserable. And without him, what would become of her? Would she keep running and subtracting from herself and trying to beat her life into lists of manageable tasks? And the worst thing—what she was sickest of—wasn't George or herself at all, but the vast expanse of years ahead of them. Time upon time during which they would surely go on changing and needing each other and being disappointed and losing things they loved and having no control, and she was terrified of it, absolutely terrified, so much that it made her want to throw up.

"Who cares?" she screamed. "Who cares?"

Then George shrieked and howled like a crazy person. He set his pack down on the ground and fumbled madly with the urn.

"Don't! What are you doing?" she yelled.

Her words bounced off the trees and vanished into the deep crimson sunset. Orange light cascaded off the clouds, which for a moment looked like great plateaus above them. When she was a girl, she'd believed that was where dead people went, fluttering around on little wings with their harps and white robes.

George looked triumphant as he heaved the great iron urn up above his head—and nearly toppled under its weight.

"What are you *doing*? Put that *back!*" she screeched.

"Irene! Irene!" he was shouting. Streaks of tears dripped from his pinched eyes. The compass. "She's a magnet!"

He was ready to fling the urn at the nearest tree. He hated it with all his might. He wanted to see it crack in half, to watch a gray cloud of soot and sediment mushroom out and disappear onto the forest floor and be gone forever. Lost. *Perdu*. But even as he stood poised at last to be rid of Irene—who had sent them on this insane journey, who had nearly gotten them killed, who he saw now had ruined the past three years of their lives—George couldn't let go.

"Stop," Sara said softly. She eased the urn away from him and set it on the ground and held her husband closely. He breathed in and then sobbed.

They sat silently and watched quietly as the sun went down and darkness fell. They felt the forest come alive around them. They each felt the other in their arms. They wished Irene were really there. They wanted to close their eyes and sleep and not worry about waking up in the morning. They watched as one by one, tiny pinpoints of stars emerged above them—some brilliant and some barely glowing—but in the darkness there were millions and millions.

George looked down at his pale, weak, pained body. Sixty percent of it was indistinguishable from the little drips of water that clung to the sides of the empty canteen. Mostly, he was just a mixture of oxygen and hydrogen. Eighteen percent carbon. Three percent nitrogen. Some calcium and potassium and other salts. All down the line, these were the same elements that he measured every day in the stars of the Ring Nebulae, the same as in the sun, as in all the stars in the universe. On an atomic level, he was constructed from fused leftovers, expelled into the void when these stars inevitably collapsed. In a way it comforted him that he was elementally connected to everyone and everything—even if, as he lay in the dirt, he felt sure there was also something to him beyond atoms. He'd seen something leave Irene, in those final seconds, and it wasn't energy or matter.

Back in high school physics he'd learned the cycle of decay and renewal over the course of millennia, and what a small footnote mankind was, when you looked at the entirety. But what he hadn't learned until much later was that for millennia, these stars, perceived by the naked eye, were thought to be, well, what they appeared to be: lonely, single points of light, isolated by billions of miles. But with better telescopes, astronomers in the seventeenth century had first noticed that some of these single dots were really two stars orbiting each other, or some common point, but in any case swirling close together. And now scientists had discovered that the vast majority, over 80 percent, of stars in the universe were these binary systems. Some were even multiple systems, three or more stars bound up in the same complex gravity.

He could hear Sara breathing beside him, and he reached over to take her hand. It was surprisingly warm. But he knew he shouldn't be so surprised. She—this woman he loved—was a great inferno of carbon and nitrogen and water, orbiting his own glowing, celestial body as it, in turn, circled hers.

"I don't think I've ever seen this many stars," she said, as awed as he was by the wide, bright swath of the Milky Way, stretching above them from one end of the valley to the other. Silently they stood up and, eyes fixed on the heavens, lofted Irene's urn from the damp earth. He held the base while Sara unscrewed the lid. Together they tipped it into the soft wind that remained of the earlier storm. In the dark they could barely see each other or the ashes as they swirled away, but they felt the urn getting lighter as they emptied it. George believed that on some microscopic level the last elemental traces of Irene would change this spot and, even if imperceptibly, affect all that would someday grow from it, just as surely as she had forever changed his life and all their lives.

Sara closed her eyes and wished Jacob and William were there with them. She began, silently, ordering all the events of the day into a story that she and George would soon tell many times. She opened her eyes and looked at her husband. He was looking up at the dippers and the North Star. He was staring into the dark place where, though the light hadn't yet reached them, 237 Lyrae V had long ago collapsed and formed a new bright white star. And George, just like the explorers of centuries past, felt the warming chill of knowing just how large it all really was and exactly where he was inside it.

"Let's go," he whispered to Sara, taking her hand. "I can find our way back from here."

THE CITY THAT IS

See gray threads of streets, dotted with the green of trees off the lanes. See glass rising, indistinguishable from sky. See aluminum herds coming down the West Side Highway and gulls circling the Battery. The ferry is just easing in. See the firecracker glow of M&M's advertisements on Broadway, where the Levi's are ten stories high. See the pine tar on the telephone poles and the chalk-dusty cobblestones. See where the careful grid begins to go off in angles, because part of this city is from before it was even a city. See, everywhere, there are children here. Everything is two or three times bigger in their eyes. See a takeout bag gusting up into a traffic light. There may be snow there, below, crusted to the curb. Or weeds driving up between the acts, to live an inch, or two, before the parade of dogs and passing feet. We are almost always about to touch. To be hit by bicycle messengers or buses. See how soon we get lost. See soot on silver, Post No Bills, snaking subway cars. Tunnels below tunnels below tunnels. See the copper skeleton city inside of it, all pipes and wires. We have this much in common. These belong to us all, like the blankets of green forests that hold pearl lakes inside and the rivers that cradle us and all that sprawls beyond them. See? It is a different city than the one we knew. It changed while we weren't looking, and while we were. We will never really understand how it changed because of us. Our words and motions moved its air and entered its vines. Still, my city is not your city, and neither of ours is the same as the city that belongs to the rest of them. To all the people elsewhere, remembering, or expecting it. There is a city that none of us knows at all. Why there is a dinosaur on the side of that building. Where all the yoga pants come from. What happened on that street corner fifty years before we were born. How that empty sports bar down the block stays in business. If anyone anywhere owns that bike that's been locked to the speed limit sign for the past nine months. There is the city where we are falling in love, and the city where we have lost all hope, and the city that never lets us down. There is the city that comes at us from all sides and knocks us down into puddles of something (we'd rather not know what). There is the city beneath the paint that coats this city. There is the city we step out into on warm days with no place in particular we have to be. Had you forgotten? There are cities where we are still young and cities where we have become very old. There are cities with just me, and cities with only you. There are cities that have vanished completely. There are cities we speak of very highly. There is a city we can never go back to, and a city we have never left and a city that was never built, and even one city that we all, each of us, believe in, that never fully leaves us.

ACKNOWLEDGMENTS

Many thanks are owed to the dozens of supporters, believers, and friends who have helped me to write this book: Chelsea Lindman and everyone at Sanford Greenburger; my editors at Viking, Chris Russell, Beena Kamlani, and, formerly, Maggie Riggs; and my publicist, Angie Messina.

Thank you to Leah, Joshua, my parents Dennis and Deborah, Oma, Jonathan, Dennis and Susan, Hanna, Chris, Theodore and all the rest of my family.

I owe a great debt to the kind eyes and hearts of Elizabeth Perrella, Andrew Carter Dodds, Neil Bardhan, Jerry Wu, Jill Rafson, Robin Ganek, Rachel Panny, Emily Ethridge, John Proctor, Jordan Dollak, Michael Levy, Andrew Bodenrader, Dongwon Song, Yaron Kaver, Dr. Aaron Prosnitz, Dr. Joel Green of the University of Texas at Austin and the Space Telescope Science Institute, Katie Peyton, and to Tom Mansell and Lenn Thompson of the New York Cork Report. Additional thanks to the good people at Bien Cuit bakery for many vital refills.

I am indebted as well to the support and generosity of Columbia University, Sarah Lawrence University, the New York Public Library, my tremendous colleagues at SUNY New Paltz College, the PEN/New England Organization, The UCross Foundation, and the Sherwood Anderson Foundation.

This book was written in loving memory of my sister, Jennifer, who pushed me first.